FUNNY PAPERS

FUNNY PAPERS

a novel by
Tom De Haven

PICADOR USA
A Metropolitan Book
Henry Holt and Company
New York

www.picadorusa.com

Picador ® is a U.S. registered trademark and is used by Henry Holt and Company under license from Pan Books Limited.

For information on Picador USA Reading Group Guides, as well as ordering, please contact the Trade Marketing department at St. Martin's Press.
Phone: 1-800-221-7945 extension 763
Fax: 212-677-7456
E-mail: trademarketing@stmartins.com

Grateful acknowledgment is made to King Features Syndicate, Inc., for permission to reprint the text of the epigraph appearing in this book. Copyright © King Features Syndicate, Inc.

Library of Congress Cataloging-in-Publication Data

De Haven, Tom.
    Funny papers.
      I. Title.
    PS3554.E1116F8 1985   813'.54   83-40681
    ISBN 0-312-42134-6

First published by Viking Penguin Inc., New York

First Picador USA Edition: November 2002

10 9 8 7 6 5 4 3 2 1

For Kate, and for Jessie and Santa

I'm grateful to the National Endowment for the Arts and the New Jersey State Council on the Arts for their generous support. Let's do this again sometime.

"A comic artist ain't no different than you or me or anybody excep' he knows how to draw pitchers an' is crazy in the head."
—*Popeye the Sailor*

FUNNY PAPERS

HOW PINFOLD
LOST HIS HAIR

Down in Awful Alley, many years ago when the sun was higher in the sky and a much brighter yellow, there lived a strange small boy called Pinfold. His mother was dead, and his father—who knows? Home was under a wooden stoop alongside a backyard tenement, and every morning out he crawled to take a leak and air his blanket, and then he was gone for most of the day, off selling condoms furtively as dope—at saloons and hotels and penny arcades, at City Hall Park, and at brothels, of course. Late in the evening he'd return carrying a pail of beer and a loaf of black bread in his wagon, and maybe in the crook of an arm some pushcart fruit or a fish wrapped in the New York *World*.

But then one time on his way back home, he ran into the Homicide Flats gang, older boys in checkerboard suits who were killing each other like pirates with stolen rolls of wallpaper and oilcloth. They jumped him and robbed him and set his hair on fire. When he finally showed up, drooling Hail Marys, at the stoop, Pinfold's ear was bleeding, and his scalp had blistered and was smoking. Overnight, he had fever. It soared and burnt to ash whatever hair he still had left, the few clumps and the stubble, so by daybreak he was bald. Then the chills took him, and his teeth made such a loud clacking sound that Albert Shallow heard it down in the tenement's coal bin, where he lived. Albert the Negro was a condom maker who supplied Pinfold with all his merchandise.

Albert came at once and peeked in under the porch. When he spotted Pinfold huddled and shivering there, he fetched dice from his coat, rattled them in his derby, then flung them hard against the wall, and they bounced off as an ice cube and a dried golden herb. Nothing to it. Things behaved differently in those days, somewhat. They just did. Why, back then rabbit blood and buffalo salve reversed human blindness, and milk-fed whales in fancy harness powered great yachts across the ocean. Sea monsters were captured and colossal forests of fungi were discovered by European princes on holiday with their American brides. Men of science could open your chest and wash your heart clean of sin. And yes, certain dice could end a fever and heal a bad burn, if your wrist was supple and your will strong enough.

Black Albert charged Pinfold twenty-five cents for the doctoring, and the boy paid in full a few days later, just as soon as he was on his feet and in business again. This all happened in late September, 1894. Winter came and passed, but Pinfold's hair never grew in, and by the following April, when he saved the fuzzy dog and his life changed, Pinfold had taken to wearing a hat, a high-crowned yellow derby with a bullet hole—a found thing.

O_{ne}

WRECKAGE OF THE WORLD

1

Park Row is a little street at the foot of Manhattan, just south of
the plaza entrance to Brooklyn Bridge, and in those days nearly all
the city's newspapers were published there. The *Sun*, the *Herald*,
and the *Tribune*. The *Times*, the *Star*, the *Mail & Express*. The *Commercial Advertiser*, the *Daily News*. The *Evening Telegram*. The *Press*.
The *Recorder*. The *Morning Journal*. And the *World*, the mighty
World. Its building—53 to 63 Park Row—was the tallest in New
York, twenty splendid stories. Everything else around it, including
the *Tribune*'s clock tower, looked puny, and the shadow that it cast
was immense. You entered, as though you were entering a castle,
through an archway. At the top of the building was a gilded dome
which could dazzle a man in sunny weather. Inside the dome, so it
was said, were leather wainscoting, and ceilings with frescoes, and
who knew what other trappings of magical American wealth. This
sanctum had been constructed for Joseph Pulitzer, the *World*'s owner
and publisher, but he had never used it, not once in twelve years.
Picture a mouse on the window seat, and everywhere cobwebs like
Florida moss.

Pulitzer controlled his newspaper by telephone and encoded cable, spending his days in soundproof mansions or on board slow

steamships crossing the seven seas. He was totally blind and a nervous wreck. Noise, any sort of noise—the scratch of cutlery, a sprinkle of salt—threw him into violent tempers which left his long, frail body thrumming and exhausted. Often it seemed to his wife and male secretaries that he would surely burst apart, sending chunks of himself whizzing in every direction.

As a young man, Pulitzer had emigrated from Hungary, arriving in St. Louis shortly after the War Between the States. Picture big side-wheelers, and levees crowded with barrels and bales, ornate southern hotels, and the Slave Market to let. He worked as a hack driver, a stevedore, a gravedigger—during one cholera epidemic he buried hundreds of bodies—and then as a reporter for a German-language daily. Eventually, he bought a newspaper of his own, merged it with another, and became editor of the *Post and Dispatch*. Work, work, work. Money! More work. His health started to fail. His vision browned. He began to look tubercular. He developed a stoop. He shouted angrily at the birds singing in the trees; their songs sounded like cannons. His nose grew beakier. His red hair faded almost to pink. Rest, his doctors warned him. Take a good long rest, Joey.

Instead, he moved to New York and acquired the *World*. A penny paper for the common man! Pulitzer launched crusades for clean government and tax reform, he lambasted the trusts and privileged corporations, but he always remembered to feature a grisly murder or a botched hanging on Page One. He widened the news to include the sordid and the sentimental, especially on weekends. Criminal Surgery! Monster Ape Men! Society scandals, homicides in Mackerelville. Is Cycling Immoral? She Drank Poison for Love.

Circulation climbed and climbed. Half a million, three quarters. . . .

Under Pulitzer, the *World* paid the highest salaries in the Row, and clever reporters were drawn there like cats to fish. Artists too. There were no halftones in the newspapers before the turn of the century, no photographs. There were drawings reproduced by zinc etching. The swearings-in at City Hall, the visiting battleships and Coochee-Coochee dancers, the shootings and stabbings and other sudden deaths were all turned out by a great crew of sketch artists dispatched every day, near and far, with large pads of cheap paper. Picture a young stick of a fellow dashing through the streets, coattails flying, pencils clutched in a fist. . . .

2

His name was Georgie Wreckage—really, it was spelled Reckage, but who was to know? "Wreckage" looked smarter, it looked plucky, and he'd always signed his pictures that way, even the ones he'd made as a very young boy on old calendars and grocery bags, on pavements and his tenement's roof. By the time he was eleven, he'd already begun to underscore his signature with a scribbled rebus of smoking ruins.

Georgie had not easily mastered the fork and spoon, but the lead pencil was a cinch. He loved the feel of it in his hand, he loved applying pressure to it, or loosening up the pressure, as he moved it—slowly, quickly, decisively, doubtfully—across paper. Zigzags, then big circles, smaller circles and stickmen, then cats and dogs and horses and fish and watermelons and apples. That's rain. See my cart? He used to copy—he never traced—news sketches and ink portraits of public officers from the penny papers that his father, a watchman at Portnoy's Brickyard, would bring home, but he much preferred doing pictures of his own. A hill of boots in a shoemaker's window. Two men in caps talking at a wine bar. A fat baby girl in a laundry's doorway with a rope tied round her waist. Scenes from the neighborhood. Germans playing scat and pinochle.

He trained himself to look closely and shrewdly at posture and gesture, at expression and clothing and context; to look, *look,* and to remember afterwards whatever it was he'd seen—except for color. (Colors didn't much matter since he used only grease crayons and pencils, chalk and chunks of carbon.) Some image would strike him, or some tableau, and he'd stop suddenly and just stare, recording in his brain a picture of, say, a blind old Jew in a sandwich board or a Bowery tough swinging a kitty by its tail. His memory drawings— which often he didn't get to sketch on paper for several hours or even several days—became more and more accurate, more full of detail, as he grew older. People said, He's a regular camera, ain't he?

He drew his mother at the spool table sewing linings into coats for Ziftel the Polack.

He drew his father down on his knees, vomiting fish cakes into an empty quart growler.

He drew his retarded brother Jack, still in diapers at five, rocking on the floor and staring at the baseboard with a thumb stuck into his mouth.

But he very rarely drew himself. Why look into a mirror when he could look across the room? When he could look out the window? Except for some flattering (eye patch added) self-portraits done in grammar school and given away as valentines, the only early picture of Georgie by Georgie was a charcoal sketch that he made when he was fourteen. And under very stressful circumstances.

He got nabbed in a drugstore one morning shortly after midnight with a gallon of root beer extract in his arms, register cash in his jacket, and an opium derivative in his back pocket. The cops took him to Houston Street station house, beat him a little with daysticks—across the back—and then one of them slipped a gallows hood over his head while another squeezed his throat and a third slammed the door shut. Let this be a lesson to you, lightfingers. Georgie tore off the hood and flung it down. He tried to act tough, but he'd peed his pants. *Chunk!* he'd heard as the door closed, and for an instant he really had been falling through space and choking. Later, after his father had come and gotten him, taken him home and worked him over with a razor strop, Georgie crawled through the front-room window onto the fire escape, then climbed to the roof. It was dawn. His thighs were sore with a urine rash, his trousers smelled like ammonia. He still felt humiliated. He'd peed his pants. Damn. *Damn.* He'd taken up some manila paper with him, and a charcoal stick, and, hunkering alongside the chimney pot, he drew a picture in the poor gray light: him wearing that black hood, his knees buckled, his fingers splayed, and three fat cops in unbuttoned tunics laughing with their mouths wide open. Then he burned the picture. Then he felt better.

When Georgie was sixteen, he took a portfolio of drawings around to the M. Laudermilch Advertising Company on lower Broadway. His pictures weren't very good, but they were good enough for an outfit on the verge of bankruptcy, and Georgie was hired, at a weekly salary of $9.53. For almost a year, he sat at a board ten hours a day, six days a week, drawing gloves and shirts, chewing gum, shaving sticks, collars and cuffs and pneumatic boats. The novelty of working by electric light quickly wore off, and the job became tedious. But it was a beginning.

The art chief there was a squashy redhead with billions of orange freckles. There were freckles on his face, on his scalp where his hair was centrally parted, on his throat, and on the backs of his hands. He dressed in cheap blue suits, the coat pockets lumpy with plums, and three times every morning and twice in the afternoon he rose from behind his table on a platform at the front of the room and went to the toilet, trudging like a tired postman. Otherwise, he never moved. He called you and you came. He used a Cornell cheerleader's megaphone. His name was Philly Finck, and once upon a time he'd been a regular contributor to the weekly humor magazine called *Our Favorite Uncle;* for half a dozen years an ink drawing of his for a short story, or a political lithograph in color, or a captioned cartoon appeared in almost every number. A sharp wit and a fluent brush line, and a very solid commercial reputation. He'd illustrated books, too. But that was then. And now he was a ruin, and radically unhappy, thanks to drink and alkaloid drugs. Forty, forty-one years old. Headaches and shaky hands.

Finck took an instant liking to Georgie and crabbed especially loud whenever his drawing was mediocre. He'd say, That's the sorriest-looking nigger baby I ever saw. We're trying to sell tar soap, not subscribe for a charity. But then he'd wink and end up complimenting Georgie for his cross-hatching. Ask if he wanted a plum. Good spots Finck would overpraise. Now *that's* a cup of instantaneous chocolate! Where'd you learn to draw steam like that?

Wednesday evenings after work, Finck usually walked up to the Penman's Club, and a few times he invited Georgie to come along with him. The Penman's Club was on Lafayette Street, in the cellar of an ink factory, and there some of the most successful illustrators and cartoonists in New York—Art Frost and Ed Kemble, F. B. Opper and Palmer Cox, Grant Hamilton, Tom Worth, Syd Griffin, and Zim—met to drink claret punch, eat Welsh rarebit, and put on skits. These were some of the fellas who drew for *Collier's* and *Scribner's, Harper's* and *Uncle,* as well as for *Puck* and *Judge* and *Life,* the holy trinity of humor weeklies, and in their company Georgie was awestruck. They'd ask him, You draw? and he'd mumble. You *draw?* Yes, a little. He stared at their hands.

During this period, and encouraged by Philly Finck, Georgie tried to break into the weeklies himself, but it was always sorry, sorry, sorry, this isn't for us. His problem? He couldn't draw pretty enough girls, or dream up jokes about insects on a picnic or Negroes or Jews, and since he didn't know any golfers or farmers or emancipated women, he didn't know how to make fun of them. And he had no aptitude at all for political satire. He'd never cared much for symbols and second meanings. He liked his wrecked engines to be wrecked engines, not the state of the union or the currency.

Finally, he decided to forget about magazines and try the newspapers, and he started leaving drawings for examination at practically every one on Park Row. But nothing doing. Finck thought Georgie ought to look older, or at any rate less boyish; editors weren't taking him seriously, maybe. He suggested that Georgie grow a mustache. When it grew in peach-blond, though, he told him to shave it off, shave it off. Is that what you got on your balls? Is it? Is it? Georgie wasn't so friendly with Philly after that.

One morning, everybody except the bosses showed up for work at the Laudermilch Company, the doors were padlocked, and there was a sheriff's bulletin on the glass. Georgie was in big trouble now, a pickle. How was he supposed to pay his rent? He'd recently moved out of his family's tenement—you leave, said his father, you don't come back—and into a boardinghouse, Mrs. Bennett's for Quality People in lower Sawdust Street. Mrs. Bennett was not a sympathetic person. You paid your rent or she locked you out, your things in. But also living in the boardinghouse were several music-hall artistes—a Female Hercules, an Irish tenor, a Metal-Eater, a human lizard, and a songbird—and they kindly helped Georgie to get a job at LeFebre & Chill's Theatre and Musee on the Bowery. As the Charcoal Caricaturist. As the fella who made great big sketches of folks like Buffalo Bill and Lillian Russell while scenery was being changed. He'd sit down on the stage apron, pull off his left shoe, stocking, and garter, fit a carbon stick between his big and second toe, and draw a dinosaur—Taller, ladies and gentlemen, than even Brooklyn Bridge!

Georgie stayed at the theatre, which he loved, *loved,* for six and a half months. Then he was hired on at the *World* by pure accident. Somebody mistook him for an office boy late one afternoon when he'd gone up to the eleventh floor of the Pulitzer Building to drop off some more art samples. Suddenly he found himself running around collecting flimsies from reporters, sweeping the floor, sharpening pencils, and slaughtering cockroaches on demand. He returned the following day, and the day after that. For almost two full weeks he worked there without any salary. Finally, an editor asked him, What's your name, how do you spell that? And next payday there was a cheque waiting for him. He earned nineteen cents more a

week than he had at the advertising company, and two dollars less
than he was making at the music hall, Ah, well. He was part of the
World now. It was the summer of '93. Georgie had just turned
eighteen.

Every now and then, and by dint of his making an awful pest of
himself, Georgie got to draw little sketches illustrating jokey news in
a Saturday edition, but he was, officially, an errand boy, a speedy
little nobody. You, George! Run downstairs to Perry's and get us a
drink. George! There's a wasp flying around in here, dammit! Say,
George, see that lady at the door? Tell her I was just sent to the
Hook of Holland on special assignment. George, George—pickup,
pickup, pickup! Until the Bits and Pieces Murder Case, the most
notable drawing that Georgie made for the paper was a phre-
nological portrait of a Tammany politician with the zones of avarice,
cunning, lust, egoism, and mother-love clearly indicated. (He'd
been given the labels and told to draw the bumps.)

The Bits and Pieces Case! Thank God (Georgie did) for that wonderful homicide—the legs turning up in Chelsea, the torso in
Harlem, a foot in Yorkville, and several fingers in the Gashouse District; one arm in Brooklyn, the other in the Bronx. And thank God
(again, Georgie did, fervently) that the poor galoot was brained and
carved in sultry mid-August, the very week that five quick-sketch
artists, a staff illustrator, and a crime reporter were away canoeing
the Delaware. Can you believe the luck?

The day after the story broke, when the headlines had grown
from an inch to an inch-and-a-half, Georgie presented himself at the
city desk with a batch of gruesome illustrations that he'd drawn
overnight, using a copy of the *Police Gazette* for inspiration. All right,
all right. Grab your hat. He was sent up to the morgue and spent one
of the happiest mornings of his life sketching a headless, armless,
legless torso. Next day, he did drawings of the bloated legs, then was
told to go out and search for the missing head. Everybody in town by
then was looking for that head—the *World* had announced a big reward. In due course, three were turned in at the paper, but none of
them fit the trunk. The right head never did turn up. The murdered
man was never identified. The case was never solved. But so what?
Before the story was abandoned, Georgie had been given a five-
dollar raise and his reporter's derby.

In his first few months as a sketchman, Georgie described in line
so many gang wars, so many boiler explosions and ferry catastro-

phes, so many showgirl suicides and bungled abortions, so many frozen vagrants, vitriol mutilations, and other acts of vengeance that his fellow artists on staff began to call him Bloody Wreckage. There goes Bloody Wreckage, dashing through the streets, coattails flying, pencils clutched in a fist. And look, he's smiling. Must be something good. Mayor get shot?

3

Georgie was antsy, waiting for the trouble about to happen. "You sure it's today, Clarky?" He picked at side teeth with a bent-out-of-shape paper-fastener. "You sure it's this morning?"

Clarky didn't even bother to reply. Was he sure? Come on. Was the earth a ball? Was the Pope a fiend?

They were sitting on a bench at Cooper Square, the two of them watching Canary Ella pester all the clerks and shopgirls and messengers who passed by in a hurry. They'd been there a quarter of an hour, long enough for Georgie to have finished a sketch of the woman: fat and bosomy, tiny legs, tiny feet. Dressed in heavy twill trousers and a man's shirt. Splayed on a camp chair with a sign next to it that read FORTUNES—5¢/AMERICAN-BORN—NOT A GYPSY. Several yellow birds hovered above her head, a few others nested in her snarled fontanelle. A card table, a baby's cradle on top.

Clarky got up now and went over and gave a nickel to Ella. She blew a kiss to a canary, and it swooped into the cradle, nipped out a piece of folded paper. The paper was blue-lined and flecked with wood fiber. The bird flew to Clarky, delivering the paper into his palm. BUY POTS TOMORROW. "I'll be sure to," Clarky said and touched a finger to his hat. "Thank you." He walked back to the bench and sat down again beside Georgie. "Any minute now."

"You're *sure* the cops are coming. *Today? Friday?*"

"Is today the twelfth of April? I heard what I heard. Just sit tight, you'll get some pictures." He glanced at Georgie's boots, and finding them dull, the uppers speckled with dried mud, he frowned. Then he stuck his fortune into his jacket. "I feel sorry for her, though."

Georgie grunted.

"Maybe we should warn her."

Georgie closed one eye and widened the other, as if to say, Get off the earth!

"Only joking," laughed Clarky, and still smiling, he looked back at the fortune-teller. "I heard she comes from South Carolina."

Georgie took out a pencil, nibbled at the wood below the point, then picked off splinters with a fingernail.

"A place called Dog's Hair. That's what I heard." Clarky thought for a moment. "Funny, her being a witch and she don't know what's coming."

"Maybe she does, she don't care."

"Could be. She's bugs enough." And if Clarky said she was bugs, she was; you could believe it. He'd know. He knew, for example—he'd heard—that she lived by herself in the old Maloney & Grue Pickleworks and that she slept, but never bathed, in a large metal tub with painted lovebirds and garlands and monograms on both sides. Wedding gift from her husband, who'd made a blockheaded wager one summer night and jumped off Brooklyn Bridge. Eleventh to jump, seventh to die. Poor Ella, Clarky thought. The things you hear.

Georgie was sharpening his pencil point against a tiny patch of sandpaper. "You sure the cops won't just pinch her?" he said. "They're going to brain her, for certain?"

"It's what I heard," said Clarky. "As a lesson. She told a roundsman to go jump in the lake. It's a free country, she has the nerve to say. It's a free street. Stupid woman, when all he wanted was five dollars a week. Five dollars is what I heard. The same cop gets ten from Mr. Next-Thursday, he thought he'd give her a break. This is America, she says. Ain't this America? Sure it's America, you stupid woman. Where you pay as you go. Or hasn't she heard?"

Well, Clarky had. Heard that, and a lot else besides. He heard things all the time. Nothing spooky about it, no secret voices—he just used the big jug-shaped ears that God had given him and listened. Eavesdropped. Asked questions. And regularly quizzed all his shoeblacks. Is that so, is that so. He would hear about it first if there was to be another strike at the meat-packers or a boxing match in a Long Island barn. He heard things. Knew things. That it was Nigger Jake, not Jimmy Dalton, that killed Annie Beck; that preferred stock in Amalgamated Greed was about to take a nosedive; that a Chinaman on Mott Street had turned three-hundred-and-two last Friday, making him the second-oldest person in New York. And who's the oldest, Clarky? The Jew of Scold Alley—you didn't know that? Where you been all your life?

Because Clarky heard so much, and because what he heard was

generally true, reporters sought him out, as did coppers, occasionally even financiers. Georgie Wreckage had put him on retainer. Three beans a week fair enough? You know the kind of stuff I like.

Clarky was twenty, a husky blond with a bad complexion. His clothes were disintegrating from constant wear, but his shoes always had a high glossy shine. He did that, shine his shoes, more often than he did anything else, except breathe. Tell you why. When Clarky was still a kid, a frail old man dressed to the nines had called to him one evening from a private carriage. Mahogany. Clarky strode up to the window, and the old man—who'd been drinking, but that didn't matter, so had Clarky—told him to mind his shoes. Just like that: Mind your shoes! He said that if Clarky minded his shoes and always kept them gleaming, he too could become a millionaire. Here was sudden wisdom, like in a Bible story. It made Clarky lightheaded, and from that night forward, he'd kept his shoes more immaculate than even the headwaiter at Rector's kept his. The rest of his attire, and the rest of him, looked pure bum.

Clarky was no bum, however. Maybe once, but not anymore. He was still far from turning millionaire, but he did have some money in the bank, a three-room flat in the Village, and a blooming little business.

Following his epiphany, Clarky had quit selling newspapers and become a shoeshine boy. There'd been several years of that. Then he rented a storefront with some money he'd saved. Bought shoe wax in quantity and slapped his own label on the tins. Clarky's— The Paste That's Remarkably Black. Then he went up to Inwood, where an insane asylum had recently burned down, and purchased three dozen white staffers' uniforms. He recruited as many teenaged boys, the majority of them Negroes and swarthy Arabs, and suddenly Clarky's Shoeblacks—You'd Have to Be Crazy Not to See the Difference in Our Shine—began showing up at train depots and ferry slips, in city parks and on the streets. And because he'd trained and drilled all his boys in the art of waxing and buffing—The Clarky Method, swift but finicky—their suits were always as spotlessly vanilla at the end of a shift of work as they'd been at the start. Good idea? Clever? Clarky thought so. He *knew* so. People were saying, I think I'll go have my shoes clarked. It's what they were saying. My shoes *clarked*. That's what he heard.

❑ ❑ ❑

A monkey man was crouched on the pavement picking up monkey shit with a fireplace shovel, while his wife, up ahead, pushed along the organ. He banged the shovel against the curbstone, and when he stood up, Canary Ella called to him. He shook his head, no; smiling, no. But she called to him again, calling, "There's one for you," in a husky drawl. "There's one for you." The monkey was pulling at its leash, straining toward Ella. And finally, after he'd checked and seen that his wife had turned down into Astor Place, the monkey man succumbed. He dropped five pennies into the saucer on Ella's lap, while his animal sniffed avidly at her signboard. The monkey man laughed when a bird selected his fortune, but as he read it, his expression clouded; he rubbed the back of a hand across his mouth, slowly. Then, starting to slump away, his monkey gabbling behind him, he crumpled up the paper and flung it into the curb. Georgie ran over and retrieved it. DON'T TRUST HER. And for a moment he was tempted to follow the monkey man—who *did* have that shovel, maybe he'd use it. Picture of the wife with her skull bashed in, the barrel organ in pieces, and the panicked monkey up a telegraph pole. Yes? No? No. Just wishful thinking.

Georgie looked around to Canary Ella, found her looking back at him.

He noticed then that one of her eyelids was droopy.

And wondered suddenly why she hadn't badgered *him* to take a fortune-paper. He would've turned her down, of course, but still. Funny she hadn't tried.

It was almost noon. In five or ten minutes, the square would be thick with clerks and managers and pinched-faced little typewriters all scurrying to lunch. So where were the cops? What did they want, an audience?

"What's all the fuss—hey!"

Two of Clarky's shoeshine boys, a skinny-belink Armenian and a big soft Irish, had just come along, arguing loudly. Clarky, on his feet, was crooking a finger at them sternly as a nun. "What's all the fuss? You're in uniform—you don't behave like jugheads!"

"Aw," said the Irish kid, pointing to his companion, "this big dope says Kernochan's got more dough than Huntington. That's a lot of bunk!"

"Bull," cried the other. "It's not bunk, he *does*. Mr. Clark, tell this dense mug who has more millions. It's Kernochan, right?"

Then, turning to Georgie, who'd just sat down again on the bench, he said, "You can get in on this too, mister. What do you say?"

Georgie shrugged. He couldn't say one way or the other; he'd just be guessing. Industrialists, even their lackeys, had great celebrity among street boys, but Georgie couldn't have cared less about them. Big shots. Big deal. *Just let me know if one of the bastards gets shot in the face or goes down with his yacht—any women aboard?*

"Kernochan!"

"Huntington! Tell him it's Huntington, Mr. Clark."

Clarky was shaking his head at the Armenian, clearly disappointed in him. "Huntington," he said. "What kind of question is that? You're nutty. Kernochan's a bankrupt, compared."

Ashamed, the Armenian lowered his eyes; then, tucking his chin against his shoulder, he walked away. But the Irish boy dogged him, jabbing him in the ribs, whispering against the nape of his neck, needling him.

"Hey!" Clarky called after them. "Come back here and give us a shine."

Georgie said, "I don't want any shine. I want the cops. I got a job, I got a boss."

Clarky said, "If I were your boss, I'd fire you. Your boots, George, are a disgrace."

The boys squatted—a Clarky Shoeblack did not kneel, ever— and started pulling cloths and tins of wax from their boxes. Georgie inspected their bright suits for speckles of paste, for any traces of soot, found none. *How the hell did they do it? What talent! Couple of street arabs. No wonder the country was crackerjack.*

Canary Ella ran out into Fourth Avenue, after a bird of hers that'd found a piece of corn bread in the street. Georgie heard her call the bird Seelie. She carried Seelie back on her wrist.

"So tell me, Clarky, what else have you heard?"

Clarky pretended not to notice the sarcasm. "Interested in the French comedienne who's got syphilis?" he said.

"No."

"Then how about this. There's a pizzeria gonna open up next month on Spring Street."

"What's a pizzeria?"

"I don't know. Nobody does. But whatever it is, it's gonna open on Spring. Maybe it's like a wop penny arcade, I don't know yet."

"What else?" Georgie's boots were done already. Clarky wouldn't
let him pay.

"What else? You know about Hearst?"

"The Senator? The Comstock Lode guy?"

"The Senator's dead, George. Holy Christmas. And you work for
a newspaper?"

"Yeah, but I don't read it." He grinned. Then he checked on Ella
once more.

"I'm talking about the Senator's son, the Senator's *son*. William
Randall Hearst. *Randolph* Hearst. Owns the San Francisco *Examiner*."

"So what about him?"

Clarky gave four bits to the Irish kid, nothing to the Armenian,
and they left. "I hear he's coming to New York. Gonna buy a paper
here."

"Which one?"

"Don't matter. He could pick up a frankfurter daily and make it
sell a million copies in three months. That's what I heard."

"He's good?"

"He's rich."

"Democrat or Republican?"

"He'll decide that when he gets here and sees the voter rolls,
won't he? But I hear he wants to take on Blind Joe, head to head."

"He prepared to lose a lot of dough?"

"He is, is what I heard. Big spender. So maybe you can get a job
when he arrives. Late summer, maybe the fall."

"I already got a job." Georgie stretched out his legs and looked at
his boots. Christ, they gleamed! "What else you hear?"

"You want fights? There's a free-and-easy at the Blade tonight."

"More like it. Thanks."

"You're welcome. And tomorrow night, it's the Filch Hall banquet."

Georgie brought his legs back, turned on the bench to face Clarky.
"At the hall?"

"Not this year. This year it's at Mother Polk's."

"On New Dream Street?"

Clarky pushed out his lips, then put his tongue through them.
"Can tell you don't dip your wick too often. She moved. She's in
Penalty Street now."

"Can I get in?"

"Were you invited?"

"Come on, Clarky. How can I get in?"

"You can't. Not tomorrow night. And don't even try, Georgie, all right? Last year, a bird from the *Sun* tried it, and somebody found him crucified on a stepladder two days later."

"You going to be there?"

"Why would I be there? Am I a crook?"

"Any of your boys work Mother's house?"

"Sure." Clarky squinted and looked Georgie over. Then he wagged his head.

"Come *on*, Clarky. I'd love to see this."

"I won't let you put on one of my suits and walk in there, no. You don't know the Method. You'd screw up. And then what happens to my reputation?"

"So teach me."

"Why you want to go to the stupid banquet anyhow?"

"Something might happen."

"It's just a banquet." But Clarky was tapping his mouth with his fingertips, scrutinizing Georgie again, sizing him. "Let me see your hands."

Palms up, palms down.

"Wiggle your fingers."

Georgie wiggled them.

"Now, walk like a duck. Show me."

"What?"

"You have to walk like a duck if you want to polish shoes." Clarky was enjoying this, so much. "Now, walk like a duck."

Georgie bellied his cheeks, then let out his breath—*whoosh!* He set aside his sketchbook and stood. Looked around. Canary Ella was pressing a heel of stale bread between her hands, filling a dish with bread crumbs.

"If you can't walk like a duck, I can't teach you the Method."

"All right, all right," said Georgie. He tugged at his trouser knees and hunkered, then up and down in front of Clarky he waddled, his face red and his fingers clenched. And he was still waddling when the police wagon arrived, from the Bowery. He heard it behind him and pivoted around to see, but lost his balance and sprawled, left palm slapping the pavement where a gob of chaw spit was. "Damn!"

"My fellas don't get distracted, no matter what," Clarky said, "and they never swear on duty."

Several officers of the law, all of them men of good height and expansive chests, were approaching Canary Ella with their daysticks waggling. Public nuisance. Code violation. Suddenly, *crash!* Over went Ella's signboard, over went the table. The cradle fell, a rocker snapped, and fortunes scattered every which way.

Ella had covered an eye with a hand—her left with her right—and, cyclopic now, she glared at the coppers till one by one their noses started to bleed. But it was feeble hoodoo and those galoots weren't afraid of a little blood; they grabbed her. Dragged her into the street. The canaries followed, whizzing in orbits around Ella's head, trying to dive into her piled hair. Standing in the back of the wagon was a young roundsman with a cowcatcher mustache and a mottled, winey complexion—his hair stuck out from under his helmet—and just as Ella was propelled through the doors, he drew a billy and clubbed her in the teeth.

There. *That.* Georgie had his picture, and before the wagon had even rattled away, he'd licked his pencil point and was making the first cursive lines. He'd rough it now, finish it later. He became so absorbed so quickly in his sketching that he never saw the little humpback who trotted out from the Cooper Union to grab Ella's table, or the newsboy with acne rosacea who ran away with her stool and her cradle. Or Clarky leave, wandering off in a crouch, picking up fortunes as he went. DRINK MORE MILK. TUESDAY WEAR GREEN. Finally, as the angelus was ringing somewhere, Georgie put the pencil in his pocket and closed his pad, then he jumped up and ran to catch a surface car.

He never saw or even thought about the canary lady again, but Clarky eventually heard that she moved to Jersey City, married a Stein named Jack, and opened a candy store. This is America, ain't it? Ain't this America? And perhaps their candy store lasted in business for years and years, through wars and world wars, a place where bookies used the telephone and truants read the magazines. A candy and newspaper store, a place to buy school stationery and cheap toys. Baseball cards. Jack's Confectionary. Or Jack and Ella's. Whatever. A place their grandchildren probably sold last year, or the year before, to a Pakistani family.

4

"Myself, I can't draw a pretty girl or a red Indian," said A.K.;
then he filled his mouth with navy beans, lifted a shooter to his lips,
and fired at the slowly revolving tin ceiling fan—*dink, dink-dink.*
"I'm just lucky neither species owns a utility. Or can run for President." A.K. was strictly an editorial-page man—drew donkeys and
elephants and tigers, and rascals with bankrolls sticking out of their
coat pockets. Everything labeled. Beef Trust. Sugar Trust. Ben-
jamin Harrison. His great gift—and that's exactly what he called it,
his great gift—was knowing how to make monkeys out of men, and
he'd become rich thanks to it. Twice a year he sailed to England to
watch the steeplechase. He owned a commercial building on Fourteenth Street and a farm in Pennyslvania. His tie pins had all been
fashioned from twenty-dollar gold pieces. And practically everybody in the art department wished he'd hurry up and get arthritis.
"But our *Georgie,*" he said now, with a big wink at Dieffer and
Stolley, a couple of sketchmen playing a hand of gin—Dieffer was
the one with the broken nose. "But you take our Georgie, here. He
can draw anybody, anybody at all. Tinker, tailor, sweet potato. So
long as they're stabbed, bashed, burnt, shot, crushed, or drowned,
eh?"

Georgie, who was at the supply closet putting some white cardboard back on a shelf, just smiled and said, "You bet. And I could
even draw an ugly bastard like you, A.K. Providing you let me take
that frigging peashooter and shove it up your nose." Arthritis? Georgie wished he'd hurry up and get run over by the Elevated. Blab-
blab-blab. The man had nothing to do, that was his problem. Every
morning an editorial writer would come down from the fifteenth floor
and tell him what to draw—the gas franchise as buccaneers, the
Republican chairman as Cinderella's stepmother—and it would take
A.K. all of twenty minutes to render. Then what? Then nothing,
except blab-blab-blab. He could insult everybody on staff, he could
loaf around during pandemoniums reading Wild West tales, he could
even invite up a lady friend with a hamper of cold chicken, then
picnic in the city room—and nothing would happen to him. You
might want like crazy to biff him in the face, but unless you also
wanted to see the cashier to collect any wages due, you didn't take
that swing; you couldn't. Because A.K. was "valuable," see. It's

what they said upstairs. His cartoons sold papers, and that made him a valuable man, it protected him. But someone like Georgie—a dime a dozen. They said upstairs.

A.K. laid down his beanshooter, then picked up today's *Evening World,* damp yet, from a stack on the windowsill. Went paging through it. "'Fortune Teller Removed'—Georgie Wreckage," he said. "'Fire Wagon Crack-Up'—Georgie Wreckage. 'Crowd of Italians Clubbing a Rapist in Broad Daylight'—*also* by Georgie Wreckage. How's it feel to have your signature on every sorrow in New York, George?"

Again, he glanced around to wink, but nobody was looking now. Dieffer was blowing his nose. Stolley was caressing the cyst on his neck with the four of diamonds. Georgie had rolled down his shirt sleeves and was attaching the cuffs. Almost quitting time. Dinner with Bram.

"Sleep well, do you, George?"

"Like a stone, thanks." Georgie looked across the art department at A.K.'s smiling mug. He tried to smile, too, but couldn't manage it. Cartoonist Plummets 11 Floors—pictures by Georgie Wreckage. "I sleep like a stone." In fact, several times a week he had nightmares, though he wasn't about to admit that, especially to A.K. Nightmares of running, chasing, suddenly bleeding, suffocating. You told people, immediately they'd figure something was the matter with you, you should see a doctor—or confess to the crime. Otherwise you'd end up drinking carbolic acid. Georgie'd been having his nightmares for years. He was used to them. And besides, you always woke up, didn't you? Woke up safe. And then didn't it feel ever so sweet to be alive?

Dieffer said, "Gin."

Stolley said, "Yer mother!"

Then A.K. put on his hunter's cap and his plaid cape, he toodle-ooed and said, "Good night, gentlemen." Left without his beanshooter and half-filled sack of beans—which Georgie right away threw into a wastepaper basket.

Just then, in burst Sid McKeon—Handsome Sid, the Art Chief—and waving high a batch of flimsies, he shouted, "Who wants the exploding horse? Who wants an airshaft suicide? Who wants to draw a machine that cures consumption, asthma, bronchitis, and catarrh?"

Dieffer jumped up and bid for the suicide, and Stolley took the horse. That stuck Georgie with the goddamn machine. Jesus H. Christ. Consumption, asthma, bronchitis, and *what?* Swap you, Stolley. Swap you, Dief. But no dice. "Hey, Sid, how am I supposed to know what this thing looks like? Should I go see it?"

"See it?" McKeon hooted. "Where you going to see it? It hasn't been invented yet. Use your imagination." He pulled open his bottom drawer, took out an unlabeled bottle of rye whiskey. Had a slug, a second. Then he crossed his arms on his desk, rested his chin on a wrist, and stared moonily at a file photograph of Consuelo Vanderbilt, his ideal, that was pinned to the wall. It was Sid's goal in life to become acquainted with a girl like her, an eligible daughter of the new wealth. Now, he was choosy but not pernickety—her father didn't have to own *railroads;* a pig-iron furnace or a spline-wire factory would do. As long as he had several millions. Sid's One Rule for Success was: Marry Money. Forget for poon tang or for love, marry for money. Sunday afternoons, he rented a gentleman's Norfolk suit and a visored cap and went pedaling up and down Riverside Drive, up and down on a borrowed Imperial, the so-called "make for modern young Lochinvars," praying that he'd find his fair Helen (or May, or Anna) stranded with a punctured tire. The hell with newspaper work! The hell with work of any kind. Sid truly believed he was destined to summer at Newport in a sixty-room marble "cottage"—because his profile was good. In all other respects, he was a rational fella. He picked up his head now and called to Georgie, "Just stick on some vacuum tubes, it'll be fine."

Georgie nodded and began reading the news story as he walked back to his table. According to that, not only had the machine been invented—by a man named Elmer Dreezle—it had been widely tested too and found to be 99 percent effective. It seemed to Georgie that he'd heard of this Elmer Dreezle before—from Clarky? Maybe, but more likely from Professor Thom. The Professor, who also lived in Mrs. Bennett's house, knew every nutty inventor there was, and downtown was full of them that year. Inventors inventing automatic shoe-lacing gizmos, better cherry stoners, philharmonic gas ranges, and concocting blacker explosives and baroque weapons of war. On a weekend, if you had nothing to do, you could ride the nickel ferry to Richmond and see a few dozen of them test their latest devices on open land. The Professor had taken Georgie and Joette Davey with him one time, and they'd all watched a friend of his who'd produced yet another death ray turn a Civil War plaque at Fort Hill to copper jelly. Could that've been Dreezle? Short old man with cueball eyes and a biblical white beard down to his privates? Maybe. Georgie worked on the drawing for half an hour, letting it take shape randomly, like a doodle, sticking on knobs and levers.

"Whoa, what's this? A Marvelous Engine That Will Convert the Heathen to Christianity?"

Georgie glanced up, grinning, at Bram Hoopes, the Sunday-supplement cartoonist. "Or vice versa, Bram."

Handsome Sid had heard Bram's remark, and over he trotted now to look at Georgie's machine. Hmm. He scratched his head and, sucking hard on his front teeth, made a frizzling sound. "You're right, Bram," he said finally. "This is too good to cure consumption. The hell with consumption! The hell with disease! What'd you call it? An engine to convert the Jews?"

"The heathen to Christianity."

"At least!" Sid snatched up the drawing and rushed out with it. "Feature writer! I need a feature writer!"

Georgie had just run a match across a striker to light a cigarette when he remembered that he hadn't signed the picture. He nearly went chasing after Sid, but then Bram said, "Leave it off, why don't you? You'll probably be glad someday you did." Meaning what? Meaning what, exactly? Georgie wondered. The picture's no good? It stinks? Then say that, Ohio. Sick and tired of these goddamn "valuable" sons of bitches cracking wise. Bram caught Georgie's sour, questioning look and started to laugh. "You won't want people to know that you drew some daffy invention, will you—five years from now when you're famous?" Oh. Well. Since Bram meant it like *that:* Georgie nodded. Leave off the signature. Makes sense. Let's go eat.

On the way down in the elevator, though, Georgie had second thoughts, elbowed Bram suddenly between ribs, and said, "What do you mean, *five* years?"

5

Bram had asked, Hitchcock's or Meehan's? and Georgie had replied, Either place—you're paying, Ohio, you pick. So they'd walked down the Row to Meehan's Restaurant, where portly Meehan himself stood in the front window carving up a corned beef. The place was crowded, busy: reporters leaning at the long bar with schooners of beer, politicians arguing by the rubber plants, a cele- brated jewel thief supping at a table with his mother and three glam- orous wives. In a booth, a pair of robust stage actresses laughed hectically while their gentlemen companions smugly puffed on tiny cigarettes. Bram ordered wine. It came and he proposed a toast: to Georgie. "My pal! And the fella to whom I owe all my good fortune. I thank you. And the hag thanks you." The hag? The Yellow Hag of Fan-Tan Street. Appearing Sundays, exclusively in the New York *World*. Very popular feature. "We both thank you from the bottom of our paper hearts."

Georgie gulped his wine, then reached for the bottle.

True, he *was* responsible for Bram's very recent success, kind of. And he felt—well, he didn't know for certain just *how* he felt about it. Amused? That, a little. Surprised? That too. Pleased? Well . . . maybe. Jealous? Jealous. You bet. Not that he wanted to spend all his time cartooning a bad-tempered old squint with a pigtail, but still. Still, Bram was now making four times the money that Georgie was, and doing one-zillionth the amount of work. Every day he had on a different suit of clothes, a new topcoat. He'd grown a mustache and kept it *waxed*. God almighty. Last week, they'd come out with Yellow Hag licorice; this week it was hatchets. That's what Bram was celebrating tonight, the Yellow Hag Hatchet o' Fun. He'd get a nickel for each one sold. Small wonder Georgie was jealous.

Bram groomed himself these days like a second Richard Harding Davis, but only three months ago he couldn't even comb his hair so it'd stay in place. Food on his shirt. Midwest twang. He drew maps at the *World*, some of them beauts. Tokyo in Korea, the Sudan as an island. And whenever such blunders were pointed out to him, Bram would laugh uproariously. *Not* an island? *That's* funny. A real kid. A country Jake. A foozle from Ohio. And then one day, out of the blue, Bram the foozle informed Sid McKeon that he'd decided to give up maps—too boring—and become a cartoonist. I'm a happy fella. Got a sense of humor. Bet I can make you laugh. Sure, Bram, sure. Go right ahead. But before you do, you think you might draw us the French Congo? And stick it in Africa, please. Poor Sid—why, oh, why couldn't he find a poor little rich girl who'd take him away from all these nuts? *Bram?* A car*toon*ist?

Already there were more than two dozen *real* cartoonists on staff, and twice as many more contributed as free lances—all of them, since Pulitzer's acquisition last year of a color press, competing like mad for space in the Comic Weekly. This was the paper's latest kicker, an eight-page Sunday wrapper full of text jokes, puns, and limericks swiped from local music halls, plus large crowded line drawings that burlesqued city life in wishy-washy pastels. The funny papers. Something new, something different and easy to swallow, like minute tapioca and the Hershey bar. A young man could make a name for himself in the funny papers. Say, maybe Bram wasn't such a foozle after all.

But once he'd started drawing cartoons and bringing them in, he sure was a pain in the ass, always trying to collar Walt McDougall and Dickie Outcault and practically every other gag artist that he spotted around the office. What d'you think of this? Have a look. And if there was no mop closet to hide in, they would, grudgingly; they'd look at Bram's poor dim yokels struck by lightning or kicked by mules, at his sheriffs in hot pursuit of hoboes juggling looted pies, at his dogs and cats being devilish to their suburban masters, and they'd think—all, right, since you *asked*—they'd think Bram should stop copying old corn and start using his noodle. This is New York, they'd tell him. This is a New York paper. What's a riot in Skeedaddle, Ohio, ain't here. Wops are funny here, how they quarrel. Micks are funny, the way they drink, and Jews because they dicker and bilk. And bicyclists, God bless 'em, are *very* funny, if they're fat and female, especially if they fall in the mud. But nobody here gives a hoot about the farmer in the dell. Understand?

Bram did; he understood that he had a problem—complete ignorance of New York City beyond Park Row. Bram was living with relatives out in Flushing, commuting to work every day on the Long Island Rail Road. Flushing in those days was very much a little village. Bram felt comfortable there—it was homey, it was friendly, and he even had a sweetheart spotted with freckles; she sang "When the Mists Have Rolled Away" for Sunday visitors and gave piano lessons. Bram had never thought that he *needed* to learn New York. Now he changed his mind and turned to Georgie for help. How about we go out some evening? What's worth seeing? Know any Irish families? Where do Italians live? Thursday good?

Thursday's fine, said Georgie, even though it wasn't, and to go out with Bram he'd have to break a date with Joette Davey; Thursday's

fine, he said, because Bram was another lefty, and in those days
lefties, like Masons, like countrymen on foreign soil, went readily to
each other's aid, no questions asked.

It was January then, though the evening of their excursion proved
to be so mild that they left off their mufflers and gloves. Georgie
conducted Bram first through several penny arcades—Irish boys at
miniature bowling—then strolled him by a stale beer dive, the
Lower Bowery Captive Balloon Port, Police Headquarters, the Pro-
duce Exchange, and Filch Hall. Then they ate spaghetti in a cellar
restaurant with chromolithographs of vineyards, Pompeii, and the
Colosseum on the walls. Bram seemed disappointed when nobody
there argued. Let's see some Jews. So Georgie took him to Hester
Street. Again, Bram was disappointed; it was growing late, and the
only vendor they saw was a fishmonger whose cart was illuminated
by torches. Where was all the *funny* stuff?

Georgie accompanied Bram next to a small park in a German
neighborhood where about a dozen health faddists were strolling
barefoot on a section of lawn they'd made sodden with buckets of
water. Bram liked that. *That's* pretty funny. What else can you show
me, George? I got time for one last thing.

And so they ended up in Pell Street, at a joss house where the
opium was make-believe for a tourist clientele and an orchestra of
yellow men played the same grand march over and over. The white
slaves chained to filthy cots in the bagnio were all hired actresses,
and the cooties in their grubby wigs nothing more than strips of
pressed bread. The gambling was bona fide, though, and grossly
rigged. You could buy souvenirs, you could buy liquor, and steamed
fish on a bed of rice. It was mostly an uptown crowd. Bram started
giggling as soon as he walked in. This is *great!* They both got drunk
on Chinese wine, and then Bram wandered away from Georgie's
side. He went upstairs, where he shouldn't have gone, and stumbled
into a private crib tiered with benches. And there, seated at the top
with a bushy orange cat asleep in her lap, was a small wrinkled
Chinese woman in a loose blouse and baggy trousers and sandals
with thick soles. She was sucking on a long pipe and her head was
enveloped in a cloud of yellow smoke. Bram asked her, innocently
enough, where the gents' room was, and she threw a hatchet. From
such misadventures fortunes are made. Or used to be.

"If I'd been standing a foot, just one foot to the left, she would've
split my skull in half," Bram said now at Meehan's, talking with his

mouth full. So far, he'd devoured three porterhouse steaks, each
weighing a pound, half a dozen warm buttered rolls, and a side order
of pigs' feet with deviled sauce. "Now, *there* was a hag!"

Georgie, slowly chewing his lobster-on-toast, laughed because
Bram did. He took out his watch and looked at it. Free-and-easy at
the Blade. But Clarky hadn't said when. He'd try eight.

"God bless her, though." Bram took a sip of stomach bitters, then
reached for the cold asparagus in french dressing. "God bless the
hag!"

Two mornings after his close call with that blessed hag, Bram had
showed up at work with a finished cartoon called "Thursday Evening at the Fan-Tan Joint," the picture a bedlam of borrowed characters and exaggerated incidents. Admit it, fellas—*now* I got the
hang of it. Absolutely! There were galloping vendors and girls
muscle-dancing with big galoots on top of the bar, at least three pickpockets, and a juggler wangling fish and candles and peaches.
Waiters with the pigtail leaping over crapshooters and dogs. A lush-
worker robbing a fancy Dan who'd passed into a torpor behind the
wheel of fortune. And two little China boys in overalls tossing cannon crackers underneath the gaming table, blasting half a dozen
cardplayers out of their seats and sending pasteboards, cash money,
and cigars flying through the air pell-mell. All of that *plus* coppers
breaking down the front door, tumbling through the windows.
Whew! And more still. Up there, in the right-hand corner—see her?
on that bamboo swing? An old woman with a hatchet in her fist, a
tomcat in her lap, and a deckle-edged cloud of smoke spurting from
her pipe, surrounding her comment: IT'S ALWAYS QUIET BEFORE
THE WEEKEND. BUT JUST LET ANYBODY GET OUT O' LINE, THEY
ANSWER TO *ME!*

Well, well, Bram *had* got the hang of it, hadn't he? Quick learner.
Now, you might quibble about his anatomy—as McDougall did,
though Lord knows, *he* was no Da Vinci himself—and you could
criticize his rendering and his indifference to the laws of light and
shadow, but you couldn't deny he'd captured the hooligan spirit of
the *World*'s funny sheets—*that* you could not dispute. Good for
Hoopes. Hurray for Ohio. Credit where credit's due.

The cartoon—hey, look what our map man did—had been passed
around the office, from Art to Editorial and finally to the press room,
where Charlie Saalburgh, foreman of the tint-laying Ben Day machines, grabbed it and ran it back to Sid McKeon. We're *using* this,

he said, to which Handsome Sid replied, Maybe—haven't decided
yet. No, no, we're *using* this, Charlie insisted. It's perfect! Aw, it's
not *that* funny. Funny shmunny, said Charlie. Just look, I counted
ten chinks. What color are chinks, Sid? They're yellow. And what's
happened every time we used yellow ink? It smeared all over the
goddamn page. Right? Right, Sid replied and conked himself on his
temple with a fist. Let me get this straight, Charlie. Yellow makes a
mess—so you want to run a picture that's almost nothing *but* yellow?
Saints preserve me, is *every*body nuts? And Charlie said, But listen,
I invented this quick drier, uses tallow, it'll dry the yellow in a jiff
and leave it bright as the midday sun. *Another* inventor. This cartoon, said Charlie, it'll be a test. A test. And if your drier *don't* work,
we got a catastrophe on Sunday, don't we? Trust me, Charlie
pleaded. Bram was standing nearby, chewing his cuticles. Trust
him, Sid, *trust* him. Sid nodded, finally, and Charlie Saalburgh
turned and gave Bram a playful poke in the arm, the left, with his
left elbow. *Another* lefty, what do you know.

The drier worked, and that Sunday you could spot Bram's picture
on the newsstand from thirty feet away. What's that all about? Let's
have a look, Oscar; let's have a look, Maggie, old girl. . . .

"Would you like coffee, George? I wouldn't mind a slice of chocolate cake, myself." Half standing, Bram looked around for their
waiter. He began to snap his fingers—service, service! Then, from
inside his coat, he pulled out a small hatchet and rapped it against
the table.

"I don't have time for dessert," Georgie said. "Really. Jesus
Christ, will you put that away? People are staring."

"Going somewhere?"

"I should."

"You *should?* What's that mean? Clarky tell you there's a big fire
scheduled for tonight, you don't want to miss it? Two pieces of chocolate cake, two coffees. *Georgie*. Skip the fire, let's do something."

"It's not a fire."

"Who cares what it is. A bomb set for nine. You run around too
damn much."

"Keeps me fit, Bram. Thirty-two waist, nice strong legs."

"They should buy your shoes."

"I can buy my own."

"Paid enough, are you?"

"*Well* enough."

Bram said, "Listen, George. Since the subject's come up naturally in the conversation, there's a question I want to ask you."

"What subject? My salary?"

"Your livelihood. Your job. I been curious how long you see yourself having one at the *World*."

"Till I screw up."

"Never happen, George. You won't do that. But somebody just might screw *you* up. In fact, I'm sure he will. One of these days."

Georgie laughed, then made believe his palm was a note pad, his finger a pencil. "Name? Address? Occupation?" he asked.

"His name," said Bram, "is whoever figures out a way to adapt halftone engravings to a perfecting press."

"Inventors," Georgie said. "Honest to God, something ought to be done about those bastards."

"You smirk, George, but it's coming. You know it is. Then what do you do? Paint landscapes? I worry about you."

"Please don't."

"Well, I do. We're pals."

"Lose any sleep?"

"No, but I still worry. Half the drawings in the paper right now are *copied* from photographs."

"You exaggerate. Typical cartoonist."

Bram smiled. "Have they had *you* do that, copy?"

"No."

"Send you out with a camera?"

"Not me." Their coffee and cake arrived.

"Not you *yet*. But they will. And then maybe next year it's photographs for real, and the hell with line copies. Sketch artist seeks employment."

Georgie was eating and listening; he nodded slightly, then shrugged. "Maybe. But I'm not gonna worry now. Don't you, either."

Bram sweetened his coffee, bent forward, and slurped. "You draw better than I do."

"Who doesn't? So?"

"Come on," Bram said, grinning. "You know what I'm driving at. You did me a favor, now it's my turn. One backhand to another: Get religion, pal. Go to church on Sunday, loaf around all week."

"I like what I'm doing. I like the news."

"The news," Bram said, "the news," and bleated. "Life is death, life is death. Very boring."

"Says you."

"Says me. You're right. I say life is full of hazards, but nobody, *nobody* gets seriously hurt. The Cartoonists' Creed." The waiter came over, and Bram asked him for the check. Then he said to Georgie, "You know that picture you have in today's paper—the fortune-teller? I saw that earlier, I thought now here's something *I* might've done, or Outcault or Drayton or Paulie or McDougall, any one of us. Birds flying around her clobbered head going *tweet-tweet-tweet*. That's Sunday stuff, George, I'm telling you."

"Thought that was a funny picture, did you?"

"Christ, no. But who draws funny pictures in the comics section? I don't. Between you and me and the wallpaper, I don't think any of the stuff I've been doing is funny. In the least. Is it funny when some poor nigger has a bite taken out of his rear end by a bulldog? No. But that's what I happened to draw last week and it was in the funny papers, so it must be funny. Look. The only difference between what you and I draw is the upshot. *Your* drunk falls off a train trestle and ends up with a busted neck. Mine goes cross-eyed." Bram smiled, then licked cake frosting from the tines of his fork. "Anyway. All I'm saying is, there's room still in the front pew with the elect. If you care to be saved."

"Saved?"

"Rich and lazy. End of sermon. Now. Why don't you just forget all about running off to that stupid fire?"

"I'm not running to any fire."

"Good. Then come out with me. We'll do something. My treat. How about it, George? We'll have some *real* laughs. Go someplace silly. I'll think of someplace."

By the time he'd drained his coffee cup, Bram had thought of the Constantinople Club, up on Twenty-fifth Street—because what could be sillier than a nightclub decked out like a pasha's palace, with Oriental lamps and sputtering torches, burning censers and bare-chested Tenderloin roughnecks bearing blunted scimitars and shod in turned-up slippers? Ha, ha! Bram was delighted that Georgie had never heard of the place. *Never? Really?* It's a Turkish smoking parlor: overstuffed cushions, nargilehs and chibouks, pretty girls in fluffy skirts and light-colored turbans. There's a Frieda called Cassay, a Sally called Ogala, and a Marguerite called Zavor. A grand place. You really never heard of it? Imagine that. Bram the cosmopolite. Lived in Chelsea now, and Flushing was a hick town. "Shall we be off?"

"Some other time, Bram."

"Sure. Some other time." He moistened a finger and started picking up crumbs of devil's food with it. "I wouldn't want you to miss any good grief. I understand." He smiled.

"Thanks for dinner. And for the sermon, I guess."

"You just think about it."

"Maybe I will."

Bram took the hatchet from beside his water glass and passed it across the table to Georgie. "A little token of my high esteem."

"What're they asking for this?"

"Twenty-two cents."

"And you get a nickel?"

"I get a nickel, the *World* gets a dime. They want the hag, they pay the price." And there she was, pasted on the short handle. "Good night, George. Happy fire." They shook lefty.

When Georgie left the restaurant, it was half past seven and full dark. An overcast night. Cabbies looked at him from their driver's boxes, reins limp in their hands. Coach lights flickering, horses standing motionless along the curb. The pavement shook from high-speed presses belowground. A few reporters hastened by. Across the street in City Hall Park, several bums were huddled around a barrel of flames, and outside the park fence, a Bohemian in a greatcoat stood hunched and forlorn behind a trestle table displaying two-for-a-nickel cigars. You could smell the river.

Georgie cut across Park Row, then strolled down to the statue of Nathan Hale at the northern end of the park, hoping to see the litle bald kid who loitered there sometimes with condoms in a wigbox; he was thinking he might buy half a dozen now, for the weekend. But the kid wasn't there, only pigeons and a young drunk curled up on a rustling pallet of newspapers, other newspapers covering him. Georgie looked down at the sleeping man, indifferently at first, but then the thought occurred to him that he had matches, that he could light one and touch it to the papers—some picture! Some *picture?* What am I, completely out of my mind? He felt stunned, he'd frightened himself, and he backed away till the statue and the figure lying at its base lost definition and became part of the darkness.

He hurried away, scribbling on his thumbs with the tips of his first fingers; scribbling, then digging in the nails till it hurt. Thinking that he should run back to Meehan's, see if he could catch Bram—go uptown, that silly place. Overstuffed cushions, girls in fluffy skirts, a Marguerite called something. He felt logy all of a sudden, and then he found himself, not back at Meehan's, but on Canal Street, near the Bowery, outside the Blade, paying his ten cents' admission. And he couldn't remember having walked over. What route had he taken? How on earth had he come to be here?

Just inside the door, and seated on a wire crate, was a clean-shaven bouncer in a bowler hat who was peeling an apple over a newspaper spread across his lap.

At the Blade, the last room of three in a row, and the one with a vast oil painting of nude bathers on the ceiling, was called the Snuggery—for bachelor parties and poker tournaments, for serious plotting to kill the Queen of England, and, irregularly, for the knife fights, the free-and-easies. That evening, Blond Robert, not-a-scar-on-'im, was fighting, and if you wanted to challenge him, the entrant's fee was fifty cents. With a hundred-dollar purse, there was no shortage of brave—or, as Georgie thought of them, foolhardy—souls. Sarsaparilla Reilly had already turned some away. Pip-squeaks and fatsos and obvious drunkards. This was to be a quality show, square and sporting. Reilly, very short and slightly over-weight, was proprietor of the Blade. He had puffy cheeks and a pitted chin, and eyes like two black taws—shooting marbles. A dark-blue suit, double-breasted with pearl buttons; there were pearl buttons even down his trouser seams. Georgie had counted exactly how many there were, all told. Thirty-six. The habit of observation.

Reilly stood at ringside, at the head of the line of challengers and next to a blackboard, wearing gloves so his fingers wouldn't get powdery from his stick of chalk. He beckoned a well-built redhead to step forward now. The redhead wasn't wearing a shirt, and his suspenders cut deeply into his beefy shoulders. He grinned at Reilly to show off a silver-plated roofer's nail where an eyetooth should've been. He plunked his money down on Reilly's barrel. Georgie was watching from the long bar.

"Name?"

"Eugene McCarthy."

Beside the number 7 on the blackboard, Reilly printed GENE THE GIANT.

"All righty. Know the rules, Gene? You have three minutes in the ring with the champ. If you so much as nick him, we stop the fight and you walk away with a hundred bucks. I should warn you, though—last time, Robert extracted two stomachs, a gallbladder, and about forty miles of intestines. Still game?"

Gene the Giant laughed and fetched out a penknife from his pants pocket. "Game," he said.

"Take a seat. We'll call you."

Reilly turned away a boy who'd glued on a woolen beard and a merchant sailor who obviously was wearing protective armor under his pea coat. Then he accepted a Negro with gold freckles—THE FRECKLED FIEND, he wrote on the blackboard.

A man standing alongside Georgie at the bar started to laugh. "God, I love this dive," he said. "You never know what you're going to see next, do you? Last time I was here? There was a priest climbed in the ring, a Catholic priest."

Georgie nodded; he believed it.

"Beats Fourteenth Street," said the man. "Beats the theatre." He was middle-aged, of medium build, had sideburns and a spade-cut beard. A chesterfield coat, unbuttoned, black trousers, black shoes with fawn-colored tops. A slummer. "You're liable to see *any*thing. Have you seen the dog?" He chuckled; then, noticing that his glass had been refilled by the barman, he picked it up and emptied it in a gulp. "You haven't seen the dog by any chance, have you?"

"What dog?" Georgie asked.

At that moment, Reilly was rejecting still another challenger, an old leathery Cuban whose eyes were amazingly blue. He had only one hand, his right. Attached to a stump at the end of his left arm was a cut-glass doorknob. "I'm sorry, grandfather," said Reilly with a friendly smile, "but I'm not in the murder business."

"What dog?" Georgie asked again.

"I don't see it at the moment," replied the slummer, going up on his toes and scanning the room. "But it was over by the candy concession a few minutes ago. A dog that talks."

Georgie didn't say anything.

"I'm standing there to get some licorice," said the slummer, picking up the white sack of it now from the bar top, "when I feel something brush my leg. In this place, you never know, it might be the
world's tallest rat, so down I look. And there's this dog, big old dog,
and the dog looks right back up at me and says, I swear it says,
'Don't worry, pal, I don't bite.'"

Georgie had to laugh.

"I mean it! That's what the dog said first. Then it says, 'What're
you getting there, chocolates?' And I say, 'Licorice,' and it says,
really disappointed, 'I can't eat licorice, sticks to my teeth.' So I buy
a bonbon, I bend over, and the dog eats it out of my hand. Says,
'Thanks!'"

Georgie's face was skeptical, but he said, "I remember this bull-
frog once. It could count as high as twenty, but it always skipped
over one number. It would count *eleven, twelve,* then skip to *fourteen.*
Or, *twelve, thirteen,* and skip to *fifteen*—I can't remember exactly.
Somebody brought it into third grade. Then the girls screamed and
Miss Bernadette killed it with her umbrella. Did the dog really talk
to you?"

"Absolutely-positively. And I wasn't the only one heard it. There
was this fella just in back of me. I asked him, 'You hear what I'm
hearing?' This is right after the dog said thanks, and the fella nods
and says, 'Polite animal, ain't she.' The dog's around someplace. Go
see for yourself."

Georgie was trying to decide whether he should do just that thing,
whether the slummer was corked or not—he didn't slur, he didn't
look bugs.

By now, Reilly had accepted the tenth, and final, contestant—
dubbed THE PIRATE, on account of the big man's gold earring—and
the first match would get under way in a few minutes. The slummer
put his shotglass down on the bar. "Time to make a few wagers," he
said, reaching into his hip pocket for his purse. Then he frowned—
"Damn"—and started to pat himself frantically, all over. *"Damn!"*

Georgie went off to look for the dog that talked.

He spotted one of Clarky's boys in the crowd, and it turned out to
be the Armenian he'd seen earlier at Cooper Square. The boy remembered Georgie, too. He still seemed abashed. There was the
tiniest smudge of bootblack on his jacket cuff. Georgie asked him if
he'd seen a dog.

"Fuzzy?"

"I don't know. Is there more than one dog?"

"You're probably talking about Fuzzy. They went into the other room."

"They?"

"Her and Billy McCord."

"Billy McCord," said Georgie. "He a dip?"

"Is Huntington richer than Kernochan?"

After the hubbub in the Snuggery, the Blade's middle room, a small plain barroom, was a relief for Georgie. It had a low timbered ceiling, sawdust on the floor, chamber-pot spittoons, and framed cards on the walls: *The Clock Is Never Right. We Cash Checks for Everyone. If You Haven't Any Money, the Hydrant Is in the Rear*. Because of the fights, there wasn't much of a crowd: thirty, thirty-five poorly dressed men, standing at the long bar or sitting around tables—smoking cigarettes and eating rye bread sandwiches, nursing Brain Dusters and Alabazams or quaffing nickel beers. Georgie saw Fuzzy immediately, at the far end of the bar. A woolly yellow mixed-breed, a large animal with a long narrow muzzle; definitely some collie blood.

A little fat man set down a saucer of raw whiskey on the floor, and the dog began to lap it up, avidly. Georgie could hear the man's delighted laughter halfway across the room. He moved closer and then saw another man, a pale young sourpuss with flickering eyelids and thyroid cartilage the size of a walnut, slide off a stool, crouch, and quickly remove the fat man's wallet. "Did you hear what it just said—did you hear it talk?" said the fat man to the sourpuss. "It said it wants another!"

The sourpuss nodded and replied, "Thirsty animal, ain't she?" Then he tossed two dimes on the bar and started back toward the Snuggery. But ten feet on, Georgie put a hand out and stopped him.

"Amazing dog you got there, William, Just amazing."

"What dog? *That* dog? That ain't mine. She's just some dog they let in."

"Talks, don't it? Don't she?"

Billy hesitated before sneering. "Dogs don't talk, pal. You better lay off the Sitting Bull Fizz." He poked Georgie in the chest and strode off. The fat man, meanwhile, was trying to get the dog to say something further and having no success. Finally, looking embarrassed and shaking his head, he climbed back onto his stool and reached for a pickle.

Moments later, Fuzzy got up and trotted across the room. She stopped at the Snuggery door. Georgie opened it for her. He winked. And he would've sworn that she did likewise, that she winked back.

The dog scooted into the crowd, and Georgie lost her; he didn't see Billy anywhere either, so he turned to the ring—what he was there for, wasn't it?—and watched a challenger with bad skin and a seaman's ponytail stumble around clutching at his throat. Killer Costello or Brave Dave? Blood flowed through his fingers. Blond Robert—what a gorilla—smiled blissfully and danced the cakewalk, taking further cuts. "D'you know, in two and a half years only one fella's ever collected the pot?" It was Clarky's Armenian, suddenly at Georgie's side. "I hear he died the next day, but he collected."

"This Costello now?"

"You missed Costello. He just left the premises in a carpet runner." The kid pointed to the rear exit. "That's Dave. That *was* Dave. You seen Fuzzy?"

"I did," said Georgie. "Neat trick of Billy's."

"What is?"

"Making it look like she talks."

"Don't be stupid. It don't *look* like she does, she *does*."

"Yeah? Go and jam one of your rags down Billy's throat, then see how much she talks."

There they were again—Billy seated on a folding chair, a few feet from where Fuzzy lay on the floor in a doughnut shape next to Reilly's blackboard. Georgie began to sketch them both, with his tongue on the roof of his mouth. From his shoeshine kit, the Armenian pulled a soiled polishing cloth. He shook it at Georgie.

"*You* do it, go ahead. Gag him up, and I bet you anything she still asks you to buy her a drink. Bet you."

Georgie raised his eyes to the oil painting. *That* dog? Talks by herself? Nuts! What could you expect, though, from a kid who'd pick Kernochan over Huntington. Now, if you'd pressed Georgie, he would've owned it was possible, even likely, that *some* dogs might do better than growl and bark, bark and whine—that one dog out of, say, a billion litters could have true smarts and a human larynx. Why not? Much of nature was still a mystery, much of Africa still was dark. But *this* dog, this Fuzzy—sure as God made apples, she was a dummy for Billy McCord. Good trick! "The Pickpocket's

Hound," pictures by Georgie Wreckage. "The Pickpocket's *Partner?*" Partner. Partner sounded better, thought Georgie.

The ring was being swabbed clean by a couple of refs in yellow
rain slickers, and the fight crowd was swarming to the betting tables.
At the bar it was six deep and dangerous. A small gray-faced man
starting to get bald on top had gone over to the blackboard. He was
studying the names. Georgie saw him glance down to Fuzzy, saw his
eyes and mouth open wide. Saw him stoop. And saw Billy step behind him.

"This dog gives tips!" exclaimed the balding man, getting up.

"Some animal, ain't she?" Billy said.

"Says I should put three bucks on Mustache Ike—he'll have the
blond man's ears in ten seconds flat."

Billy looked at the blackboard and rubbed his chin. "Ike?"

"How come a dog talks to me?"

"Why shouldn't she? You don't look like such a bad fella."

"It's yours, this dog?"

"Not mine. Guess she belongs here. Ike, says she, huh?" Billy
waited till the man had gone and joined a betting line; then he gave
Fuzzy a light boot in the haunch. She stood. Billy turned around.
Georgie was right there, grinning.

"Ike," he said. "I seen Ike. He couldn't cut a boiled potato."

Billy shrugged, so what. "You a dick?"

"God, no."

"So why you following me?"

Georgie kept smiling and didn't reply.

"Listen, chump, if Connie sent you, you don't scare me and he
can go to hell. Straight to hell." He swaggered off, buttoning his coat
up, then pulling a cloth cap down over his eyes. The dog followed
him across the Snuggery and out.

Georgie wished they'd done something more special, those two.
What he'd seen was all *right*, but it was Page Eight stuff. Filler. Gee,
they could do better than that. Who was *Connie?*

Blond Robert was sharpening his long knife on a whetstone. Now
he plucked a hair from his head and split it, for the applause. Reilly
was calling, "Number four—Slippery John. Slippery John! Where
is that piece of beef?"

Georgie decided he'd seen enough. Of this.

❑ ❑ ❑

He never let the man and his dog get farther ahead than half a block, and they seemed totally unaware that he was shadowing them. The dog pissed against a fence that advertised beers and catsup and Franco-American soups. Billy stopped at a penny coffee stand, gulped down a cup. Then they strolled on, past the dime museums, the cabarets, and the glass-fronted saloons. Georgie was smoking.

The Bowery at that time of night, that time of Friday night, was mad with noise and confusion. Surface cars clanged. An El train clattered overhead, spewing hot oil and a fusillade of glowing coals. Rifles popped in the shooting galleries, hurdy-gurdies wheezed. There were Chinamen and Galicians, Russians and Poles, and young Italian men in Old World suits who flashed their hands, describing women. There were soldiers and sailors, and bums cooking chuck steaks over campfires along the curb. Prostitutes hollered from their windows. Vendors roamed, crying Peanuts! Hot corn! Carpet samples! Collar buttons! Suspenders! Smooth-faced Bowery boys wearing pearly fedoras and loud-checked jackets and pink-striped shirts walked arm in arm with their current rags, all dolled up in flowered hats with ostrich feathers. And a huge, barrel-chested, black-whiskered vampire, clutching in one hand his growler of blood from the slaughterhouse, leaned against a bank building and read *The Prisoner of Zenda* by yellow arc light.

Beyond McBirdie's Museum of the Amazing and the Lower Bowery Captive Balloon Port was a triangle-shaped park called Vest Pocket Wedge. Georgie was hoping that McCord and Fuzzy wouldn't cut through it, because it was poorly lit, it was *un*lit, because on any night of the week you were very likely to find at least one suicide dangling at the end of a rope tied to a Dutch elm, and because it was Devil Boys' turf—but they did. Now what? Go home? Georgie leaned against the balloon port's corral fence and finished his smoke. He watched one heated bag go up carrying several laughing passengers in its gondola, and another bag come down. The operators of the great winch were all Frenchmen. Some evening he'd take Joette for a ride; he'd been promising her and promising her. He stamped out his cigarette. So? Was he going home, or was he going on? Make up your mind, George. Well, since he'd come *this* far. . . . He plunged into the park. He could hear a water fountain gurgling but couldn't see past his nose.

Then the dog fell in beside him, her paws going *tip-tap, tip-tap* on the paved walk, and Georgie jumped a foot.

The dog said, "Connie Dwyer *did* send you after us, didn't he?"

Georgie whirled around, shoving his arms out straight: no Billy. "Who's Connie Dwyer?"

He was talking to a dog.

"Come on! You tell Connie that Billy had nothing to do with that thing on Fourteenth Street. Nothing at all. You tell him." The dog's voice: soft, breathy, vaguely southern—there was a drawl—but neither masculine nor feminine.

"I don't know any Connie Dwyer."

The dog wasn't buying that. "You tell Connie, he has some quarrel with Billy, he knows where to find him tomorrow night. But don't go sending any more cheap cutthroats after us."

"Cutthroat?" Georgie laughed.

"Cheap and *dumb,*" said Billy McCord, here now from nowhere. "You come after me again, sport, you might try holding onto your weapon."

Georgie would've asked, What weapon, *what?* but before he had the chance, he was conked on the head and knocked cold by it. By the Official Yellow Hag Hatchet o' Fun, *that* weapon. Guess Billy didn't know it was supposed to be a toy.

7

"When I was eleven and twelve," said Professor Thom as he fitted Georgie with the Headache Abater, patent pending, "I attended All-Souls School in Hoboken. Red brick building with separate entrances for boys and girls. Fat nuns standing on the front steps every day at eight twenty, hurrying pupils through the proper doors. 'G'morning, sister.' 'G'morning, sister.'" He smiled, attaching wires to the circlet. Georgie was still sick at his stomach, and his temples throbbed. "The Mother Superior came outside at eight twenty-nine. Eight thirty, she rang this golden altar bell of hers. Then you were late. Big trouble." From a cabinet he took a large zinc battery. "She was a small woman—barely five feet, as I recall. Face covered with freckles, and she wore a black leather glove on her right hand.

Mother Angelus. Could bring down great chunks of plastering on the heads of secret talkers, just by squinting at the ceiling. I remember *that* about her. How could I forget? Now, take a deep breath, George. Hold it." He connected the wires to the dry cell, and there was a buzz. Georgie's eyes bulged against their lids. "Feel better?"

Georgie lifted the metal band off his head. It was warm. "I don't know yet." He touched the lump, size of a fig and just as soft. His complexion was as white as white butter. "I think it's a little better."

Professor Thom frowned. "Just a *little?* Let's try it one more time. You got a nasty crack."

"I'll be fine."

"Whatever you say." Indoors and out, Professor Thom—it was Thomas Thomson—wore a homburg and a topcoat, the hat crushed and the coat mangy, and he smoked a pipe home-made from a wooden toy soldier and a bullet mold. He relit the pipe now. "But I was telling you about Sister Angelus."

"Is there a point to this story?" Georgie squeezed his head between his hands.

"Certainly there's a point. I'm getting there. I'll come to it." He wrapped the circlet in a piece of flannel and put it back into a hair trunk at the foot of his bed. "What I remember best about Sister Angelus was how she used to communicate by what she called 'psychogram' with her first cousin, who was a missionary priest in East Africa."

Georgie got up suddenly from the hard chair and went to the window and raised the sash. He stuck his head out and breathed deeply. Don't let me be sick. The heavy clouds had rolled on. The night sky had become clear, starry. Across Sawdust Street, there were shops, most of them taxidermists, all closed now. In front of one, and bright under the moon, a stuffed grizzly reared on its base. In front of another, a mastiff stood guard, only it never moved a muscle. And in the window seat of yet another, a small and unprosperous-looking shop, a single stuffed white rat was on display.

Professor Thom said, "Father David."

Georgie said, "What?"

"Father David was the man's name. The nun's cousin. 'I heard from Father David last night in my dreams,' she'd tell the entire student body from the auditorium stage. During weekly assemblies. 'He thanks us for our prayers. There's a flood in his village.' Or if not a flood, then a scourge of flies, or a sudden violent madness in some of the older wives."

Georgie closed the window.

"I loved hearing about that Father David. His latest adventures. Father David Shoots the White Panther, Wrestles with the Evil Witch Doctor of the Bush, Enters the Lost City of Gold. Oh, boy!"

Georgie smiled. The headache hadn't gone away entirely, but it was better, much, much better.

"Father David trekking here, trekking there. What a white fella! On the Mountain of Demons. In the Valley of the Pagan Dogs. They all talked," said the Professor, winking. "Like the one you met tonight. Father David tried giving those pagan dogs catechism lessons, Mother Superior told us. But they chased him off before he even got to why God made us. So he poisoned their streams. I wonder if Fuzzy is East African, by any chance."

"East Fourth Street, more like," said Georgie. "I told you, Thom, it was all a big trick. Sucker stuff. He had to be throwing his voice, this Billy. That brained me." He felt around his lump again. Be tender for a while. "Skinny bastard."

Georgie had come to in the park, his vision speckled with glowing threads, when a whore had tripped over him; he'd begged her pardon. Billy had left the hatchet but lifted his wallet. *Bastard!* Georgie had scuffed home to Mrs. Bennett's. Knocked on the Professor's door—a chunk of ice? The Professor, of course, had had something *even better than that!*

He said now, as Georgie was about to go on up to his own room, "I know this fella lives on Avenue A—been working forever on a mechanical dog. This Fuzzy wasn't mechanical, was it?"

"No."

"Just a thought." Thom unshot the bolt and opened the door. "You know, George, I always was under the impression you were supposed to draw the news, not make it. Going to be all right?"

"Yeah, sure." There was too much quivering gaslight in the hall, too much shadow, and it all hurt Georgie like pins to the brain. "Thanks again."

"Did the Abater help? At all? Tell me the truth."

"Did, indeed. You'll make a fortune."

"I doubt that. But I'm glad I was here. Good night, George."

"'Night."

❑ ❑ ❑

He'd splashed his face with water, undressed, and stretched out on the bed, intending to rest a few minutes, then get up and draw the knife fights so he could run the pictures over to Park Row first thing in the morning. But he'd fallen asleep, and when he woke, it was half past two by the alarm clock hanging on a nail in the wall. He heard talk and laughter coming from down on the porch; Female Hercules was telling a story. The music-hall people were home. Joette would've come back with them. He listened carefully but didn't hear her. So maybe she was on her way upstairs right this minute, to see him. Georgie put his trousers back on and grabbed a fresh shirt from his dresser. Then he rolled a couple of cigarettes. He waited five minutes. The front door opened and closed several times. He heard the Metal-Eater, who had a room just down the hall, come up and go in; he heard him groan.

Finally, Georgie went down.

Phil Ward was sitting on the porch steps, alone. He was the Human Lizard—performed in only a pair of trunks, to show off his beaded red pores; he'd wriggle on his stomach across the stage and gesticulate with his tongue while his pretty young assistant fed him actual dead flies from a jar. Sweet guy. Back when Georgie was the charcoal artist, Phil had taught him how to win at poker and fire a pistol.

"Where's everybody?" Georgie asked him now. "Sounded like you were having a party."

"No party. Franny got drunk." Franny was Female Hercules. "Sorry if we woke you."

Georgie sat with him. "Joette come home with you?"

"She went right upstairs. Looked pretty tired tonight." Phil smiled, then leaned toward Georgie and suddenly frowned. "What the hell's the matter with your forehead?"

"What?" Georgie touched it and felt a row of small blisters, just above his eyebrows. "Jesus," he said.

"Let me guess: Professor Thom?"

"I had a bad headache."

"That's why God made druggists. I stay away from Thom and his contraptions—ever since he convinced me to spend a night in his Vitalizer Hammock and I felt twiddly for nearly a week afterwards."

Georgie asked, "You ever heard of a ventriloquist named McCord?"

"Alvin?"

"Billy."

"No, I'm thinking of McCoy. I was in a traveling variety show with a ventriloquist named Alvin McCoy. Dummy was named Foggy the Clown. Billy McCord? No."

"Uses a dog."

"In a show? Never saw *that* done. Saw it done once with a hen. But it was no good."

"Why was that?"

"Should be obvious. Everybody could see its mouth wasn't moving at the proper time."

Georgie shut one eye and tried to think: had Fuzzy's mouth moved at the proper time? Think hard. Come on, George. *Remember*. That's what you do, it's half your job. But at the Blade, first in the barroom and then at ringside, he hadn't been close enough to the dog to have a good look. And in the Wedge, it had been too dark. So that was that. Next time, though. He'd make sure he noticed. And there would be a next time, you bet. Guy swiped his billfold. He'd find them. Clarky would know where to look.

Phil said, "It was no good and it didn't work out, this hen. So the ventriloquist killed it and roasted it, and then he went and got himself a pinewood nigger. And what an improvement! Live things? They just never, never cooperate."

She was very pretty, slim as a cypress, yet full-breasted. She had a small mouth, pale green eyes, and a faint line of freckles across the bridge of her nose. She had hair the color of corn bread, and fragile hands, and she was waiting in Georgie's room when he returned. "Are you just coming home?"

"I went downstairs to look for you. I been in all evening. Practically." He'd expected her to notice the blisters immediately, and when she didn't, he felt hurt—he went and peered into his shaving mirror. Perhaps they'd disappeared already? No. "I was on the Bowery earlier tonight." He could see Joette reflected in the glass. She was smoking one of the cigarettes that he'd rolled. Sitting on a wicker stool. "I passed the theatre."

"Really? You should've stopped in?"

"Busy with something."

She nodded. "It's too bad you didn't come by? You would've enjoyed what happened?" Joette had a habit of uttering most of her statements as timid queries, and when Georgie had first met her, he'd thought it showed a promising weakness in her character. But it hadn't taken him long to discover that it was only a quirk, signifying nothing.

"So what happened?" he asked.

Joette bent forward and tapped her ash into a saucer. It was on top of the small footlocker where Georgie stored his professional souvenirs: a buffalo-plaid shirt with five bullet holes, a derringer in pieces, a Mason jar of pickled fingers, a gallows rope, a scarf that smelled faintly of chloroform, a hammer whose ball head was flaky with old blood. "Do you know Lorenzo the Magician? Well, at the second show, he was pulling out rabbits from his opera hat? One, two, three, and so on, till he reached out the seventh and it was dead as a doornail. He burst into tears and cradled the rabbit against his heart. His heart? I thought of you," she said, squinting against the cigarette smoke. "I wonder if it happened when you were passing by?"

Georgie hesitated, then said, "Probably. And I'm damned sorry I missed it, too. Never get a chance anymore to draw a dead rabbit, and I do a good one. Just ask anybody." More and more, it was like this between them. She'd throw him a baited line, and he'd nibble, but only nibble, never take the hook. What do you want to do today, George, go out in a rowboat and look for drowned babies? Fine idea, Jo, I'll pack a lunch. Are you wearing scent, George, or is that formaldehyde? Formaldehyde! Do you really like it? Jesus God, did cops have to listen to these kinds of gibes from *their* girls? Did medical men? It was so unfair. Did he ever crack wise to her? Mock her job? Tell her how preposterous it was to sing "Love's Old Sweet Song" dressed in red tights and spangled stockings? He did not. Yet she needled him, all the time. Sketchmen could call him Bloody Wreckage forever, it wouldn't bother him; A.K. and Bram Hoopes, even the Professor, could get in their worst digs, and half the time he wouldn't even hear them. But Joette, when she came on like this, all sarcasm, it cut. Not that Georgie would ever let on that it did. It cut and made him want to kick out a window, punch the wall. He always checked *those* impulses, though. Checked them quick. And played the ghoul. Safest thing to do. He said now, "It was only *one* rabbit? Just the one? Now, *all* of them—there's a picture. Can you see it?

Two or three lying on a table. Few more at his feet. One still in the hat. And the one in his arms. Yum!" He rubbed his hands together, he bugged his eyes and panted noisily, and Joette shook her head but finally smiled. What Georgie called her Maid Bridget smile. Just loaded with sex appeal, and innocent of cunning—or maybe not. Beautiful.

Two years before, when Georgie had believed he could sell pictures to the weeklies, when Philly Finck had him convinced he could do funny business, Joette used to pose for him in a black-and-white costume, a genuine domestic's uniform, that he'd rented. Is this what you see me as? she'd asked. As a girl in service? They'd laughed about it. At the theatre, Joette Davey was Amanda the Songbird, but in Georgie's room, on his model stand, she was Maid Bridget. He'd drawn her listening at a keyhole, cowering on a ladderback chair on account of a mouse, dusting with her fanny in the air, sneaking a smoke in the kitchen pantry, and gulping Sir's cocktail while Sir lined up a shot at the billiard table. "Maid Bridget—The Wreckage Girl." Georgie had made some thirty-odd pen-and-ink drawings, hadn't sold one. You can't draw a pretty girl, young Wreckage. At *Puck*, at *Life*, at *Judge*. And they were right, he couldn't. Even Joette hadn't liked the pictures. Am I really cross-eyed? Are my nostrils so *large?* Are my bosoms that *low?* I thought I've been smiling up here for an hour, George, and look what you've drawn. What *had* he drawn? A sneer. A crooked little sneer—unintended, mind you, but there it was. Again and again. Infuriating! And Joette wondered why he'd chucked that comic stuff in favor of calamities! Criticized him for doing it. Of all people, she should've understood. He'd given her the full Maid Bridget portfolio, and she'd rolled all the pictures into a tube and tied them with a ribbon, and as far as George knew they were still at the back of her wardrobe where she'd stuck them.

He'd worked the cork out of a half-empty bottle of Moselle and was starting to pour. The glasses, the only clean ones that he could find, the *tumblers*, each bore a stenciled portrait of the Yellow Hag. Bram had given him a boxed dozen some weeks ago, as soon as they'd gone on sale. Joette was amused when she saw the picture; she scraped at it with a fingernail. A Yellow Hag—one of the chorus boys, in saffron makeup and a sack dress—had recently been added to the bill at LeFebre & Chill's. Just ran about the stage for a couple of minutes ranting in sham Chinese. Very popular, though.

Georgie said, "Now that we've disposed of Lorenzo and his bunny, what else shall we talk about? What's an appropriate topic at three in the morning? Love?"

Joette frowned and looked at Georgie, grinning because he'd said "love." The wine tasted old and terrible. "George? Your face is breaking out?"

"It's blisters." Finally she notices! "I had a headache and the Professor fixed me up."

"You're not serious? Don't tell me you're serious?"

"It was a *bad* headache."

"You let him put that thing on your head? Oh, George. I would've thought you'd learned your lesson." After what had happened, she meant, the time he'd walked to Washington Square and back in the Professor's refrigerated boots: he'd nearly lost a pinky toe to frostbite. He was *such* a little boy, was her George. In *some* ways. "Did it help, at least? I hope?"

"Certainly," he told her. "Want to hear how I *got* my headache?" He bowed his head. "Can you see a bump?" Pointing.

"No."

"No, you can't see it? Or no, you don't want to hear the story? Or both?"

"For heaven's sake, George. It *is* three o'clock in the morning. And I thought you wanted to talk about love."

"Well, sure," he said. "If *you* do."

She had grown up twenty miles outside Baltimore, in a town called Dieppe Springs, the daughter of a Metho preacher—*Caroline Davey*. She'd picked the name Joette—saw it on the awning of a notions store, liked it—shortly after she'd arrived in New York City as a girl of seventeen. She'd run off with one of the Magruder twins—Mal, the wild one—but their liaison had not traveled well. He'd left her within a month, sneaked away in the night, taking what little money she had, her suitcase, her jacket, even her bits of chewing gum, and Joette, to keep body and soul together, had had to roll cigars and sew pants.

If she hadn't had her good looks, certainly she would've ended up—well, *you* pick a fate, any sorry fate will do. But she did have those looks, and they saved her life, so to speak.

Young men would follow her on the avenue, asking her to slow down, to wait up, and unless they were too obviously shady, she usually did. She was no fool for the soft sawder, but she was willing to listen—what harm was there in that?—and she was always *very* willing to spend Saturday in a beer garden with a nice Karl or a nice Stephen or a nice James, or to pass the evening at a penny arcade with a lively Chimmie or a lighthearted Jack. It was a Michael who'd gotten Joette her first theatre job—ballet girl in the Whirligig Burlesque Company. She was one in a squad of sixteen, and she galloped and marched, countermarched and high-kicked on the stage of the Whirligig Theatre for a year and a half, till *another* Michael, this one a comic, arranged a singing audition for her with Johnny Chill, the impresario. You sing like a songbird, Johnny had told her. Why, *thank* you. Thank you very much? And what do I fuck like? Johnny had blushed. Of *course* he had—even with trousers down and cockadoodle up, a true gentleman reddened at vulgarity. Such language, he'd said, and Joette had curled her lip before giving him fellatio. Such language? Jesus goddamn Christ, it was the least of things she'd picked up after living two years in New York.

And now, after almost four years in the city, and as a seasoned woman of twenty-one, she wanted out. Or if not out, then she wanted to move uptown, at least as far as Murray Hill. Quit the music hall, get married—marry a man she'd enjoy watching, every morning till kingdom come, as he shaved and dressed and topped his egg, and whose politics she would memorize like a difficult poem, without comprehension and with a touch of scorn; a man with money in the bank—how much, which bank, none of her business—and generous with her allowance. Get married, have babies. She wanted children. She wanted to plan birthday parties and look forward to Christmas. She wanted to put peppercorns on tiny cavities in tiny teeth, blow pipe smoke into sick ears, and make asafetida bags. She wanted to sign report cards. She wanted to change her life. Wanted to need half an hour just to wind all the clocks. To go into Macy's and buy a good service of blue plate, and have use for it. These hankerings of hers weren't a lot of hooey back then, they were perfectly natural. They were thrilling. . . .

All the lamps were out now, there was a rich, almost underground darkness to the room, and Georgie was saying, " . . . and I went

looking for him by the statue. He's almost always there when I go
by, but tonight he wasn't," talking about the condom boy. "Do you
think we could—?"

"No," said Joette. "But it's fine. It's fine. Let me just be sweet to
you?" First marriage, *then* babies. Maybe Georgie's, but maybe not.
"Just let me be nice?"

Georgie kissed her—he'd expected her lips to be there; instead, it
was the nape of her neck. "I love you," he said. "Jo? I love you."

She smoothed his hair, ran a finger down his jawline. It had always amazed her, and sometimes it even bothered her, how easily
he could say that. Other men she'd known would gulp just telling
her, I think you're swell. But Georgie—pledging his love seemed no
more difficult to do than ordering a steak. It was charming, it was
troubling. Love you, love you. Once, he'd told her, not realizing how
awful it sounded, not seeing her goose bumps, that he knew he loved
her, really loved her, because every single time he imagined her
dying or dead, he clutched up inside. Clutched right up. It was the
Test, he'd told her; as a boy, he'd used it to determine that he loved
his mother, not his father. Love you, Jo, love you. And she believed
him. She believed he was truthful. She only wished she didn't also
believe he was dangerous. "Just let me be nice," she said. "Make
you feel good?"

Joette was a righty.

WHAT BROUGHT PINFOLD TO MOTHER POLK'S HOUSE

The annual trophy supper for the badmen of Filch Hall was scheduled to get under way at nine, but Pinfold came early, showing up at Mother Polk's house in Penalty Street—it was the big brown one that slouched to the left as you faced it—just after seven thirty. A cadet named Frankie let him in at the kitchen door. Frankie was plump and ham-jawed, a real galoot who'd tell you that he'd grown up in Texas and used to rob banks and mail trains in Kansas and Oklahoma. Oh, yeah? Well, he'd always sounded Avenue C to Pinfold. Avenue C and Thirteenth. His left eye was bum, almost blind, shot with red and like to pop right out—somebody had once flung cleaning salts into his face. He was dressed that evening in a dark tweed suit, a cowboy hat. "Mother's upstairs," he said as Pinfold wiped mud from his boots and pulled off his oilskins. There'd been thunderstorms all day. "She's waiting for you."

Cook stood by the stove stroking her chin and sampling an end piece from a roast of beef, and a girl Pinfold didn't recognize was seated at the kitchen table using her slim hands to frost a big yellow cake. She looked thirteen or fourteen—Pinfold's age?—and had very oily skin and long plaited hair blacker than tar. There were rope burns on both her wrists. When Pinfold tipped his derby, she frowned at him bitterly.

Another girl, Mo the Irish, had just removed a pan of nuts from the oven—now, where could she set it down? Odd Og's lattice-

backed invalid chair was parked near the sinks, and Mo stuck the
pan on its seat. Odd Og, the parlor boy, had died yesterday afternoon—ruptured appendix—and that's why Pinfold was here. To
take his place during the banquet. Mother hadn't had the time to go
out and shanghai a permanent replacement.

The topmost hallway in the house was plastered with yellow-and-
green flowered wallpaper, and still lit by gas, and the runner was
badly worn. There were oil paintings of sea storms almost too dark
with grime to look at. Mother's private office was the last room on
the right, her door the only one unnumbered. Pinfold knocked. "It's
Pinfoo, Mother. Pinfoo's here." That's what she'd always called
him: Pinfoo. A chink name to go with his chink eyes—he had a
perpetual squint because his vision was poor—and his chink ears
that stuck out. She thought he even dressed chink: those white laun-
dryman's blouses, those roomy black trousers, those rope-soled
shoes of his. Someone, she'd crack, must've bleached you as a baby,
Pinfoo, and he'd shrug. He didn't care. She could call him anything
she pleased. She could call him Pinwheel, Pinhole, she could call
him Pinprick if she liked, and he'd only grin. A name was only so
much noise, and besides, Mother took a gross and a half of Albert
Shallow's plainest condoms from Pinfold every other week. "It's
Pinfoo, Mother—you wanted to see me, Frankie said."

"Door's open!"

Mother had been riding her safety bicycle around the room in the
dark, but when Pinfold came in, she dismounted and leaned it
against a wall beneath a clock. She turned on some lamps. The door
of a wardrobe was open, and hanging inside were several cloaks, a
woolen shawl, and the habits of a mother superior, a tan one, a
brown one, a white one, a black one.

"You're early. That's good. I like that," she said, sitting down
behind her desk. Mother's desk was immense. She was a tiny
woman with a doll's face and red hair, the syrupy red of a sundae
cherry. Her desk was covered like a banker's with green felt and a
thick layer of glass. The green of the felt matched her formal gown
exactly. There was a deep rich-red Persian carpet, red draperies and
a mahogany sideboard, and a chair for Pinfold. He shifted in it till he
got his spine fitted comfortably between two spindles. He set his
wigbox on his lap. He'd found it a long time ago in a carton of court-
house trash with an exhibit tag—Exhibit D—still attached. He'd
never snipped it off.

A long legal document of some kind, several of its paragraphs scored out boldly in blue, lay on Mother's desk. She glanced at it for a moment before pushing it aside. In the glare of so many incandescent bulbs, the powder on her face looked an inch thick; you could see fine cracks running through it. The lights bounced off her greasy rouge and off the top of Pinfold's head. He'd hung his derby up. Mother said, "We don't expect the party to end till very late—maybe as late as five. If you like, Mo'll fix you up with a cot somewhere, afterwards."

"Thanks. But I think I'll just go on home." Mother smiled often, had a sunny nature—but she had a darker nature too, and whenever she felt slighted or disrespected, she could turn suddenly mean and hurtful as a drake. Pinfold wanted to be careful. "But thanks!" He leaned across the desk now and placed his wigbox directly in front of her. He took the lid off and set it aside, then he dipped a hand and started flipping out condoms, novelty condoms—some with devil tips, some with cupid wings. "Albert thought you might like to give these out at the banquet," he said. "No charge." That Albert, he had business smarts. Pinfold admired him for them.

Mother sheathed an index finger with a condom that was flame-red, then pointed it at Pinfold. "Just remember later—in the front parlor, anybody wants oranges or candy or peanuts, they pay for it. That's not part of the dinner."

Pinfold said, "Sure, I know that. I'll remember."

"And also remember, every buck goes into the cigar box. You know the difference between your pocket and a cigar box?"

"I sure do, Mother."

Mother pushed her chair back and unlocked a drawer. From the drawer she took a cashbox, and from the cashbox two dollar bills. She dropped them into Pinfold's wigbox. It's what they'd agreed on yesterday, for tonight's work. She looked at Pinfold for a long moment. "Did you think about what I said? About taking Og's job for good?"

"Did. And I haven't changed my mind." He shook his head emphatically, no. "Thanks for the offer. But the way I see it, it ain't too healthy living indoors all the time." When you worked for Mother, you stayed under her roof. She ran a controlled house.

"I really do need another parlor boy."

"Not me. But thanks! Find another cripple, how about? I just like being out and around."

"Selling scumbags and picking garbage," said Mother. "Quite a life, Pinfoo."

"I don't intend to do it forever," he insisted. "Just till I find what I'm looking for."

"And what's that, a hat that fits?"

"A million bucks," he said, "in twenty-dollar bills. Somebody's *bound* to lose it one of these days."

As he left her, he closed the door carefully behind him.

Two

THE BOOTBLACK AND
THE PARLOR BOY

1

Georgie Wreckage was feeling mighty proud of himself: all day long he'd polished shoes, dozens of pairs, and hadn't gotten so much as a particle of bootblack anywhere on his white suit. He'd carefully followed Clarky's instructions—how to crouch, how to pivot—pushing his coat sleeves back "suavely" and remembering always to use only the tip of the cloth. The trick was to concentrate.

This morning, Clarky had been surprised and delighted at how quickly Georgie learned the Method, and when finally he'd sent him out on his probationary rounds—surely, Georgie hadn't thought Clarky would let him go *untested* to Mother Polk's house—he'd included, as a kind of reward, a few stops certain to be of interest to a newspaperman. Thus, Georgie had shined shoes at three social clubs (two Italian, one Lithuanian), at the longest-running bachelor party in New York City (three years, seven months, six and three-quarter days, according to the profligate bridegroom), and at a house of sissies, where gentlemen in women's dresses sat chattering noisily on divans.

Clarky had even included on Georgie's itinerary a visit to Filch Hall, in St. Mark's Place. It was a brick building, painted blue, for-

merly the gymnasium of a Carpathian Catholic school and now, of
course, union headquarters for the Brotherhood of Hooligans and
Lawbreakers. Georgie had stayed there almost a full hour, watching
thieves drift in with booty sacks slung over their shoulders; several
had arrived still wearing slender raccoon-style masks. They'd all
tramped up to the stage and emptied their sacks on a table. After the
union's treasurer, a grizzled old man with spotty white hair and a
cheesy yellow scalp, had drawn the organization's cut—snatching
one bankroll out of three or dividing a mountain of precious stones,
cameos, stickpins, chokers, and wedding rings into two equal-sized
hills—the thieves helped themselves to a buffet lunch. There was
cold chicken, bread and butter, ham, pigs' knuckles, and sour
pickles.

Georgie had shined a lot of shoes at the hall—fellas wanting to
look sharp for the banquet later—and he'd overheard some lively
speculation concerning who might walk away that evening with the
award for Best Swindler or Sharper or Bad Check Passer or Green
Goods Merchant, about who had a real shot at being honored as
Fence of the Year, and about who was most likely to be recipient of
the Jesse James Medal for Outstanding Achievement in a Life
of Crime. (Most of those Georgie had listened to figured a counter-
feiter named Caesar Sergio for the medal, since he was dying of
c-a-n-c-e-r.)

Now it was just eight o'clock when Georgie, feeling so proud of
himself, returned to Avenue B and to Clarky's storefront with its
bright red awning. Inside, along a wall, crates were stacked almost
to the ceiling. Another wall was lined with plank shelving, each shelf
filled with tins of polish. A bar top served as a desk—invoices
weighted with bricks. More than a dozen white suits hung on a gar-
ment worker's rack. Some boys were playing cards. They said
Clarky was in the back. But there was a guy with him—private
business. So Georgie slipped off his india rubbers, hung his slicker
on a hook, and waited, and the other bootblacks looked him up and
down.

Ten minutes later, a blocky Irishman in a thigh-length coat, a
good one, of black alpaca came through the curtain separating the
store from the back room and walked quickly to the door and out;
Georgie had noticed immediately that the man's pinky and ring fingers, left hand, were only stumps, purple as eggplant. Clarky appeared then. "I'm so successful," he announced to everyone, "I'm

even paying off Tammany already. Can you imagine!" He laughed but made belligerent fists. "Georgie!" He came over and strolled around him, around and around, hunting paste stains. "You did great," he said at last, and clapped his hands. "But enough of that. Now we gotta talk. I heard something and we gotta talk about it, right now."

In his office, Clarky had an icebox, a poker table with four chairs, a Currier & Ives print of the Crystal Palace that used to stand in Bryant Park, and a line cut torn from the *Police Gazette* and framed. It depicted a handsome young metropolitan detective grabbing a goateed man in a top hat and a Prince Albert coat and dark trousers. The caption read, "'Here's our murderer, Inspector! Trying to pass himself off as the Ambassador from Hungoslavia—ha! Well, his *shoes* gave him away!'" Of *course*—all that cross-hatching meant they were *scuffed*.

Georgie took out a handkerchief and swiped at the seat of his chair before sitting down.

Clarky had a fresh stain—brown sauce—on his green necktie. He was wearing a red flannel shirt and dungarees. He said, "George, I changed my mind. I'm not letting you go to Mother's. You want to shoot me, right? But listen first."

Georgie mentally sketched Clarky, exaggerating the teeth, horsing them up, beetling the brows, bunching the nose, and sizing the nostrils like energy pills; giving him ears like dinner plates and small moron eyes. "I'm listening," he said.

"This morning you told me a story and asked me some questions. What'd I ever hear about a cutpurse named McCord, who's Connie Dwyer? I told you what I knew." That McCord had been in town maybe a year, a year and a half; that he had some talent, people said. But a bad temper. Cocky little punk. And Connie Dwyer— nothing but a shitpot gangster out of Mackerelville. Used twenty sticks of dynamite to blow a ten-pound safe. Had a few twitchy characters he called an organization. "But what I hadn't heard this morning," said Clarky, "and what I heard since is that your friend McCord used to belong to Dwyer's gang. Used to. He works out of the hall now—they gave him a turf, him and the dog."

"But what's that got to do with tonight?"

"McCord'll be at the banquet."

"So? That's no problem, that's perfect. I'll have a look at the party, and I'll get my purse back." Then he said, with a dismissive wave of his left hand, "And if he won't give it over, I'll kill the sucker." Saying it as he might say, I won't eat in that restaurant again, the food's poison, or, I'm not voting this time or next time or any time, they're all crooks. I'll kill the sucker.

"And spoil my good reputation? Like hell. It comes out that Clarky sent a spy, I'm ruined."

"All right, already, don't have a brain seizure. I'll leave my business with Billy go till another day. Happy? Deal?"

Clarky smiled. "But see, George. There's the sad part, as far as your having a crack at McCord is concerned. I won't let you near him tonight. And tomorrow it'll be too late." He went over to the icebox and got out a bottle of milk, fumbled the paper top off. He scooped cream with two fingers, then licked them. "There's going to be trouble later at the house, and it's all Billy's." He offered the bottle to Georgie.

"No, thanks. What sort of trouble?"

"The sort we hope don't happen to us till we're ninety-nine. All because Connie Dwyer has this dumb idea that Billy suckered him. This is the latest thing I heard, and I been asking everybody I could think of."

"Something about Fourteenth Street."

"A cigarette factory." Clarky nodded. "Connie had it all figured to do the safe. This was last October. But when he got there, him and two or three other fellas in the middle of the night, guess what? He found the friggin' safe already blown. Pieces still warm. Billy was supposed to've gone along on the job, then never showed up. No explanation. And the next thing Connie hears, a day later, Billy's joined the hall." Clarky drank the quart of milk. He wiped his mouth on his sleeve and said, "So what do you think Connie concluded?"

"Did he do it? Billy?"

"What I hear—no, he didn't. It was Connie's own brother-in-law. Tell that to Connie, though, and he'll take your head off. He don't want to hear it. Billy did it. Billy did it. And he's been sending word to Billy for half a year that he wants that money, and Billy's been sending word back to go jump in a lake. And what I hear now, he's run out of patience finally, Connie has. He wants justice. So Billy goes down tonight at the banquet."

"Maybe Billy's heard, he won't show up."

"*George. I* hear things. Mugs like Billy McCord don't even hear their own shoes squeak."

"Does Connie Dwyer figure on busting in on all of Filch Hall?"

"He won't be anywhere near Penalty Street. But that don't mean Billy McCord's gonna walk out of that house alive."

"What's going to happen?"

"You want details, go ask Connie. And be ready to duck. Don't *really* ask Connie," he quickly added, just in case Georgie didn't realize he was being a smart aleck.

"You can't expect me to stay away from the banquet now," Georgie protested. "Not after what you've just told me. You can't."

"But I do. And you're not going. There's no way you can get through Mother's door tonight unless you got that suit on, and I'm not letting you wear it out of here."

"You promised."

"When did I ever?"

Georgie looked at Clarky, then looked away. He stared at the magazine illustration on the wall, then at the icebox. Then he stared at the illustration again. Drummed his fingers on the card table. "What're you afraid of? That I'll interfere? Warn McCord?"

"You? Never!"

"What, then? That I'll pick a fight with him? I'm telling you I won't. Word of honor. I'll stay clear."

"Clear! What do you think Mother's place is, Madison Square Gardens? You'll stay clear of him. And what's to make him stay clear of you? He'll recognize you, George. And I don't want to be responsible. Like you told me, he thinks you're Connie's boy as it is. He sees you, what happens? You disappear, there goes a good suit." Clarky smiled.

Georgie said, "But if he doesn't recognize me, nothing can happen. Right? So how about if I went disguised?"

Disguised! Clarky shut one eye, giving the idea a serious think. It wasn't a *bad* idea, it wasn't, and not in the least outlandish. In those days, ministers frequently disguised themselves as tramps to see iniquity first-hand, and strong girls cut their hair and disguised themselves as laboring men to earn a living wage; even Theodore Roosevelt, the Commissioner of Police, disguised himself in a sombrero and a gaudy blanket one evening every other week to roam the city streets looking for policemen on the loaf. A disguise!

Might work. Could. Clarky said, "What kind of disguise do you have in mind?"

And Georgie replied, "Well, you have all this bootblack around—I'll go as a Negro."

And so he did.

2

"Good evening! I'm your Clarky's shoeshine boy. Clarky's is the paste that's remarkably black."

The front parlor of Mother's house was stuffy and dark, much smaller than Georgie had expected. It reminded him, a little, of an undertaking parlor—a pair of maroon couches and a lot of wooden folding chairs. The carpet was faded and threadbare. A couple of idle whores had brought out their pyrography and were burning pictures into cutting boards—one doing Hansel and Gretel and the other, St. Joseph. A piano player was chopping sentimental favorites with his hands in boxing gloves. And off in one corner, behind a long counter, sat a parlor boy in charge of oranges and cherries, bars of milk chocolate and peanuts in paper sacks. Everything for sale was priced the same—that's what the big dollar sign meant daubed in red paint on the boy's white blouse. As soon as Georgie had walked into the room, he'd spotted the yellow derby and recognized the boy as the condom vendor from City Hall Park. A bad moment. What if *Pin*head? Pin*dot?* recognized *him* through his blackface? But he hadn't. Busily coating his supply of oranges with tallow and wrapping each one in tissue paper, he'd given Georgie only the briefest glance. Pinguid? Pinto?

It was already half past ten, but there were only three Filchers, puffing cigars to aid digestion, up here in the parlor. Everybody else was downstairs yet. Supper was finished, but the awards were still being presented. You could hear loud clapping and foot-stomping; also, once in a while, the shrill blast of a post horn, followed by laughter and then a drum roll—whatever all that meant. Georgie had counted on being allowed into the banquet room, but the rough-neck cadet who'd met him at the front door had said no dice: What're you gonna do down there, crawl under the tables? He'd called Georgie dinge, and Georgie had tingled with relief and ego—

fooled ya! He'd stayed sore, though, about having to miss the main event.

"A Clarky's shine will last for days and days, in all kinds of weather," said Georgie now, smiling at the languid trio of cigar smokers. "Who wants his first? You, sir?" The big Swede on a couch. Georgie stooped in front of him. He groped through his shoeshine box, taking out paste and rags and a buffer, and as he was doing that, several more whores walked in. The Swede gestured to one—a girl with bulging stomach and large breasts, and her hair done up in a wavy pompadour—and she promptly came, her thigh brushing Georgie's arm before she sat down. Her legs were smooth and skinny. She wore a string of phony pearls, a camisole, and carpet slippers. Georgie saw the Swede give her a round token minted Good for a Sexual Intercourse. She dropped it into her yellow string purse.

Over the next five or ten minutes, the parlor filled up with banqueters and whores, everybody squiffed. Georgie kept getting bumped, especially once the dancing started. Time to fade back and lamp the goings on.

"Gentlemen? Gentlemen? You may also purchase Clarky's remarkably black polish for use at home. Ten cents the tin—and that's real value! Anybody needs me, I'll be right over there. Gentlemen? If you need me."

Georgie folded his arms and leaned against the wall, and nobody paid him any mind—except for the little parlor boy, who kept looking over now while pulling on his bottom lip.

3

As he'd figured would happen that evening, Pinfold got the fantods and started wishing he were someplace, anyplace else. Because of the crowd. Any crowd he was part of gave him jitters, but indoor crowds made his heart knock wildly; they caused his palms to sweat and his mouth to go dry. What if somebody went berserk? A fire started? The floor collapsed? Could he get out? Could he save himself? There's the window and there's the door. But could he reach either in time? It was a worry. He'd been stupid, he'd been *crazy* to say yes to Mother—sure, it was only for the one night, and like

Albert told him, it never hurt to do a little favor for somebody bigger than you, but Jesus Christ, he felt crawly, and it was getting worse. There was nobody here but armed toughs—so what that they'd all shaved and clipped the fuzz in their nostrils, slicked back their hair with laundry soap, and put on twenty-dollar suits, they were still dangerous. One of them suddenly decides *he* should've won a Golden Bludgeon instead of so-and-so, and *bang! bang!* Pinfold could just see it. Didn't matter that everybody was laughing and carrying on; trouble was coming—Pinfold just knew it. If not a shoot-out, then something else. What? Who? That shoeshine fella. Now, who was he, *really?* Clarky's boy, my foot! It had taken Pinfold a while to realize that something was fishy—Clarky's boys never wore *gloves,* they never kept their hats on indoors. What else did he have in that shoeshine kit? Bayonets? A bomb? God, let me get out of here!

He had a grown man's sense of the haphazard, Pinfold did, and a terror of dying that belied his age. From the night his hair had been torched, when, lost in fever, he'd floated away clutching a yellow balloon by its string and thinking he'd never come back, never. He'd floated past the silvery crescent moon, the Big Dipper, then splashed through, nearly drowned in, the Milky Way. Finally, a comet had showered his balloon with chips of heavenly ice and popped it. He'd fallen a hundred miles, into Awful Alley. Albert Shallow had been there to catch him, but ever since—because you couldn't count on a nigger to catch you twice, they were constitutionally unreliable—Pinfold had been afraid of dying, very much afraid. He wanted to live forever. He had been born in the month of May—his was an earthbound nature, and he wanted no more of the sky, ever again.

"Kid? You don't look so good. Kid?" Blinky Conroy, the piano player, had come over for an orange. He was holding a slab of beef in napkin linen. "You sick?"

"Ain't!" Pinfold frowned at the suggestion. "I'm swell. Where'd you get that meat?"

"Downstairs. There's lots."

"Mother let you?"

"Mother's busy."

"Any cake left?"

Blinky shrugged. "You hungry?" He was batting his eyelashes a mile a minute, like he was sending rapid code. "I said, you hungry?"

"I might be. I'm not saying I am."

"Listen, Pinfold—you want to run downstairs, see what you can scrounge, go ahead. I'll sit here for you."

"Five minutes."

"Take your time," said Blinky, coming around the table.

Although he was almost positive that Blinky would help himself to chocolate bars and not bother to pay for them, Pinfold took him up on his offer—he had to get out of the parlor for a while. With any luck, the coming mayhem would break out while he was safe in the dining room. It occurred to him taking the stairs down that he could easily slip out through the kitchen, tell Frankie he had to get something from his wagon, and then not return. But, nah, Mother'd have his head.

Coming along the hallway, he passed a Filcher spunking up that new girl, the dark one with long braids and sore-looking wrists. They didn't even notice him. The fella, skinny fella, seemed dressed for Asbury Park in the middle of July—a black-and-white striped seaside coat, white trousers and shoes of white buck, and a flat-brimmed straw hat with a wide band. Pretty silly for April in New York, Pinfold thought, though he had to admit that he liked those shoes. If ever he saw a pair like them in a barrel of trash, he'd grab them in a second. As he was turning into the dining room, he glanced back, seeing the fella's hand go to the whore's breast, seeing him kiss her brutally hard, and his Adam's apple, big as a marshmallow, bob up and drop down.

Pinfold was reminded of the time, the first and still the only time, he'd coaxed a girl into the coal bin. A thirteen-year-old Lizzie from Dingley Flats. For a fresh-killed hen and a bottle of codeine, she had given his little penis a slow licking with her tongue, but then Albert had suddenly barged in and spoiled it. He'd chased away Lizzie and cuffed Pinfold again and again, and then he'd made Pinfold dunk his pecker into a glass of rubbing alcohol. Don't bring no bad-luck bitch in here again! But why was *Lizzie* bad luck? Lizzie, Elsie, Mary— they're all bad luck, Albert had said.

Pinfold strolled from table to table, finishing leftover drinks and picking through ashtrays for cold cigars. Those he threw into his wigbox. He tore a piece off a crusty bread and soaked up beef juice. Tasted good. He wiped a carving knife clean on his trousers, then cut himself a big wedge of the banquet cake. Before he could take a bite, though, he heard something, a slight thump. He tensed up and turned around and saw a dog, its large and woolly face sticking out from under the skirts of a tablecloth. Historic moment.

Pinfold laughed, he was so relieved that it was only a dog, then sat down on the floor and reached out slowly with his left hand; if it didn't growl, he'd pet the mutt. He liked dogs. It didn't growl. "What're you doing here?" he said. "You a bad guy too?" The dog bellied out from beneath the table and stood up. "Huh? You a bad guy?"

Upstairs, everybody'd started singing Ta-ra-ra-*boom*-de-ay. You could hear it loud and clear. Ta-ra-ra-*boom*-de-ay. But if Blinky was playing piano, who was minding the store? What the hell. Pinfold took a bite out of his cake finally. And, from the way the dog was sadly watching him eat, he got the idea that she—it was a girl dog, he'd checked—that she might like a piece herself. "Came to supper and nobody fed you? What a bunch of mugs!" He put her slice on a dish, the dish down in front of her. And what an appetite! He was cutting her a second piece—why not, if she was hungry?—when the fella in the sack coat suddenly breezed in and said, "Hey!" There was bright red lip cosmetic on his neck, his shirt collar, and his bow tie. He called the dog Fuzzy and told her to hurry up and get a move on. Hurry up, hurry up! And just when Pinfold was beginning to have a nice time, too. Was thinking he'd look around, see if there was any champagne. Or run back to the parlor, even, for a bar of chocolate. Since she liked sweets so much.

The young whore was standing in the doorway now.

The skinny-belink dressed for the New Jersey shore smacked a palm against his thigh and said, "Come *on*, Fuzzy, we're all going upstairs."

And the dog, as she was turning to leave, a jot of yellow frosting on her nose, said to Pinfold, "Maybe I'll see you around, kid. Thanks for dessert."

Pinfold gaped. Then he touched a finger to his derby. "Don't mention it," he said.

It was Pinfold, the kid's name. Georgie was surprised that he hadn't been able to remember it, that he'd ended up having to ask somebody. Usually, he was pretty good at names. Pin*fold*, sure. "Decent little arab he is, too. As far as they go," said Blinky, the piano man. "You probably *have* seed him around, like you say. You being a nigger that must spend plenty of time on the street yourself."

Georgie cocked his head and nodded. He was down applying wax to Blinky's boots.

"Maybe you haven't noticed, on account of that derby of his. But he don't have a hair on his head, not one hair." Blinky made a sad face. "I heard Mother tell he had cooties so bad, he tried to burn 'em out. I hope that's not true. But it just might be. He's crazy enough."

Georgie nodded again. Then he spat on each boot and started to buff.

Clarky had told him don't stay any longer than thirty, forty minutes, somebody might get suspicious, and already Georgie had been at the house close to an hour. He'd watched plenty of arm wrestling, heard plenty of dirty talk, he'd listened to a yegg named Paddy Foyle drunkenly bang out songs on the upright and bellow the lyrics: Casey would waltz with a strawberry blonde. Ta-ra-ra-*boom*-de-ay. Three girls had performed acts of self-abuse—but what good was that? You couldn't draw such a thing for a daily paper. You couldn't draw it, period. Waste of time, coming here tonight. Georgie hadn't seen anything worth a damn—you could've mistaken this for a file clerk's banquet, for crying out loud. Big waste of time. Billy McCord hadn't even shown up—so much for Clarky's ears, Clarky's apprehension. Georgie had just about decided to leave, to walk on over to the Bowery and drop in on Joette at the theatre—she might get a kick out of seeing him in his white suit and coon-faced—when Blinky Conroy, back on his piano bench, had called him over and wanted a shine. For church in the morning.

"Give you some idea just how crazy that Pinfold is," said Blinky now. "You might've noticed, I sent him downstairs so he could get something to eat."

Georgie shook his head—though he'd noticed, all right.

"He comes back all excited. Just five minutes ago. Met a dog down there, he says, and it talked to him." Blinky laughed. "I know exactly what dog he means, too. I seed it. And it didn't talk to *me*. He's just a crazy arab. They're all crazy. But what do you want? They don't eat too good, their brains get small. A talking dog!"

Blinky thought for a second, then said, "At a state fair once I seed something alive in a box that I can't describe, it was so horrible. Partly human and very female." Then he shrugged.

5

When the kid left the parlor again, skulking out with his wig-box, Georgie followed. He passed two of Mother's cadets in the front hall, and neither of them so much as frowned when he suddenly turned and started up the stairs, thirty seconds behind Pinfold. Like nearly everyone else in the house by this time, they were pretty snickered—sprawled on a deacon's bench, blowing smoke rings. An hour ago they would've grabbed him, for sure.

A thin, nervous-looking fella with a bristly mustache passed Georgie coming down; his forehead was flush and damp, his lips had a sticky glaze. He glanced at Georgie's shoeshine kit. Georgie quickened his step. When he reached the first landing, he checked the hallway—no Pinfold, only a fat man and a whore. The fat man, with a silver medal pinned to the seat of his trousers and a breadstick in his mouth, was creeping on his hands and knees. The whore stood outside her bedroom and watched him with a bored expression. She was naked on down from her pelvis, corseted above. There were penknife scars on her cheeks and across the bridge of her nose. Through the open doorway behind her, Georgie saw a hamper, a wastepaper basket, a chest, and an iron bedstead. He continued up the stairs.

Pinfold was waiting for him at the top, hugging his wigbox to his chest. "I'm loud," he said. "I'll yell, I don't care. I'll yell like a girl."

Georgie tried to look puzzled. "What're you going to yell for? I just come up to see if anybody needs his shoes done."

"Heck you did. You followed me."

"All right, so I did. So I did. But only to ask you something."

"You couldn't ask me downstairs?"

"Could've. Didn't want to."

"So what's the question?"

"Piano man tells me you saw a dog," said Georgie. "Know where she went?"

"She?"

Georgie smiled. Then he looked up the hall and frowned, noticing a sandy-haired man sitting tensely on the edge of an upholstered bench. His coat was folded across his lap. He finished knotting the ends of a short length of clothesline, then raised his eyes and stared at the bedroom door directly opposite him. Was Billy in back of it? Georgie wondered. And was the man on the bench from Connie Dwyer? But then the door opened, and a girl stuck her head out and nodded. The man stood up and went into the room.

Pinfold said, "You're pretty nosy."

Georgie didn't reply.

"Tell me. All right? Just tell me. You don't have to say what. But just tell me, is something gonna start?"

"You tell me something first. *Do* you know where they are? The dog and the guy that owns her?"

"Now I know this stinks! Should I skedaddle? Be a pal, just tell me. I won't say nothing." Pinfold squinted hard. "I think I'm gonna get."

Georgie took a dollar bill from his pocket and crumpled it in his left fist. Then he reached out with his right hand and lifted up the lid on Pinfold's wigbox. He dropped the money in.

"Twelve over the door," said Pinfold. "Down here at the end."

"Sure?"

"It's a new girl he's with, the skinny guy. I asked in the kitchen where they put her, what room. Says twelve over the door."

Georgie nodded. "And why'd you come up here?" Christ—the thought had just occurred to him—what if the *boy* was from Connie Dwyer, and his fidgets were all an act?

"I'm telling you everything," Pinfold said, shaking his head slowly, "and you still haven't told me yet—should I leave?"

"Don't on my account. I'm harmless."

"Somebody gonna steal that dog 'cause it talks—that it?"

Georgie said, "Like that dog, do you?"

"She's all right. Maybe I do."

"Well, stick around then. She might need another owner by to-morrow morning."

Pinfold grinned. "No fooling?" he said. But then, right away, he looked scared.

Peeping through a keyhole—and that's what he was doing now, crouched at the door of Room 12—was something that Georgie had done a lot of in the past several months. Covering an actor's suicide, he'd squinted through one and seen a bare foot dangling off a bed and two cops helping themselves to the contents of the dresser drawers; after a murder trail, he'd squinted through another, watching jurors vote with jelly beans—pink for acquittal, yellow for conviction. He'd even squinted through the keyhole in Joette's door, the time he'd suspected she'd brought a man into her room. (Lucky for her, it had turned out only to be a music-hall chimp she had agreed to mind so its trainer could go to a wake in Brooklyn.)

Pinfold whispered, "What d'you see? See anything?"

For an additional dollar and fifty cents—and against his better judgment, he'd wanted Georgie to know—the boy had agreed to station himself against the wall alongside the door, with one foot planted on the shoeshine kit. That way, if somebody appeared suddenly, Georgie could pivot and pretend that he was blacking Pinfold's boots—which, incidentally, weren't a matched pair.

"See anybody?"

Georgie nodded. He saw the girl, some of her: she was putting on stockings. And he saw McCord too, stretched out naked on the bed. His eyes were closed, he was smiling, and his lax penis was jacketed in a glistening red prophylactic that drooped at its tip. Georgie leaned away from the door. Well, he was in there, and he was alive. Now what? Go back to the parlor and wait for Billy to come down? It was growing late, though—and maybe Connie Dwyer's assassin hadn't been able to get into the house. Or maybe he was waiting out front.

"What about the dog," said Pinfold. "See her?"

In fact, Georgie hadn't, so he took another peek. Oh, there she was, lying on a hooked rug at the foot of the bed, and chewing on something bright yellow. Georgie mistook it at first for a glob of scrambled egg—pretty damn unlikely, so he strained his eye to make it out better. It was the whore's purse. Several tokens, he saw now, had spilled out.

"She's there," he told Pinfold.

"Let me have a look."

"This isn't a kinetoscope, you know."

"Just let me have a look."

Georgie shrugged and stood up, and Pinfold took his place at the keyhole. He was still there ten, fifteen seconds later when the shots came, and he saw the dog's throat explode in a cloud of blood.

7

The dog, whether she lived or died, was Pinfold's now. And don't anybody say different. If worse came to worst, he'd bury her, but if she pulled through—if he could keep her alive and she still had a voice—well, Pinfold just might have himself a goddamn good summer, at the very least. Hire on with some carnival in South Jersey, where people probably had never seen an actual talking dog before—that'd be fine. Sleep in rooming houses, squeeze in a swim once a week, pick trash in a dozen small towns and resorts. Live, dog, live.

But whatever happened, Fuzzy was his. During all the craziness, the hubbub—the new girl screaming it was self-defense, that she'd been cut up with a razor, and the cadets trying to fold Billy McCord into a hair trunk without getting themselves sticky, then tossing in his clothes, and the Filchers beating it from the house, some of them with their shoes in their hands and their shirttails hanging out, and Doctor Narcoticus racing up the stairs in back of Texas Frankie— during all of that, Pinfold had lifted Fuzzy into his arms and carried her down to the kitchen. She'd thrashed once and tried to bite Pinfold's wrist. She'd even got her jaws locked around it, but then she'd lost her strength and her head lolled.

He'd brought his wagon in from the yard and lined it with newspapers and made a bed for the dog. Then, from his wigbox, he'd taken two plain condoms, slipped one on his thumb, the other on his first finger. Of his left hand. He'd dug around in Fuzzy's wound, found a bullet, and gently worked it out. She had barely stirred.

"She's mine now," he told Mother, who'd come in with Frankie just moments ago. "She's mine," but when he saw Mother's lips purse and the muscles bunch along her jawline, he said, "If that's all right with you." Stooped by the wagon and using his sleeve to blot Fuzzy's throat, Pinfold was fairly covered with blood—his hands and shirt glossy, the rest of him stippled.

Mother stepped closer and peered down at the dog. She skimmed a palm along Fuzzy's flank, then abruptly removed her hand and wiggled the fingers till Frankie dabbed at them with a handkerchief.

She pulled a chair out from the table and sat. "Start with what you were doing upstairs," she said.

Pinfold fumbled out a wad of tissue paper from his trousers, unwrapped it, and showed Mother three big lumps of dark chocolate. "I was gonna give these to the dog. I thought maybe the guy left her in the hall—I'd just go up and give 'em to her," he said. "She likes sweets." He smiled. Mother did too. What a relief! Pinfold's shoulders slumped, and then he said, "Hey, Mother, I heard this dog talk. It's no lie! What do you say to that? Here's this fella has a talking dog. Had." He smiled wider. His heart pounded.

Frankie said, "The kid is bugs," and Mother leaned sideways on her chair and thumped him on the chest. Then told him sharply to go see if the Doc had any salve in his bag that could be used on a dog. He was still with Anna. Knock first.

As soon as Frankie had gone, Mother looked at Pinfold again. "So you brought the candy upstairs. Then what?"

"I met the nigger—the one that's been shining shoes all night. He'd went up to look for business."

Mother lighted a cigar. "That so?"

"It's what he said. And I told him he could do my shoes, if he wanted to. So there we were. That's how we both happened to be there."

"What did you see?"

Pinfold looked at the sinks, the tin ceiling, then stuck out his underlip. "Same as what you did."

Mother exhaled smoke, watching it go scribbly, then vanish. "Anna says the man turned crazy, that before he took the razor to her, he started talking wild. Called her filthy names. You hear any of that?"

Pinfold shook his head. He shrugged. He said, "Maybe, I don't know."

"You were right *there*."

"Not *exactly* there, Mother. We were down the hall a ways."

"You're not lying to me?"

"I swear!"

Mother rubbed her forehead, she pinched the skin at a temple. Then she nodded finally and stood up.

Pinfold said, "Is it all right if I keep the dog?"

"Here?" She looked at him with dismay.

"I'll take her home in the morning."

Mother shrugged tiredly, turning to go. Then she walked back over and gave Pinfold the rest of her cigar to smoke.

She'd slobbered it, but still it tasted good.

Pinfold was alone in the kitchen now, and after he finished the cigar he helped himself to a slice of bread and butter and a bowl of tea. He checked on Fuzzy every few minutes, listening to her heart. It seemed to beat satisfactorily. He was reminded of how he used to press an ear to his mother's chest, when he was five or six and she lay dying, and of how her heart would thud like a drunk on the stairs, then hiss like a steam valve.

Frankie came back after quite a while with a wad of cotton wool and an unguent from Doctor Narcoticus. Pinfold slathered on some of the ointment, pressing the wound closed as best he could. He covered it with the cotton and then with a red napkin, which he knotted. The dog growled but stayed unconscious.

Around midnight, the doctor himself came down in his long cape and five-and-a-half-gallon black felt hat. He hunkered alongside Fuzzy and felt various pulses. He poked her organs, thumbed her eyes open. He shook his head this way, that way, undecidedly. Maybe she'd pull through, maybe she wouldn't. He told Pinfold, "I asked the girl, 'Why'd you shoot the poor animal—*she* wasn't cutting you with a razor, for God's sake.'"

"And what'd the girl say?"

"That she doesn't even remember shooting the dog. She guesses she lost her head."

Pinfold made a face.

They both looked at Fuzzy then.

"Mother tells me this used to be a talking dog."

"Still is. But don't spread it around."

The doctor smiled. "All right. I promise." Narcoticus was a name that he used just at the house; elsewhere, he had another, distinguished name. At Mother Polk's he was principally an abortionist, but he would also drop around if a girl had the croup or the clap or needed some dope.

Pinfold said, "There used to be one lived over on New Dream Street."

"One what?" Narcoticus picked up the bullet that Pinfold had dropped into the wagon.

"Talking dog. I forget its name. A big black dog. But this was a real long time ago. My ma took me to see it." Pinfold could remem-

ber it vividly—the day they'd gone, the sidewalks had been sloughy
with caterpillars. "Lived in a shop, this dog." A store that sold reli-
gious goods. The sign above the door showed God's palace in the
clouds, and displayed in the window were crucifixes and carved
ivory martyrs, hair relics of Italian saints, novena booklets, and
powders that you stirred into water—his mother had told him—to
materialize your guardian angel; white first missals and black rosary
beads. Inside, the place smelled like a church: candle wax and incense. The dog had sat in a cane chair, a cane chair with a high fan
back. "It could say word for word the Sermon on the Mount—that's
the one goes, Blessed are these guys, blessed are those guys," Pinfold said to Narcoticus. "And you know why it could talk? Ate a
bunch of splinters from the True Cross. You can look that up. It
musta been in all the papers."

The doctor laughed, his narrow head moving up and down, his
pointy beard stabbing at his collarbone. Then he took another peek
at Fuzzy. A dog that talks? Could be. There's room, he thought.
There's room yet. Years before, in Heidelberg where he'd gone to
medical school, he'd been shown a werewolf. Brought to a locked
cell, he'd peered through a slot in the oaken door and watched as the
creature, entirely covered in a reddish fur, tore apart a large gray
rabbit and consumed it. Later, after moonset, Narcoticus had entered the cell and shaken hands with a pale naked Russian in his late
forties, a well-known philosophical novelist. "Well, even if this dog
of yours talked once, I doubt very much that she'll talk again."

Pinfold moved his shoulders, then he crossed all his fingers and
made an X with his thumbs.

Much later, some of the whores came in their petticoats to see the
dog. Ohh, poor thing, they all said about Fuzzy, and then three of
them—they were very drunk—pulled a wooden tub in from the
back porch to give Pinfold a bath, as a giggle. He was so gummy,
they said, and his clothes were disgusting—burn them! Pinfold let
himself be undressed, and didn't mind it, sort of liked it, when his
pecker was tweaked, when someone goosed him. He sat down in the
water. The girls found a sponge and a two-pound bar of soap. They
took turns scrubbing him, joking that it was a good thing he was
bald, bet you he would've been just full of head lice otherwise. After
he stepped out of the tub, they wrapped him in a tablecloth. Then

one of the girls—called Baby, because she always dragged around a porcelain doll—went up to her room and found a nightshirt for Pinfold to wear, an ordinary white flannel nightshirt, nothing sissy about it.

By then it was after two in the morning, time for everybody to go to bed. Pinfold didn't like the idea of staying over at Mother's, but what could he do? He couldn't move Fuzzy, not now; that would've been stupid. Nor could he walk back to Awful Alley in a nightshirt—he'd never make it there alive. So he had to stay. He pulled two chairs up next to the wagon. Before turning in, though, he got his wigbox from the kitchen table and took out the pair of white bucks that he'd looted from Room 12. Tried them on. Way too big. He stuffed them with newspaper and then they fit okay. Finally, he went to sleep, waking often to listen for the sound of Fuzzy's breathing. When he was sure that she wasn't dead, he'd sit back and doze again.

The cadets who'd taken Billy McCord's body away returned to the house about half past three. They came in through the kitchen, the four cadets and Georgie Wreckage. Drunk.

After having been with him for a chunk of time—the first hour of it difficult but the next several a lot of fun—Mother's boys had concluded that Jim—Georgie's *nom de polish*—was a pretty decent fella, all in all, for a coon. Spit especially had cottoned to him. Spit was called that because of a funny absence of pigmentation—in streaks running from the corners of his mouth down his chin—which made you think at first that he was drooling. And why had he ended up feeling so warmly toward Georgie? Because they'd shared a burden. The two men had carried the trunk with Billy McCord stuffed inside it from Mother Polk's house to the Church of Eleven Martyrs and One Virgin, a walking distance of roughly one mile. Spit had volunteered for the job; he was the newest of Mother's cadets and eager to court her favor. Georgie had been dragooned. His own fault, for being right there when the shooting happened: You, boy, grab an end. End of *what?* Of the trunk, nigger. Take an end! Which he did, after slipping Anna's pistol—one more souvenir—into his waistband.

❑ ❑ ❑

At the church, Georgie and Spit and a cadet called Punch and another called Three-Nut Case had stayed with the trunk while a cadet named Luther ran to the rectory next door to get a priest. Three-Nut lit every votive candle in the place, walking around to each tier of red cups with a sliver of wood that held a flame. Georgie massaged his fingers and wandered from one station of the cross to the next, looking at the pictures. Spit stretched out on a hemlock pew. And Punch—Punch undid the belts on the trunk and gingerly raised the lid.

Clearly, he intended to help himself to Billy's purse. And he meant to do it on the sly—didn't want any mouth from the others—but the moment he turned the seaside coat inside out, he was so astonished by what he saw that he yelped involuntarily. There were thirteen pockets sewn into the lining, and in each pocket was a bill-fold. Oh, murder, will you look at *this!* Because of Punch's excla-mation, Three-Nut came trotting up the center aisle, and Spit clambered over the back of his pew, and Georgie glanced away from the Women of Jerusalem Weeping. Punch, laughing and gleeful, started to flip all the billfolds into the air, and when they fell they smacked loudly. He was feeling generous now, old Punch, and he said, "Everybody gets three, but I get four, since I found them."

"I'm not gonna take just any three," said Spit. "What if I get three empty ones?" Then he picked one up off the floor and peered inside, and his eyebrows jumped. "I'll take this one and two others. But what about Jim? Jim should get something."

Three-Nut crouched and scooped up a purse for himself. It bore the logo of the New York *World,* twin globes separated by the Statue of Liberty and cushioned by clouds, and Georgie, recognizing it as his own—Pulitzer had given one to every man on staff last Christ-mas—felt a keen impulse to walk over there and just grab it. But he didn't. He wasn't Georgie now, he was Jim, and he only stuffed his hands into his pockets and said, "I don't expect nothing, gentlemen. You go right ahead and take your four, Mr. Punch."

Punch grinned, winked at Spit.

Three-Nut tossed aside Georgie's purse after ripping all of the cash from the moneyfold. Georgie bent and looked to see where it had skittered to. All right. Under the kneeler: two, three, *fourth* pew from the rear.

Spit said, "No, this Jim carried that frigging trunk all the way over here with me—he oughta get something. Jim?" He looked into

a square and shabby black billfold that he'd just taken from Mc-
Cord's jacket; then he pitched it underhand to Georgie. It contained
a lock of blond infant's hair, pinned in a cigarette paper, and a five-
dollar bill.

"Why, thank you, Mr. Spit, thank you so much," said Georgie,
doing a low bow.

Punch looked annoyed but didn't object; he set aside three wallets
for Luther, then closed the trunk and belted it again.

"I say we should take all the money from all the wallets and split
that," said Three-Nut, obviously less than pleased by the ones he'd
picked.

Spit told him to go jump; he'd begun to smooth out several tens on
top of the poor box. Then, what the hell, he rolled one up and
pushed it through the slot.

Luther returned with a roly-poly father whose cassock hem in the
back, Georgie noticed, was sooty gray from being stepped on. He
had a big iron key in his fist, and he glanced at the trunk, and
scowled at the hat on Georgie's head, but he didn't speak a word, he
just kept walking, straight up the nave and through the chancel rail.
Luther snapped his fingers, then hurried after the priest. Three-Nut
and Punch hurried after Luther, and Georgie and Spit lifted the
trunk again.

They carried it across the altar—passing in front of the taberna-
cle, Spit did a half genuflection—and into the sacristy; then through
a door and down a long flight of stairs to a crypt. The priest opened a
gate with his key. Luther had lighted a kerosene lantern. Spit and
Georgie put the trunk down next to a similar trunk, behind a lifesize
statue of the Blessed Mother. Georgie counted nine hair or steamer
trunks and fifteen sepulchers.

On the way back up the stairs, the priest said to Luther, "That's
the third this year. You tell Mrs. Polk that if she can't keep her house
in order, someone else will be found who can. The same goes for
you."

Luther cringed like a schoolboy, and Georgie started to grin, but
then suddenly he was shaking, all over. To stop it, he hugged himself, and then he went tight across the chest. It became difficult to
breathe. He was gulping. He had to sit down just as soon as he
reached the first pew in the church. He squeezed his hands between
his knees. Spit gave him an odd, questioning look, and Georgie

shook his head—nothing's the matter. He freed a hand then and blessed himself, so that Spit would think he was saying a prayer.

Easter was still a week away, and the statues on the main and side altars were draped in purple. There was a cruit on the ledge of the pulpit, an officiating stole coiled like a rattlesnake on a kneeling bench, and there was a desiccated apple core in the drip pan of a candlestick. Seeing these things, just by looking at them, Georgie was able to collect himself, finally. But why had he gone fizzy like that? Why? What happened? He was ashamed.

Leaving to rejoin the others outside, he remembered to pick up his billfold.

9

Pinfold said, "I didn't expect to see you back here tonight." He checked again on Fuzzy, then covered her with a black slicker that he'd found in the pantry. "I thought you were long gone." The boy caught Georgie gawking at his dome, so he walked over and took down his derby from a hook beside the kitchen door and popped it on. He jerked a thumb over his shoulder at the wagon. "You were right. She needs a new master. Guess who's it?"

Georgie, seated at the table and butting the salt cellar against the pepper grinder, raised his eyes and nodded. He was liquor-woozy. Spit had insisted that he join the boys for a drink, at a dive right around the corner from the church. One drink—you deserve it! Georgie had felt he needed it, too. But one drink had led to another, and before Georgie knew it he was drunk and laughing at all of Three-Nut's jokes—hear about the rabbi that lost his pecker? And then Georgie was telling jokes himself—this sailor wants to get laid, see, but every time he drops his drawers he starts to hiccup. . . . At one point, Georgie unthinkingly had taken off his hat to fan his face; when he realized what he'd done, he nearly jumped up, ready to run for his life. But the cadets were too pissed by that hour even to notice that "Jim" wasn't nappy on top, that his hair was straight and biscuit-brown.

"She's my dog now," said Pinfold.

Georgie nodded again. He wondered what time it was. Spit, and wasn't he a grand son of a bitch, had gone upstairs ten minutes ago?

fifteen? to look for Georgie's shoeshine kit. The other men had gone to bed.

Pinfold sat down opposite Georgie at the table. His smile moved around, bending higher now on the left side of his face, now on the right. "You're the first Clarky's boy I ever seen spoilt his suit." He pointed merrily at all the bloodstains—there, there, there . . . there! "Gonna lose your job?"

"Doubt it."

"Me too." Pinfold took the crumpled butt of a cheroot from his wigbox; then a safety match, then a friction strip. "This ain't your job really, is it?"

Georgie didn't reply.

"You knew that whore was gonna shoot the fella. And Fuzzy." He was accusing, but he did it with his head cocked and his eyebrows up and that locomotive smile, just to be on the safe side. "You knew."

Georgie tapped the salt cellar too hard, and it tipped; some spilled. "No," he said. "No, I didn't. I knew somebody was planning to do something. But I expected it to be one of the crooks at the banquet. And I thought the dog was safe—honest!"

Pinfold pursed his lips, blew smoke, and the cloud of it came out resembling a straight razor. "Your man didn't try to cut her," he said. Then he puffed again, plucked the cigar from his mouth, and blew a fancy casket. "It looked like he was snoozing, to me."

"I know," said Georgie. "You saw everything?"

"I saw the girl cut *herself*, is what I saw. I didn't see her shoot him. She turned her back, she was blocking the bed." Pinfold had dropped his voice to a whisper. "And I saw Fuzzy get it."

Georgie exhaled noisily and frowned. What *he'd* seen—after the girl had come running from the bedroom, a revolver still in her hand, the right, and her chest scored with trifling cuts; after she'd slammed into him and ruined Clarky's suit, and he'd scooted around her and crossed the threshold: Billy McCord, lying spread-eagled on the bed, a tiny red hole—slightly off-center—in his forehead. The dog trying to stand, her legs collapsing under her, her paws slipping in pools of her own blood. The yellow money purse and a straight razor on the floor, and across the room, stuck to the dressing mirror and dribbling, the bright red condom.

"What happened to the girl?" Georgie asked now. "Anything?"

"Not that I heard. Mother believed her. I think." Pinfold laid the cigar down and rose from his seat and walked to the wagon; from habit, but in vain, his hands searched out back pockets to plunge into.

"You didn't tell anybody what you saw?"

"Why should I? Anyhow, say I did—you would've been in the soup. So thank me."

"Thank you," said Georgie, and looked at Pinfold's cigar, the coal just over the table edge, burning toward the oilcloth. Then he looked at Pinfold: derby on his big head, white buck shoes on his bare feet; that nightshirt, those skinny legs, shins bruised. Then: the yellow dog in the red wagon, unconscious, a raincoat blanketing her, a red dish towel tied around her throat. Derby, bucks, nightshirt, dog. Dog, wagon, raincoat, dish towel. Holy smoke! The picture was so grotesquely poignant that Georgie's eyes dilated with pleasure; he very nearly clapped his hands together. A boy and his dog. "What're you going to do with her?"

"All depends. We'll have to talk about it, but I got a few ideas."

Georgie didn't understand right away: *We?* Why should we have to talk about it? But then, ah, *then* it hit: Pinfold meant Fuzzy and him, *that* we. "Think she'll have very much to say?" His meaning was clear enough: Ha-ha. And the boy caught it.

He came back across the kitchen scowling and stood watching Georgie's left pointing finger scribble rapidly on the tabletop; it made a slight crackling sound because of the salt. Pinfold said, "I figure she'll have a lot to say. But that's none of your business."

Georgie casually licked salt from his finger pad. "I guess not," he said.

The night through the kitchen window already was turning gray by the time Spit finally returned. He came down with a whore—she was carrying Georgie's shoeshine kit—whose yellow hair was full of paper curlers. She seemed more asleep than awake; her neck and shoulders were swollen and whisker-burned. Spit had keys and unlocked the door to let Georgie out. "Be back tonight, Jim?"

"It's Sunday," said Georgie. "I don't work on Sunday." As he was going, he glanced around at Pinfold, back in his chairs for another drowse. Nose, he thought, no bigger than my pinkie tip.

Walking to Sawdust Street, Georgie stopped twice to throw up in the curb. He didn't pass anybody all the way home, or at any rate he didn't notice anybody, and the tins of polish rattled in his box, and the brushes thudded. With the end of the rain, hours ago, the skies had cleared, and there was a big fat Man in the Moon.

10

"I heard he was over there last night," said Clarky, meaning Pinfold, looking at Georgie's large sketch: The boy in his derby and nightshirt and that trig pair of shoes stooped beside the wagon, a hand poised to stroke the dog's forehead. "How come you haven't drawn the other business? Where's the murder? Where's the trunk, where's the priest? Where're *you?*"

Georgie's eyebrows crawled into a frown. He was using his fingers, clustered, to scrape at the shoe wax in his sideburns. He'd slept in his clothes, woke up a little before ten very depressed and badly hung over. He'd wiped his face clean, almost clean, on several towels. He'd finally taken off the bloody white suit and hung it up. Then he'd brewed green coffee and sat at his board to draw. He'd felt he had to. Though his hands shook and his eyes kept losing focus, he'd persisted and forced the work out. Not that he was much pleased by any of it. He was glad when Clarky arrived. It gave him an excuse to quit. Clarky had glanced at the suit—he'd heard it was a total ruin— and then looked daggers at Georgie. "Where's the murder, I said. Where's the trunk? Haven't drawn any of that yet?"

"You heard about what happened, then."

"Is that supposed to be funny, George? Are you making a joke?"

Georgie smiled feebly; then, picking up a hand mirror from the bureau, he used it in conjunction with his dressing mirror to look at the hair at the nape of his neck, hard-caked. There was black wedged under all his fingernails. What a nuisance! As a boy, he'd read quite a number of frontier tales in which white men passed among savage Indians by smearing themselves with wild-growing berries. And all *they'd* ever had to do to get clean was sponge off or jump in a river. Georgie grabbed a tie pin from his jewelry box and began to dig the wax from under a thumbnail; to dig and flick. He avoided meeting Clarky's eyes. Clarky seemed very annoyed. About the suit?

"I asked you how come you haven't drawn the murder."

"I didn't see it."

"Oh, no?"

"No. Pinfold did."

"But you saw everything else. You had to go upstairs where you didn't belong, didn't you?"

"It's what I do."

Clarky sighed.

"I'll pay for the suit."

"You bet you will!" Clarky threw the cardboard, the picture of Pinfold and Fuzzy, down on the carpet. He noticed a quill pen left uncleaned and cleaned it on a cloth. "Are you stupid, are you dumb?" he asked. "Are you crazy?" and Georgie laughed. "Just *how* crazy are you, George? That's what I want to know."

Georgie lifted his eyebrows. The suit—that's not what Clarky had come about, was it? What, then?

Clarky stood now with his arms dangling at his sides; he pursed his lips and very slightly raised his shoulders. "You have to tell me something, George. All right? Are you gonna go and draw a *Clarky's boy* lugging a dead body around town in a trunk? Is that one of the pictures you got in mind to draw for Monday's first edition? Because if it is, George, I'm saying to you, dead serious: Don't."

Georgie had no expression: he was simply listening.

"Don't. All right? I'm saying don't. We're talking about my reputation now. We're talking about my trademark here. That's a registered trademark, that suit." It was no such thing. "You want to ruin me?" Clarky was glowering; his fingers were flexing, unflexing. His cheeks were puffing out, collapsing, puffing out, collapsing.

Georgie used the tie pin to scratch at a black spot on his knuckle: not paste there, ink.

Clarky said, "We're friends, George. Do a friend a favor. You won't be sorry."

Georgie looked at the tie pin, then flipped it away.

Clarky sat down on the studio couch. On the floor was a box labeled GRAPEFRUIT and crammed with a few dozen periodicals. Clarky knew that at the bottom of the box were several mounted photographs of naked women—with no hair on their pudenda— posed against painted sylvan backdrops. Usually when he visited, he sneaked a look at them. But not today. He grabbed a batch of magazines and set them on his lap. He looked at Georgie—who'd resumed cleaning his fingernails—then glanced at a back issue of *McClure's*. Paged through it for half a minute, then pitched it aside and picked up a weekly called *Truth*. A propos. Because there was a truth that Clarky hoped Georgie would come to realize, and quickly. That he, Clarky, was not about to let Georgie Wreckage scotch his entire business for a lousy newspaper sketch. If Georgie insisted that he was going to draw the episode of the hair trunk, and draw it with all *five* carters, then Clarky would take the necessary measures to stop him. In his shirt pocket was a loaded pistol that was an exact copy of a maduro cigar, and to fire it all you had to do was squeeze the foot. Clarky had purchased it from an inventor named Elmer Dreezle. He'd use it if he had to, he could. He *could*—couldn't he? Georgie was his friend and all, but still. Still, he wasn't his *brother*, anything like *that*. Don't make me, George. Clarky was looking at a copy of *Judge* now, at an Antville cartoon by Gus Dirks. Say, Farmer Rabbit, who gave you permission to plant potatoes right on our main street?

"George? So what do you say?"

Georgie made a pained face.

As soon as he'd had his first cup of coffee that morning—and after he'd chased from his mind the dream of waking to discover Billy McCord leaning over him and digging mushy fingers through the pockets of his uniform jacket—Georgie had decided to forget about the killing. At least to forget about drawing it for the *World*. And he'd decided that reluctantly, because this time he'd got too close to things. He hadn't just watched last night, he'd participated. He'd never done that before. He'd stepped into the picture, so to speak, and ended up with blood on his clothes, five extra dollars, aching shoulders, and the katzenjammers—the jangled nerves and the bad taste in his mouth on account of his drinking. And what he'd done, even though he hadn't volunteered, presented him in the light of day with a moral dilemma, something he was unused to. Also, there was a legal problem maybe, and nothing, certainly no sketch in the paper, was worth the risk of being hauled into the cop house. Unless he was dispatched to cover a particular story, Georgie was under no obligation to draw anything. So never mind the banquet, forget the killing, to hell with Billy McCord. To hell with him! Which meant Clarky was all upset for no good reason. Look at him fidget. Georgie grinned, a little. Most of the time Clarky was smart. But not today. He'd seen the pictures Georgie had drawn earlier, and if he'd used his brains he would've realized that had Georgie intended to draw up the murder story he wouldn't have wasted time illustrating a crowd of hoodlums and whores dancing three sheets to the wind.

And he certainly wouldn't have drawn the dog unconscious in a
wagon. He would've drawn her bloody in the bedroom.

"Well?" said Clarky. He snapped his fingers. "Well?" And took
out his cigar.

Georgie was at the window, holding back an edge of the curtain.
He saw Professor Thom coming home from South Dump, his wheelbarrow loaded with tap handles and clock guts, fly cams and pot
valves, a teapot, a bell buoy, a laundry mangle. The Professor
looked up and squinted, and waved. Georgie turned to Clarky and
asked him, "How much do I owe you for the suit? What do you want
for it?"

"Eighty trillion dollars and forty-nine cents. Or your solemn
promise to forget all about last night."

Walking over to the bedside table, Georgie picked up a billfold—
not his own, the other one, the one he'd gotten from Spit. He opened
it and looked inside. Big stagey frown. "All I have is a five," he said,
and smiled, and then crossed his heart with his left thumb. "So I
guess I promise. You want the five?"

"Keep it, George. The five *and* the promise, okay?" Clarky
passed his cigar under his nose, faking a sniff, then stuck it back into
his shirt pocket. "And George? There'll be other things. I'll let you
know what I hear."

And Georgie said, "Sure," but without much enthusiasm.

A happy man, Clarky left to have his Sunday dinner, and immediately Georgie flung himself down on the couch and in a blue funk
smoked cigarettes, occasionally pressing the heel of his hand against
his forehead. He'd read *Trilby;* who hadn't? After a long while, he
got up and took the old brown wallet, and leaving the fiver in the
moneyfold, he tossed it into his souvenirs footlocker. Then he
jammed in the white suit. Then he laid Anna's pistol on top.

11

Sunday evening, way up high in a captive balloon, Georgie
counted nine small clouds and sighted the planet Mars, and Joette
said, as she'd said at least once every half hour since she'd come

across the sketch of Pinfold and Fuzzy on Georgie's floor, "I hope that dog hasn't . . . passed away? Can you find out for me? Can you?"

Earlier, astounding himself at how easily, how *instantly* he could fabricate the lie, Georgie had told her that Fuzzy was shot in anger by an old coot, a coot named, named Slippery John—had a cut-glass doorknob instead of a left hand. But *why*, George? Well . . . seems the dog ate Slippery John's dinner off his plate when he wasn't looking. Scrambled eggs. Some thief, that Fuzzy. Where was this? A restaurant. But which one? You don't know it. Last night? Late last night. Holy gee, she'd asked so many questions about that cheesy little picture! How come the boy was wearing a nightshirt? What happened to the shooter? I don't know, Georgie had finally said, his imagination flagging. I don't know. I don't know. What do you mean, you don't know—you were *there*, weren't you? Hey, Joette, it's Sunday. Day of rest. I don't want to talk about all this stuff on my day of rest. Buy tomorrow's paper. Being a wise guy, but it'd worked. But now, in the swaying gondola, she was starting up again: "Can you find out for me, George? If the dog's okay?"

The French balloonist burned another handful of straw, and when the bag suddenly lifted, he sneered at Georgie for cringing; decay ran like an ore through his front teeth.

"Joette? Can I ask you one question? And I don't mean it to sound nasty—all right?—but you must've seen two hundred pictures of mine, two hundred times you've made a face. So how come you care so much about this fat old dog and a street arab?"

"I don't know," she replied, looking off at a dumb barge drifting toward Brooklyn. She pressed Georgie's hand. She smiled at him warmly, did Maid Bridget. "I don't really know. Isn't that funny?"

WHEN PINFOLD WAS FAMOUS

The tenement at the head of Awful Alley was called Calamity Flats, and down in its coal cellar lived Albert Shallow. As soon as you stepped through the basement door, you could smell the sulfur that he used in producing condoms, and party balloons occasionally, and dishwashing gloves. In Albert's poky stall there were fish skeletons and lumps of coal underfoot, and hills of coal in every corner. There was a kerosene lamp, and a Bunsen burner, and a round wooden table with two chairs. An army cot. A physician's cabinet with a scale on top and chemical bottles on all its shelves. Half a hundred condoms or more were always drying on a clothesline.

Albert was six-foot-six and weighed 270 pounds. He was as deeply black as printer's ink, and his eyes were green. Once upon a time he'd been a bare-knuckled fighter at the Bleecker Saloon, and his fingers were permanently swollen. Still, he could do careful, pernickety manual jobs adroitly as a jeweler. He was born the same day President Lincoln died, which made him exactly thirty, but he looked much older, as old as fifty. Because of his gray hair, cropped close to his skull, and because he had practically no teeth in his head, only a few busted brown ones.

It was two Saturdays after the banquet at Mother Polk's. About noon. Pinfold came to see Albert and found him hunched over his table playing with a jigsaw puzzle he'd constructed himself by gluing a news illustration from the *Police Gazette* to a backing of stiff cardboard, then cutting it into pieces. A train wreck at Long Branch. Albert fitted two pieces, areas of dense cross-hatching, into the picture; they were parts of the locomotive's steam dome. Then finally he turned in his chair and acknowledged the boy. The dog, surrounded by tin plates of scrambled eggs, sat in the red wagon. Ever since the sketches and the stories began appearing in the *World* newspaper, people—strangers mostly—had been coming around to the alley with scrambled eggs for Fuzzy. She wouldn't touch the stuff. She liked chicken broth and, of course, anything sweet, dark chocolate especially. Albert liked scrambled eggs, though, and Pinfold had been giving him whatever he couldn't finish. But the two of them had just about had it with eggs. Albert glanced at today's platefuls and shivered.

Pinfold handed him a copy of the morning paper.

"You in here again?"

"We are. Page number six. They got us at the vet's today."

Albert frowned.

Pinfold shrugged. "I don't know! I'm just telling you where they got us."

Albert unfolded the paper and rattled it; then he moistened an index finger and turned the pages.

Eagerly, Pinfold asked, "What's it say?"

Albert hummed as he read, then, "It says this doctor named Thomson—not a vet, a doctor—checked over your dog yesterday and there's no damage to the larynx."

"What's that?"

Albert pressed two fingers against the hollow of his throat. "What's here that lets a body talk. Vocal cords."

Pinfold turned to Fuzzy. "Vocal cords!" he said gaily. "See? Just let somebody say you don't got 'em now!" He folded his arms across his chest. "What else does it say, Albert?"

"It says the prognosis—that's what's likely to happen—the prognosis is supposed to be good. And it says be sure to buy Sunday's paper. Fuzzy might say a word or two to all her friends in New York."

"No!" Pinfold jumped. "It says that? Where?" He came around the table and peered over Albert's shoulder. "Where's it say that?" Albert pointed. Then Pinfold said, "Gee!" and grabbed the paper back. "Tomorrow!"

He looked again at the picture; he'd been looking at it every two minutes since seven o'clock this morning. Four columns wide, a half page deep. Fuzzy stretched out on a long examination table, Pinfold pacing in the background. The doctor was dressed in a morning suit and wore a parabolic mirror on a headband; he was holding a tongue depressor, he was smiling.

"Hear that, Fuzz? By tomorrow morning you might be saying a word or two. Well, that's good news!"

Albert scratched the side of his head. Daff, this whole business. Daff. He looked over at Fuzzy, and she looked steadily back at him, her big fleecy head bobbing up and down, her green eyes as melancholy as a widow's. Absolutely daff.

A couple of Sundays ago, late in the morning, Pinfold had rolled the dog into Albert's stall. Look what I found! She can talk! Talk? The animal was almost dead. While Albert slathered her neck with a mixture of tar and western Pennyslvania healing grasses, Pinfold told him the story. Sounds like you had quite a time for yourself at Mother's. Albert had never had much use for dogs, but he hoped for the boy's sake that it lived. This dog is special, Albert. This dog is the best thing I ever found. I love this dog! Love? For Pete's sake, why? It's only a *dog*. And Pinfold said, But I got a feeling she's my *lucky* dog. Albert shook his head. Lucky. Shot in the neck is lucky? Then up is down, back is front. So to Albert it was slightly daff even from the get-go, was Pinfold's adoption of Fuzzy.

But come that Monday morning, the adoption turned into a public rigmarole.

Albert was on his way through the alley to the street when he saw a dozen kids from the tenements milling at Pinfold's stoop; two were squatted on their hams and calling under the stairs, demanding that Pinfold come out with his dog—or at least let them come in to see her. What's she talk? English? Why it say you live in a cardboard box when you really live here? Pinfold! How come you never told us you wash dishes? You wash dishes? Where's that dog? Let's see her. She ain't dead yet, is she? And then Albert saw a small girl go and set down a plate of watery scrambled eggs; warily, she pushed the plate under the stoop. Overhead, a woman on a fire escape laughed and shook out her apron full of bones. They're not talking about *our* Pinfold, she hollered. It must be another. And one of the children called back to her, That ain't possible. There can't be two. Everybody laughed. Albert finally went on his way, and when he returned, perhaps an hour later, there was an even greater crowd at the stoop, and four or five plates of eggs on the ground.

Pinfold and Fuzzy were in the coal cellar, waiting for Albert in his stall. Fuzzy was still lying in the wagon and covered with the raincoat, but she was conscious. Her eyes were runny, and when she breathed she made a bubbling sound. Pinfold was leaning over Albert's table, his palms braced against the edge. He was studying a big drawing in the newspaper. Albert glanced at it, and his eyes widened.

Pinfold asked, What's it say, Albert? I heard what everybody tells me it says. But *you* read it. Albert did, reading out loud: A Boy and His Dog That Used to Talk. *Used* to! *Used* to? You want to listen, Pinfold, or do you want to yap? I'll listen, Albert. Just read. A boy and his dog that used to talk. Story and picture by Georgie Wreckage. Then Albert hummed and hummed, reading to himself, while Pinfold gnawed his fingernails. What, Albert, What? You wash dishes? *That's* what it says? Says you wash dishes, Pinfold, at this restaurant called the Snuggery. Sounds like a dive. I work in a restaurant that sounds like a dive—I *do?* You live out back. Since when do I? Have a dog named Fuzzy. Well, that's so. Been telling everybody she can talk, and count as high as twenty. I never said she could *count.* I don't *know* if she can. I *guess* she can. Only to twenty? Albert sniffed and hummed some more. I thought you told me some whore shot the dog. She *did;* she *didn't?* Slippery John did. Over scrambled eggs. *Bang!* What a riot that must've been, said Albert. Everybody dove for cover, it says here. It says that, Albert? It says Slippery John? Who's Slippery John? You don't know him? Jeez, Albert, I don't *think* so. Pinfold looked once more at the newspaper sketch. That's me, all right. That's my wagon, my wigbox. That's Fuzzy. He took off his derby and put it right back on again. There's nothing about Mother Polk's house? Nothing. Nothing at all. I *was* there Saturday night, Albert. Sure you were. I *was.* And I'm telling you, I know that. So what's all this? Albert said, It's a picture in the newspaper. That's what it is. Cut it out and tack it up. Listen, Pinfold, this happens all the time. It does? Sure, somebody gets the wrong information. I seen a picture of dinosaurs in the paper last month. These two fellas were supposed to've found a herd of them running around in Colorado. No fooling, said Pinfold. But listen to what I'm saying, boy: It was the wrong information. It wasn't Colo-

rado? Albert laughed. Sure it was Colorado, he said. But there
hasn't been a dinosaur there in a hundred years. Pinfold said, Oh.
And Albert said, Sometimes the facts get mixed up.

It didn't end there, though, with the one picture of Pinfold and
Fuzzy. Three days later there was another, even larger than the
first. Why do they keep drawing me in a nightshirt, Albert? I wore it
once. Albert hummed. You wear it to wash dishes, he said after a
minute. I *do?* You wear it instead of an apron. Ah, said Pinfold, I
guess that makes sense. So what else does it say about me? It says
you're twelve—are you? Pinfold lifted one shoulder. That sounds
about right. But what am I supposed to be doing in the picture?
What am I giving Fuzzy? What's in the spoon? Codeine syrup. Does
it help? It doesn't say, Albert told him. And what else? It says you
don't live behind the restaurant anymore. You moved. Really? said
Pinfold. Where to? Here, said Albert. Here? I live *here* now? Albert
shut one eye and looked at the boy. Yes, you live here now. Pinfold
nodded. Well, *sure!* And what else? It says a lot of people been writing letters to the *World*, asking about you both. They hope Fuzzy is
getting better. Pinfold laughed. He turned to the dog. Hear that,
Fuzz? People hope you're okay. Fuzzy was napping with her snout
on her paws, in the wagon. That's mostly what she'd been doing,
taking naps and long sleeps; but she was beginning to drink more
water now, and to swallow a little broth. And what *else* does it say,
Albert? Nothing else. Nothing? Pinfold scowled. Gee, he said, I
wonder what's going to happen to us next.

Albert said, Guess you'll have to buy the paper and see.

And Pinfold said, I guess I will.

Albert rolled his eyes.

There was another picture the Tuesday after Easter: She's Back
on Her Feet, Folks! And that one caused Pinfold considerable vexa-
tion. I don't know what's wrong with her, Albert. She should be
walking, like it says, but she just won't do it! She's still in the wagon.
Everybody's coming around saying congrats and I don't know what
to tell them. Tell them the paper got it wrong. I can't do *that*, Albert.

By this time, Pinfold had bought himself a white nightshirt and
was wearing it around over his clothes. People smiled but they didn't
laugh.

Albert was hungry and so he tried to eat a bit of today's cold eggs,
but he gagged on the first mouthful and roughly pushed away the

plate. "Why couldn't it be steaks?" he said. "Why couldn't they say
she liked porterhouse steaks?"

"But it *wasn't* a steak," Pinfold replied. "It was the guy's scrambled eggs." He had picked up a puzzle piece, and bending over the
table with it in his fingers, he tried to see where it might fit. He tried
here, he tried there. Finally, Albert took it and snapped it into
place. It was a section of a boxcar upside down.

"Do you still work for me? Or are you too busy nursing that dumb
animal?"

"I still work for you, Albert."

"Well! I'm glad to hear you say that." He rose then from the table
and walked around the stall, yanking condoms from the clothesline
and tossing them into a paper sack. Fuzzy watched him. Pinfold
watched Fuzzy.

"You know, Albert, every day I been telling her. Like it says in
the paper I been telling her. I tell her maybe she should spend a few
minutes thinking about who saved her life. Is that too much to ask?
And every night I tell her, You might try to say my name, at least.
It's Pin-fold. I tell her, It's just an idea. Think about it. But I don't
know, Albert. Am I doing this all wrong? Nothing works. In the
paper she's already licking my fingers. I show her *that* picture, and it
don't make any difference."

Albert held the sack out for Pinfold to take. "If I were you, I'd
roll that animal someplace and dump her. She ain't going to do nothing but lay around and shit in your house."

"You know that's not true. You know that, Albert. Come on. Her
prognosis is *good!*"

After Pinfold left, pulling the dog in the wagon, Albert Shallow sat
back down at the table and took up his scissors and cut out today's
Boy and Dog picture from the paper. Then he got a piece of cardboard and his glue pot.

Wherever Pinfold went lately, he was noticed and pointed at;
often he was followed, usually by children, and from time to time,
especially down around Wall Street and City Hall, prosperous-
looking men would throw nickels and dimes into the wagon. Oddly
enough, though, very few people who recognized him and Fuzzy
from the newspaper actually tried to speak to him. Even the kids in
Awful Alley weren't pestering him any longer: they always stopped

what they were at when he and the dog came out from under the steps, and they stared, but they'd turned strangely quiet. Just the other night, Pinfold had gone outside to have a smoke, and there were two fellas having a piss war. When finally they'd emptied their bladders and buttoned up, they sat down against the tenement wall, and Pinfold went over and joined them. They lit their cigarettes off his, but then there was an awkward silence for about a minute, till one of the boys—Carmine something—suddenly said, My old lady thinks Pinfold shoulda gone to the cops and had them pinch that bum Slippery John. There's laws, she says, against shooting dogs. The other boy—everybody called him No—No said, Maybe he shoulda. And Pinfold said, Aw, he probably thought the cops woulda just laughed. You think so? said Carmine. Pinfold shrugged. I don't know for sure, he said. But maybe. Then No and Carmine got up and drifted away, leaving Pinfold sitting there all by himself and feeling suddenly lightheaded and badly mixed up, as though he'd gone too long, a few days, without any sleep. I don't know for *sure?* But *maybe?* He made a fist and banged himself hard on the side of his head.

Since the pictures started, Pinfold's business in condoms had fallen off sharply. He'd go out and stand by his wagon at the usual corners and he'd see any number of his regular customers, only these days they just weren't buying. They'd smile at him—in the past they hadn't done that—they'd smile at him like he was a valentine card, but then they'd pass him straight by. Maybe they thought he was no longer a vendor? That he was just out taking the air? That he'd given up selling condoms to scrub pots in a kitchen? Very possible. Sometimes Pinfold even thought it himself: He'd be traipsing down some avenue and suddenly think, Wait a minute! Am I supposed to be working tonight? Am I supposed to wash dishes? Whenever that happened, Pinfold was left feeling shaky and a little angry. Disappointed. I don't work in any restaurant! According to the newspaper, the Snuggery was on Second Avenue, near Second Street, and twice Pinfold had tried to find it. There were plenty of cheap eating places over there, but none called the Snuggery. Like Albert said, though, sometimes facts got tumbled around; names too, Pinfold figured.

If it hadn't been for the dollar, dollar and a half in small change that he was taking in from strangers almost every day, Pinfold might've worried more about his dwindling business receipts. He was concerned, but not unduly, not enough that he couldn't enjoy his celebrity, even if it did make him feel isolated. He just hoped it lasted until Fuzzy got her voice back. *Then* he'd have something to offer and could start charging money for it. Then he could walk around with his wigbox open, telling everybody to drop it here, drop it here, and meanwhile, groomed and bright-eyed, Fuzzy would be standing in the wagon reciting, "And somewhere men are laughing, and somewhere children shout/But there is no joy in Mudville— mighty Casey has struck out."

That Saturday afternoon, Pinfold spent several unprofitable hours on the streets and in the arcades, then after the sun left for China and a wind kicked up, he started for home. By then he was quite a distance from Awful Alley; he was over by the ferry docks. He stayed on West Street for a while, then veered eastward, negotiating narrow transverse streets and pulling the wagon past hash houses and saloons and haberdasheries, chandleries and barbershops; merchant seamen and sandwich men and customhouse officials all glanced at him. He passed markets that sold eggs and butter, markets displaying hams and quails and squabs and trout, markets full of cheese. Some were closing down for the night, others were being resupplied. He cut through a neighborhood of Syrians, and the air smelled of frying dough and honey and attar of roses, and dusky men eyed him from the doorways. They pointed to Fuzzy. Pinfold felt safe.

On the way through Guld Alley, Fuzzy began stirring in the wagon, noisily. When Pinfold glanced around and down, she was struggling to stand up; she'd shaken off the raincoat, she was whimpering. Pinfold's face lit. He stopped in front of a clapboard tenement. An old woman—to Pinfold she seemed as old as petroleum— sat at the top of the wooden stoop, on a milk crate, mumbling in a language of Eastern Europe. She was saying the rosary. Her bony fingers jiggled like a telegrapher's on the beads. She half stood and called something unintelligible, addressing Fuzzy, and all at once the dog barked and jumped from the wagon and ran up the stairs. She disappeared into the tenement. Pinfold shouted for her to come back, and when he realized that she wasn't likely to, he lifted the wagon into his arms, as though carrying cordwood, and followed her inside. The old woman wagged a scolding finger at him as he went by. He climbed through the building, stumbling on worn treads. "Fuzzy! Fuzzy!" The place was swept clean and had hallway toilets that were padlocked, but what you breathed wasn't air at all, it was cabbage fumes. "Fuzz-*zee!*"

At the top of the house, Pinfold came upon a man in an invalid chair blocking the head of the stairs. Broken veins in his cheeks and popped capillaries at the tip of his nose, deep lines across his forehead. He wore a dark gabardine suit which hadn't been laundered, it looked like, or even off his body, in several years. A narrow bottle of white liquor was jammed between his legs at the crotch. He leaned to one side and peered around Pinfold. "Where's Delannoy?"

Pinfold turned and looked behind him.

"He's not with you?"

"I don't know what you're talking about. My dog ran up here. I'm trying to find my dog."

"*Your* dog? What's going on? That's not your dog, it's his. Where is he? He coming back?"

Pinfold was standing three steps below the landing, and the wagon in his arms was getting heavier and heavier. "Say, you mind letting me come up so I can put this down?"

The man considered for a moment, then he released the brake and rolled the chair back, just enough that Pinfold could squeeze through holding the wagon over his head. He set the wagon on the floor. Down the hall a door stood open. "Fuzzy! Fuzzy? She go in there, mister?" Pinfold started walking.

"Where's Delannoy?" the man called after him. "He's not coming back? Where's Billy?"

Pinfold stopped. "Billy?"

"How come you got his dog? What's going on? Fuzzy ain't yours."

Pinfold couldn't help feeling a mild scorn for the man. Sure as a horsehair in a jar of water turned into a snake, this old cripple was reading the wrong newspaper. Fuzzy not mine? Go chase yourself. Pinfold said, "I'm looking after her."

"Then you know Billy?"

"I know Billy, sure. I only didn't know his last name was Illinois."

"Delannoy. So where is he?"

"Away." Pinfold jerked a thumb at the open door. "That his room, hey? She go in there?"

"It's been open for a week. With the lock busted like that, you can't keep it shut. It just opens by itself."

"How'd the lock get busted?"

"Four micks done it. I got a good peek at 'em, but they didn't see me. I don't know what they were looking for—they didn't take away nothing that I could tell. Four of them. Somebody named Connie, somebody named Daniel. And two others. I could describe 'em to Billy, when he comes back."

"He'll appreciate that," said Pinfold. "I bet."

"When's he coming?"

"I don't know exactly."

"He go back to Chicago?"

"No."

The man narrowed his eyes. "You sure you're his friend?"

"Didn't say he was my friend. I said I was taking care of his dog."

"You said he was coming back when—next week?"

"I said I didn't know. But he took a trunk with him, so he might be gone awhile."

"Well, I hope he's not away *too* long. He's a nice fella. Say—you be staying in his room, will you? Till he comes back? You play checkers?"

Pinfold said, "No," and walked down the hall. The doorjamb was splintered around the lock; chunks of wood still lay on the floor where they'd fallen. Before he went inside, he turned his head and looked back, and the man in the chair was taking a belt, the bottle trembling in his hand.

The room had been thoroughly tumbled. The bed was stripped and the mattress slashed, and wads of stuffing were everywhere. The bureau was on its side, its back pried off and its drawers out. On the floor—bicycle clips, a stick of chewing gum, a copy of *The King in Yellow*. A shirt and several collars, a chipped shaving mug, a woman's handkerchief, an electromagnetic toothbrush, a bottle of gargling oil. There was an artist's easel, and that had been knocked over too; someone had driven a fist through an oil painting of yellow wildflowers in the sentimental light of early evening. There were other paintings of other fields, all torn from their stretchers, their edges voluted and full of tacks. Pinfold accidentally stepped on one canvas, and the thick pigment crunched. Scattered around, as many as a dozen billfolds, each turned inside out.

Fuzzy was curled up in a tin-plated washtub below the window.

"This where you used to live, huh?" said Pinfold. "You two? That where you slept?" He bent and picked up a fresh bar of soap; the crumpled wrapper—Santa Claus brand—was lying a few feet away on a rag carpet, next to an iron, a pliers, and a blue cloth cap. He put the soap into his wigbox, and then the pliers and a woolen scarf. "Well, come on, Fuzz, you don't live here anymore. Come on."

But Fuzzy made no effort to get up; as a matter of fact, she seemed to be settling in for a nap. Pinfold sighed, then wandered around the room seeing if there was anything else that he wanted. The wardrobe was open. Three cheap suits were lying in a pile on the floor of it. Pinfold took a cursory look—nah, nah, mmm? nah—then noticed a gold picture frame stuck way in the back. He reached for it. A branching crack ran through the glass. It was a photograph of a man, a woman—a good-looker too; blond—and a small boy-child in a fancy shirtwaist posed in front of the Egyptian Obelisk at the Chicago Exposition. A couple of years back, Pinfold had seen plenty of sketches of the fairgrounds in all the New York papers: sketches of the great Ferris Wheel, the Moorish Palace, the Japanese Bazaar, the Ice Railway, the Congress of Beauty. And a week hadn't passed without another pen-and-ink portrait somewhere of Little Egypt in her veils and metal breastplates. It took Pinfold several seconds now to recognize the man in the photograph as Billy McCord, or Delannoy. Because in the picture Billy was smiling happily, and at Mother's he'd been pretty sour. He had one arm around the blond woman's waist, and he was holding the child in the crook of the other. Pinfold clamped his teeth and sucked on them and made a simmering noise. He frowned. That Billy McCord, or Delannoy, or whoever was dead struck Pinfold now as . . . sad. Sad, he'd have to say that he felt sad about it. He thought of his mother. Put in a word for the fella, Ma. If it's not too late. Amen.

He tossed the photograph back into the wardrobe, then went over and squatted by the washtub. "Come on, Fuzz. You don't live here anymore. Come on." She wouldn't on her own, but she didn't struggle when the boy finally lifted her and carried her back to the wagon and set her down into it. "You come from Chicago too? Huh? Jeez, Fuzz, you're gonna say a few words for all your friends in New York tomorrow—how about just one word for your *best* friend. No?"

No.

Pinfold shrugged; then he went and got the stick of chewing gum—it was Juicy Fruit, and Albert liked Juicy Fruit—and at last he picked up the wagon handle, ready to go. He was dreading the climb back down the stairs, not sure at all that he could lug the wagon *and* Fuzzy.

Just as he was leaving, the man in the wheelchair appeared again, rolling through the doorway, and there on his lap, sitting up straight on his lap, was the same small child Pinfold had seen in the World's Fair picture five minutes ago. The same child, the same happy expression, the same frilly shirtwaist. "If you see Billy before I do," said the man, "tell him Little Joe's okay. After those four bastards come up and done what they did—well, you see how they left the place—I brought Joe into my room. Just to be safe. I didn't want somebody else maybe coming in here, since you can't lock the door, and stealing the little fella. I know how much Billy cares about him."

It was a pinewood dummy, a ventriloquist's dummy, the features painted on but the blond hair genuine and silky, and seeing it, Pinfold let out a terrible moan, then propelled himself across the floor and ripped the thing from the old man's lap and flung it, hard as he could.

And this is how Pinfold lost his wagon and his wigbox: He ran away and left them behind.

He lost his wagon and his wigbox, but not his dog.

She followed him all the way home to Awful Alley.

Pinfold sat under the stoop in the dark. The corners of his eyes were raw, and his head throbbed something awful. He was beginning to feel hungry and knew that he could just reach outside and there'd be a dish of eggs—he'd heard somebody come by earlier and leave it—but he didn't believe that he could keep eggs down. He took the stick of chewing gum from his pocket and licked the sugar from one side. Finally, he lit a candle jammed into the neck of a wine bottle and then he could see Fuzzy, curled up tightly on a pile of damp blankets. And he let himself cry again, but just a little bit.

He felt confused and dreadfully let down. Fuzzy wasn't ever going to talk again—she never had! A ventriloquist's dog. He'd gone kerplunk for a ventriloquist's dog! She was a fake, and he was a dope. A dope! She was nothing special, and neither was he. No matter what the newspaper said.

Fuzzy got up then and warily approached Pinfold from the gloom at the back of the hovel. She regarded the stick of gum still in his hand and then began to lick the side that had sugar yet. She kept licking, licking, and then she was licking Pinfold's fingers, and he didn't pull his hand away. She stopped suddenly and returned to her blankets.

Pinfold smiled, he couldn't help it, and he went on smiling for some time, until at last he walked on his knees over to his dog and said, "You didn't have to do that. I wasn't going to throw you out." He stretched alongside her, and they both went to sleep.

Next morning everywhere you turned there was a Pinfold. Here a Pinfold, there a Pinfold, everywhere a Pinfold. And all the Pinfolds wore bright yellow derbies and clean white nightshirts and white buck shoes, and they roamed around the city with bundles of newspapers, *World* newspapers, under their arms, and they hollered, "Fuzzy talks! Fuzzy talks today!"

And what she said, in a half-page drawing on the front of the color wraparound, was, "Sure I talk! Dis is America, ain't it? Ain't dis America?"

"Jesus Christ, Albert," said *our* Pinfold when he saw it, "they stuck us in the funny papers!"

Three

WALTER

1

Aboard the ferry crossing the Hudson River, Manhattan to Hoboken, Georgie Wreckage stood on deck, his back to the railing, and eye-sketched some of the other passengers: that young laborer there, whose head was shaped like a coffeepot . . . the Italian kid with a broken nose, a broken jaw, and hostile lights in his black eyes . . . the bent crone in purple skirts, her hands concealed in a net reticule. *She* caught him staring and stared right back with a deep and malevolent suspicion. Georgie looked away.

Because in New York you couldn't legally drink on Sunday and in New Jersey you could, the boat was dangerously overcrowded. And slow. Everyone was carrying a beer pail, at least one, and you could smell cheeses and garlic and fresh bread. The day was a beauty, the temperature mild, almost seventy degrees. The clouds were pure white and piled luxuriantly.

Georgie turned and glanced down toward the Battery, and just for fun he pictured a green sea serpent with a long serrated neck rising to the surface and capsizing a steamship or a fireboat. Wouldn't *that* be something! Joette was beside him, watching him, and when the grin broke suddenly across his face, she reckoned she knew why. "Pinfold & Fuzzy" and all that hoopla. And the fifty-dollar raise in salary, of course—he was probably thinking about that. And the cable that he'd got last night from Joseph Pulitzer himself in Genoa. Genoa, *Italy!* THREE CHEERS FOR YOUR BOY AND DOG BOW WOW WOW.

Professor Thom met Georgie and Joette as they came down the gangway. He had a large picnic hamper, and he was smiling jovially, showing his teeth. He shook hands with Georgie, and when Joette extended a hand, he shook with her as well. He had spent the last several days in Hoboken visiting a boyhood chum, Doctor Will Geebus, an eye-ear-nose-and-throat man who'd invented, in his spare time, the celluloid price tag. The Professor had left New York on Thursday evening, but before going he'd stopped by Georgie's room in the boardinghouse to invite him over for Sunday afternoon—Joette was welcome too, naturally, if she cared to make the trip. The Professor had promised Georgie a "treat." "We're to join my friend Geebus at Elysian Field," he said now. "There's a streetcar or we can walk. What's your preference?"

Georgie was all for walking—he'd never been to Hoboken before—and Joette was agreeable to that. Whatever Georgie wanted. Had he suggested they hop to the park, she would've hopped. She was very proud of him today; excited for him and by him. Fifty extra dollars a week and a transatlantic cable? You bet she was proud of him. My Georgie! She felt slightly giddy. She hoped she looked as good as she felt. For Georgie. She wanted him to think she looked pippin. She had on a short blue jacket over a white blouse with a high neck, and a plaid ankle-length skirt. She wasn't sure about Georgie—he seemed awfully distracted today—but other men certainly were appreciating her.

"Well then," said Professor Thom, "if we're going to walk, let's be on our way. Don't want to be late for the baseball game."

Baseball game? Joette turned and gave Georgie a private, quizzical look, and he shrugged. Then he took her by an elbow and steered her through the crowd. They followed Professor Thom down the length of the pier to the street.

Hoboken, in those days gone by, was a brewery town, and you smelled the sharp, almost bitter odor of fermenting lagers everywhere, all the time—as you were falling asleep at night, and first thing in the morning; in the schoolroom, on the job, at church, where it was stronger than incense; you smelled it while you waited to board a train, during sexual intercourse, when you were having a

baby, or dying in your bed. Nobody seemed to mind. Sundays in
Hoboken, oompah bands played in the German beer gardens.

Professor Thom had grown up there, and he acted as Georgie and
Joette's sightseeing guide. He took them past clapboard tenements
and low cramped rowhouses where the working class lived, and then
he took them through neighborhoods of big frame houses with sta-
bles in back, and neighborhoods of brownstone and yellowstone and
whitestone houses belonging to physicians and attorneys and company managers, and to the politicians who were helping themselves
to much of Hoboken's railroad and waterfront money. He pointed
out bakeries and churches of merit, brewery after brewery, a cemetery, a national bank with French gargoyles, and, behind tall
wrought-iron fencing, an old monastery whose monks were rumored
to have no feet and no ears. The grounds were untended, as wild as
any jungle.

"I wonder if they use crutches," Georgie said. "Or if they crawl."
He walked up to the gate and pressed his face between the bars.

That's when Joette asked the Professor, "Did you happen to see
the paper today?"

"No? What's happened?"

"Georgie's picture—I mean, the picture that Georgie drew. 'Dog
Day in Awful Alley'? You didn't see it?"

"Doctor Geebus doesn't take the *World*. Won't have it in his
house—he's Republican." Thom smiled. Democrat, Republican,
Martian, Venusian; he had no patience with politics and parties, it
was all so much balloon juice. Was Cleveland still President? Was
Strong still Mayor of New York? Don't ask the Professor. He'd never
voted in his life, and never would—unless Thomas Edison became a
candidate for something. "So, George. You've done still another picture of that ragamuffin and his old dog, have you?"

Georgie nodded, having come away from the fence. "Another picture," he said. Then he rolled his eyes.

"It's not *just* another picture," Joette protested, "it's so *big*, and
it's filled with all *sorts* of funny things. Isn't it, George? And dozens
of people, it *seems* like dozens, and dogs and cats and goats. There's
a goat jumping through a hoop. And there's boys and girls doing
tumblesaults. And there's *pennants*. And—oh, it's wonderful. You
must see it when you get back."

"You could paper your *room* with it when you get back," said
Georgie, shaking his head. "She must have twenty copies. And she
bought 'em all."

"Why not? It's just so good!"

Georgie looked at Joette and grunted, then he looked away—he looked across the street at a shabbily dressed man sitting on the base of a copper statue memorializing dead firemen; he had several mangled trumpets on his lap. Georgie grunted a second time.

"It *is* good." Joette pursed her lips and tipped her head to one side, lifted her brows. Young Woman Exasperated.

"It's a picture," Georgie said. "It's a picture." He looked unhappy.

"It sounds like a circus," Professor Thom said.

Joette gestured to strike up the band. "It *is* a circus! That's exactly right. That's what it's all about, Georgie's picture. It's a celebration. Isn't it a celebration, George? Because the dog talks today. And it's all in color!"

"In color, is it? I've never seen a news picture done up in color."

"It's not a news picture. Said the news artist with blazing cheeks and self-disgust," said Georgie. And thought: *Former* news artist.

"Oh, George—you just don't like it because it's so *happy*."

"Because it's so full of baloney."

"So happy."

"And in the comic supplement."

"Over there," said the Professor, "is the laundry my mother used to work in when I was small."

They were approaching the northernmost part of town now, and suddenly a parade came noisily out of a side street. They stood a few minutes to watch. As parades went, this was a stinker: barely forty marchers, some ragtag flags, a few horns, a single drum. The flags bore very intricate symbols—snakes, birds, flowers, zebras—but no words, so it was impossible to determine what the parade was all about. At the end of it was an aged white-haired man of tremendous girth riding in an open carriage. Bunting and streamers adorned the carriage door. "The poor coot looks dazed," said the Professor, and Joette nodded that he did indeed, and Georgie wondered smugly if either one of them noticed the old man had a small Christmas candy cane tightly clutched in a fist—bet not!

Shortly, they arrived at the park. The trees were beginning to get leafy, squirrels were out. So where the cyclists—sportily dressed men and women pedaling on old-fashioned English ordinaries and on the popular newfangled safeties, on tandem tricycles, even quadricycles. Wheels hummed, bells rang, cyclometers clicked off the

miles. Small children sat in a circle near a duck pond, playing Hot
Handkerchief with a First Communion veil. Two teams of older boys
darted and tagged and screamed across a greening field—No-Man's
Land for a game of Prisoner's Base. Bocce players, checkers play-
ers, kitists. Girls in pretty dresses jumped rope: Solomon Grundy,
Born on Monday, Married on Tuesday, Took sick on Wednesday,
Got worse on Thursday, Died on Friday. . . .

The Professor brought them to a baseball diamond. Around it, a
large crowd milled. There were sausage-and-beer pavilions. A vendor with metal canisters of soda water and flavoring strapped on his
back struggled to keep his balance as he trudged up and down.
Cherry! Strawberry! Cola! A kid in a railway cap danced around a
balloon man, stabbing the merchandise with a straight pin. "Ah,
good," said Professor Thom, "we're just in time," and he pointed at
a middle-aged man who was trundling what seemed to be an extraordinarily large trash barrel on wheels out to the pitcher's station. He
was broadly built, with heavy shoulders and a very short neck; his
head was large and round and sandy-haired. He had almond-shaped
spectacles, was dressed in a navy-blue high-necked pullover—a
biker's sweater—and blue-and-white checked knickers, thick wool
socks, and golf shoes with spiked soles. A teenaged boy ran after him
carrying a bushel basket filled with baseballs. Everyone started to
laugh and clap. Players drifted out then and took the field. "That's
my friend," said the Professor. "That's Doctor Geebus."

"In that getup?" said Joette? "A medical doctor?"

"It's Sunday afternoon, dear."

Doctor Geebus raised the hinged lid on his trash barrel, and the
boy poured in all the balls.

Batter up!

"A pitching machine," said Georgie, laughing. "For heaven's
sake, why?"

"Why not?" said the Professor. "This is America, ain't it? Ain't
this America?" Then he laughed and blushed when Georgie and
Joette both turned and gaped at him, astonished. "Excuse the vul-
garism. I picked it up from the doctor's boy. Something I heard him
say." At breakfast that morning. There'd been Professor Thom,
Doctor Geebus, and Geebus's son, Walter, at the table. The doctor
and the Professor had had stewed prunes, lemon, and oatmeal, and
the boy—just a bowl of a new flaked cereal. Why on earth do you
insist on consuming that wretched stuff, Walter? It can't be good for

you. It can't be wholesome. So why must you eat it? Why not, Father? This is America, ain't it? Ain't this America?—filling his mouth with another spoonful and chewing hyperbolically. "That's Walter there," said the Professor. "With the bushel basket."

The pitching machine was semi-automatic—Doctor Geebus stood by with a mallet and, to send a ball hurtling, gave the contraption a solid knock on its side, directly on a small rubber bulb. Time was called after three consecutive balls popped into flames on their way to the dish. The doctor made some minor adjustments—his son ran a toolbox out to him—and then play resumed. Strikeout, strikeout, then a hit, a two-baser. Then another strikeout. When the side retired, Doctor Geebus stayed where he was. This was an exhibition game, and both teams—the Bayonne Go Braghs, who'd led off, and the Hoboken Brezels—were to have a crack at the wonderful device. Unfortunately, though, even before all the Brezels had come across the infield, the pitching machine malfunctioned. There was a loud grinding sound, then *whump!* Baseballs started firing all by themselves, one right after the other—high, low, and fumbling through the dirt. Then the lid blew: thirty feet into the air, forty. Players ran for their lives and so did Doctor Geebus, his arms crossed on top of his head, shouting, "Next Sunday, same time!"

The Professor, who still hadn't stopped chuckling at the debacle, led the way up several gently climbing hills, and at the top he tossed down the hamper and threw off his coat. "This is a good spot, I think." Joette turned around and around, saying yes, it really was nice there; you could see most of the park, all of the treetops; you could see the baseball diamond, you could see the field where the kitists ran, you could see all the way back to town, the rooftops and the church spires and the hulking breweries; and look! you could even see that little parade they'd passed. It was a swell spot for a picnic, she thought. Georgie sat down and unlaced his boots and pulled them off and flexed his toes.

After he'd spread a blanket on the ground, Professor Thom unpacked his hamper: two loaves of bread, a roasted chicken, lemonade in a vacuum flask, and half a pound cake; also napery, glasses, and—should we have some music?—a windup bear cub that tooted a horn.

"Is your doctor friend going to come join us?" Joette asked.

"I told him where we'd be. But I suspect he's not in a picnic mood at the moment." The Professor grinned sympathetically; then, glancing at Georgie, stretched out with his fists jammed behind his neck and his elbows sticking up, he said, "You're very quiet all of a sudden. Why so?"

Georgie pushed out his bottom lip. "No special reason." But he was thinking. Wondering, really. About something odd that had happened—or maybe not?—down at the baseball field, after the machine expired with a Glorious Fourth finale of red and blue sparks. A hundred or more spectators, Georgie among them, had surged across the infield laughing and chattering and cracking wise. Hope he's a better doc than he is a mechanic! I wasn't scared, did I *look* scared? Say, Geebus, can you fix my watch? Georgie was halfway to the pitcher's box when he realized that Joette and the Professor weren't with him. He looked around and, instead of his two companions, saw a player for the Bayonne club sprawled on the grass, bleeding from the nose and mouth. Apparently, he'd been struck in the face by a wild ball. Both his arms were outstretched, one knee was raised. The crowd rushing past to have a close look at the broken-down pitching machine ignored him utterly, but Georgie saw him. And then Georgie saw a girl of five or six with filthy yellow hair stoop and pick up several of the man's teeth and toss them down the front of her dress. He was just about to go chase the girl away and help the poor fella to his feet when Joette suddenly called his name. He turned at the sound of her voice, he raised an arm so she could find him in the swarm, and when he turned back the baseball player was gone. So was the little girl. At most, ten seconds had passed. Oh, come on. The man had been *stunned*, flat on his back, and now he was *gone?* A tickling started, like carbonated water, at the base of Georgie's spine, then spread quickly. He *had* seen the man. Of course he had. And he could see him still, and the child: the picture in his mind was absolutely clear. Give him a pencil and he could sketch it; take him five minutes. There'd been a red gumdrop wedged between two cleats on the player's left shoe, a pebbly rash on the girl's throat, snot glazed on her cheek. How could he have imagined such picayune stuff? He'd *seen* them. The girl—all right, she could've raced off, but the baseball player? Georgie was mystified, and he buttonholed a teenaged boy in overalls, then a fat lady pulling a Skye terrier on a leash, and finally a big whiskery umpire

in frock coat and parson's hat. No, mister. No, sir. No! They hadn't
seen anybody carted away. Somebody got hurt? News to them.

Joette had jostled her way to Georgie at last, and she'd taken him
by the arm and they'd plunged together through the crowd. They'd
watched a maddened Doctor Geebus, his hand swaddled in towel-
ing, pull out a smoking ratchet wheel from his machine, and they'd
smiled at the doctor's son, who stood behind his father, flapping his
arms and making funny faces, and then they'd left the field and
waited by a water fountain for Professor Thom. He'd wanted to
speak a few words to his distraught friend—wanted to tell him, Oh,
don't worry, half the fun is finding out what the deuce went wrong.

As they ate their picnic lunch, the Professor talked excitedly
about his trip yesterday to the Hoboken city dump—so many cotter
pins! so much mattress wire!—and Joette smiled at Georgie and
talked about the newest spectacle at LeFebre & Chill's, the Civil
War reenacted by chimps, and Georgie didn't talk at all. Didn't eat
much, either. A few bites of chicken. (I *did* see them: the girl was
barefoot, the man's cheek was dark purple.) And when Joette tried
to pass him a slice of cake, he shook his head, then sat up so he could
reach a hand into his coat pocket and get out a pencil and one of the
small squares of cardboard that he carried with him all the time.
Used his thigh as a drawing table, squinted toward an old hemlock
tree, then began to sketch lightly, rapidly. The ballplayer, the girl,
the devastated pitching machine. Both Joette and the Professor
looked over at the tree and nodded. Sure. Interesting. Artists always
liked trees, stuff like that. The Professor poured lemonade. "And
these monkeys at the theatre, they do Antietam?" Joette laughed—
no, no, they didn't get that *specific*—and then she leaned over to
peek at Georgie's drawing. But he covered it with his right hand.
Finally, he folded it in half and stuck it away. Then, frowning, he
scratched at the ground with the shoulder end of his pencil.

He'd made the sketch because—well, just because he'd felt like
making it (I did *so* see them). For himself (they were there!). Out of
habit (they *were!*). But not because he'd had it in mind to render the
scene later, render it properly and then submit it to the *World*.
There'd be no point to that. At the paper, they didn't expect, they
didn't *want* any more news sketches, any more on-the-spot drawings
from him. They'd made that clear this week. Let Dieffer and Stol-

ley, let Cooper and Ahearn and Sullivan and all those other dime-a-dozen hands worry about the barge fires and the homicides, the atrocious assaults. From now on, Georgie Wreckage was to concentrate only on his boy and dog. His "Pinfold & Fuzzy." His Sunday panel, his *funny*, for crying out loud!

Tell you what *Georgie* thought was funny, and it wasn't any big, busy colored picture; it wasn't "Dog Day in Awful Alley!" It was all the newsboys masquerading as Pinfold, and all the posters—"She Talks, New York!"—slapped on walls and telegraph poles, and it was the Free Scrambled Egg Breakfasts that the *World* had sponsored in twenty different neighborhoods, and it was Bram Hoopes too— Bram Hoopes tramping into Georgie's room earlier today, downhearted as a groom left waiting at the altar. They knocked me to the second page, George. They knocked back the Hag. How could they *do* that? Now, I'm not holding it against you—you had nothing to do with it, George, I know that. But still, the Hag is *funny*. What's so funny about that ugly kid of yours and his ugly dog? This is America, ain't it—is *that* supposed to be funny, George? If it is, I miss the humor completely, it's over my head. And it sounds a little sarcastic, if you don't mind me saying so. This is America, ain't it. Ain't this America. Sounds sarcastic to me.

Bram's complaints weren't funny? Sure, they were. Very funny— as funny, almost, as Joette's giddy behavior. Good lord, if she swelled with any more pride, *ka-boom*, she'd burst. You'd think Georgie had climbed a mountain, discovered a river, slaughtered a nation of Indians single-handed! Twenty copies of the goddamn newspaper—she'd gone out and bought twenty copies. What was she thinking? What was she planning to *do* with all of them? Well, Georgie, we'll *keep* them, of course. Some for the friends we make later in life? Some for our children? And the rest to look at when we're old and gray? She'd been *serious*. That wasn't funny? *Our* children?

So, with all that real-life funny business, all that comedy, how come Georgie wasn't laughing? How come he wasn't even smiling? Why the long face as he scratched in the dirt with a pencil? Why the funk? He'd woke up in it today, he'd gone to sleep in it last night. Part of the reason, he kept telling himself, was nerves. Something he'd been comfortable doing, that he'd been familiar with and good at, had been taken suddenly away from him. He'd been a good news artist, a good sketchman, and now he wasn't that anymore—he was

a cartoonist. Just like that: You're a cartoonist. And he had no idea if
he could do it, draw cartoons week after week. Whenever he'd tried
drawing funny pictures before, he'd failed miserably. It was partly
nerves, then, his mood today. And partly what else? Guilt? Guilt for
playing crooked and then winning the grand prize? Maybe guilt.
Maybe so.

Georgie wished—and this had to be the funniest business of all, he
told himself—he sincerely wished that he'd never turned in that first
sketch of the boy and the wounded dog. He wished now that he'd
torn it up with the other sketches he'd done of the banquet. And he
wished he'd never invented that cockamamie story about the restaurant, about Fuzzy getting shot over a plate of eggs. Even though
reporters, the drunks especially, were always making stories up, and
even though it was standard practice to pump out fiction and call it
tidings on slow news days and days of inclement weather, still
Georgie had been ill at ease—he'd felt like a perjurer—dictating
that story to Paragraph Jones, the rewrite man. He'd never fudged
before, he'd never fabricated, and probably he wouldn't have done
it then, but for the fuss that Joette had made over the picture. She'd
loved it, it had touched her, and Georgie had wanted to get it into
the paper to please her. He should've realized—Joette's rhapsody
should've *made* him realize—that a boy and his dog was as potent an
image in those maudlin times as a mother and child or a child on
crutches, but he hadn't; he'd never dreamed the picture would get
any kind of reaction from subscribers—nothing he'd drawn before
ever had—and when it did, when the letters of sympathy began to
pour in, and especially when Sid McKeon passed along the Editor's
demand for a follow-up picture, Georgie turned pale. Stayed pale.
Panicked. And finally confessed to Sid, fully expecting the art chief
to rag him down, then haul him by a coat sleeve to the city desk,
where for certain he'd be shouted at and maybe even sacked. But
Sid had only shrugged. So you made up the story—the *whole* story?
Well, the kid's real, the dog's real. The dog was actually shot. In the
neck. George, that's good enough for *me*. This paper's reported entire wars with less substance. So you go ahead, do a second picture.
But I *can't*. Why the hell not? Because it's all phony, Sid. I'd
feel . . . I'd feel funny. Georgie, Georgie, pray give over. *You* draw
the pictures, let *me* worry about any travesties of journalism. Draw
whatever you like, just don't let the dog croak or make the boy too

much of a thug—they're selling papers. And not incidentally, so are
you.

By this time, by the time of the second picture, "The Doctor Pre-
scribes Codeine for the Dog That Used to Talk," Georgie knew—
because Clarky had told him—that Pinfold and Fuzzy were living in
Awful Alley, so he put it into the story, a truth to ease his conscience.
And he'd hoped that picture would be the end of it, but no, there was
to be a third picture, a fourth, a fifth. And then, incredibly—at any
rate, it was incredible to Georgie—word came down from the fifteenth floor: Enough suspense. Let the dog speak again, for heaven's
sake. Georgie had followed orders—drawing, he'd imagined his conscience angel packing a bag and leaving the premises in a puff of
smoke—and when he'd handed in that sixth picture, Handsome Sid
brought out several tablets of watercolors and said, Indicate where
you want the reds, the blues, the yellows. Will you do that, George?
Because come Sunday, Pinfold and Fuzzy are going to be part of the
Comic Weekly. But I've been drawing them as *news,* Georgie protested, to which Sid replied, Ah, George, but you can't copyright the
news. A cartoon, you can. Thus Georgie became a cartoonist, and
Pinfold and Fuzzy became "Pinfold & Fuzzy"—a copyrighted feature of the New York *World.*

Several times during the last week, Georgie had been tempted to
go look for Pinfold, to drop by the alley—he'd have to traipse there,
since the boy no longer could be found at City Hall Park—and see
how the dog was, but he'd always managed to talk himself out of it.
What would he say, really? How do you like the pictures? How do
you like seeing yourself? Don't you remember me, I'm Jim?

Day before yesterday, Georgie had run into Clarky on Ann
Street, and he'd asked him what he'd heard about Pinfold and the
dog. Tell you, George. I've heard a lot of things. But I don't know
what to believe. Frankly. I've heard he's been abducted by the
Children's Aid Society—and adopted by Hetty Green. I've heard
he drowned—and saved somebody from drowning. I've heard that
he tried to murder a cripple over in Guld Alley. That him and the
dog are delivering milk for a dairy in Jersey. That the dog's addicted
to codeine. Is gonna have pups. That she has a pirate map tattooed
on her leg. Georgie had taken notes. Delivers milk? Milk and *eggs!*
There might be a picture in that. Pirates? In Awful Alley? Could be
a picture in that, too.

And the thought suddenly occurred to Georgie now, as he half listened to the Professor talk and talk about a new-style toaster he'd recently designed, that there might also be a picture—a "Pinfold & Fuzzy" picture—in what he'd seen (the barefoot girl—she'd worn a scapular, a *scapular!*) here in the park this afternoon. "The Calamitous Pitching Machine of Awful Alley!" Substitute a slum dweller for the ballplayer, Pinfold for the little girl. Sure, Georgie could picture the kid going around collecting teeth. Yeah, he could picture that, easily. Well, what do you know. Already I'm thinking like a Sunday man, Georgie thought. A Sunday man.

He sat up and began to sprinkle tobacco into a cigarette paper, and Joette looked over at him—her lips greasy from the chicken, her lap full of cake crumbs—and then she clapped her hands and said, "At last! At last! A smile!"

Presently, Doctor Geebus's son appeared, topping the hill with his bushel basket loaded with scorched baseballs. He was tall and well-built, sandy-haired; his blue eyes bulged slightly, were pouched. His complexion was flawless, like a child's. He smiled at the Professor, at Georgie, at Joette; when she smiled back, he looked away quickly, and his ears turned red.

"So he's not coming?" said Professor Thom.

Walter Geebus laughed. "No, no, not coming. He and Bull McCarthy took that infernal thing back to the house in Bull's wagon." Walter laughed again, then clucked. "But first they had to wait till it cooled." He set down the basket, then stared at the cake on the blanket, waiting for the Professor to offer him a piece. When he got it, he stuffed it entire into his mouth; then, talking with his mouth full, he said, "Papa . . . Papa'd like to meet your friends . . . if they care to come back with you later . . . they're welcome . . . for lemonade."

"Fine!" said the Professor. "And speaking of my friends, Walter. This is Miss Davey. And George Wreckage."

Walter struggled to swallow, nearly choked; when at last he could speak again, he exclaimed; "Pinfold!"

And Georgie blushed.

2

Young Walter Geebus, who would be seventeen in October, lived with his papa, the medical doctor, in a handsome four-storied house

of red brick with a high stoop and an arched door on the corner of
Morning Street and Afternoon Place.

Walter's mother was dead. So was his twin, a sister. Both had
perished four summers ago on an excursion boat which had caught
fire in the Harlem River and sunk. That morning, Walter had waked
with a sore throat and a slight ear infection, and Doctor Geebus had
said, You stay at home with me, my little man—I'll read you *The
Mysterious Island.* So he hadn't drowned. The tragedy made Walter
bitterly unhappy for about a month, but then he seemed to forget
that he'd ever had a mother and a sister Judith. He never talked
about them again, and it wasn't in his nature to consider, either at
the time or later on, just how close to dying he himself had come.
Reckon with a twist of fate? Not Walter Geebus. Mrs. Meerebott,
the housekeeper, called him a nice boy, by which she meant he was
uncomplicated, always smiling, making jokes; bright. A nice boy was
Walter Geebus, she said.

Mary Meerebott—Nana Mary to Walter—gave you the impression of being hollow, brittle. She was slight, auburn-haired, a woman
in her late forties with pinched, plain features and a waxy complexion. She was a secret smoker of cigarettes, a person of profound
melancholy. Her husband was locked away in an insane asylum and
had been for nearly sixteen years—once a brakeman for the Morris
& Essex, he'd lost his mind following the accident in which he'd lost
a foot. She had a daughter who'd married a traveling coal furnace
salesman at the age of fourteen; that is, she *thought* she still had a
daughter, she didn't know it for a fact. The ungrateful thing had
never written. Just about the only thing in Mrs. Meerebott's life that
gave her any pleasure was Walter. Walter, nicotine, and masturba-
tion, those were the only things. And baking. And sometimes a well-
crafted sermon. But Walter gave her the *most* pleasure, by far. She
liked a nice boy, a good-looking, round-faced nice boy. She liked
Walter.

Frankly, she didn't care for his father, although she slept in his
bed half a dozen nights a year—on the doctor's birthday, on New
Year's Eve, and once at the beginning of each new season. On most
matters, from the butcher's bills to the Free Silver Question to Walter's artistic temperament, they were natural antagonists. It's only a
phase, Doctor. He's really a nice boy. Mary, for heaven's sake, Walter is *not* a nice boy. He's a young man, and he's driving me to
distraction. So he enjoys drawing, is that a crime? You *tinker.* Mary!

Normal young men do not paint Gibson girls on the backs of their
hands. Normal young men would not bother even to *look* at Gibson
Girls. Oh, Doctor Geebus, *really!* That's quite enough, *Mrs. Meerebott.* Quite enough of that tone, thank you. My son is driving me to
distraction. And you're making things worse—cooing over him all
the time!

This morning, Doctor Geebus had informed Mrs. Meerebott that
she needn't prepare an afternoon meal, only a picnic lunch, since he
would be at the park for most of the day—with that idiotic machine
of his and that bughouse inventor-friend, and with poor Walter
dragged along to help. But all right—the doctor didn't want dinner?
Fine. The day was hers then, to do with as she pleased; she planned
to spend it seated at the kitchen table smoking cigarettes and reading the newspaper, Walter's newspaper.

Every Sunday, Mrs. Meerebott attended early mass, and on her
way back to the house she bought Walter his New York *World.* Walter
usually went to the ten o'clock with his father. Once home, he'd race
downstairs and Mrs. Meerebott would have the paper waiting for
him, safely hidden away in the pantry. Had Doctor Geebus ever
discovered their little secret, he would've promptly confiscated the
newspaper like a customs official and torn it to pieces. Walter had
enlisted Mrs. Meerebott in his smuggling scheme a year ago, to
avoid suffering through any more of his father's excruciating lec-
tures; he'd listened to enough of those, boy, the doctor waggling a
finger as he pompously dismissed—dismissed? condemned!—the
World and its publisher, that foreign Jew, for espousing Democratic
platforms and radical reforms—the very idea of taxing luxuries! in-
heritances! large incomes! monopolies and corporations!—and then
ridiculed the paper for glamorizing actresses and for reporting, as
news, adventures which Doctor Geebus considered patently fantas-
tical. If the morons of New York chose to believe in immortal pyg-
mies and garlic snails the size of buffalo, let them. But he would not
have his son exposed to such rot. We live in the real world in this
house, Walter.

Some time ago, and just before he'd been driven to his weekly
deceptions, Walter had tried to strike a deal with his father. He
would purchase the Sunday paper with his own nickel and then immediately throw it away, all of it except the Comic Weekly. But
Doctor Geebus would agree to no such thing. The so-called funnies
were as indelicate, as preposterous as the rest of the sheet. The doc-

tor was not opposed to humor—lord, no! he'd always enjoyed a good
joke—but what, please tell him, what was so funny about injury,
and people constantly were being injured in those awful cartoons.
And what people! The dregs of society—bums and immigrants,
shirkers and mischief-makers. And the pictures themselves! Crude,
though even to call them that was to be overkind. Crude and un-
sightly, and atrociously colored. If Walter needed to look at pictures,
he ought to go to a picture gallery.

Fiddlesticks! Walter had turned to Mrs. Meerebott, recruiting her
to be his Sunday morning smuggler.

It was half past three, and Mrs. Meerebott was still reading the
World—she'd just finished one story, about the Mikado's uncle sailing from Hiroshima to China, and was beginning another, about
John Wilkes Booth being alive in Brazil—when Walter suddenly
burst into the kitchen. "Nana! You'll never believe who I walked
home with—who's sitting with Papa in the garden right this second!"

"Buffalo Bill?" Walter had recently read a collection of Ned Bunt-
line's lurid tales about that famous death-dealing Indian scout and
then had synopsized them all, breathlessly, for Mrs. Meerebott.
"John Philip Sousa?"

"Mr. George Wreckage—who drew that swell cartoon we both
loved this morning!" Walter reached around in front of Mrs. Meerebott and spread out all the sections of the newspaper, then snatched
up the colored supplement. "This!" The picture with eleven,
twelve, thirteen, *fourteen* toothless shaggy children, some backflip-
ping, others dangling by their ankles from the fire escapes, and *allez
oop!* a screaming red-faced baby in a christening gown seesawed
through the air. A black cat on a wooden fence, its tail strung with
bean cans and a cow bell, a nanny goat ready to blast a poor copper
in the seat with her hind legs. There were drawers and bloomers and
a mended handkerchief flapping on a washline, and triangular pennants on crisscrossing wires, and a geranium pot in mid-fall from a
window ledge. There was a booth—of plankboards and rain barrels—with a crowd of slum toughs and mustachioed papas huddled
around it and a sign that read Place Yer Bets! Do She or Dont She?
And in the middle of all this commotion, and high on a slantwise
platform, there was a funny-looking dog and a funnier-looking boy.
The boy—wearing a bright yellow derby clumsily lettered I'm Wit

Her and a nightshirt lettered And She's Wit Me—stood grinning
with his arms stretched up like a triumphant ring boxer, and the dog,
her nose in a plate of scrambled eggs, glared down at a Negro in a
bone-white suit and said—her remarks crowded inside a balloon
above her head—Sure I talk! I got a right to! Dis is America, ain't it?
Ain't dis America?

"*This* cartoon," said Walter. "And do you see the name down
there in the left corner—on the shoeshine kit against the wall?
Georgie Wreckage. And he's here! I walked him here! I met him!
The fella that did this!" Walter held up the picture, smiling at it.
Grand, wasn't it? Just grand! Pinfold & Fuzzy. He liked them—
already!—much better than he'd ever liked the Yellow Hag. Since he
took the *World* newspaper Sundays only, today's color cartoon was
Walter's introduction to Pinfold and Fuzzy, to Awful Alley, to Georgie's work. He had no idea why the boy was wearing a nightshirt, or
that the red scarf tied around the dog's neck was there to conceal a
bullet hole, and the straw effigy labeled Slippery John meant nothing to him. But being ignorant of the earlier pictures, the "news"
pictures, the background to this picture mattered not in the least.
Not in the least. *This* picture was funny—that's all that counted. It
delighted him, everything about it: the energy, the extravagance
and confusion, but especially Pinfold and Fuzzy, the dog that
talked. He wished like anything, he would've given anything, to be
able to draw like that.

"It turns out he's a friend of Professor Thom. A friend! I'm going
to show him some of my own pictures before he goes!"

"Have you asked him if it's all right?"

"Nana! I'm sure he'd be happy to take a look. We're both artists!
And he's about my age."

"Your age?"

Walter shrugged. "I guess he's about twenty. It's not that big a
difference. Twenty-one. And you should see his lady friend—she's a
queen! A regular queen!"

Mrs. Meerebott reflected, then frowned. "Walter. Tell your father
I'll make lemonade and bring it out."

"Oh! That's what I was supposed to tell *you!* Make lemonade,
Nana, and bring it out. There's five of us." He touched her on the
wrist, smiled, winked, took another glance at the funny sheet, and
raced away.

Mrs. Meerebott shook her head, taking a package of pre-rolled cigarettes from the table's cutlery drawer. She puffed and thought fondly, He's such a nice boy. She just loved him. And then she thought about how he blushed like a flame whenever she walked into his bedroom—to wake him up or with his folded laundry—and saw him naked. Handsome boy. Handsome build. Lately, she'd noticed flaky matter in his chamber pot some mornings; dried semen. He was such a nice, nice boy, and he was growing up so fast. A queen, was she, the lady friend? A regular *queen?* He was growing up so fast. Like the doctor said. *Puff, puff, puff.* Finally, Mrs. Meerebott went to cut and squeeze lemons.

Georgie wanted to be off, he wanted to get back to New York; if he and Joette caught a ferry in the next half hour, forty-five minutes— it was almost five o'clock now—they might avoid the beery crowds, they might even get a seat. Another reason he wanted to leave, he was bored stiff. With glazed eyes and a fixed smile he'd been listening for well over an hour to Doctor Geebus and Professor Thom, Tweedledum and Tweedledee, yammer about the Age of Invention—it *is*, y'know!—about patents, about cap screws, collar screws, skein screws, and lag screws. The doctor had talked about his dentist friend who'd invented the burglar alarm, and the Professor about a stenographer he'd heard of who'd invented an electric can opener, and about the Episcopalian priest who'd invented photograph film. Just now, the doctor had explained that his pitching machine—the Geebus Hurler, presently under the chestnut tree at the rear of the garden and covered with a blanket of quilted bombproof—had been commissioned by the owner of a summer amusement park at Lake Hopatcong, as a novelty, something more of a challenge than anvil-pounding and more manly than tennis or croquet. He'd spent, he said, every evening of the last three months at work on the confounded device, and he was doubly determined after today's embarrassing fiasco to see it operate perfectly—to deliver it by June. The Professor said, "Don't worry, William, you'll make it," then launched into a story about mechanical legs. It seemed that a soda-

water vendor had been cut in half by a surface car, and for less than
the cost of an invalid chair, Professor Thom had fitted him with two
shiny tin legs—ball-and-socket kneecaps and feet like isosceles triangles. Storage compartments in the calves and shins, and spigots on
the thighs, facing out. "Beautiful! Beautiful!" said Doctor Geebus.
Georgie smiled. Joette smiled. But Walter suddenly exploded into
wild laughter, spraying himself and his father with lemonade.

"Walter! For the love of Mike!" The doctor pulled out a handkerchief and dabbed himself, the back of a hand, a sweater sleeve. "For
the love of *Mike!*"

"I'm sorry," Walter said, chewing his grin away. "I'm really
sorry. But I saw those spigots in my head—and, well, I'm very
sorry. Honest. It sounded funny."

"Everything sounds funny to you. That's one of your problems. I
don't like to harp, Walter, but *Walter.*"

Walking along River Street fifteen minutes later, Georgie said to
Professor Thom, twitting him, "I notice you didn't tell the end of
that story."

"Didn't get the opportunity, did I?" The Professor smiled crook-
edly over at young Walter, who'd insisted on coming along to the
ferry slip; under an arm, he was carrying a bulky tan envelope with
his name carefully printed across the face of it. "And besides,
George. That's not part of *my* story. That's *your* story. I made the
legs. What happened to them later had nothing to do with me."

"What happened?" Walter asked. Eagerly.

Georgie looked at Joette, then he widened one eye, shut the
other, and finally shook his head. "Never mind."

"Please! I'd love to hear it, Mr. Wreckage. Is it funny?"

"No," said Joette. "It's not." She'd already heard the story—or
rather, she'd seen the picture. Unusual Vendor Attacked.

Professor Thom said, "Well, you might as well tell him, George.
It's not fair to Walter. Since you brought it up, tell him."

Georgie smiled. "You put it that way, all right." Then turning to
Walter, he said, "This soda vendor that went to the Professor here,
his name was Richard Silky."

"I thought it was Robert," said the Professor.

"Richard. Names I can always remember. Almost always. Richard Silky, from Mulberry Street. And"—giving Walter his full at-

tention once more—"after he got fixed up with those new legs, he
was some spectacle, I mean to say! He could walk pretty good with
them too, up and down—slow, of course, but pretty good. And
whenever he came clanking into a neighborhood, people gathered
around, kids gave him pennies for drinks left and right. Just to see
him turn on the faucets. Everybody laughed, had a time. I saw him
myself, once or twice. And then one day, a gang of Bowery boys
came along, and—well, they just couldn't resist. Could they? Found
brickbats and sticks and for sport began to whack away—*bang!
bang!*—at Silky's legs. Crumpled them right up; the fruit juice and
the flavorings and a gallon of seltzer water gushed out all over the
pavement. I got there maybe five minutes after it happened. Just
lucked onto it. I'd been up the street at a gas explosion." Georgie
nodded, remembering. Then he said, "I got one of the spigots home.
Saved it." He winked at Walter. "So that's what happened to Professor Thom's miraculous legs."

Walter, whose eyes had opened wide in astonishment, who
seemed truly shocked by the story, frowned now and asked, "Did he
get a second pair, this Silky fella? I hope."

The Professor shook his head, smiling sadly. "I never saw the
poor man again. Whatever happened to him, George? Do you
know?"

"Oh, gee," said Georgie, "I don't." He shrugged. "I really
don't." A squirrel ran across the sidewalk, and Georgie watched it
scoot up a tree. "Come to think of it, I believe I have *both* of those
spigots."

Joette sighed noisily.

Just before Georgie and Joette took the ferryboat to New York—
Professor Thom would be staying on in Hoboken for at least one
more day, to comb the dumps of Jersey City and Weehawken and to
help Doctor Geebus make some repairs on the Hurler—Walter said,
"Mr. Wreckage? Mr. Wreckage, I wonder if you'd do me a very
great favor." He thrust his envelope into Georgie's hands. The Professor was up the pier tearing apart, for the wire, a broken umbrella
that he'd spotted sticking out of a carton of trash, and Joette had
wandered into the railroad terminal to watch a German and his big
wife at a table fashioning paper dolls—the woman did the scissors
work, her husband the brisk folding and the pasting. Georgie looked

at Walter's package, then, partly amused and partly dubious, he looked at Walter. "What's this?"

"Pictures."

"Yours? You draw?"

"A little," Walter replied, grinning. "Would you look at them? I'd be ever so grateful. Papa thinks I'm wasting my time. But I don't!"

Georgie pressed his lips together, he cocked his head; he struggled against an urge to roll his eyes. "Walter. You should've asked me this before."

"With my father there? He'd've called me impudent or rude or one of those finky words."

"But I don't have the time now. I really don't." Georgie tried handing back the envelope. Walter jammed his hands down into his coat pockets.

"Take them with you," he said. "I'll see you again."

Georgie smiled. Oh, you *will*, will you? "I'd prefer not to do that, Walter. Please don't be offended. But perhaps the next time I'm in Hoboken . . ."

"Mr. Wreckage, I know you're probably afraid to even look at my pictures—you're afraid they're terrible, they stink, and you won't know what to say. You don't want to hurt my feelings. Am I right?"

Right, but Georgie said, "Not at all. I'm sure you have talent, Walter."

"Well, I do!"

Georgie laughed. "Have you ever had any instruction?"

"Oh, no, I just do them. My pictures, Last year, I went to Luna Park—just to give you a for-instance—I went to Luna Park on my school trip and I came home with a picture I'd done of two bathers that's just the most wonderful thing. Even Papa says so, and he hardly ever says anything nice about anything of mine. Wait'll you see it—two fatties in their bathing costumes. It's very funny. It's in there," pointing at the envelope, using his left hand.

"Are you a lefty, Walter?"

Walter slowly grinned, he nodded slightly, then said, "I noticed that you are. Too."

"Oh? And when did you notice that?"

"At the park. You'd just lighted a cigarette and it was still in your right hand."

"Very good! Sherlock Holmes!" Walter blushed. "All right, Mr. Geebus, I'll take your pictures home with me. I'll have a look and mail them back. How's that?"

"Wonderful. Or I could come pick them up." Joette was walking toward them with two dolls that she'd purchased, a Dutch boy and a pickaninny girl. "I appreciate this, Mr. Wreckage. I can't tell you how much. You're the first real cartoonist I've ever met!"

Georgie frowned and said, "Is that so."

As the ferry left, Joette waved and waved at Walter and Professor Thom, waved as lustily as if she were sailing to Europe; Georgie stood next to her with his hands clamped on the railing. "He's a nice young man, the doctor's son, don't you think?" she said, once they'd gone belowdecks and sat down on a bench.

Georgie said, "Sure. I suppose." Not much of a crowd this crossing; surprisingly few passengers, a couple dozen, everybody sitting quietly except for one tall thin man with several blue-black fingernails—perhaps someone had shut a door on them—who leaned against a bin full of life preservers and drunkenly sang an Irish anthem. Georgie counted the knots in the fellow's shoelaces: three and four—three in the left, four in the right.

"What's in the envelope that he gave you?"

"A bloody shirt and a kitchen knife. He asked me to throw them into the river when we're halfway across. Didn't say why."

Joette made a face and took the envelope from Georgie. She unwound its string. Then she tipped it and a sheaf of pictures—soft pencil on good textured paper—slid into her lap. Georgie had been expecting—oh, a lot of schoolboy stuff. Ugly teachers, boys in dunce caps, girls in tears, their pigtails dripping ink. What do you see if you're the son of a physician and you live in Hoboken, New Jersey, in the good section? What do you know? Ice skaters. Ice skaters, blacksmiths, boys in dunce caps—and two fat bathers, of course. Certainly he'd never expected a picture of a big-bellied, cow-eyed, self-important city copper kicking butts and swinging his daystick, scattering pedestrians from the path of a dangerously careening streetcar. He never would've expected it from Walter Geebus—who was so, so *well-groomed,* so middle-class—but there it was, the top picture. Streetcar bulging with terrified hoi-polloi, ragamuffin kids pointing and laughing with idiot glee from their perch on a bronze war hero, mangy dogs racing about.

Georgie grinned. Joette raised her eyebrows, then she pulled out another picture, from the bottom of the pile—a pantomime series, eight panels, the characters a husband and a wife who had exceedingly large heads. Georgie instantly recognized the models, and so did Joette: Doctor Geebus and that wraithlike woman who'd appeared briefly in the garden to bring out lemonade and a tray of cookies. The situation revolved around a lost pair of eyeglasses. The husband was blind without them, and the wife was in a dither trying to locate them. While she ransacked the parlor and the bedroom, he walked into walls, fell over a chair, and finally toppled out a window. Ended up in traction. The spectacles had been on top of his head all along.

Georgie shrugged. Joette laughed out loud.

"What do you think, George?"

"He can draw."

"He can?" But she meant, he *can,* she agreed.

"Too much cross-hatching, though."

"Well, I wouldn't know about that. But he's good?" She slid the pictures back into the envelope. "What does he want you to do for him?"

"I don't really know. *Tell* him he's good, I expect." For a moment, Georgie thought about Philly Finck, from the Laudermilch Company; poor Philly Finck. He was living in Stapleton these days, working for his brother-in-law at a small lumber and millwork company, Clarky said.

"So you're going to tell him that he's good?"

"I'll tell him he has talent." Georgie smiled. "But he already told *me* that."

"I didn't like his father, did you?"

"No, but then, he probably didn't like me, either. Or you. Neither one of us knowing a filament from a philodendron. And if Thom had properly introduced us, he would've liked us even less." Because Doctor Geebus disapproved of newspapermen and of women who worked in the theatre, Professor Thom—after apologizing in advance to his friends and cautioning Walter to keep quiet—had introduced them as Mr. Wreckage, an artist, and Miss Davey, his fiancée. "An artist!" said Georgie, and snorted.

"Well, you are, George. You're an artist."

"Maybe," he replied, then started playing with the string on Walter's envelope. After a while, he looked back up and smiled at Joette. "Maybe I am an artist. But are you a fiancée?"

Her cheeks reddened. "Not that I'm aware of," she said. "*Am* I?"

Georgie shrugged. "Not that I'm aware of, either." Then he
nudged her playfully with his elbow. But she wouldn't look at him
then, she wouldn't speak to him.

"Hoboken's pretty nice, eh? You think you'd like to live there—
say, after you got married?"

The ferry was docking, and the other passengers were all on their
feet and moving toward the gangway, and Joette turned swiftly to
Georgie and told him to drop dead, drop dead, drop dead.

"I was only trying to be funny," he called after her. "That's what
I do now. I'm a cartoonist!"

A small man wearing a stovepipe hat and a dark suit and carrying
a heavy satchel approached Georgie on the street. "Are you Mr.
Wreckage? Mr. Wreckage, Jilly Clark told me that if I waited here,
eventually you'd come off one of the ferries. My name is Mr. Fein."
He put out a hand. Georgie hesitated a moment before shaking it.
Mr. Fein had big-lidded watery eyes and a boot-shaped crimson
birthmark at his left temple; he had a prodigious mustache and was
redolent of bay rum. His suit wasn't cheap—it wasn't expensive, but
it wasn't cheap. "You've heard of, maybe, Fein and Dandley—of
Brooklyn? We make toys, Mr. Wreckage. Could we talk? You're on
your way home—let me get a carriage." He looked over at the two
dolls Joette was still holding and said, "We do better than that, miss.
What child could fall in love with a piece of paper?"

Mr. Fein sat opposite Georgie and Joette in the cab; he'd placed
the satchel on his lap and as he talked he undid all the buckles—
Georgie counted six—and opened several locks—Georgie couldn't
be sure how many of those there were—with a variety of tiny keys.
"Your friend Mr. Clark, he's very careful. He wouldn't tell me where
you live. That's a good friend. But I didn't mind waiting at the
ferry—I use my time; I think. I think, Someday, Mr. Fein, you're
going to die, like your father, your grandfather. And I think, Tomorrow, Mr. Fein, get cracking on those sleds, those Christmas or-
naments. I *think*." He tapped on his temple, not the birthmark
temple. "And this afternoon, all afternoon, I thought, Mr. Fein, just
wait till Mr. Wreckage gets here, wait'll he meets you. You'll make
his day, his week, his month! Who knows, maybe his year. It's not
out of the question." Eyes bright—moist—Mr. Fein carefully lifted
from his satchel a pot-metal statuette of Pinfold pulling Fuzzy in a

slat-sided wagon. "Do you have any children, Mr. Wreckage? No? Well, then, you might use it for mints." He passed it across to Georgie, who was surprised by how much it weighed—a couple of pounds.

"Let me see," said Joette. "Let me see?"

Georgie gave it to her, then turned back to Mr. Fein, still beaming, and said, "For mints or as an ashtray."

Mr. Fein wasn't amused. "It's only too bad our timing was off. If you'd started drawing your little boy and dog before Easter, we could've done fancy eggs. *Next* year."

"Mr. Fein? Excuse me," said Georgie, "but I don't understand something. Do you intend to sell this—toy? You're making others?"

"Of course. A week and a half from now, God willing, it'll be in all the stores."

"But I haven't given you the permission to do that. I haven't *signed* anything."

Mr. Fein looked puzzled, then indignant. "Believe me, Mr. Wreckage, everything is legal, everything is licensed. Maybe *you* didn't sign anything, but *I* did. I have a contract with the New York *World.*"

"So what are you telling me, Fein? All I'm to get out of this is a *gravy boat?*"

"It is *not* a gravy boat, Mr. Wreckage. Where would you put any gravy? Show me. A gravy boat! It's Pinfold and Fuzzy Number One: The Wagon. And you needn't worry—as Pinfold's daddy, you're going to get a fair shake." Mr. Fein took out his billfold and, from that, fished a bank draft. It was payable to Georgie—the sum of 400 dollars and no cents. "Nobody's chiseling anybody here. This is America, ain't it? Ain't this America?"

4

Later, up in Georgie's room, as Mr. Fein was about to raise his glass in a toast, the lid of his tall hat—which he'd declined to take off—sprang open suddenly and up popped a cardboard cutout of Abraham Lincoln in profile. Georgie gaped and Joette broke into giggles, and Mr. Fein lifted an arm and felt around. He tsked, pulling the hat off his head. "It's not supposed to *do* that—unless you pinch the brim." He slapped the lid back down; there was a soft *click*. "Now, then," said Mr. Fein, smiling sheepishly, "let's drink to your funny, Mr. Wreckage. To the boy in the derby and his dog that talks. Cheers."

Joette found a sack of peanuts and poured some out—not very many fit—into the pot-metal wagon, then everyone sat down at the table. Mr. Fein took out a small pad and a pencil. He licked the pencil point. "All right, let's have a good think, let's all think. Shall we? And I'll tell you my *first* thought, shall I? I think your little characters should be around for at least a year. I'm told by Mr. Winkle at the paper, George—may I call you George?—that current plans are to run a picture every Sunday. He anticipates a solid eight to ten weeks before interest flags. I'm more optimistic. Look at that other regular character in the supplement, the Yellow Hag. She's been around since last winter, and it's only recently that she's started to lose appeal."

That was news to Georgie, and he said as much.

"Take my word, she won't last till Christmas, which is a shame. Not that *we* do any of that merchandise. Biggs and Company has the exclusive on her. But you hear things in the business, and I've heard that the hatchets they just put out have been a large disappointment. And they're not going ahead with the glass candy container or the cast-iron roly-poly. Don't cry for Biggs, though; they've made a bundle off that old chink. I still kick myself for missing the boat. And that's why I moved so quickly on your characters, George. Two weeks ago, as soon as I saw the first picture—my wife pointed it out to me—as soon as I saw that, let me tell you, I *ran* to the Pulitzer Building. Put those two in color, I said, and we have ourselves a deal. But—I've been talking too much. And when you talk, you can't think. We need to think. Let's think."

Everyone was quiet then. Georgie lit a cigarette. Mr. Fein broke open a peanut shell. Joette ran her tongue around and around and around her lips, then finally asked, "What're we supposed to be thinking *about?*"

"Products," said Mr. Fein. "Products! For example, I've just been thinking that the derby, the boy's derby is a natural. Yellow derbies. Like the ones the newsboys have been wearing all day. It's catching on already—why, this afternoon when I was waiting for you at the ferry, a boy came by, *not* a newsboy, and he was wearing one. A little street boy. I'd tell you, George, what he tried to sell me,

but we're in mixed company." He smiled at Joette. "So yellow derbies are a natural. We can even put that big dot on the crown, make
it the *official* derby. I can guarantee good sales."

"That's not a dot," said Georgie. "It's supposed to be a hole."

"A hole?"

"A bullet hole."

"*Bullet* hole? God help us, George, please don't mention that in
any Sunday picture—we'll lose the suburbs. A hole. We couldn't
very well sell any derbies with holes in them!"

Georgie shrugged.

Then Joette suggested, "Why not a circle on the crown? Would
that be all right? Sort of a compromise?"

"A circle! A big circle! I like that!" Mr. Fein wrote it down. Then
he rubbed two fingers across his mouth. "You're a thinking woman,
miss. Congratulations!"

Joette glowed at the compliment. "And how about nightshirts,
how about white shoes?"

"Those are clothing," said Mr. Fein. "Brighter Brothers of
Broadway will be doing any clothes."

"Derbies are clothes," said Joette. "Aren't they?"

"Not how we'll make them, miss." He nodded at his stovepipe
hat.

"Nothing's going to pop out of this derby of yours, is it?" Georgie
asked.

"Well, let's think about that."

Georgie shook his head. "I don't want anything to pop out."

Joette said, "Georgie, don't be so quick. As Mr. Fein says, let's
just *think* about it?"

During the next half hour, Mr. Fein covered three pages in his
notebook with further merchandising ideas—ideas of his, mostly,
though Joette did contribute a few, such as the Pinfold pinky ring
and the Fuzzy feed bowl. Georgie didn't come up with anything; he
didn't really try. He smoked cigarettes, he drank glass after glass of
red wine, and he kept getting up from his chair and walking to the
window, sniffing the night air. "I think I smell smoke," he said at
one point. "There's a fire someplace."

"Well, I think we've thought enough for now," said Mr. Fein,
putting away his pencil. "We've got wagons, kites, dog collars, dog
leashes; we've got buttons, handcars, banks, box cameras, maybe

watches. All righty. It's back to Brooklyn for me. And then I'll think
some more about what we've thought about."

Joette suddenly slapped the table. "Oh! We *forgot!*"

"Forgot? What?" Mr. Fein took out his pencil again.

"The wigbox," she said. "There's that wigbox. We could sell wigboxes."

Georgie stopped pouring yet another glass of wine for himself. He
looked at Joette in amazement. *We* could sell?

Mr. Fein was moving his head slightly this way, slightly that: he
wasn't excited by the idea. "I thought about it already, the wigbox, I
did. But how could we sell a wigbox with a picture on it of a boy and
his dog? It doesn't make much sense. It's . . . unnatural. Besides,
children don't *buy* wigboxes." He turned to Georgie. "Will that be in
other pictures, the wigbox?"

Georgie pushed out his underlip. Then he swallowed his wine.

"I don't mean to question your art, George. I wouldn't think of it.
Only I wonder about that wigbox. Why did you give him one? Boys
don't carry wigboxes."

"This one does. He really does."

Mr. Fein smiled indulgently. "He *really* does?"

Georgie nodded. "It's where he keeps all his things."

"Well, why not change it to a *suitcase?* A little toy suitcase we
could retail at two dollars, possibly two and a quarter. I think that's
a good idea, a suitcase—don't you, miss?"

Joette indicated that she did, yes.

Georgie frowned.

"The last thing in the world that we want, George, is for people to
start thinking your little boy is a pantywaist. Don't you agree, miss?
And the wigbox just might do that, start them thinking *bad* thoughts.
But a suitcase, now. We could slap his picture on it. An address tag,
too. Be cute. Reading 'The Alley, New York City.'"

"It's Awful Alley," said Georgie. "It's a real place."

"I think simply *The* Alley would be wiser." Mr. Fein smiled, then
he jotted *suitcase?* on a fresh page in his notebook. Then he got his
coat and put on his hat.

On the landing, Joette shook his hand and smiled warmly and
thanked him so very much. Georgie walked him downstairs. The
Human Lizard was sitting on the porch rocker, smoking a cigar and

tapping the ash into a cracker tin. "Saw your picture in the paper this morning," he said. *"Big* one. Good one."

Mr. Fein started down the front steps, then stopped, turned around all of a sudden, and came back. "I just had another thought." He leaned his satchel against the porch railing and spent half a minute opening it. At last he reached in and brought out a long canary-yellow billfold. "What's your little boy carry his money around in? Have you thought about that, George? And what do you think of *this?* We have a thousand of them on hand—originally they were supposed to tie in with a series of novels for young readers. Yellow Billy of Sioux City. But then the publisher changed the title at the last minute. *Yellow* Billy made the hero sound like a coward. Too close to yellow *belly."* Mr. Fein held the billfold up to the moon. "It's really nice-looking, isn't it? Imagine a picture of Pinfold right here, and the dog on the other side. To me it sounds like a good idea. You might think about giving your little boy a billfold just like it in your picture next Sunday. Why not? He has to carry his money around in *something."* Then Mr. Fein took a hundred-dollar bill from his own purse and stuck it into the yellow one, which he pressed on Georgie. "It's been a pleasure." He went down the steps and walked briskly to the gate. There, he turned and waved.

Georgie looked at the billfold in his hand. He shrugged and stuck it into his hip pocket. "You smell smoke?" he asked the Human Lizard, who plucked the cigar from his mouth and waved it back and forth. "No, I mean fire smoke. There's a fire somewhere."

"Is there?"

Georgie nodded. And then he went to find it.

Several weeks later, A.K. the editorial cartoonist dropped by to see Georgie Wreckage in his private room—and a very nice one it was—at the *World.* A.K. was dressed that morning in a yellow-and-black checked suit with a carnation, and when he came in—he hadn't knocked first—he discovered Georgie stretched out on a mohair sofa, smoking a cigarette and clicking smoke rings at the ceiling. The window was open wide—it was the end of May now, the weather fine—and through it you could see the river, the great bridge, and Brooklyn in strong yellow sunlight. Besides the couch, there were several chairs, two of them big and upholstered, an excellent rolltop desk, and a large drawing table. Georgie slowly turned his head and, seeing who'd come in, muttered, "Shut the door. I don't want anyone to know I'm being visited by the likes of you." Since he was now at least as valuable as A.K., Georgie felt free to insult him whenever and however he pleased. Indeed, that freedom, and his exercising of it, had become one of his very few daily pleasures. On-the-job pleasures.

"Game of checkers, George? Poker? Know any word games?"

Georgie sat up, swung his legs around, and planted them on the floor. Felt lightheaded for a moment. He reached out, crushing his cigarette in the ashtray stand. "What time is it?"

"Almost eleven. Want to go to lunch early?" A.K. had walked over to the board, and he stood now peering down at a picture, secured with tape, that was tightly penciled and only partly inked. Pinfold in a free-for-all with half-a-dozen other street arabs, everyone scrambling, clawing, and slugging his way toward an oversized purse lying on the pavement, a five-dollar bill sticking out of its moneyfold. A purse which Fuzzy the dog was about to snatch into her jaws. All the talk balloons were indicated, but none were lettered. "Lunch?"

"With you? Not on your life."

"I'm not really hungry yet anyway." He was still looking at the drawing. "Why've you taken the nightshirt off your little friend? I liked it. I liked it better than overalls. Overalls are so common."

Georgie picked up a glass of yesterday's seltzer, took a sniff, then a sip. "Brighter Brothers think they can sell more overalls than nightshirts."

"And overalls cost more," said A.K. He clearly approved of the change now.

"They do. The fasteners are yellow, and the cuffs too, once they're turned up. If you lose a couple hundred pounds, I'll see to it that you get a free pair."

A.K. grinned and sat down on the couch. "Were you ordered to retire the nightshirt? Or asked?"

"I'm to get fifty cents for each pair of overalls sold."

"Asked, then."

"Ordered. But nicely."

"Nicely is always better than not-nicely. And you get used to it. Being ordered, I mean. I was ordered this morning to make the Queen Regent of Spain a great big ogress—something out of the Household Tales, they said. Something you'd be afraid might be lurking underneath a bridge. I said, How about the Hansel and Gretel witch? They said, No, make her much worse than that. A witch is still a woman. And all because of Cuba. Cuba! Who cares about Cuba? I hated to do it. The Queen Regent seems like a nice old lady. But that's business."

Georgie dipped a brush, inked several bricks in a chimney. Then he laid the brush down and blew on the picture; he made a pained face.

"Spain's a lovely place—ever been there?" A.K. was lying down now, feet crossed.

Georgie squinted at him sidelong. "Sure, dozens of times."

"Watch that sarcasm, George. One of these minutes I might lumber over there and destroy your pancreas. But about Spain. About travel. Pretty soon you'll be able to afford more than a trip to Coney, won't you? I mean, if the kiddies buy those overalls. Incidentally, George, I saw a Pinfold *clock* the other day in Macy's."

"Buy one?"

"And put twenty-five cents in *your* pocket?"

"Thirty-one cents."

A.K. raised himself and looked at Georgie over the back of the couch. "I'm impressed. Maybe you'll get to Spain on the clocks alone. And Italy's nice—but I could do without the Italians. And England, of course. England. That's *real* swell. They have a lot of old places, you'd like it. I guess it's quaint." He got up, stroking the back of his neck and rolling his head. "That old Victoria—the Queen?—I seen her once. She's got a figure like the Liberty Bell. And no taller than a child. I say she looks like a little ugly girl. Talk about your ogress under the bridge. Wears a bonnet. I did some pictures of her sitting on a throne, but I made it a potty chair, an elimination seat. Funny? And I sketched in some toys, a ball, a dollhouse. The idea being, she's in her second childhood, see? I tried to sell them to the *Times,* the one they have in London, but they threw me out. Glory be to God, you never saw such a bunch of stuffed shirts, them editors, in all your life. They all wore top hats and burnsides and had fancy teacups on their tables. Sissies!"

"What time is it now?"

"Just eleven."

Georgie sighed and flopped back down on the sofa.

At two o'clock that afternoon, in a little eating house on Spring Street which had only recently opened for business, Georgie and Clarky sat hunched over their table, both of them staring mistrustfully down at a red gooey thing in a cast-iron pan. When Clarky had seen it come out of the oven a few minutes ago, he'd exclaimed that to him it looked like bleeding bread. And even though he'd heard that it was supposed to taste all right, pretty good, he still didn't like the looks of it. Pizza? Now, what the hell does that mean in American? And what was all that black stuff on top? Sorry, he didn't like its looks; give him a frankfurter any day, with sauerkraut. Georgie tentatively poked the thing, then licked his fingertip. "It's only gravy," he said.

"Yeah?" Clarky picked up his knife and fork, then immediately put them down again. He looked at Georgie, then he looked around —the place was half empty, the clientele entirely male, everybody in a work shirt and sturdy trousers, speaking Italian with his mouth full. "Let's have another glass of wine, shall we, George? Let this thing . . . cool." He poured.

Georgie propped his chin in a hand, then regarded all the little bits of cork floating around in his glass.

Clarky said, "You know those Cuban exiles who hang around that lawyer's office down on Broadway? The place everybody calls the Peanut Club? I heard they're planning another invasion. Get a boat and sail to Havana, all sixty of 'em, and kick the Spanish right out. There's some fellas down there, they'd just love you to draw 'em. Bring out their machetes."

Georgie continued to look into his wineglass.

"All right. Let's try this, then. There's a rich girl in town right now, she's from Milwaukee. Staying at the Fifth Avenue Hotel. At four o'clock this afternoon, she's going to get a note from her mother to meet her at Lord and Taylor's. Only she won't make it. Her brother's going to kidnap her as soon as she gets into a cab and take her up to St. Saviour's Sanitorium. Him and the mother both figure she's crazy. I do too. She plans to marry a man who writes chastity pamphlets. How's that, George? A kidnapping's right up your alley."

Georgie finally raised his eyes. "I'll tell Stolley about it, if I see him."

"What is it, you're not doing *any* news stories these days?"

Georgie took another look at the pizza—at least it wasn't burbling like a sulfur spring any longer—and then he sat back in his chair. "They won't send me out. And if I turn in pictures I did on my own, they get someone to redraw them. They don't want my signature on anything but the Sunday comic."

"So have them run your other pictures *without* your signature."

Georgie said, "No." That was that.

"Well then, George, I'm not going to keep taking your money every week. What's the point? You don't use nothing."

"Sure I do. Didn't I use what you told me about the kid who made wings out of newspaper?"

"You put it in your funny sheet! Pinfold lands head first in a barrel full of ashes. The kid *I* told you about they had to scrape off Fourth Street."

Georgie shrugged. "I used what I needed."

He cut a wedge of pie and tried to lift it from the pan; the cheese strings wouldn't break, though, and he kept lifting the wedge higher and higher. Finally, Clarky cut them with his knife.

"What do you hear about Pinfold—the other one?"

"The real one? I heard—do you know Albert Shallow? Makes condoms? I heard from somebody knows Albert that Pinfold and Albert, and the dog too, I suppose, went down south. But then I also heard that Pinfold got a job playing your version of himself at a shoestore on Second Avenue. And *then* I heard he got into a lot of trouble for braining some Negro girl in the head with a golf club."

"That was last Sunday's picture."

"What?"

"Pinfold braining a Negro—it was a boy, not a girl—in the head with a golf club."

"So you heard that too, did you?"

"I made it *up.*"

Clarky said, "Oh." Then, his forehead ridged, he watched, solemnly, as Georgie took a bite of the pizza pie.

Georgie chewed and swallowed. Then he pushed out his lips. "Not bad."

"Salty?"

"No. Try some, Clarky."

"I'm still working on my wine here. I'll get to it."

"So tell me—what else have you heard?"

"About Pinfold? Nothing."

"About anything. Anybody."

Clarky tipped his chair back, smiled ear to ear. "I heard some things about you! I heard you're now a valued depositor at the Corn Bank, for one thing."

Georgie laughed. "They open the door for me if they see me coming, yeah."

"And I also heard how much you're making—"

"Whatever you heard, it's way too high. And where'd you hear this stuff about me, anyway?"

"Around."

"Around where, around who? I hardly talk to anybody. Or hardly anybody talks to me, is more like it. You wouldn't believe what it's like at the paper. I feel like a ghost."

"It's jealousy, George. Enjoy."

"Do you know Bram Hoopes?"

"Heard of him."

"A friend of mine. And now the man won't even look at me. I meet him in the elevator, he turns and faces the wall."

"On account of you, George, he's page two now. It's jealousy."

"He's page *four*. Or will be Sunday. *Half* of page four. And I had nothing to do with *that*."

"Excuse me, George, but I notice you didn't take a second bite of the pizza. What's wrong?"

"I'm not hungry. Honest. Clarky, it's all right. You can eat it."

"Maybe I will." But he didn't. "And I heard something else about you, George. Is it true? I heard you're getting married."

"Who told you that?"

"I forget."

Georgie wiped his mouth on a napkin. He looked past Clarky and saw the pizza baker whack the countertop with a flyswatter. "I'm getting married, yeah."

"When?"

"I don't know. This summer. Next fall. I don't know. Soon enough."

"Rich, famous, and engaged, all in a season! Congratulations." Clarky went to refill the glasses, but the bottle was empty. "Should we get another?"

"I don't think so. Well, all right. I'm in no hurry, if you're not. I got nothing special to do."

As Clarky was standing up—there was no table service—he said, "Just don't forget. That kid from Hoboken's coming by to see you at five."

Georgie's jaw dropped. "Christ! How the hell did you know *that?*"

Clarky winked and swaggered off to get another bottle of cheap red.

Georgie had completely forgotten. Walter Geebus *was* coming in from Hoboken later with more drawings to show him. Walter had been over three or four times already, maybe five. He was *always* coming over, it seemed, and Georgie wasn't altogether pleased about it. Oh, he liked Walter well enough, and he didn't mind taking a look at his drawings—they were good, for the most part—and he certainly had the time these days to do that, to look and comment, make suggestions. It was just that, well, Walter Geebus was god-damn *presuming*.

The first time he'd showed up at Georgie's door—this was the Tuesday after they'd met and he'd come over on the ferry with Professor Thom—he'd acted as if he'd been invited. Walked right in. Hi, George. Suddenly it was George, not Mr. Wreckage any longer. Have some more pictures with me to show you. You get a chance yet to look at those other ones? Joette had been there, and she'd laughed.

He'd come again the following Saturday. Do you think we might go sketching together, George? It's a nice day. You don't have other plans, do you? No, Georgie hadn't, and since Joette was at the music hall, for the matinee, he'd taken Walter around, showed him places —Park Row, the Fireboat Station, the Aquarium. They'd sat together sketching, at the Battery Cannon, at Fulton Market, Trinity Church, and then they'd compared sketches.

The next Saturday, Walter had come yet again. Walter, really, I might like the afternoon to myself—if you don't mind. Sure, and what would you like to do, have a nice lunch? George, let me buy you lunch today. Let me buy you lunch uptown. We can take bicy-cles. And let *me* rent them, I want to do it. But Georgie—why? he wondered—had insisted on paying for the bicycle rentals. They'd pedaled to Central Park. Walter had never been there before, though he'd drawn it often, basing his pictures on prints that he'd seen, and on newspaper and magazine sketches. In the first batch of drawings that he'd given to Georgie, there'd been a series of ten cartoons entitled Central Park Cavalcade.

It was a funny thing about Walter. He knew everything second-hand, practically everything. He clipped line cuts all the time. He drew a good picture of a picture of a horse. And even when he did go out and sketch something directly, he never saw it—or at any rate he didn't put it down on paper—as it actually looked. Walter would see a barge and draw it heaped with garbage and circled by gulls, when in fact it was loaded with crates and not a gull was in sight. Georgie would ask, Now why'd you do that? and Walter would reply, I think it looks better that way. They went over to Riverside Park and there was a group of health faddists leaping about in Roman togas, and Georgie drew them as they were, but Walter just had to depict them as grossly fat or pathetically skinny or walleyed, which none of them were. He said, It's funnier that way. They're crazy people, right? They should *look* like crazy people on a page. *I* think. Georgie would be turning through Walter's sketchbook and he'd comment, You only have four fingers on that hand, and Walter would shrug, he didn't care. They would look at the same things on their days together, but what they each saw was totally different. It's vision, Walt would say, and Georgie would roll his eyes. Vision is for saints. Walter was kind of a dope, Georgie had decided. He *liked* him, but still, he was kind of a dope.

Clarky had returned and filled their glasses; he was combing back his hair with his fingers and grimacing again at the pie. Georgie smiled. My pal! My pal Clarky, he thought, and realized, when his eyes misted, that he'd become slightly drunk. Unusual for him even to be drinking in the afternoon, much less drunk—though come to think of it, he'd got drunk *yesterday* afternoon too, a *little* drunk—spent an hour, or two, in a saloon on Spruce Street, drinking with reporters from the *Tribune*. Evenings, lately, he'd been drinking a lot. At Jack's mostly, on Forty-third Street. Standing at the bar from eight, eight thirty to around midnight in the company of writers like David Graham Phillips and Stephen Crane and Clyde Fitch, and notables of the Metropolitan Opera, and members of the underworld aristocracy; nobody knew who he was, but he dressed appropriately and spent money, he bought rounds, so he wasn't freezed out—he wasn't talked to, but he wasn't freezed out. Georgie never tried making any conversation himself, he only listened and watched—how did these people behave, he wanted to know, what did they care about? These people with money, with celebrity. These people Joette had been telling him he ought to get to know. Finally, after several hours and too much whiskey, he'd grab his hat and stagger outside semi-delirious and flag a hansom cab. And then riding down Sixth Avenue—down through the most openly immoral midway in New York, past the chophouses and saloons of assignation, past the Haymarket with its abundance of young pretty whores milling in front—Georgie would sit slumped with a cheek pressed against the shaky window and gulp air. He'd go down to the Bowery and meet Joette after the show, and then they'd have a late dinner and he'd drink some more. Get home after three. He used to arrive at the *World* at eight o'clock every morning; now it was closer to ten. Make your own hours, George. Fine. So long as we get your picture to the engraver by Wednesday. Thursday at the latest. Friday? Think we could have it by Friday, George? Before noon, do you think?

"George?" They'd finished the second bottle of wine and were smoking cigars, and Clarky had just finished talking about having gone to the Barnum and Bailey Circus and seen all 1000 Wonderful Sights including the Twenty-four Wise Elephants and Joanna the Great Gorilla, and now, wrinkling his nose as once again he scrutinized the pizza pie, he said, "George? Do you plan on eating any more? No? Great." And he used the pan as an ashtray. "It's no use. I look at that thing, it reminds me of somebody's back after forty lashes plus one. You about ready to leave?"

Walking east on Spring Street a short time later, Georgie was telling Clarky about the kid from Hoboken, about how Joette thought he was so adorable—pushy, she said, but adorable—and then Clarky interrupted him suddenly, saying, "Across the street. Don't stare, but you see that fella in the long brown coat? That's Connie Dwyer."

Georgie looked, and Connie Dwyer—a big sloppy man, his yellow hair long and dirty, his face pale, his expression, his entire demeanor, furtive—was pacing back and forth just inside the narrow alley between two brick buildings with cast-iron ornamentation, a hatmaker's and a textile firm. He then stepped out onto the pavement, glanced up the street, down the street, and immediately ducked back into the alley. He kept his hands in his topcoat pockets. Then a redheaded messenger boy came out of the hatmaker's carrying his bicycle, and before he could mount it, Connie trotted over to him. They exchanged a few words. Connie took his hands from his pockets, and the boy looked at them, and he laughed. Then the two of them disappeared up the alley.

"What the hell's going on?" Georgie asked.

"You really want to know? Okay, all right. Let's walk around the block."

At Crosby, they turned south, strolled to Broome, then turned west, Georgie asking again and again what was going on, and Clarky being mysterious—he'd only say that Connie's game had nothing to do with the blackjack. "He's not strong enough for that, George. Afraid he'd pick the wrong fella and find himself flattened. No, he's not robbing anybody. And it's not gambling, either—no peas."

"What, then?"

"Just wait. We'll go back on his side of the street and see what he says to us."

Georgie nodded, thinking about Billy McCord—how could he *not* think about him, seeing Connie Dwyer? He was remembering Billy at the Snuggery, then at Mother Polk's, how he'd looked there, first as Georgie had seen him through the keyhole, asleep in bed, and then as he'd looked with the small red hole in his forehead. A month and a half ago? That was all? It seemed like a year, a couple of years. Then Georgie thought about Spit, and about carrying the trunk, and about the priest with the dirty cassock. And then he thought about Fuzzy, as she was in the red wagon in Mother's kitchen, and about Pinfold, the way he'd put his derby on when Georgie had looked too steadily at his bald head. That night. And Georgie wished now, walking up West Broadway, that he hadn't drunk so much at the pizza restaurant—he wanted very much to feel sober and clear-headed. But he didn't know why. And Clarky was saying, "Connie's fallen on hard times, I heard. You remember me telling you about his brother-in-law? How Connie wouldn't listen to anybody bad-mouth the guy? Connie should've listened. That pickpocket you knew would be alive today—and Connie might still have himself a gang."

Georgie stopped and squeezed his eyes tightly shut; when he opened them again, he didn't feel any more sober. He said, "What?"

"People that don't listen end up with cannon crackers in their ass-holes, is what I'm really saying. The brother-in-law took all of Connie's boys, every single one of them, and they're working for *him* now, and *he's* working for Shag Draper, and Shag Draper, I'm sure you've heard, runs everything crooked above Fourteenth Street."

"So how come the brother-in-law didn't just take Connie too?"

Bluh-bluh-bluh: that's what Georgie's question had sounded like to his own ears, but apparently it had come out clearer than that, because Clarky replied, "Who the hell wants some cluck in his gang who won't *listen?*"

They were turning back into Spring Street now.

Clarky said, "I think it's kind of sad—everybody cutting out on Connie like that. Even though he *is* a shitpot."

Georgie frowned. "Shitpot? The son of a bitch! He had somebody killed for no reason."

Clarky looked at him queerly. "He thought he was a big shot, George. Everybody does, sometime or another."

Georgie nodded—and then went on nodding, nodding, nodding.

"You feeling all right, George? You want to forget this? It's really no big deal. Come on, I'll walk you back to the Row."

"I'm feeling fine."

"You don't look so good."

"Let's go see Connie. Let's go see what's so sad," Georgie said, and Clarky shrugged.

As they approached the alley, Connie stepped out to the pavement; he smiled amiably, then, after glancing over a shoulder, he said, "Gentlemen. Could I have a word with you both?" He pulled his hands from his pockets and held them up, and clutched in his fingers were snippets of curly hair, pubic hair, black in his left hand, brown in his right. He passed the brown snippet under Georgie's nose, the black under Clarky's, then he grinned lasciviously and jerked his head toward the alley. "Five cents if you'd like to see more. Apiece. Five cents apiece."

Clarky looked to Georgie, who seemed thoroughly confused and unsteady on his feet all of a sudden. "What do you say, George? A little afternoon diversion sound good to you?" Georgie opened his mouth. Then he closed it. Clarky took out a dime. They followed Connie into the alley. At the end of it, where there was a recess, two young girls stood leaning against the brick wall. They were smoking. They looked profoundly bored. They were identically dressed in gray shirtwaists and dark-green skirts. The one with brown hair managed a smile when she saw Clarky and Georgie—she was missing a front tooth—but the other one, the one with black hair, tossed her cigarette away, as though in anger, and pouted. Georgie gaped. It was Anna, the girl who'd shot Billy McCord.

"Ladies, if you'd be so kind . . . ," said Connie Dwyer, and immediately both girls drew up their skirts—they were, naturally, wearing no undergarments—and held them bunched at their waists, and then they turned slowly around on skinny legs, around again and again and again. Seven revolutions in all, before they let their skirts drop and went back to leaning against the wall.

Now Connie was holding out a small stiff card for Georgie, another one for Clarky, and he said, "If you'd like to see either of these fine young specimens of female beauty in a more intimate setting."

Georgie thought, I can't spit—too drunk. If I could spit, I'd spit in his face. And then he snatched the card—his card; Clarky had accepted the other and was perusing it, chuckling at its tiny pornographic silhouette—snatched the card and tore it in half and flung the pieces at Connie's chest. He turned and walked up the alley, trying not to lurch, not to stagger, hearing Clarky in back of him say, "Don't mind him—I hear he's engaged to be married."

Two minutes later, Clarky found Georgie almost at the corner of Crosby Street, sitting on the steps of a fireplace-and-stove supply. "What was that all about? I'm sure you've seen much worse."

Georgie smiled coldly.

"We all must make a living, George."

"The girl with the black hair—know who she is?"

"Of course."

"How'd she get out of Mother's house?"

"I don't hear every little thing, George. But I'd guess money. And it couldn't have cost Connie *too* much—he doesn't have much, and besides, she's no Anna Held." Clarky looked back up the street; Connie was standing watching them, frowning. "Let's go, eh? I've got to get a sandwich someplace. I'm starving."

Georgie had taken out his pencil, one of his little squares of cardboard. "You go ahead. I want to do something first."

"Why bother? You told me, I heard you tell me they won't take none of your street pictures anymore."

Georgie started picking away at the pencil point with his thumbnail. "You go ahead, all right? I'll see you soon."

Clarky said, "Okay, sure, I'll see you," but hesitated—what was the matter with Georgie all of a sudden? Was he ill? He *looked* ill, he looked almost white, and his eyebrows kept moving up and down, up and down. And he was breathing funny. Too much wine, maybe. Or Christ—that pizza thing! "So I'll be seeing you then. Talk to you in a couple days." Clarky took out a soft cloth from his coat, bent over, and swiped at the tops of his shoes. *Georgie's* shoes—and it was the first thing that Clarky had noticed when he'd met Georgie earlier, before they'd gone to the restaurant—were new, expensive, and very shiny. Buckskin oxfords with tips. "Will I be invited to the wedding, George?"

But Georgie had begun to sketch and he was paying no more attention to Clarky, he hadn't heard the question, and at last Clarky shrugged. Then with a worried look he drifted away. Strange to say, but he'd liked Georgie better when his shoes were scuffed.

Georgie had to get up three times to let customers pass in or out of the fireplace store, but even so, he roughed a picture in ten minutes—the two girls, with their skirts *down,* of course. Finished, he held the sketch at arm's length, and it wasn't any good. The figures were stiff, their proportions all wrong, their postures approximate because, hard as he'd tried, he couldn't remember exactly how they'd stood; not a single line was juicy. He'd drawn in anger, drawing to ease it, and now that the picture had turned out so poorly, he became even angrier. He felt that inside him everything was shut off, except for that anger. Up the street, Connie Dwyer had accosted a gaunt, foreign-looking man who was trying to light a cigar as he listened. Georgie crumpled the cardboard and lobbed it across the pavement and into the gutter. At that moment, the door in back of him tinkled open again and a woman came out. He stood and moved aside to let her pass, and then he noticed the display of merchandise in the store window, the shovels and andirons, the fancy coal scuttles, the canisters of lighting sticks, an unpainted pinewood mantel, a Baltimore stove. He smiled and went up the steps and into the store.

Connie Dwyer's dour expression turned mocking as Georgie approached him. "So you're back, are you, Mr. Prissy? Or maybe you're not as prissy as you acted, eh? Want another look? Cost you five more cents." And then he spotted the poker in Georgie's hand. His eyes opened wide and his hands flew out of his pockets, but he couldn't get them up to his face quickly enough. Georgie swung his

arm high and then brought the poker down, hard, and it split open
Connie's forehead on a diagonal. Connie screamed. Georgie hit him
again, on the shoulder. Connie stumbled into the alley, tripped over
his own feet, and fell. Georgie dragged him up the alley by his coat
collar.

When the two girls saw Georgie come trudging toward them, they
paled and pressed themselves flat against the brick wall. The one
missing her front tooth began to cry. Georgie looked at her, nodded
to her, then he pointed, using the poker, toward the street. Slowly,
she came away from the wall, her eyes darting from side to side;
then suddenly she ran. Georgie let go of Connie. He crawled away
and balled himself up against the fence at the back of the alley. He
stared at Georgie over his knees. Blood streamed down his face,
beading on the tip of his nose, on his chin.

The dark-haired girl, the girl who'd shot the ventriloquist, took a
step away from the wall, a step toward Georgie, and he lifted the
poker again. She stopped. "Do you want me to come with you—
what do you want?" she said, her voice cracking. "Say something!"

Georgie very nearly struck her then. His heart was beating like
crazy, his temples pounded; he tried to swallow and couldn't. His
throat was sore. He wanted to strike her—God knows, at that instant he really wanted to—but he couldn't bring himself to do it, and
finally he said, "Go on, get out of here." And she did, stumbling as
she ran and making a high, keening, hysterical sound in her throat.

A few seconds later, and not even bothering to look at Connie
Dwyer again, Georgie turned around and left the alley himself. Out
in front of the hatmaker's was a large cardboard box filled with fab-
ric remnants, and as he passed it he threw in the poker, which had
for its handle a five-inch Pinfold made out of brass.

"Walter. Walter, Walter." Doctor Geebus was seated behind his
desk with his hands folded on the green felt top. There were several
long postal envelopes lying in front of him, and a silver letter
opener, and, to the side, the daily Hoboken *Call*. At the front of his
desk, one on each corner, were large three-dimensional models of
the human eyeball. Mounted high on the paneled wall behind him
was a colossal, and aristocratic-looking, nose of painted plaster.

"Nana said you wanted to see me," said Walter.

"She's not your nana, she's our housekeeper."

"She said you had something to talk to me about."

"Yes. Sit."

"Will this take long? I have to go to the library and read about the French and Indian War or something."

"Sit."

Walter smiled and took a seat in the chair alongside the desk that patients used.

The consultation room was filled with golden sunlight and smelled of camphor.

"Walter. This came in the mail today. For you." Doctor Geebus picked up one of the envelopes, which bore a fancy logo—*Our Favorite Uncle*—on its upper left-hand corner, and threw it across the desk. The envelope had been sliced open, and discovering that, Walter frowned, then glanced out the bay window. "Are you aware, Walter, that this particular magazine champions Democratic candidates and platforms?"

"No."

"I thought not."

"But who cares? I sent them cartoons, Papa, not bouquets to Grover Cleveland."

"That's enough of that. You sent them cartoons. Well, they've sent them all back. Walter. With a letter, which is what I really want to talk to you about."

"You read a letter to *me?*"

Doctor Geebus sighed. He removed his spectacles and pocketed them, and Walter became a smudge. "The letter mentions a Mr. George Wreckage of the New York *World*. Who apparently wrote a note to the editor asking him to have a look at your pictures. This Mr. Wreckage, I presume, is the same one who was at our house several Sundays back?"

Walter nodded.

"It's very peculiar. I was under the impression he was a painter. I was *given* that impression."

"*I* didn't give it to you, sir."

"I know you didn't, Walter. I'm not *saying* you did. But what I would like to know is how you and this Mr. Wreckage of the New York *World* have gotten to be such good friends. Good enough that he would try to help you place your . . . pictures. Kindly enlighten me."

"I asked him if he'd look at some of my drawings, that's all."

"Rather bold of you, Walter. But that shouldn't surprise me. And he looked at them while he was here? Your pictures? I didn't see him doing that."

"He took them home."

"And have you seen him since then?"

"Once or twice."

"You've gone to New York? To his *house?*"

"Professor Thom lives there too."

"That's not the point. I disapprove of your associating with this person. He's a newspaperman—Walter, close your mouth, you'll swallow a fly!—and newspapermen are about as admirable as . . . as *housebreakers!*"

"He's not a newspaperman, Papa, he's a cartoonist. Gee whiz."

"I've told you before, Walter, I don't wish to hear that expression. It's a vulgarization of Our Lord's name and I won't have it."

"I'm sorry."

"Don't let me hear it. Is that clear?"

"Yes, sir."

"And you won't gallivant off again to see this Mr. George Wreckage of the New York *World* without my permission. Which I might as well tell you now you won't receive. Is that clear?"

"Yes, sir." Walter crossed his legs wearily and read an eyesight chart that was propped on a decorative easel, starting at the bottom line: D L O F N I P. "But not everybody can be a doctor, sir."

"Not everybody, no. But you could be."

Walter laughed. "Not me. I don't have the doctor stuff, Papa. I don't. I'd probably only cut healthy people's hearts out for no good reason."

"Oh, don't speak like a juvenile! You're almost seventeen years old, Walter. Talk like a grown man."

"I was only trying to be funny."

"Well, you're not amusing." Doctor Geebus took an examination instrument from his desk drawer—a long, thin steel cylinder with a tiny monocle on top. He squinted through it and saw his son reduced to a speck. He grimaced and tossed it down. "And obviously your *pictures* are not amusing either. I've been telling you that for two

years. And now this"—gesturing toward the envelope that Walter
had taken from the desk and was holding in his lap—"only confirms
what I've been saying. You're simply not talented."

"I have to go." Walter stood up. "May I leave?"

Doctor Geebus leaned back in his chair and closed his eyes for a
moment. "From now on, you stay away from this man Wreckage, is
that understood? Is it?"

"He's Professor *Thom's* friend."

"I'm not concerned about Professor Thom, I'm concerned about
you."

Walter said, "Yes, sir."

"And please don't think I'm being cruel, Walter. Please. But this
young man—I don't know him, really, and he seemed pleasant
enough—but Walter, he draws cartoons for an obscene newspaper."

"It's not obscene!" Obscene? Didn't that mean naked women?

"It's a Democratic newspaper full of crimes and nonsense and
chatter about an income tax, and I won't have your head filled with
such things."

"But that's not at all fair. We talk about art, Papa, not politics.
Don't you want to be fair?"

Doctor Geebus folded his hands. He pushed out his lips. He
slowly wagged his head. Be fair? That was a useless appeal for Walter to make. The doctor was a Republican, and all Republicans
knew that life wasn't fair. Knew it and drew comfort from it. When
you were correct-thinking, you needn't be fair. "Walter," he said, "I
believe we've finished our discussion. Now, run along to the French
and Indian War. But just you mind my wishes."

With a nod, Walter left, closing the door after him and crossing the
waiting room. There was a patient seated on the davenport playing a
magnifying glass back and forth over stock quotations in the press.
Fluffy white hair, thought Walter. Skinny neck, veiny hands, gray
worsted suit. Spats over his shoes. His hat is a homburg. Trying to
observe carefully, as Georgie had been pressing him to do. Walter
glanced at the bright red goldfish in the bowl of water on the windowsill. And he couldn't help it; he imagined a cat up there, fishing
with its paw.

Mrs. Meerebott had been waiting anxiously outside the reception
parlor, and she intercepted Walter before he could get away—took
him by one arm, led him into the parlor, and sat him down in a
rocker. She had his school satchel, which he'd left in the entry hall

before going upstairs to see his father. "Off to the library, are you?" she said, pulling out roller skates by the ankle straps, then a heavy envelope of drawings. She made believe she was digging around in the satchel for books, then acted surprised when there were none.

"Why'd you open that?" said Walter. "It's not yours. Everybody thinks they can open anything of mine they like." He still had a smile on his face, but it wasn't blandly friendly anymore, it was ice cold.

"Walter," said Mrs. Meerebott, and then she touched his cheek lightly with her fingertips, "I just don't want you getting into trouble."

Walter sprang from the chair, grabbing his skates, his portfolio, the satchel. "I have to go. And don't you say anything to him!" But he knew there was no chance of that. Nana Mary tell on Walter, her nice boy? Not a chance.

At the bottom of the front stoop, Walter fitted his shoes between the skates' metal clamps, tightened the clamps, then pushed off. A man and a woman were arguing loudly as Walter skated past Violin Park, and glancing at them, he thought, Big noses on the two of them—his hat's too small. And he could almost hear Georgie asking him, But how are their noses *different*, Walter? What *kind* of hat is it? Look, Walter, *look*. It was ever so difficult, though, for Walter to do that, to look with such scrutiny. A face or a building, a crowd or a streetcar, a decorated Christmas tree, whatever it was that he happened to see, Walter would remark only its most striking features; the finer points of a thing hardly ever made an impression on him. He would see a man's bald dome and heavy chest, never the man's cuff links—unless they were diamond and sparkled. His father, the eye specialist, probably would've called it a form of myopia, but Walter, as he'd already told Georgie, called it vision and deemed it a gift. He saw things simplified.

Walter just missed catching the four o'clock ferry to Manhattan. Now he'd have to wait fifteen minutes for another. Gee whiz, and he'd told Georgie he'd be there at five. Well, he might make it still, why not be optimistic? He went into the train station and tried to buy a cigar—it might impress Georgie if he smoked—but because he was still wearing his school uniform, the news dealer wouldn't sell him one. So instead of that, Walter bought a copy of *Life* and a copy of *Puck*—he'd already seen this week's *Judge*, and he wouldn't spend another dime, not another dime on *Uncle*, since they'd rejected all of his cartoons; he hadn't yet summoned enough courage to look at the editor's note. He found a bench and sat down and started paging through *Life*—he never read any of the lampoons or reviews—smiling at a caveman cartoon by Kemble and a barnyard panel by Sullivant, glancing at a story illustration by Michael Angelo Woolf, then pausing to admire—look at that linework!—the double-spread drawing by Charles Dana Gibson. A pretty long-necked girl in a formal monobosom gown seated on a couch with her timid suitor. She reminded Walter, a little, of Joette Davey. Joette Davey, Joette Davey—Joette Geebus, Walter thought. He began to perspire—with sudden ardor, but also because of that damnable school uniform, short jacket and knickers—woolens!—in springtime! Come sit nearer to me, Walter? Thanks. Thanks, I believe I will. Now why don't you kiss me, Walter? Make love to me! Are you sure? Of course I'm sure! Well then, I'd be glad to. Walter closed the magazine and fanned his face with it. One of the fellas at school had told him just the other day that women had beards between their legs. Could this be so? He glanced at the big terminal clock—time to run! But he couldn't, he couldn't stand up, and he very nearly missed the four fifteen, waiting around for his erection to go away.

7

It was half past five, and Walter was still waiting on the front porch of Mrs. Bennett's boardinghouse. He'd arrived in Sawdust Street at five minutes before the hour—he'd nearly killed himself trying to get there, racing on skates all the way from the ferry—only to discover that Georgie wasn't home. That was funny. He'd *said* five, Walter had. He'd said he'd come at five. Though he knew he didn't have any right to be annoyed with Georgie, he was nevertheless. He took out his watch again.

"Walter!"

But it wasn't Georgie, it was Professor Thom, awkwardly steering through the gate his wheelbarrow freighted with a large metal bathtub.

"Come lend a hand, Walter. Help me carry this thing upstairs."

Only that past Sunday, Walter had seen a cartoon in the *World* in which a tiger, a baby elephant, and a bull moose had voyaged to the moon in a bathtub fitted with bicycle pedals and a leg-of-mutton sail—so, coming down off the porch, he asked the Professor, "Are you inventing a flying machine?"

The Professor laughed; he must've also seen the cartoon. "No, this week I'm trying to be practical. This is for my toaster!"

Walter could visualize it clearly: the World's Biggest Toaster for the World's Largest Slice of Bread. He took an end of the tub, and together he and Professor Thom carried it up the stairs and into the house. Mrs. Bennett—a fat woman with pouched eyes, and black hair in a French braid—stalked out from the parlor and frowned. "There's a tub in the hall, Mr. Thom," she said crossly. "I don't want you bathing in your room; you'll ruin my floor." She planted her fists on her hips.

"Keep walking, Walter," said the Professor. "I won't be bathing in this, ma'am. I plan to cut it up and use the metal. I'm making toasters."

Mrs. Bennett raised her eyes to heaven. Then she came across the hall and looked at the tub as it went by, reaching to touch one of the bluebirds, blistered now, that were painted on its side. Bluebirds, garlands, and a monogram "E." "You're going to cut this up?"

"With a saw. I have a saw for every occasion."

"I'm sure you do, Mr. Thom. Just you clean up after yourself."

"I promise. This is Walter Geebus, by the way."

"I already know Mr. Geebus," said Mrs. Bennett. "And if he comes around here any more frequently, I just may start charging him rent." But she said that with a smile—he was, after all, such a good-looking boy. Young man.

"I have celery pop—interested? It's warm, though."

Walter declined. He was scrutinizing half a hundred or more small cylinders of red paper with short fuses jumbled on the worktable— they looked like cannon crackers, but since this was the Professor's room, he figured they probably weren't.

"Can you stay and have a sandwich with me?"

"I'm not hungry, thanks," said Walter. "I've been waiting for George. I hope he's coming back."

"Can't say." The Professor dropped into a chair and began to unlace his boots. Walter didn't notice, but there were tiny corks in each toe. The boots were filled with water. Professor Thom had

thought that water-cushioned footwear might be a great comfort to
people who had to walk long distances each day—postmen, for example—but he'd discovered that the extra weight made every step
taken seem like a slog through snow; also, there was some leakage.
"I haven't seen George in a few days. Have you talked to Joette?
She might know where he is."

Walter blushed—did the Professor imagine that he might've gone
to her *room?* By himself? "No," he said. Then he said, "What're
these?" picking up one of the red cylinders.

"Light one and see."

"No, thanks." Walter laughed nervously and tossed it back on the
pile.

"Go ahead." The Professor pushed himself out of the chair and
came over to the worktable in damp-stockinged feet, grabbing an
ashtray from the gas mantel on his way. He dropped several of the
red sticks into the ashtray, then patted his coat till he found a safety
match and a striker. To his great amusement, Walter stepped back,
squeezed his eyes shut, and stuck a finger into each ear.

There was no explosion, however. Instead, the cylinders yielded
an inky-black film, slowly at first and curling toward the ceiling, then
belching and diffusing, until finally all the incandescent bulbs were
swallowed up in the murk, and then the Professor vanished from
Walter's sight, along with the table, the bedstead, the wardrobe, the
window, everything. It was like being in a cavern, that dark.

"Artificial Midnight, Walter! What do you think? For people who
want to nap during the daytime. No more heavy drapes. No more
blinders. What do you think?"

Walter never got a chance to say—because suddenly his throat
was burning, he was choking, and he began to cough.

Joette had been away shopping in department stores all afternoon. The beribboned sailor's hat she was wearing now, coming
back into the house, was new, and she'd also bought several blouses,
three pairs of cambric drawers with ruffles, two skirts, and a pale-
blue combing sacque; for Georgie she'd bought a half dozen wilt-
proof celluloid collars and a dozen cuffs, fancily embroidered
suspenders, a smoking jacket with a single braid fastener, and a bottle of Macassar oil—it was time that he groomed himself better,
parted his hair in the middle. Georgie had given her a hundred dol-

lars, two fifty-dollar bills, this morning—to raise her spirits, since
she'd waked up, sneezed herself awake, with a head cold, the poor
girl. When they'd gone to bed last night, she'd felt fine.

She was burdened down with all her packages as she came
through the front door and started up the stairs. On the first landing,
she ran into Walter, but she didn't recognize him immediately and,
in fact, he gave her quite a start. With his face so begrimed, she
mistook him for a Negro. "Walter! Why on earth are you wearing
blackface?"

Walter coughed and took several of the bigger boxes from her
arms. "Ask Professor Thom," he said miserably.

When Joette, instead of going to her own room, went directly up
to Georgie's and unlocked the door, Walter felt sexual pangs. And
they felt especially sharp once he'd stepped inside and saw flannel
bloomers and a camisole strewn across the foot of Georgie's bed. He
began to put the packages down there, on the bed, but changed his
mind suddenly and put them on the table, after shoving aside breakfast dishes. "Do you think he'll be back soon?" Walter couldn't bring
himself to look at Joette—she was so pretty! "I hope he's coming
soon," talking at a crazed, hand-painted Oriental teapot—expensive. As soon as she'd laughed at his appearance out on the stairs,
he'd been struck abysmally shy and wanted to run away. Hearts.
He'd been afraid that she might see them all, afraid they might
really have *been* there: hearts fanned out above his head, like on a
Valentine's Day card.

Joette was hanging up her jacket. "I'm surprised he's not here?
He should be?" She came up behind Walter then and touched his
elbow lightly, and he jumped. She smiled. "Why don't you find an
old towel and wipe that soot off your face?" She tapped her front
teeth with her tongue, scolding. "You and Georgie," she said. "You'd
let that Professor Thom *shrink* you if he had a shrinker."

Walter's ears blazed.

Joette made tea for herself and Walter, and they sat down together at the table. All she could find to eat were soda crackers. She
asked Walter how was school, how was his father, how was his father's baseball machine, was it getting fixed? and Walter did a lot of
shrugging, a lot of guessing that everything was . . . okay. Eventually, she gave up trying to make conversation—and wasn't it odd,
his reticence? With Georgie around, he was positively gabby: I got
some really good things to show you. I did an elephant right out of

my own head, without looking it up in the *Illustrated Book of the
Known World*. George, it's all one continuous line, except for the
ears. Gab, gab, gab. Gab and boast. But today, *without* Georgie
here, Walter was quiet as a cat. *Very* odd. Unless he's sweet on me?
Is he? If that was the case, Joette was flattered but by no means
surprised.

She asked Walter to let her see his new pictures—"May I,
please?" Walter's pleasure. And then oh! how she liked his funny
gnomes, she loved them, and his Noah's ark too, with its silly me-
nagerie, and his black cannibals in polka-dot loincloths seasoning a
white missionary for the dinner pot. She smiled, she laughed, the
corners of her eyes crinkled.

Watching Joette go through his cartoons, obviously enjoying
them, Walter wished that *she* were the editor of *Our Favorite Uncle;*
then, maybe, he'd get somewhere. Whoever the real editor was,
though, he was an idiot. An idiot! So what if *he* doesn't like my pictures! He's a blankenhead, he doesn't count. So thinking, Walter
finally took out that idiot's, that blankenhead's, letter to read. And
gee—gee, it wasn't so bad, really. Certainly it was nothing at all like
what Doctor Geebus had led him to expect—he'd almost expected
the editor to suggest he cut off his hand, or something. His talent
wasn't dismissed or even questioned. It was, in fact, acknowledged.
You draw well, sir. *You draw well!* Nothing here is quite right for
OFU, but do try us again. Best Wishes. P.S. Although we can't use
them, we were all amused by your pictures of the Bread Witch—
any relation to Hetty Green?

Walter laughed out loud when he read that. Any *relation?* It *was*
Hetty Green . . . changed around some.

At that time, Mrs. Green was the richest woman in America,
maybe on earth. An ill-tempered financier and a miser's miser—the
Witch of Wall Street, the newspapers called her. She had millions,
millions and millions of dollars, yet she lived—under an alias,
though everyone knew who she was—in a squalid Irish tenement in
Hoboken with her small yappy terrier. She dressed entirely in black
and walked with her hands always in a net reticule—a finger on a
loaded derringer? Walter would often pass her on the streets of Hoboken, and last February, late on a weekday afternoon, he'd seen
her slip and fall on a patch of ice in front of a bakeshop. She'd irritably refused any aid from passersby—Walter hadn't gone to her assistance; instead, he'd hung back, watching. She eventually had picked

herself up and was flicking slush from her skirts when the baker came running outside with a large white sack full of bread. He'd offered her his apologies and then he'd offered her the sack. Mrs. Green had snatched it rudely from the baker, she'd called him an ass, threatened him with a lawsuit, then—and Walter had thought this was just about the oddest, *funniest* thing—she'd remained there on the street corner *selling the long loaves*, at a nickel each, till the sack was empty. At last, she had continued on her way up Washington Street, thirty cents richer.

Ever since then, whenever he'd seen her, Walter had said to himself, Here comes the Bread Witch, there goes the Bread Witch. And he'd drawn her into several pictures—riding a loaf instead of a broom, her familiar a Skye terrier instead of a cat. A small bonneted beldam, her cheeks puffed like biscuits, her nose as round and flat as a scone.

He'd included two illustrated jokes featuring the witch in the batch of pictures he'd taken—along with Georgie's introductory note—up to the Uncle Building on West Nineteenth Street last week. BREAD WITCH (to a beggar she's threatening to strike with a pumpernickel): "Well, you're a fine specimen of a man!" DOWN-AND-OUT-DAN: "T'anks, really; I couldn't so easily classify *you*." And BREAD WITCH (at the zoo, regarding a hippopotamus and musing to herself): "My! of all the ugly creatures!" So, they'd liked those pictures, had they? Not enough to *buy* them, but still. Still, they'd liked 'em!

Joette was watching Walter across the table. When he realized that, when he looked up from the editor's letter and found her staring at him, he blushed again. "I'm just thinking," she said, "that you have a very nice smile."

Reflexively, he lifted a hand to his mouth. "My father says I smile too much. Well, I guess he doesn't exactly say *that*. What he really says is, I *laugh* too much."

Joette laughed then, and Walter said, it just popped out, "You have a nice smile too." And his head buzzed.

"Why, thank you, Walter. Thank you?" She kept staring at him, her eyes merry, perhaps a little mocking, even flirtatious—staring till finally Walter believed he might, at any moment, burst into flame, like one of his father's baseballs. He leaped up, banging the table with his knees, and went to the window. He put his head out, looking up and down Sawdust Street. Where was George? He wanted George to come back, he wanted him to *be* here. And at the same time, he did not. The moon and the sun both were visible.

Walter let the curtains fall, he turned around, and there was Georgie standing in the doorway. A huge tipsy grin on his face, both eyes blackened, the left swollen shut, and an arm around the waist of one of those four-foot-high Pinfold nursery dolls that Walter had seen advertised—$5, mail orders only—in last Sunday's *World*. "Look what *I* found!" Georgie said.

And then the doll winked at Joette, nodded howdy-do to Walter.

WHERE PINFOLD MET HIS MAKER

Pinfold was never sure just where he'd been: North Carolina? Or South? Was there another one? Was there an *East* Carolina? Because East, East something, stuck in his mind, afterwards. But maybe the place itself, Albert's hamlet, was named East something. East something, North Carolina. Or South. But whatever it was, wherever it was, it had taken Albert Shallow and Fuzzy and Pinfold two and a half days of traveling on freight cars to get there. They'd brought along enough to eat, so the trip hadn't been too bad—they'd never gotten hungry, none of the hoboes they'd met were mean or Miss Nancy, and the nights weren't cold now. Albert had kept slipping in and out of a blue funk, though; he'd be sharing a cigar with Pinfold one minute, showing the boy how to blow smoke horses, smoke fish, and the next minute his eyes might glaze sorrowfully and he'd start to moan; it was a hum and a growl, together, his moaning, and it made Pinfold uneasy.

They'd left New York on a Tuesday. The letter had come on Monday. From Albert's brother. Somebody died. Named Velma. Got lockjaw. Thought you'd like to know. Who's Velma? Pinfold had asked. Nobody. She must be *some*body. I said, *no*body. Albert, who's Velma? My worst mistake. And going down south, Albert had cried some, he'd cried a lot, over the death of his worst mistake. But in between, he'd acted as if nothing was the matter; acted, in fact, as if everything was specially fine. Standing at the slats of a stock car, he'd shout with joy at how beautiful the passing countryside looked in golden light; he'd say, Pinfold, get over here, boy, and take a squint at this; he'd say, I'm glad you came, with a big, happy grin. And Pinfold too had been glad; he'd never been away from New York before—he'd never even been to Brooklyn! Also, he'd felt proud that Albert had wanted him for company. Sometimes now he would imagine his unknown father in Albert's image—strapping and gruff, enthusiastic when you least expected it, mysteriously sorrowful, skillful with his hands, privy to a little magic—only white.

All the way down from New York, Fuzzy either had napped or had wanted to be petted—except when there'd been a train to hop or quit, and then, ears back, eyes bright, tail bristled, she'd fairly quivered with pep. She'd enjoyed herself. Old Fuzz. Good girl, good girl.

They jumped train for the last time in late afternoon and some five miles, Albert said, from where they were going; then they had to hike through woodlands—yellow pines, mostly—which spooked Pinfold after daylight. Over there, where I'm pointing to, that's tobacco, said Albert as they came out of the forest cover at last. I don't see nothin'. It's too dark. *There!* It's tobacco. You smell? Can't you smell? Guess so—can we pick some? No, Albert said, and then he said, It's not too far now—twenty minutes?

In the woods, Pinfold had looped a rope around Fuzzy's neck and she hadn't minded. She suddenly started to, though, when they got to Clarence's poky board shack. Clarence was Albert's brother. Fuzzy planted her paws, then pulled to go back—up the road? back to New York? Pulling and whining. Pinfold finally had to give her a swat on the haunch. But in his heart he felt as fussed up as she was behaving. Maybe it was all the stars, or closer, the sawing, clicking country sounds. Or maybe it was the way the kerosene lamp that he could see through the cabin's only window flickered ever so weirdly. Or maybe, maybe he was just tired. Clar-rinse! Clar-rinse! Albert hollered, and then his brother lumbered out onto the porch, swearing oaths and with a rifle lifted. And Pinfold's heart stopped; he believed he was as good as shot dead, since Negroes could see, see *best* in the dark.

Clar-*rinse,* it's only me, Albert. Point that thing away—you stupid? It's Albert. And Clarence said, I know who it is, you think I don't? What you come for? You *wrote* me, Clarence. Don't you remember? Nice letter too—you write that all yourself? Nice letter.

Albert's voice sounded strange, strangled, and he started rocking on his heels, and Pinfold could hear his thick fingers clenching and un-clenching—none of which gave the boy much hope. He crouched and slung an arm around Fuzzy. Wanted like hell to run. But you don't run. Man has a rifle, you don't run. Clarence, *Clar*-rinse, I come to pay my respects. And Clarence laughed. Respects? You the strangest man, Albert Shallow. Am not! Are too! Am *not! Are* too! And Pinfold whispered to Fuzzy, It's all right now. Fuzzy twisted her head around and gave his knuckles a lick.

Albert had to admit that he *was* the strangest man, maybe, and then Clarence let them all come into his house. Inside, there wasn't much: a chair, a table, a lantern, a cookstove, and—kneeling up on an iron bed in white nightshirts—two girls, twelve and fourteen, about. They looked scared. And there was a sickly woman in a rocker—she held a bowl in her hands, close to her face, and the bowl was filled with several wet gray bags that resembled mice, and she breathed them, and she never looked up. Clarence frowned at Pin-fold and asked Albert who's that, and Albert said, Some boy I know and you don't, and don't need to. Boy, said Albert—and Pinfold felt like crying; his eyes tingled—boy, you just go over there and lie down with that dog, and I'll see you tomorrow. So Pinfold had thrown his blanket on the floor, then he'd curled up around Fuzzy, and the night air coming through the chinks had blown across his face. Albert and Clarence had argued. Velma this, Velma that. And the boys this, the boys that. Pinfold dozed and woke, dozed and woke, missing most of everything—he'd wake when the shouting got loudest. You crazy, Albert, coming all the way down here. Albert saying, You still only got the two girls? Must be using what I send you. And Clarence saying, Honey-bee too *sick* for more children, Albert, I got no *choice*—but you changing the subject now, you crazy man. And Albert saying, No, not really. . . .

Next day, Pinfold got up when Albert came and roughly shook him. Clarence was gone out already—Pinfold never did learn what Clarence did, but he did something, because most of the time they stayed there he was away—and the ailing woman still was in her rocker, but sleeping now, the bowl on a shelf above her head. They had corn bread and red beans all mushed up for breakfast, Fuzzy too, and then Albert said, Come on, if you're coming with me.

Walking down the road, Pinfold spied one of Clarence's girls, the older girl, sitting in a tulip tree, and as he passed underneath it, he

looked up, to see her underpants, but she hadn't any on. His heart
lurched. Albert cracked him on the ear, which sent his derby sailing
off his head. Keep your eyes to yourself! The girl laughed—Boy,
what happen to *your* hair?—and Fuzzy started barking loudly, racing around and around the tree trunk.

Half a mile on, they came to a cemetery. This where she is? Pinfold asked. Albert hesitated at the gate, which hung by a single
hinge, the other one rusted to flakes. The fence, low and made of
unpainted pickets, sagged badly. Grave markers were generally of
wood; only a few were limestone, the dates on those blurred beyond
reading. Grass was high. This where she is, Albert? Velma? Don't
you talk anymore, said Albert, the heartbreak coming into him
again. Pinfold nodded; then he said, You go on. I'll wait for you here.
Won't we, Fuzz? Just come back the same way you went in, Albert.

Albert disappeared, and Pinfold found a good shade tree nearby
and sat down; he reached out and plucked a blade of grass and stuck
it into his mouth. Country folks are always chewing on grass: that's
what he told Fuzzy, who seemed disinterested, sniffing about. 'Least
that's what they do in *cartoons*. Last time Pinfold had looked. Which
hadn't been very recently. Albert had warned him, a month ago, You
keep looking at them, you going to go crazy. Of course, Albert
hadn't meant *all* cartoons, he'd meant *that* cartoon. But even *not*
looking at . . . that cartoon, and he *did* stop, Pinfold had thought he
might still go crazy—just on account of it. Everywhere he'd been,
everywhere he'd turned, he'd seen pictures of himself—he'd seen
his picture on the *seat of a bicycle,* he'd seen it on a package of cigarettes, a bottle of whiskey. A lady's *fan.* A tin of crackers. And the
kids—New York was full of kids in yellow derbies now, and it was
full of kids who had dogs they'd dyed yellow in washtubs. People
would see Pinfold on the avenue and they'd smile, they'd say,
There's *another* one of them! Another! Or he'd tell somebody his
name, and he'd get back, guaranteed, a chuckle. *Sure* it is—and
what's it like living in the funny papers, *Pinfold?* Mondays must be
tough on you, always going out with the potato peelings! It'd got so
bad that Pinfold hadn't much felt like leaving the alley anymore.
But even there, things had turned strange again. Instead of treating
him special, as they had at first, instead of treating him any longer
like he was their own version of Steve Brody, the bridge jumper, the
children of the tenements—whose derbies now were yellow too and
whose dogs, even the bull-terriers and mastiffs, were called Fuzzy—

had begun to look upon Pinfold almost with contempt. Just 'cause he
has the same name, he thinks he's the real thing. *If* it's his real
name. Short memories. Pinfold had become so disgusted at last that
he'd quit wearing that nightshirt, bought painter's overalls at a charity store—and *then* what? Then his cartoon self had changed to the
very same thing. Crazy. I'm going crazy. You *are,* Albert had said.
And then Albert had said something else, said, You ought to get some
money out of all this, you know. Go on over there and see the man
that's doing all these pictures—make him give you some money.
Stick out your hand, get tough. You think so, Albert? Really? *Know*
so. But after giving the matter some thought, not much but some,
Pinfold had decided to do nothing. He did not know why. He did *not*
know why. He only knew that the idea of meeting the man who was
drawing his picture filled him with fear. Wasn't that funny?

So Pinfold thought, and chewed on his grass, mincing it, till he felt
a shadow touch his cheek. He assumed it was Albert back already,
but when he looked around, it was the girl from the tree. A straggly
blue ribbon in her hair, the sack dress on her nearly as dark a brown
as she was, and she was barefoot.

Can I put on your hat?

Pinfold shook his head, no. He squinted up at her. She had
breasts. Sorry, he said, but you can't.

Where's Albert? With Velma?

Pinfold glanced toward the boneyard. Who's Velma?

Velma his wife.

Pinfold nodded. He'd figured that out for himself, sure. He got up
then, dusting off the seat of his trousers, and Fuzzy came back, net-
tles in her coat.

What's his name?

Her. Fuzzy.

And what's yours?

Pinfold.

Pinfold? That ain't a person's name, it's a place for animals. The
girl laughed at him again; it was becoming a habit with her. There
were bug bites on her calves. How come you got a name like that?

I just got it, I don't know.

Your daddy mustn't a thought much a you. A name like that. My
name's Amalina—it means clean as a whistle. My daddy *always*
like me.

Pinfold was edging away, moving into the road, and he kept looking across it, for Albert.

Velma step on a rake, you know. Then she get a headache. Then she yawn all the time, then she get stiff, and then she smiling but she can't stop it. You open the door, she scream. Then she died. All her boys *still* crying. I won't hurt your old hat, place-for-animals, just let me see it.

Pinfold ran across the road and through the cemetery gate, Fuzzy after him.

Even in the brightness of morning, *brrr!* the cemetery gave Pinfold jitters. He'd been in only one other, where they'd buried his ma. He could remember a small stone house with iron window bars, Michael the archangel in granite, and he could remember peeking under a tarpaulin and finding picks and shovels and somebody's lunch pail. He could not remember, though, where, in what cemetery, his mother was buried, and there'd never been anyone to ask.

Looking for Albert now, he wandered around, ignoring the headstones as best he could, frightening a garter snake in his path, tramping through a cold campfire and stepping over a scorched army mess kit. And then he heard a voice, loud and spleenful: Shut up, shut up! You shut up and let *me* speak! The ground rose slightly, and over that rise, Pinfold spotted Albert, ten yards distant, jumping up and down, shaking his fist, then snuffling noisily and spitting on a fresh grave. I don't want to hear about your suffering, I got my own. So you suffered. Well, I'm sorry, but I don't want to hear it. I just come to say good-bye. Let me! Shut up, why don't you, Velma, forever and just let me say good-bye.

Pinfold turned away in confusion and deep shame and went back the way he'd come. He didn't want to see such a thing.

Boys! Don't talk to me of the boys—they can take care of themselves now.

Or hear it, either.

A short time later, when Albert finished and left the cemetery, his face and throat glistened, and his shirt, sweat-dark, clung to his body. He was staggering, he was panting, and he looked cross—combustible. Pinfold thought it wise to say nothing, and he let Albert walk ahead a good dozen feet all the way back home to Clarence's shack.

That afternoon, the boys came. There were four of them, the smallest seven or eight and the biggest, the one that looked most like

Albert, about thirteen. Pinfold was on the porch fanning himself
with his derby; he hadn't seen them arrive, he hadn't heard them—
he just happened to look out toward the yard, and there they were,
standing silently together, holding one another's hand, at the foot of
the steps on the hard-packed dirt. The eyes in their heads were
puffy and bloodshot, distressed; the youngest two were crying big
tears but without so much as a sob. They stared unwaveringly at
Pinfold. 'Lo, he said with a cautious nod. Then the biggest boy came
up onto the porch. His shoes weren't a proper pair, but they'd been
wiped clean of dust—they were, in fact, still damp—and his blouse
and trousers were freshly laundered; Pinfold smelled the soap. Who
you?

Pinfold thought for a moment. Joseph, he said. It means, fella
that minds his own business.

Joseph, you please go on inside now and tell our daddy his boys
are here. Will you do that?

Your daddy? And who's that?

You just go do. Please. Poking Pinfold above the heart now with a
finger almost as big around as Albert's. *Please.* The boy went back
down into the yard and stood with his brothers.

Albert sat hunched over in a chair by the stove, his forearms
across his knees. I'm supposed to tell you, your boys are here.
There's four of them. Amalina laughed. She was brushing her mother's hair. The mother was inhaling from the bowl again. *He* know
how many boys he got. Telling him *four.* Like he mighta forgot. And
she laughed again. Albert raised his eyes and looked at Pinfold;
then, sighing, he shook his head. Tell them go away—they ain't my
responsibility. Pinfold said, Why don't you do that? Please? The
hairbrush crackled.

Pinfold took his sweet time going back outside—he stalled so long
that Amalina finished grooming her mother and walked over to him;
then she laughed—again!—and gave him a nudge to follow. These
my cousins, she said. Sure, said Pinfold, I know that. She jumped off
the porch—Pinfold stayed there—and she grabbed one of the middle boys by an ear and gave it a tug, she kicked the other middle boy
in a shin, she kissed the littlest on the head, and finally she said to
the oldest, He says go 'way, Dick. Y'all ain't his responsibility.

Dick rubbed his face, all around, with an open palm, and he said,
Why he come back then?

Amalina opined that she didn't know. But my daddy say he crazy.

Don't you talk about him that way, said Dick, and then he bent down and picked up a stone and threw it at the shack. The other boys did the same, one stone apiece. Pinfold had got out of the way, quick, but Fuzzy was struck in the flank by a ricochet, and she fired herself off the porch and chased Albert's sons from the yard, yapping a blue streak. They fled up the road and stopped running only when they were certain the dog wasn't coming after them; they linked hands and solemnly looked back.

Amalina said, Let me try on that hat, come on.

Pinfold said, No. He was watching the brothers: they were huddled, talking, their heads bobbing up and down in unison. Then Dick led them away through the woods. Where's your sister?

I don't know, said Amalina. Why?

Pinfold shrugged. He'd only asked to fill the quiet, and because he was nervous. He walked into the house. Albert, I want to go home. When're we going?

Soon, Albert said. He was still in the same chair, in the same posture. Soon, he said, and that's all he would say.

That's a old dog, ain't she? You have her a long time?

Not long. She ain't *old*.

She is, said Amalina. She is too.

Amalina had brought out a little taped-up ball; she'd thought she might throw it and have the dog chase after it and fetch it back. But Fuzzy wasn't chasing anything, anywhere. So Amalina and Pinfold had gone down to the water pump for a catch. She threw hard. Pinfold wasn't used to playing ball, and he dropped it more than he caught it, and when he did catch it, it stung his hand. She is *too* old.

Pinfold said, You want to know something?

I always do.

That dog used to talk.

No! Why don't she anymore? Run out of things to say? I think that what happen to my mama.

Fuzzy got shot, it's why *she* don't talk. You want to see the hole? It's not a hole now, but you can see the scar.

However, before he could loose her neckerchief, Fuzzy ran away—ran back up to the shack and crawled under it.

She don't like me showing her scar, Pinfold said.

That figures, she a girl, said Amalina. Then she said, I like that hat you got. I don't know why. You buy that hat?

Found it.

You found it? I never found nothing good as that in my life.

I found these shoes too.

I don't like the shoes so much. The hat's what I like. You want to sell it?

No, I don't.

Swap it?

What for?

Something a mine you might wanna wear.

You're a girl. What do you got I'd want to wear?

Oh, I got something. And it fit you perfect. Amalina laughed, and then she slapped Pinfold across his cheek. She raced away, up the road and into the woods, and Pinfold touched his face and his fingertips were moist. He gave chase.

And that's how Pinfold lost his derby.

In long shade, Albert knelt behind his brother's house, digging with a spoon. Pinfold wandered up from the road, his head yet woozy with excitement, and peering into the bucket by Albert's hole, counted five, six, seven—maybe eight, was that another one?—long slinky earthworms. Going fishing after dark, said Albert, smiling—somehow, he'd got happy again—smiling over a shoulder at Pinfold. And tomorrow we leave. Albert noticed then that the boy was without his derby, but he made no comment. He continued his digging.

Pinfold lay down on his belly and crept under the shack, tearing at spiderwebs and looking for Fuzzy. It was cool and the ground was damp. Fuzz, you still here? Yes, and her eyes, in the gloom, shined like jade. She began to growl as Pinfold slithered near. What's the matter, girl? Growling louder, and there was a real menace to it suddenly. Fuzz? Pinfold reached to stroke her, and she snapped at him, puncturing the skin at his wrist—deeply enough that the small holes filled with blood, though not enough so the blood ran. Cheesus, Fuzz! What the hell! He sucked on the bite and could smell Amalina's juices on his fingers. Cheesus. Then he backed away. Stay here by yourself then. I don't care. Backing away a few more feet, turning over, making a cigarette, then squinting up through a crack in the floorboards. He could see Amalina's mother's toes, clenched and scabby, and listening hard, he could hear her still breathing at her catholicom. He touched his skull. He missed his hat, sorely. He dozed, and woke with a jolt. At first, he thought it was something he'd dreamed, some fall or ghost, but then he realized there was a commotion in the yard. He crawled that way, and, concealed behind the steps, he peered out.

The four brothers had returned, and like stone pillars they were standing watching Albert rant at them and crisscross his arms clumsily and stamp a foot as though trying to scare, and chase away, a cat. I got nothing I want to say. You got nothing I want to hear. I got nothing *for* you. But then, forcing a laugh, Albert suddenly began to empty all his pockets, flinging a rabbit's foot into the dirt, his pair of dice, a bit of candy, a little book—*The Procedures of Chemistry*—and a black tooth. There! See what your daddy can give you? Take it. He turned his back on the boys and folded his arms across his chest. *Take* it. And his sons did—three of them did, diving for the things and fighting for them. Dick refused to join the fray. He smiled. That's a start, he said. It's a start.

Pinfold had been holding his breath for so long that he began to see speckles of black dancing in the air.

Clarence came in not long after nine o'clock, and Amalina, wearing Pinfold's derby—she hadn't taken it off since she'd first put it on—served him his dinner. I see your boy Adam by the road near Celie's place—he got hisself a rabbit's foot, said you give him.

Pinfold was back in the corner—already he thought of it as *his* corner—and he glanced to Albert, catching the tiniest smile on his lips before a frown drove it away.

Said you was hollering at 'em all, then you give 'em everything you got. I said, *Albert* give you? You must be lying to me. You musta all jumped on him.

Just let them try jumping on me.

Adam say Dickie say you staying on. Say Dickie say you know you got a obligation now. Say Dickie saw it in your face.

Albert leaped to his feet, scaring off Fuzzy, who'd been napping beside the chair. He's crazy!

Clarence sopped up red gravy with a piece of bread. Albert, you my brother, but I wish to Almighty God it was you dead and not Velma.

I expect so do the boys.

Clarence shook his head. I expect they *don't*. Much as they loved that woman, you still first. Sons for you.

Albert sat down again. What do you know about sons?

What do you?

Nothing, said Albert. Nothing.

Amalina's sister was washing her hair in a basin of water; leaning over it now, one of her elbows tipped it, and it crashed to the floor. Nobody even looked, not even Fuzzy. Albert said, Nothing, again, and Clarence made a sound of disgust deep in his throat.

Pinfold thought, If I close my eyes now, it'll be tomorrow in two minutes, and we'll be on our way back home.

But he'd forgot about the worms dug earlier, and about night fishing, and just when he'd got comfortable—he had a pair of rag-stuffed woolies for a pillow and a pea-green blanket that was stained badly and smelled of kerosene; Amalina had given them to him—Albert called, Come on, get up, lickety-click!

Where we going? Pinfold asked on their way across the dooryard. Ocean?

Ocean! You see any ocean 'round here?

I don't see nothin', you want the truth, Albert.

Nothing except a little bit of the road ahead and some of the brush alongside it, where the light from Albert's lantern swished.

We're going to a lake, said Albert, and Pinfold thought, A *lake!* He'd never seen one before, except in pictures—college men with jackets off but skimmers on rowing dinghies, simpering at their honeybuns. They walked perhaps a quarter mile, and Pinfold was relieved they didn't have to pass by the cemetery; they cut off the main road before there, traipsing down a stony fork and passing a few shanties similar to Clarence's, crinkum-crankum chimneys in silhouette, cook smoke hazing the roofs. One place, you could hear a family yelling in prayer. Pinfold realized that he hadn't seen another white face in more than twenty-four hours. Fuzzy stayed in step with Albert, and the boy resented her for it.

The lake was black as petroleum, fringed by tall pines, a couple hundred yards wide. Out in the middle was a boat with two hatted figures leaning toward each other, fishing poles sticking up. Big high clouds nibbled at the moon, occluded it, passed. Albert had brought along just one pole, and sitting down on sere grass, he baited the hook with a worm. Threw out the line—*plip!* I thought you might tell me what happened to your hat.

Nothing happened. Still looks about the same to me.

Albert said, Don't wise Albert. Why's that girl wearing it?

Pinfold gazed at the water over the tops of his knees. You don't tell *me* nothin', he said, so vehement that he startled himself.

Albert tensed; the boy felt it. You came along, said Albert. Just 'cause you did don't mean I owe you the story of my life. I don't owe you my life's story. You talking about Velma and the boys?

I guess.

I don't owe you my life's story.

No, said Pinfold, you don't.

No, I don't.

Pinfold said, You don't owe me nothin'.

Albert said, No, I don't, and fished.

There were flies the size of raisins and clouds of gnats, and Pinfold kept slapping at himself, especially his neck, and Fuzzy kept rolling around on the ground, thumping. Albert fished, motionless. So what happened to your hat? But the edge was off the question now. Albert didn't seem to care, to care to know, and Pinfold stubbornly refused to say another word about the goddamn derby. Where *you* going? Pinfold had stood up. Don't you try to go back without me. There's a seven-foot man with a rusty saw—grabs children.

Then I got nothin' to worry about, said Pinfold and went to take a piss. Fuzzy remained.

Despite Albert's caution, possibly on account of it—seven-foot sawyer, eyewash!—Pinfold wandered much farther off than he'd intended. He'd gone into the woods but stayed mindful of the lake's direction, so he couldn't get lost; the lake was over that way. That way? He frowned. Or *that* way? It was that way. It was that way. He finally unbuttoned his trousers and took his leak and then, instead of buttoning right up again, he got a match from his shirt pocket, lit it, cupped the flame, and used it—careful, now, careful—to illuminate his pecker. Where that had been! Where that had *been!* He scratched some flaky stuff from the glans, and by then the match was curling, almost scorching his thumb and first finger; he snapped back his wrist, about to shake the flame out, when somebody guffawed suddenly and said, Looks like a hour-old *mouse* to me.

It was Dick, Albert's oldest boy.

Pinfold couldn't see him, it was too dark for that, but he recognized him by the smell of laundry soap, and after he'd unstuck his tongue from the roof of his mouth, he said, You're lucky I don't have a gun—woulda blowed your head off, sneaking up on me like that.

Scared you.

Didn't, neither! Well, maybe a little. Fingers yet shaky, Pinfold did up his fly buttons, clumsily. What're you doing here?

I *live* here.

Here?

Close to here.

Pinfold got the impression, suspected, that Dick was pointing. But what're you doing *right* here?

Followed you. I followed y'all from Clarence's. Then suddenly Pinfold could see Dick's face; it was right up close in front of his, and Dick's teeth were as white as eggshells. Albert's eyes, Albert's nose. I want to talk.

Your brothers here?

No, they ain't.

What do you want to talk about? Bacon; Pinfold smelled bacon on Dick's breath.

Let's sit. Dick steered Pinfold gently by the elbow, to where there was a tree down, and they both sat. Dick took out a pipe and said, You got 'nother match?

Talk about what?

Dick said, Well. Then after a pause, Dick said, Well. Then Dick said, He adop' you?

Pinfold laughed and found a match, lit it, and held it at the pipe's bowl, loosely packed with uncured tobacco, and he listened to Dick greedily draw on the bit. He'd expected it to be a corncob; instead, it was a fancy Sherlock Holmes. I ain't adopted. Albert's my friend. Then Pinfold thought for a moment. I work for him.

He pay you?

Well, sure.

Sure?

Sure, who works for nothin'?

If it was for him, I would. Me. Dick exhaled, and Pinfold's eyes started to water—he decided, though, to think it wasn't on purpose, the smoke in his face. He got other people work for him?

No, said Pinfold. Just me.

Just you? How come you? Dick said; then he said, What? and
Pinfold said, I didn't say anything.

He got a wife? In New York?

No.

You lying?

Why should I?

Dick stood. You can't stay.

What do you mean, stay?

You can't. When he come inside our house, you can't. In case you
thought you could.

Don't want to, said Pinfold.

I don't care, said Dick.

Albert don't want to, either. Seems to me I heard him say something.

Albert, said Dick. Albert. Albert. Speaking it like it was a sound
that he'd never made before in his life. Al-bert. It don't matter what
he say. Don't matter what he want, what he don't. Say he don't. All
what matter, he got a obligation. Why you think he come back here?
He know that. Don't care what he say. He know it, someplace. Then
Dick said, I got a million questions, but just one more for you,
Joseph. When he sit down and eat his supper, he like you to make
talk or he like you to shut up?

Pinfold said, Damn, I don't know. Ask him your damn self.
Thinking, What million questions, what about? And wondering if
they shared any questions in common, he and Dick. A million. They
must.

Albert was still fishing when Pinfold returned and cautiously sat
down next to him—or, rather, next to the catch bucket next to him.
There was no catch in it. Albert's cigar glowed just below his nose. I
thought maybe the sawman got you, you been gone so long.

Dick had said, Don't tell.

Albert, we really are going tomorrow?

I said so, didn't I? I got a business.

The boat fishermen were rowing back to the opposite shore; the
squeaking of the oarlocks carried across the lake. Pinfold yawned.
The biting insects made vapors. The crickets were loud. Albert?
How long you want to stay out here?

What's the matter? You don't like fishing?

I ain't fishing. You're fishing.

Albert grunted, and Pinfold lay back and disturbed Fuzzy, who
was stretched out behind them, licking her forepaws and sleeking
her muzzle with them. Pinfold could see the tip of Albert's pole—
from this vantage, it seemed to stick the moon—and he watched it
jiggle, and then, at the very moment the line went taut, he suddenly
remembered, with an almost fearsome clarity, how his mother used
to tie a rope around his middle when she took him out walking. He
was three, four, and couldn't be trusted not to run into the street.
And he remembered—as Albert cackled and jumped to his feet—
the time he'd tangled himself, deliberately, around a telegraph pole
. . . and oh! the time a woman behind the counter in a findings store
had upbraided his mother for leading him around on a leash—like a
dog, the woman said. How red in the face his mother had got! How
confused and flustered, so apologetic, and she'd untied Pinfold's
rope then and there—and Pinfold had run away down an aisle with
his arms straight out, a T amok, knocking boxes of ribbons and buttons from the shelves, pulling out flat drawers full of pattern papers,
knocking over bolts of cloth and interfacing. And he remembered,
another time, being on a street corner, waiting to cross, and his
mother began to scream and curse at a man who'd just come up from
a barbershop below pavement level. He'd never heard his mother
shout so loud, so angrily, never heard her use such language, and
he'd never seen the man before. Man in a derby hat, squinty, with
pitted cheeks, a lusterless brown mustache, and long-lobed ears that
stuck out, a little. He'd given Pinfold the goose bumps and, at the
same time, an awful and confounding grief. A horse-drawn wagon
full of roped-down fireplace mantels had come up the street—Pinfold remembered that, the wagon passing noisily as the man in the
derby spat to insult and flung his arms wildly about. Then he'd
shouted back at Pinfold's mother, half his words not English, and
he'd called her a liar, a lunatic and a liar in front of the crowd that
had gathered, and finally he'd scuttled away. Pinfold had tried to
run after him, but his mother had yanked on the rope. And now as
Albert pulled in his catch, streaming black water, Pinfold remembered all the nights that he'd lain awake in his bed—a dresser
drawer lined with newspapers and a window curtain, alongside his
mother's pallet—imagining what he might've done if the rope had
not been tied around him and he'd caught up to the man from the
barbershop. Sometimes he imagined he would've kicked him in the

leg, or bit it, but other times, the times he was left feeling anguished, he imagined taking the man's hand in his and them walking away together. And sometimes, sometimes he even imagined tying a rope of his own around the *man's* waist and then dragging him back to his mother. Man with the derby, the mustache, the long ears that stuck out, man with the dab of shaving soap on his jawline. . . .

Albert moaned, laughed, moaned again, and then Pinfold laughed—what Albert had caught was a big old lace boot, and after all this time! But when he grabbed hold of it to disengage the hook, the boot jumped in his hand, jumped out of his hand, and then, soon as it hit the ground, one, two, three, four small catfish, in an ooze of bottom clay, flowed onto the grass, where they flipped and they flopped. They purred. Their barbels flickered. Fuzzy became excited and barked at them, while Albert—Albert seemed bewitched by them. He squatted, sat on his heels and stared. Pinfold went and grabbed the bucket, but Albert said, Put it down, and then one by one, taking each by its short dorsal, he flung the fish back into the lake.

How come? said Pinfold.

Too little. You got to let them get big. It's the fair thing.

That's a fact?

I wouldn't call it a fact. It's not a fact, a fact's different. It's a rule, kind of. Something a person just does.

Something a person just does, Pinfold repeated softly; then he nodded and, turning toward the lake, watched the ripples smooth away. It's a rule, he mused. Kind of a rule. Then he asked Albert, How little is too little? and Albert said, Oh, and he spread apart his thumb and first finger maybe five inches, but cautioned, It depends, though, on the fish. Some are little but grown all they're gonna get, and some are big but still are fry. You got to know.

Sure, said Pinfold, sure, and he smiled. Albert. Could I fish now? Could I?

Albert considered, shrugged, finally said, Okay, letting the boy bait the hook, throw out the line, and then correcting his cross-handed grip on the pole. You want to break a wrist? Do you?

No, Albert. Thanks, Albert. This way, Albert? said Pinfold, and then he fished till he drowsed. Not a nibble.

He was logy and he stumbled frequently on the walk back to Clarence's later, and his mind kept slipping from wakefulness to dreams, from a stubbed toe, an itchy bite, to Albert's coal bin glamorized with mirrors and electroliers. He'd hear Albert impatiently urging him to get a move on and then hear Fuzzy perfectly recite "The Man with the Hoe." When they came at last to the shack, Albert stopped him by the porch steps; he shook him. You awake?

And when Pinfold nodded, Albert slapped him. That's for losing your hat. Now go on in and lay down.

Pinfold went quickly, keeping his head ducked so that Albert wouldn't see him grin.

He woke after nine, sunlight in his eyes. Clarence was gone already, and Amalina's sister too—now, where'd she disappear to all the time?—and the sickly mother was dressed and sitting in her chair and inhaling deeply from her bowl. He sat up, blinking. Fuzzy was curled near his feet; she was awake and watching him. Albert? Pinfold said, Albert? Amalina was at the table, she was wearing the derby, and when she saw that Pinfold was up, she laughed. You hungry?

Sure I am. Where's Albert?

She pointed with a thumb. The porch. He waiting.

For me? Pinfold threw off his blanket. There wasn't much he had to do before leaving. He'd brought a traveling sack, it was still where he'd leaned it night before last. Maybe he'd change his shirt. Fill his water flask. He'd eat something quick and be ready to go in ten minutes. What're you laughing at *now?*

He ain't waitin' for you. He waitin' for *them.*

And they came while Pinfold was drinking a big glass of buttermilk and trying, in vain, to get back his derby. Give you fifty cents. Give you this. It was a small lumpy stone that vaguely resembled a human skull—Pinfold had had it for years. Give you a penknife that killed a colored man, I swear to God, in New York.

Keep it. Keep your old junk, said Amalina. She turned in her chair and looked through the window. They here.

Albert stepped inside then. Get your stuff. Get your dog. We're leaving. And he went right back out again.

Give you fifty cents and a nightshirt. Good one.

Don't want fifty cent and no nightshirt. Gimme a kiss.

And you'll give me the hat?

No. But gimme a kiss anyway.

Pinfold thought about just taking the hat, about just snatching it right off Amalina's head—he could do it; if she bit, he'd bite, too. Only it wouldn't be the fair thing, taking it. He'd made a swap, so he had to stick by it, he figured. Was that a rule or a fact? A rule, probably what you'd call a rule. He gave Amalina a kiss good-bye, and she gave him a chuck under the chin, like he was a little baby. He didn't appreciate that.

Albert, they're following us.

I know it.

Pinfold looked around, and the boys were just ten feet behind them in the road. Dick leading his brothers. Dick rolling up his shirt sleeves. Dick calling now, You wait up!

Albert kept going.

Pinfold had tied the rope around Fuzzy's neck before they'd left Clarence's; Albert had said to. And he'd said, Keep a tight hold. And now as she struggled at the end of it, crouching on her hind paws, springing off and barking at the boys, Pinfold had to do just that.

Wait up, Daddy. Or you like Pa? You don't wait up, Pa, I have to make you. Then Dick came at a run and jumped on Albert's back, his legs scissoring around Albert's middle, his arms crossed around Albert's throat. Albert staggered, to this side, to that. Then he let go of his suitcase and chopped at Dick's fingers, banged Dick's ears, grabbed Dick's ankles and spread his legs. Dick fell in the road. Albert shook his head. Never go after a man like that.

Dick said, No?

Albert said, Never. He picked up his suitcase and started walking again.

A few minutes later, when Pinfold turned and looked back again, the boys were no longer behind them. Pinfold saw Albert look too. They continued. In the pine forest, they met the two youngest boys, who handed Albert a tin plate of cold flapjacks spread with jam. As soon as they'd given it to him, they backed away, eyes down. Where's the other two of you? Albert asked them.

We don't know.

We don't know.

Don't you know nothin'?

Albert waited till they'd run off before he put the plate down for Fuzzy.

Pinfold balanced himself on the rail, blindingly shiny in the midday sun, and walked ten feet, turned carefully, and walked back. When's the train?

Soon.

Albert sat astraddle his suitcase—it was a mystery to Pinfold why it just didn't crush under his weight—and he picked on the shell of the hard-cooked egg that his second oldest boy, appearing just before they'd come out of the pines, had given to him. He split the egg open and offered Fuzzy the greenish-yellow yolk ball. She didn't want it. In fact, the very sight of it drove her up the embankment to join Pinfold on the tracks.

I sure hope it comes soon, said Pinfold, stepping off the rail onto the ties. He looked back down at Albert, then a sudden movement caught his eye, in the brush to Albert's left.

Albert tossed the egg away, said, It's coming. I hear it. Then he laughed and said, That's a fact. Be ready to jump, now, Pinfold. You be ready to jump. When you see an open door, jump. Don't think.

Afterwards, riding with Fuzzy in boxcars to New York, there was plenty of time to think. There was too *much* time: it took Pinfold a full week to get home since he didn't know what he was doing and twice ended up on a train going the wrong way, going back down south. Time to think, and mostly he thought about Albert, about Albert and Dick, about Dick sucker-punching Albert with such potency that Albert couldn't get up again. What else was there to think about? Nothing else seemed to matter. He thought and thought, and often he thought so hard and for so long that finally he just had to *talk*, and so he talked to Fuzzy, and that was good.

He'd say, Now what do you suppose, Fuzz—you suppose he *let* Dick knock him down? and Fuzzy would stare at him raptly with those shiny green eyes of hers, and sometimes her mouth would open and her long pink tongue would spill out. *I* think he knew Dick was hiding there. He knew everything else. Or maybe not. I don't know. Once I seen Albert get hit back of the head with a *plank*, he didn't go down *then*. I don't know. I don't know.

And then he'd stop talking, think some more. He thought a lot about what Dick had said to him when he'd come crunching up the cinders and while Dick's brothers, down below, were lifting Albert onto a pallet made of coarse rope. Dick had said, When you get back, you put everything of his in a big cracker box or something and nail it shut. We all come up one day, we get it. Fuzzy? Pinfold might say after he'd thought about that for a while. Fuzzy, how come you didn't bite him then? Before, all you wanted to *do* was bite him. And Pinfold would think, Well, why didn't I *sock* him?

Dick had said, He wake up, see he got a obligation. Everything be fine.

Last thing Dick had said: We got a obligation too, o' course. We be loyal and take everything he got. Don't you worry about it, Joseph. All be fine when he wake up. Sit on the porch. All be fine.

When the train came, Pinfold jumped.

Now he missed Albert, terribly. And he missed his hat. He'd have to find another. He'd have to find a replacement.

When at last the boy made his way back to Awful Alley, he was dismayed to find that the Agel sisters, Patsy and Mary Queen of Heaven, had moved under his stoop while he'd been away. Those Agel girls! They'd been fixtures around the neighborhood for years, missing only in the final weeks of their frequent, and simultaneous, pregnancies. They would disappear big as pianos and reappear empty-armed, and if you looked carefully through a newspaper on the day you first saw them both again following an absence—as the folks in Calamity Flats, those who could read, always did—you were certain to come upon a squib concerning newborn "twins" discovered in flimsy wrappers by a milkman or a clergyman. The sisters were close in age, early twenties; they were bad-smelling and bad-tempered, as peppery as they were promiscuous, and more often corked than not. And they were as muscular as smithies. They chased Pinfold off; they threw rocks at Fuzzy.

Pinfold had lost not only his home but his only means of support as well. But he chose not to worry about that just yet. First things first. He did what Dick had asked, *told* him to do, gathering Albert's personal belongings and emptying his cabinet and packing everything into a crate. With a crayon, he drew skulls and crossbones all over it. He spent the night in the coal bin, going to sleep on Albert's cot but

getting up and moving to the floor in the middle of the night when his
dreams turned loud and troubled. Next morning, he collected what
few condoms were lying around, the very last of them, and with
Fuzzy took them to Mrs. Polk's.

On the way there, he pondered, thinking that maybe, maybe he
should accept Mother's offer and become, at least for the time being,
her parlor boy. But it was too late. She'd already got herself a new
one, a nine-year-old she'd spirited away from the Annual Presbyter-
ian Youth Picnic. When Pinfold saw him, he was by himself in the
main parlor, down on his knees and playing with a spinning top.
Seemed quite content. You had your chance, Mother said, and Pinfold replied, Aw, I didn't really want the job anyway. They were in
the kitchen, and on the table was a canister for tea with Pinfold's
cartoon image on the lid. He picked it up and looked at it. That's the
boy in the Sunday funny—you *must've* seen him, said Mother. And
Pinfold gaped at her.

He decided now to make a clean break from the alley, and over
the next several days he and Fuzzy vagabonded, looking for a new
home. They spent one night under the banana docks, one night in
Tompkins Park, and one miserable rainy night they went over to the
World Building and huddled by the press vents. The morning after,
Pinfold came down with a bad cold and ran a fever, and by nightfall
he was feeling like death, so he tried to get into the Newsboys' Shel-
ter—he wanted badly to sleep in a bed. They would've taken him
there, but dogs weren't allowed, so he and Fuzzy ended up in the
vestibule of a small church.

At this point, Pinfold was down to less than three dollars. Time to
think about a job, and he thought about selling papers—he'd done
that once before—and he also thought about trying to get work as a
dishwasher; while he'd never done that, he was *pretty* sure he hadn't,
he felt that it was a logical thing, something he could handle, and
kitchen smells and warm water up to his elbows seemed very ap-
pealing. He decided eventually to canvass restaurants, beginning
with those on Second Avenue, where else?, and he was on his way to
do exactly that when he was spotted, then accosted by Mr. Spatterdash, owner of the Spatterdash and Son Footwear Emporium. A
large and large-headed man with thick black hair and a coping of
dandruff across his shoulders, a man with swift gestures and ani-
mated brows, who said, Here, you blind thing, *here's* where you're
going! Can't you see the sign? Pinfold glanced up at a shoe of wood

the size of a carriage door. Where's your hat? I thought you'd be in full whatever—costume. Where's your hat? Well, we can get one, suppose, easy enough. What's your shoe size? They didn't tell me you came with the dog—but I like it, that's nice. Don't bite, does he?

She, said Pinfold, puzzled and suspicious but allowing himself to be dragged into Mr. Spatterdash's store, where he was fitted with a brand-new pair of white bucks. Then Mr. Spatterdash dispatched his son, a round slovenly boy who was eating caramels one after the other, up to the corner five-and-dime for a Pinfold derby—the cheap kind, you fat thing, not the kind with the pop-up top. And twenty minutes later, Pinfold was outside again on the pavement, strolling back and forth in a sandwich board that read THEY'RE HERE, KIDS! THEY'RE HERE! SHOES WIT' MY PITCHER INSIDE! TELL MAMA!

Later, when a midget in blue overalls and a bright yellow derby, fella from the theatrical agency, appeared at the shoestore, Pinfold sicked Fuzzy on him; she clashed her teeth and took a big chunk out of his calf. Quite a team, those two!

When the store closed that evening, Mr. Spatterdash told Pinfold—you bald thing—that he could return the following morning, even though his presence had not been responsible for the sale of all that many pairs of white buck shoes. Pinfold took a half-day's wages, half a dollar, and then he and Fuzzy walked down the street and around to the kitchen door of a restaurant. He bought a sack of fried potatoes. They passed the night in the narrow alley between the shoe emporium and a hardware store.

Pinfold traipsed with the sandwich board all the next day, Friday, and then again on Saturday, when he and the dog were pestered almost constantly by small children. You ain't him, really. You really him? If that's Fuzzy, why don't she talk? I seed the real Pinfold at Macy's, and you ain't him. Fake! Fake! It was trying. Sales on the Pinfold Three-Star Shoe were good, though, and Mr. Spatterdash was well satisfied now; he invited Pinfold to come back on Monday. Pinfold said that's swell, but he wasn't at all sure that he wanted to. He'd have to think about it. There must be something better than this.

That night he went over to Canal Street and found a ruined chair on the curb; he carried it back to the store alley and repaired the caning as best he could, then he affixed a candle that he'd bought to

an armrest, and so he had a parlor. Sunday, he trash-picked. He
didn't find a million bucks in twenty-dollar bills, only a blanket, a
soapstone dragon missing its tail, a cardboard suitcase full of string,
and the morning's *World*. Back in his parlor, he turned through the
news sections, looking at the sketches: there was a sketch of an au-
topsy, a sketch of Grover Cleveland fishing at Buzzards Bay for
tautog and weakfish, a sketch of an almshouse girl who'd broken her
neck escaping, a sketch of a tidal wave as it rolled in upon Japan. He
skipped looking at the funny papers—Albert would've been proud
of him.

When it got dark, he lit the candle and drew the blanket up to his
chin. Fuzzy was stretched out on the ground alongside the chair. Her
breathing was raspy. Pinfold suddenly leaned over and said, There
was ease in Casey's manner as he stept into his place. There was
pride in Casey's bearing and a smile on Casey's face. Say that. Want
to try? Can you just say, There was ease in Casey's manner? There
was? *There? Casey?* He waited, and then he shrugged, and then he
blew out his candle. Fuzzy killed a rat overnight, a big one.

Monday, Tuesday, Wednesday. Thursday—a full week. He'd
been walking in the sandwich board for a full week now, and already
he'd worn out two pairs of shoes from the emporium's stock. Cheap
things! Pinfold had asked Mr. Spatterdash several times if he could
please wear his own shoes, *they* were white bucks too, and *so* much
more comfortable. But no, for one thing, they looked ridiculously
big on Pinfold's feet, thought Spatterdash, and for another thing,
they weren't the *official* white buck shoe. Pinfold's heels were raw.

Because of his suffering feet, and because he was going bugs just
walking up and down, up and down, walking *nowhere*, Pinfold had
decided that tomorrow would be his last day on the job. Fuzzy too
had grown bored with the strict regimen. A few times she'd trotted
off, gone down the street and around the corner, disappearing for as
much as an hour. The first couple of times that she'd wandered
away, Pinfold had chased her and brought her right back. Sit. Sit—
you understand English? Sit! But then he decided to trust her. He
was always nervous, though, very nervous, his stomach upset,
whenever she was out of his sight.

Late on that Thursday afternoon, just after four, a stately wreath
of yellow roses was delivered to an Italian funeral chapel across the
street, and scarcely a minute later the entire front of the building
exploded.

Pinfold ducked, vanishing between the advertising boards, and Fuzzy dove in on top of him, and glass splintered, and shingles, bricks, lathing, and slabs of burning wood clattered down all around them. People ran, shouted—Chodash from the hardware shouting the loudest, shouting, Help! my brooms! Smoke crossed the avenue. Pinfold breathed against his shirt sleeve; he pinched his nostrils closed. A police wagon came, and then the fire wagons, three of them, their water tanks sloshing, their horses big as calf elephants. And then came the newspapermen, a swarm of them, their press cards, some red, some blue, but most of them yellow, stuck into hatbands or dangling on string from coat buttons. *Nice* blaze! Gas leak or a blood feud? Anybody white killed? What're *you* doing here, George? Don't even look. Shut your eyes! Go draw a joke.

Very cautiously, Pinfold raised himself from his crouch and peered over the top of a board; he saw a tall freckled cop in the middle of Second Avenue reach down to pick up a coffin pillow, then saw the coffin pillow burst suddenly into flames; he saw firemen in rubber caps and capes and goggles and respirators rush at the funeral chapel with crowbars, sledges, plaster hooks, and wall-cutters; saw, turning his head, Spatterdash's dimwit son, a carton of bonbons in a pudgy fist, smiling happily at the tumult; and saw, only a few feet away and sitting on the curb, a hatless young man in an expensive black suit with blue and red threads. The young man stared, transfixed, at the burning building, while his left index finger moved rapidly, making zigzags and circles, on his knee. Next to him, in the street, stood an older man who was taking snapshots with a box camera. Say, George, better pick up your feet. Water's coming. You don't want to ruin those fine new shoes. Pinfold looked—they *were* fine shoes, beauties. But the young man left his feet just where they were; then, when the hose water came, he splashed and kicked and started to laugh. The older fella with the camera made a sound of disgust.

Finally, the young man stood—whoa! his knees buckled and his arms flew up, for balance. He turned around, and seeing Pinfold crawl out from underneath the sandwich boards as though from a tent, his mouth fell open. And then seeing Fuzzy, still in between the boards, he grinned. How *are* you, girl? He pulled himself erect, he straightened his shoulders—Pinfold realized now that the young man was drunk—and he came over, reeling a little, then got down on one knee. He stroked Fuzzy's head, and she let him; he picked up one of her paws and shook it. Meanwhile laughing like a nut. So you made it! Heard you did! Good for you! And then he said, Pinfold, I'm very happy to see you again.

Again? Pinfold was squinting hard—the young man was familiar now, sort of, but he couldn't place him. George? He didn't know any Georges. Then: Holy Christ, you used to be a nigger!

And things have only gotten worse. Now I'm a cartoonist. I'm Georgie Wreckage, Pinfold. Maybe you know the name?

And when Georgie put out a hand to shake, Pinfold biffed him in the eye, biffed him in the nose, the nose again, then the other eye. Left, right, left, right. Suckered him good.

Four LEFTIES

1

The imaginary Mrs. Cuff was a cripple—aged, of course, and all alone in the world—and since one of the things you were supposed to do was visit the sick if you wished to go to heaven, Walter Geebus visited her regularly; he'd been doing so for a couple of years. Glad to. Walter! his father would thunder at him when he came home late for his supper from a long gallivant through the backyards of Hoboken, taken to glimpse ladies' foundation garments on the wash lines, or after playing Bogeyman's Loose in a chum's dark spooky root cellar—Walter, where have you been? To see Mrs. Cuff, Papa. She asked me to read to her. I've been reading *Allan Quartermain*—or *A Connecticut Yankee* or *Plain Tales from the Hills* or *A Scandal in Bohemia*. And since the doctor had been telling Walter all his life that charity was admirable, that it was a necessary chore, let's say, like putting up and taking down storm windows, he couldn't very well turn around now and punish his son for practicing it. But why on earth had Walter picked an *Irish*woman to practice it on? An old Irishwoman who lived far across town? Doctor Geebus had never even *heard* of her street! Surely there were wretches much closer to home. Judge Murray, to name one. Walter couldn't read stories to poor Judge Murray, whose paresis qualified him, you'd *think,* for adolescent sympathy? The judge, besides living only two doors away, was a patient of Doctor Geebus. And who attends your Mrs. Cuff, Walter? Oh, she don't like doctors. Doesn't, Walter; she *doesn't* like doctors. That's right, Papa, she doesn't. Well, if you feel that you must visit this person, then go ahead. Go ahead. But you're not to bathe or dress her. It would not be correct. Doctor Geebus repeated that caution time and again, and time and again, Walter blushed. Once, the doctor had asked what Mrs. Cuff looked like, and Walter had replied, after a long moment's thought, She's got black hair and a big mole. And, um—a port-wine stain. And what's her house like? Oh, it's not a house. She's very needy. It's a room. It's got—it's got a chair, a table, and a bed. And it's got a window. Then, smiling, Walter had added, She can't afford a shade, so she tacked a newspaper onto the roller. Republican, I think. And Doctor Geebus had actually smiled. Sometimes Walter *could* be amusing. Imagine: a woman, a woman named *Cuff*, a woman named Cuff living in a single room, a woman named Cuff living in a single room and unable to afford a window shade—a *Republican?* Ha, ha, Walter! *Good* joke!

It was poor, sinking Mrs. Cuff and her enthusiasm for *Huckleberry Finn* that saved Walter from corporal punishment the night he returned from New York City at half past ten o'clock. "Doesn't this woman *know* that you go to school, Walter?" Doctor Geebus had been in his workshop—his late wife's bedroom, converted—and the moment he'd heard Walter trudging up the stairs, he'd rushed out into the hall with a flat rubber timing belt. He was wearing a mechanic's duster and protective goggles of buff leather with glass lenses; the lenses were flecked with metal shavings. "It's a school night, my tardy friend. Couldn't you open your mouth and inform the woman?"

"She was enjoying the story, Papa." Walter tried now, just in case, to remember the novel—what he'd actually read of it, months ago. He owned a copy, Mrs. Meerebott had given it to him last Christmas, and he prized it, though for the line drawings by E. W. Kemble, not the adventure. Probably he'd read no more than three or four chapters, chapters here and there. It was his custom always to, as he put it, dip. "I'm sorry if I've worried you."

"You told me you were off to the library."

"And I went. But then I went over to Mrs. Cuff's."

"Walter, you've gotten into a habit of making the strangest friend-ships. Really and truly. Do you want people thinking *you're* strange?" The doctor sighed. Then he shrugged, and Walter con-tinued up the stairs.

Five minutes later, as Walter was sitting at his desk unpacking his school satchel, Mrs. Meerebott barged in, bringing him a plate of graham crackers and a bowl of tea. "I doubt very much that the Cuff woman fed you." Wink. "You must be starving."

"I had a frankfurter." He forced a belch. "See?"

"Walter!" Mrs. Meerebott set the tray on the window seat. "I wish to goodness you'd told *me*, at least, that you wouldn't be home for dinner."

"I didn't think I'd be this late. Honest, Nana." He looked toward the door, making certain it was closed. "But what an evening I've had!" Laughing, he opened his desk drawer and threw in his port-folio of drawings.

"I want to hear all about it. Tell me!" Mrs. Meerebott plopped girlishly on Walter's bed; she patted a spot beside her. "Come sit here and tell me."

Walter decided to remain where he was, however. "I went to see George."

"Mr. Wreckage. I knew *that*."

"But he was terribly late. I had to sit around for an hour, and when he finally came, he brought home this little fella. At first, though, I didn't know it was a fella. I thought it was a big doll."

"A doll?" Oh, *Wal*ter.

"You remember that advertisement we saw last Sunday in the pa-per? For Pinfold dolls? I thought it was one of those, only it wasn't. It was the genuine article."

"What're you talking about, Walter?"

"It was Pinfold *himself*, is what I'm saying. The clear McCoy. Isn't that wonderful? It's like—well, just think if you looked out the window later and you saw a boy and a girl walking up Morning Street leaving a trail of bread crumbs behind them. Wouldn't *that* be wonderful? Same thing. Birds eating all the crumbs. Wouldn't *you* be excited?"

Mrs. Meerebott frowned. "Wonderful? Why would I be excited?"

Walter glared; then he pushed out his lips and shook his head, sadly. "Never mind."

"No, please. Tell me."

"I can't *tell* you. So just never mind. There's a real Pinfold, that's all. That's all. And a real dog named Fuzzy."

"Are you talking about models, Walter? That Mr. Wreckage uses when he draws? Is that who you met? Is that what you mean?"

"I mean the *real* Fuzzy and Pinfold, you silly thing! *That's* what I mean. And Georgie brought them home. They've moved in!"

2

Temporarily, Joette dearly hoped. She could not imagine *what*, besides foolishness, had possessed Georgie to take in that little ragamuffin. *And* his dog! Soon as Mrs. Bennett found out about the dog, a dog in her house, there'd be trouble. Oh, to hell with Mrs. Bennett, Georgie had said to *that*. If she makes a fuss, I'll move out. You're not *ser*ious. Ain't I, Jo? I don't *have* to live here anymore. I got some money now. I don't need this dinky room. If Mrs. B don't like my dog, she can just go hang. Oh, George, you sound so silly. And Pinfold had jumped from his chair and exclaimed, That ain't *your* dog, Jim, it's mine!

When Georgie had sent Walter Geebus out to have a growler filled and to buy a sack of frankfurters, he had asked him to stop by Phil Ward's room on the way downstairs—tell him, would you, that Joette has a cold and won't be going to the theatre tonight. All right with you, Jo? Stay, let's have a party. I should go to work, really? Oh, stay—you *do* have a cold. But they won't like it, George; let *them* decide I'm too sniffly to sing. *Them*, Georgie had said. Pif! You're staying. I'm throwing a party. And if they fire you, they fire you. Who cares? We got money now. We. He'd said we with such deliberate emphasis that Joette's toes had reflexively curled in her shoes and she'd felt a tingling back of her ears. Of course she'd stayed, then.

It hadn't been much of a party, though. Georgie almost right away had got the hiccups, and to stop them, he'd held his breath, but for too long—he'd turned a little blue, then he'd gone completely white, and then he'd fallen into a chair and passed out. Pinfold had eaten frankfurters, he'd fed several to Fuzzy, and he'd helped himself to Georgie's machine-mades, demonstrating a facility for blowing smoke rings. That looks like a smoke *bird,* said Walter, who seemed to be having a grand time. It *is* a smoke bird, said Pinfold. But Joette, squinting, cocking her head, just couldn't see it. Sure, said Walter, those are the wings, that's the beak. Still, Joette couldn't see it. Or the smoke *lady,* either.

So Pinfold had blown his smoke, and he'd smiled constantly, even while chewing his food, but talk? He hadn't talked much. Not much to say? Or perhaps, Joette had thought, he's dimwitted. She had asked him, You don't work in that restaurant anymore, do you? All in an instant, his expression had gone from happy to guilty to angry to—blank. And then he'd shrugged. Guess not, he'd said. She had asked him, What do you think of the pictures in the paper? and he'd replied, I seen a tidal wave I kind of thought was good. And Walter, just before he'd left for home, had asked him, What's the alley really like? and he'd answered, Empty except for this chair I got with a candle.

Walter was gone now and Georgie was still sleeping, sawing a log, and it was only the boy, the dog, and Joette, and she said, "What happened to his face? He didn't fall off a curb, did he? He only said that for me. But you don't get black eyes falling off a curb. Was George in a fight?"

"He wasn't in no fight."

"Well, what happened? I won't say that you told me."

"Somebody hit him, lady."

"Who? Who hit him? Were you there?"

"I was there."

Talk about pulling teeth! "Then who hit him?"

And Pinfold, drawing up his shoulders and dropping his head, replied, "Me."

Joette was so utterly amazed, so unprepared for the answer, that for a long moment she could only gape. Then—"How *dare* you?"

"It seemed like a good idea. It's what I thought of first." He was looking into his ashtray, moving butts around with a fingertip. "And I guess it *was* a good idea. Since here I am. Here *we* are. Don't be mad, lady. Jim isn't."

"His name is George, you little—scab!"

"*George* isn't mad. *George* wasn't mad. *George* thought it was funny," said Pinfold. "*George* laughed."

Joette stood—*she* wasn't laughing, you can be certain of that—then, pointing a finger as though pointing a gun, she said, "And I felt

so sorry when that man shot your dog, I felt so . . . bad!" Then she
threw a blanket over Georgie—she resisted the urge to shake him or
pull angrily on his ears—and just before storming out and going
down to her own room for the night, she grabbed Georgie's package
of High Life cigarettes from the table *and* the box of matches. Fuzzy
watched all this from on top of the bed. Her mouth was open.

3

Late next morning, when Pinfold stuck his head through the doorway and called, "Hello," Professor Thom howled in pain—and
snatched from his head a bowler hat with a built-in hearing trumpet.
He then strode across the room, stepping over cartons and cartons of
miscellany—into one he threw the hat—and skirting the big metal
bathtub that Walter had helped to get up the stairs. "I've been expecting you," he said, and with a smile of delight drew Pinfold in
from the hall. He closed the door. "Where's your doggie?"

Doggie? Pinfold made a face while gesturing up with a thumb.
"George says she better stay hid for right now. Till he talks to the
lady that owns the house." He gaped beyond the Professor at the
long worktable laden with doodads and dry cells and greasy motors
of various sizes. "What do you *make* here?"

"Things."

"Do they work?"

Professor Thom laughed. "Some do."

Pinfold walked to the table and picked up a wide leather belt—if
you overate, bells in it rang—and a bracelet you could wind with a
key and it would tinkle "I Don't Want to Play in Your Yard." The key
fell out. "Sell anything?"

"Occasionally. I sold a pair of artificial legs. Last year. And you
must've seen those glasses George had on this morning. Those are
mine. With the dark-green lenses? Let me find my coat and we'll be
off." They were going shopping. Would you take the kid, Thom?
I've a feeling he's the type gets grabbed going *into* a store and
turned around. Pinfold had forty dollars to spend—on new clothes
and anything else that he wanted. It's the least I owe you, Georgie
had said to him earlier before leaving for work. And Pinfold, finger-
ing the two twenty-dollar bills, had laughed giddily and said, That's
a start. Saying it flippantly, so Georgie would laugh too.

As soon as the Professor's back was turned, Pinfold scooped up several red cylinders of Artificial Midnight and stuffed them into his pocket. "You ever make condoms? Know what those are? If you made condoms, you could sell them easy. I could sell 'em *for* you."

The Professor's eyebrows shot way up. "Condoms?" he said. "Why on earth should I waste my time making *condoms? So* uncreative!" He snickered at his own joke, but he snickered alone. Pinfold didn't get it.

"Maybe so, but people *buy* condoms."

At Kyle's Department Store on Fourteenth Street, Professor Thom recommended that Pinfold look at turtleneck and open-collar sweaters and knee breeches and long stockings, in dark colors, of course, but the boy stubbornly refused. "All right, then. It's your money, you pick." And Pinfold did, buying four summer blouses, all of them white, and a couple of pairs of denim trousers with rivets on the pockets, a black derby, and sturdy black "hard-knock" brogans. He told the sales clerk, "You can burn these others for me," meaning Billy McCord's—Billy Delannoy's—stuffed-with-newspaper white buck shoes. Then, for Fuzzy, he bought a dog brush as well as a box of chocolates with cherry centers. And at last he said, "I think I'm done."

But he wasn't, not quite. As they were leaving the store, he suddenly stopped at a counter and stared at a row of blank wooden heads displaying hairpieces for gentlemen. He grinned, he pointed —and that's how Pinfold got his wig.

The Professor liked Pinfold, and he suspected that the boy liked him too. Maybe it was because, partly because, they shared a common passion for scavenging. Going home, they'd both spotted at precisely the same instant a cheap, cracked atomizer lying on a sewer grating; a block farther on, they'd both pivoted simultaneously to have a second look at a plaster swan, a centerpiece, jammed into a barrel of sand. They'd left that; they'd taken the atomizer—Professor Thom had. Pinfold had said to. I don't really need it.

Turning into Sawdust Street now, Pinfold asked, "What was the best thing you ever found, Mr. Thom?"

The Professor gave the question some thought. "A T-handled socket wrench. When I was five. What about yourself?"

"My dog, so far. What about the strangest thing?"

"A live baby."

"You found one of those too? Where'd you find yours?"

"At the dump. In a burlap clothespin sack."

"Found mine up the alley where I used to live. You ever find any money, Mr. Thom?"

"A jar of pennies, once." The Professor opened the gate and let Pinfold go through first. "Two hundred and thirteen."

"I found eleven dimes last year, in a matchbox. But that's nothing."

"Well," said Professor Thom, "I'd say it was more than nothing. I'd say it was one dollar and ten cents."

"Sure, but what I really want to find is a million bucks. It's been done, too! Seems like there's always some story you hear about, about this lucky fella or that."

"This is America, ain't it?"

"Left in a bedroll, maybe. Or a pillowcase." Pinfold nodded. "Twenty-dollar bills'd be best."

Back in Professor Thom's room, Pinfold tried on the yellow wig. He stood on a dry-goods box and looked at himself in the shaving mirror; he made faces, a variety of serious ones, and examined himself in profile. Then he put on his new derby. Then he took it off. He leaned closer to the mirror.

"How do you like yourself?"

"I don't know," said Pinfold. "I never realized something before."

"What's that?"

"I got dark eyebrows." He jumped off the box.

"I think you look very handsome."

"You do?"

"Yes, I do."

Pinfold was embarrassed. "I best go on up and see Fuzzy. Hope she hasn't eaten the door." He pulled off the wig and stuffed it into the wigbox—a small gray one, nothing like his old one, which had belonged to a showgirl. Then he stuffed the wigbox and his derby into the bag with his dungarees. And then, straight out of the blue, he said, "A fella that has bad dreams, bad enough that he shouts himself awake all night long—is that fella liable to do somebody harm? Is he bugs? You can maybe tell me."

The Professor regarded the boy. "Is this fella George?"

"I guess it is. All night long."

"I wouldn't worry about George. Use cotton wool."

"Maybe I'll try it. But I don't suppose I'll be staying too many nights anyway."

The Professor gestured Pinfold into a high-back chair, then he leaned against the edge of his worktable. "You shouldn't feel uncomfortable about being here. If that's it. You really shouldn't. George is happy to have you. I think he felt kind of rotten for not looking you up in the first place. I *know* that's so. He *told* me so when I saw him this morning. When he came down for the dark glasses to hide his eyes." The Professor grinned.

"I'm not uncomfortable," said Pinfold. "I'm not even *surprised* to be here. What you don't expect to happen, happens more than it don't. So you get almost to expect it. But I'm glad you tell me that George is all right. Because I don't mind saying—to you—I had some doubts. Fella says, I owe you a good dinner. Buys frankfurters. Fella says, You need a place to live? Live here. Then he keeps me up all night shouting in his sleep. Ain't it my luck? I say to myself at three o'clock in the morning. Four o'clock in the morning. Five o'clock. Ain't it just my luck?"

Professor Thom frowned and said, "He *did* give you forty dollars, my friend."

"That he did." Pinfold smiled.

"And it is a *little* more pleasant here—isn't it?—than in an alley somewhere. There's a roof, for one thing."

"There is," said Pinfold. "But ain't it also my luck to get lucky in the summertime? When a roof don't count for a whole heck of a lot."

Professor Thom unscrewed the top of the atomizer, blew into it; dust and insect bits whirled out.

Pinfold laughed, took up his packages, and started for the door. But whoops! he stepped into a pile of shirt hangers, stumbled over pieces of a stove, then banged a hip against the big metal bathtub. "I know where you found *this*, Mr. Thom." The tub. "Maloney and Grue's, right?"

"Maloney and what?"

"The old pickleworks. You don't know the old pickleworks? I lived
there once, time this kid in the alley beat me up whenever he seen
me. Somebody stabbed him in the heart finally. Figured *some*body
would. I just had to wait for it. At the pickleworks." Pinfold kicked
one of the claw feet; chips of white paint sprinkled his new shoes.
"This used to be Ella's. You didn't find it at the pickleworks?"

Professor Thom shook his head. "Who's Ella?"

"Big fat hoodoo lady. Fortune-teller. Had a lot of canaries. But
she's not around anymore. She used to sleep in this tub. At the
pickleworks."

"You're fooling me."

"Am not! She did. This was her bed."

"Is that a fact?" The Professor came and looked. The monogram:
"E"—for Ella. "I'm going to cut it up for the metal. To make
toasters."

"Toasters! Well, that sounds like a pretty good idea. You should sell
a few of those, huh?"

"What do you think about a toaster that's also an electric heater?
While you're having your breakfast it *warms your kitchen!*"

"I think it's swell! And you could move it around, too—heat different rooms!"

"Certainly!"

"So you could make toast in your parlor! Or your dining room—if
you had one!"

"You could."

"And you could make toast in the middle of the night—I mean,
you could even bring it into your bedroom. Heat your bedroom. And
make toast. If you woke up and you were hungry. And if you'd
thought to bring some bread. Say! That's pretty good, Mr. Thom."

"I think so. I think so. The Toaster of Tomorrow!"

Pinfold nodded and nodded—it *was* a wonderful idea! He took
another look at the bathtub. "I got a fortune from her one time," he
said. "Written on a piece of paper."

"Oh? And what did it say?"

"I don't know. I can't read. But it was short."

4

"Ex-tree, ex-tree! All the latest news! Police at work on murder
clues! Knockout drops, a hot prize fight! Cleric held up in broad

daylight! 'Nother bank has gone to smash—teller skipped with all
the cash! Rich man poisoned eating hash! Crime and bicycles, scandal and booze! Comic section for all the blues!'' The poet-newsboy—
who just five or ten minutes earlier had been Yuma Bill lighting
penny candles with blasts from his six-shooter and before that had
sung baritone in the Tinnymint Quartet—looked over his right
shoulder and began to gesture peevishly. *"Comic* section for all the
blues! *Comic section for all the blues!"*

And in the wings, down on one knee next to a flat of scenery which
depicted a lighthouse, a lifeboat, and a shipwreck, Pinfold was hur-
riedly tying a shoelace. Fuzzy kept butting him in the hip. The lace
broke. Oh, the hell with it! He raced out onto the stage—tripped,
fell, and got a laugh from the audience. Fuzzy trotted right over to
the scrambled eggs—pieces of yellow flannel—in a big salad bowl on
the apron beside the prompter's box. And there she stood, her tail
swishing a mile a minute. "Ladies and gents!" hollered the newsboy.
"Direct to you from the funny pages! *Pin*fold! And his wonderful
dog that talks! (Miss your cue again, kid, and I'll cut your dick off.)''

Pinfold was dressed in a lemon-yellow derby that had a large
white circle on the crown, in a yellow blouse, in blue overalls with
yellow fasteners and yellow cuffs, and in white bucks. Parked just in
back of the footlights was a shiny red wagon; in it was a blue valise
sized for a child with yellow grip, rivets, and beading. Everything
was exactly as it was in Georgie's funny, as required by the terms of
license.

Pinfold raised a hand and waved at the audience. Pinfold! Pinfold!
Hooray! Hello! Smiling, he picked up the valise, carried it over, and
set it down a few feet upstage from the dog. Then, standing on his
chalk line and shouting as he'd been trained to do, he said, "Hey,
Fuzz? Fuzzy, I was talkin' wit' Cohen da tailor and he tells me dat
he bites ev'ry dime he takes." And Fuzzy—the rum-nose prompter,
speaking through a megaphone—said, "But ain't he afrait of mi-
crobes?'' And Pinfold said, "Well, sure, but not so much as he's
afrait of bad money!" And *bang!* went a pit drum: *tsss!* a cymbal.

"Hey, Fuzzy—what d'you t'ink o' John D?''

"Not much!''

"Me neither. I seen 'im on Wall Street yestiddy. Asked 'im for a
nickel. He says, Are you a professional beggar? I says, For your
information, no, I ain't. And he says, Then I won't give you nothin',
for fear of *makin'* you one!''

Boom! Tsss!

Then Pinfold took out his yellow purse—six inches by four, the official dimensions—and the audience cheered. From the money-fold, he pulled a big tissue-paper moth—he frowned at it, flipped it away. "Hey, Fuzz, I wish I had enough money to take a Turkish bath."

"What? You'd take a Turkish bath?"

"Never! I'd buy a keg of beer wit' it!"

Boom! Tsss!

"Say, Pinfold, say, kid, speaking of money," said Fuzzy. "Ain't you never goin' t'*make* any? You oughta go out and find a job—I wanna eat t'morrow."

"Funny you should mention a job, Fuzz. Had a fella offer me one just t'day. Sure! Walks straight up t'me and says, What will you take t'clean out the sewers?"

"And what'd you tell 'em?"

"Oh, I says any old kind of dope, just so's I won't know wot I'm doin'!"

Boom! Tsss!

Meanwhile, upstage, a tall thin man in a dark suit, a top hat, and a long waxed mustache was slinking around the tenement backdrop, a revolver in his right hand. He had no left hand—just a large glass doorknob. It was—Slippery John, the cur who'd shot Fuzzy! Every-body in the house recognized him and hissed and booed; some women leaped up and shouted warnings. And just in the nick of time, just as Slippery John was cocking the hammer, Pinfold glanced behind him. He goggled, threw back his arms in exclama-tion, then he ran to his wagon, grabbed a rubber baseball bat, and chased that villain clear across the stage, striking him again and again in the duff. *Wap! wap! wap!* Down went John like a ton of bricks, and Pinfold triumphantly planted a foot on the small of his back.

And Fuzzy said, "It's a wonder dat little fella can take on dat big galoot and win. But—dis is America, ain't it? Ain't dis America?"

And then Joette Davey came out and sang "America the Beau-tiful," closing the show. . . .

The Saturday following Pinfold's arrival in Sawdust Street, Joette had performed in the matinee at LeFebre & Chill's, then returned to

the house in late afternoon. She'd had news. That half a hundred
street boys—*most* of them boys, but some of them midgets, all of
them with shaved heads and each of them with a dog on a leash—
had showed up at the theatre to audition. Apparently, there'd been
a notice in the paper: LOOK LIKE PINFOLD? MAKE BIG $$! What a
crowd of rowdies! What a tumult of barking! Chester Dimock, the
fella who played banjo with a straight razor, had been attacked com-
ing through the stage door by a water spaniel. Georgie said, No *kid-
ding*, and Joette said, Well, he wasn't bit *that* badly, George, thank
goodness—so don't get that look in your eye. I'm not thinking about
Chester Dimock, Jo. I'm thinking, I'm thinking. . . . He glanced to
the floor: Pinfold was downstairs in the Professor's room, helping to
saw up a bathtub. (Fuzzy was outside in the yard, snoozing in the
meager shade of a big ailanthus tree: Mrs. Bennett's orders.) I won-
der if the kid would be interested. He might like it. And Joette said,
They already hired somebody. Don't matter, Jo. If the kid wants to
do it, I'll see that he gets it; I *can*, too. George, you don't know if he
even *could* do it—go on stage. Oh, he could do it, Jo, he could do it. *I*
did it. And if I did, *he* could.

And as it had turned out, he could. Surprised everybody—not
Georgie, but everybody else, especially Joette. She'd grudgingly
admitted, after seeing him perform several times, that he was good,
very good. He'd memorized all the jokes—he'd complained about
some of them, those he didn't understand, and since he didn't talk
like that in real life, he'd bristled at having to deliver his lines in
gutter dialect, but he *had* memorized the jokes, and quickly. Just as
quickly, he'd learned to shout with inflection. And once he'd satis-
fied himself that, in the event of riot or fire, he could beat it off the
stage and plunge through the back door in ten seconds flat, eight if
he really scrambled, he seemed perfectly at ease. Fearless. He en-
joyed himself. Well, sure, Georgie had said. *I* always did.

Fuzzy seemed to love the work too. She was—well, she was just
marvelous. Everybody said it. Always traipsed right over to where
she was supposed to stand, always looked up at Pinfold when he
spoke. She never pissed or shitted, she never growled if some nitwit
beaned her with a licorice drop. But what was so truly amazing was
her stage business at the end of the act—when she had to address
the house once Pinfold clobbered Slippery John. She'd look over her
shoulder at the boy, then she'd look back at the faces in the or-
chestra, she'd look up at the balcony, and then, just as the hidden

prompter would begin to speak her famous lines, she'd wink. People swore that she did! Dis is America, ain't it? Ain't dis America? She'd lick her chops and wink. Beautiful!

The other performers all thought she was a wonder—they often gave her cider and beer and candy; Female Hercules gave her a dish of vanilla ice cream almost every night. Cosy Wilson, whose trained chimps did the Civil War, was convinced that Fuzzy had worked in a theatre before. Absolutely convinced. And the Pretzel Lady—Alice Rose—seemed to recall a dog named Fuzzy who'd appeared, some three or four years back, with a magician—or was it a juggler? a ventriloquist?—in a Philadelphia theatre directly across from the arcade where, at the time, she'd been doing her contortions. Was that possible? Pinfold said no. Fuzzy grew up in New York, he said. Always lived here. She's a New York dog.

One night, during Pinfold's second week as a performer, Georgie Wreckage, for a bit of fun, had made a surprise appearance as Slippery John. He was slightly drunk and not at all in character—came out, in fact, smiley as a political man on the Fourth of July. After being clubbed, he pulled off the wrist stump and the doorknob, jumped up, and took a deep bow. Introduced himself. And I'm so glad you like my boy! You *do* like my boy, don't you? Yeeeeeessssss, sir! *And* my dog? Yoooooooooo bet! Pinfold rolled his eyes, made a sour face, finally laughed. What the hell. Thank you, said Georgie, thank you! Then he'd gone over and embraced the boy, and the two of them had done the Hard Walk. Fuzzy had barked. And *then* Joette had come out to sing. . . .

"America, America, God shed his grace for thee, Till nobler men keep once again, thy whi-ter ju-bil-ee!"

Joette, in her spangled red tights and Lady Liberty crown, bowed, blew kisses, and strutted a little; then she nodded to Pinfold—throughout her song he'd stood next to Fuzzy, patriotic starch in his spine, his right hand over his heart—and together they left the stage. Her nose in the heap of flannel, Fuzzy stayed till the curtain fell.

This night, as soon as Joette got backstage, she put her face into her hands and sobbed, and her shoulders heaved. The old coot who swept up walked over to her and touched her on the elbow, kindly, and she suddenly flung herself against him. She hugged him like he

was somebody special and long-lost. Then she sniffled, kissed him on
his forehead, where his psoriasis wasn't, and ran downstairs. The old
coot noticed Pinfold staring, and he leered, rubbing his chest lightly
with his palms. "Lord," he said, "I haven't felt bosoms in thirty
years. I'm exaggerating—twenty years. But they felt nice." He
went off hugging himself.

Joette shared a dressing room with Pearl Conselman, a plump,
pretty bundle with reddish-gold hair, the Human Lizard's assistant.
She was devoted to him—she called him Philip—and he was in love
with her. He wrote her poems in Latin, promising to translate them
if she'd only promise to marry him. But how could she marry a man,
no matter how sweet, who for his living slithered around a stage
eating flies?

What do you *want* me to do? he'd say. Sing? Sing what? Casey
would waltz with the strawberry blonde? "You're so lucky," Pearl
said now as Joette was changing into street clothes: white blouse,
ankle-length brown culottes, then a double-breasted jacket, finally a
jockey cap. "Marrying a nice-looking fella with a nice-looking future. I know people think I won't marry Philip because of how he
looks, but that ain't it. It really ain't. It's because of how his *future*
looks. A girl'd be crazy to marry somebody whose future wasn't
nice-looking." Joette shrugged. "Philip will always have a job. It's
human nature to want to watch a fella crawl, but that ain't exactly
my idea of . . . a nice-looking future. Oh, honey, I'm gonna *miss*
you!"

Tonight's show had been Joette's last. The wedding was day after
tomorrow. Saturday, July the twenty-seventh. "I'll miss you too?"
said Joette, crying again.

Pearl got up and went to the door. She opened it a crack, looked
into the corridor. Then she shut it and sat back down at the table,
resumed dipping long strips of cardboard into a pot of honey. There
were half a dozen of those strips hanging from the ceiling. Throughout the summer Pearl diligently trapped flies—so that her Philip
would be sure to have plenty for the winter months. In boxes
stacked behind the changing screen were jars full of dead flies. Pearl
said, "What's gonna happen to your friend now? He gonna live with
yiz?"

Joette sighed. "Please, Pearl," she said, "if you don't mind, I'd
rather not talk about that?" She pulled a chair up to the table and

sat; then, frowning pettishly, dipped a finger into the honey. She licked it off and sighed again.

It had not been an easy couple of months for Joette. She'd tried—honestly!—but she just hadn't been able to warm to Pinfold. Oh, for God's sake, Jo, are you *still* mad at the kid for hitting me? Forget it, would you? *I* would've hit me too. But she really hadn't held a grudge about that; no, she simply—didn't like the boy. It was his presence that bothered her. At the house. At the theatre it was different; she didn't mind him at the theatre. Pinfold was always very polite to her, everywhere, and he stayed out of her way as much as possible, and she appreciated that—but. But he frightened her. That was silly, she knew it was silly and unreasonable, he was only a boy, but he frightened her. And she resented him. George, you're very kind, and I love you for being kind to him, but I do think you've gone a little too far. You've drawn the mayor, you've drawn Roosevelt, you've drawn the man in charge of the city morgue, you've drawn the President of the United States—do you give them twenty dollars a week, did you invite *them* to come live with you? Jo, come on—it's not the same thing. Oh, why not? It's just not. I didn't steal the mayor, I didn't steal T.R. You didn't steal the boy, either. What a stupid word to use, *steal*. You borrowed his hat. More than his hat, Jo. And I did more than borrow. Well, all right! All right! All right! she'd finally shouted in anger. *All right!* Call it whatever you like. But just answer one question straight. Just how long do you intend to keep your pets around? They're not my pets. How *long*, George? It's up to Pinfold, what he wants to do. And after we're married, George—what then? I mean, have you invited him to move into the new house with us? I haven't, no. But I took him over there last weekend—to show him the place? He just loved the wine cellar. That'd be okay, wouldn't it, Jo? You'd never see him if he lived down there. Being sarcastic. Well, *you* would, for sure, Joette had replied. I expect you'll be living in the wine cellar too. Saying that because Georgie's drinking had gotten quite out of hand recently. If it hadn't been for Walter Geebus coming by so often now, a good number of the drawings that Georgie had contracted to make might never have been finished. Why, just the other week, Walter had done *all* the pictures for an 1896 "Pinfold & Fuzzy" calendar that a coal company would be giving away to their customers. Georgie'd been too hung over even to lift a pencil. . . .

Pearl went to the dressing room door again, and this time, after peeking out, she flung it open, and all the talent from LeFebre & Chill's, assembled in the corridor, broke into song:

> Georgie, Georgie, pray give over,
> Georgie, Georgie, you're too free.
> Stop your palaver, else I'll tell Father,
> Georgie, give over and let me be.

Then Phil Ward, bearing a brown-sugar pie that Alice Rose had baked, marched in, cleared his throat, and said, with a wink and a sad smile directed at Pearl, "Isn't anybody here with a nicer-looking future than yours, Jo. And you deserve it. God bless." Then everybody was kissing Joette, hugging her, thumping her on the back, crying with her, laughing. Brian Byrne, the Irish tenor, squeezed through the mob with bottles of champagne in—oh ho!—a baby's cradle. *Pop! Pop!* Then came the gifts: a box of recipes, a Butterick pattern for a fancy bonnet, a copy of *A Young Lady's Preparation for Marriage* with the book ribbon placed at the chapter titled "The Sex Question," a coffee grinder, a hair-waving iron. Thank you, thank you. You're all so—sweet! Miss you, miss you. And then Pinfold was standing before Joette, holding out a box to her. It was clumsily gift-wrapped in bright green paper with small yellow flowers, and Joette hesitated before accepting it. It was very heavy. She lifted an eyebrow. "Thank you?" she said in a small voice. She tore off the paper and opened the box flaps. And then she frowned. What's *this?* A heavy electric cord. And a shiny metal contraption with two long and narrow slots in the top and a toggle at the side.

"It's a toaster," said Pinfold, smiling. "The Toaster of Tomorrow! It'll heat a room too, twelve by fifteen."

People were craning to see, saying Toaster? That don't *look* like a toaster, toasters got doors, and Joette said, "Thank you," once again, before putting the toaster aside.

It was after midnight, and usually Georgie would've arrived at the theatre by that time, either to take Joette to supper or, if she wasn't hungry or he was too loaded, to walk her home. Pinfold never went out to eat with them, but if they were heading straight back to Sawdust Street, he and Fuzzy would tag along. This night, however, Georgie wasn't expected. He was nearby, just up the street, in Gombossy's Crystal Palace—at his bachelor party, which Clarky had arranged. The Lizard, the Metal-Eater, Byrnsie, Cosy Wilson, once he'd got his chimps bedded down, and a few other fellas from the theatre would be heading over there shortly. Pinfold had considered going; though he hadn't been specifically invited, certainly no one would've stopped him at the door. But finally he'd decided to skip it. If he went, he'd be a log in the morning, and tomorrow he was supposed to help move Georgie's and Joette's things from Mrs. Bennett's to the new house that Georgie had rented on West Ninth Street. Besides, he was never happy in a crowd, especially a drinking crowd—and besides *that*, Fuzzy disliked gin mills. True! Whenever Georgie—who did almost all of his drawing lately at home—sent Pinfold out during the day for beer, Fuzzy refused to go with him into the corner saloon; she always waited on the pavement. Teetotaler, Pinfold would call her and laugh. That's funny, Georgie had said about the dog's quirk, I'd imagined she used to live in saloons, practically, before you got her. Pinfold had grunted, not wanting to talk any further about *that*. And Georgie, his expression clouding, had dropped the subject and gone back to work.

Pinfold was waiting for Joette at the stage door when she came upstairs carrying all her gifts in a borrowed net bag. "Let me take that stuff," he said and pointed to the red wagon he'd got from the property closet. She handed him the bag, then went out and down the steps and, not bothering to wait for the boy, walked through the alley to the street. Pinfold didn't hurry to catch up. And when Fuzzy loped ahead, he called her, sharply, and she turned and came back.

It was a hot, hot night; for the past two, two and a half weeks the weather had been oppressive—every day you woke filmed in sweat, feeling listless, the bedsheets twisted around your legs, and every day there were pictures in the newspapers of horses that had exploded—and as Joette walked home now, turning off the Bowery as soon as she could, she thought about how lovely it would be to get away to the country. She and Georgie were going to a resort in Sullivan County. Sunday to Sunday, or maybe even longer, if Georgie could catch up on his work before the wedding. There was yet another style of juvenile wallpaper he had to design, and a candy box, the wrapper for toilet paper—and a package for toothache gum. Had he ever finished the advertising art for the Pinfold Crack-Shot Rifle? She'd have to ask Walter. Walter would know. It was so hard to keep track of everything—so many endorsements, so many prod

ucts. Everything from ginger snaps to dog-powered cream separa-
tors. There was even a book, *Fuzzy's Advice for Stammerers,* which
Georgie—and Walter, *or* Walter—had illustrated with fifteen pen
drawings. And Georgie used to complain he didn't have enough to
do! The weekly funny was the least of it now, the very least of it.
God, Georgie would groan after spending a full day creating the
bottle label for Pinfold's Asthma Cure or working up the medallion
Fuzzy head to be used on a line of plush robes—God, what I
wouldn't do to draw a nice ax murder again!

Joette was nearing her corner when a nun suddenly approached
her—a nun? alone? at this hour of the night?—and, smiling, tried to
press a holy card into her hand. The Assumption of Mary into
heaven, and a poor picture it was too, Joette saw by streetlamp.
Typically sentimental—baby angels and shafts of golden light. "No,
thank you," Joette said. "You keep it, sister? Thank you, but I don't
have any money?" The nun was very small, almost tiny. Her habit
was brown, and it had a white bib and a triangular wimple that cut
across her forehead just above her red eyebrows. She followed Joette into Sawdust Street, continuing to smile but saying nothing, and
all the while she kept trying to make Joette accept the card. "No,
thank you. I'm not Catholic?" The nun wouldn't give up, though,
and at last she managed to stick it in between Joette's fingers.

Then suddenly Pinfold was there, saying, "You can't have this
one, Mother," and he grabbed the holy card from Joette's hand and
tore it into pieces. The nun said, *"Pin*foo?" and began to shake with
loud laughter; her girdle of heavy beads clacked. "Whatever are you
doing in that awful, awful wig, you little arab?" Joette gaped, then
all at once blasted with terror, she peed, a little, and turned to run—
and ran straight into a big, heavyset man who'd come up from somewhere behind her. He was dressed Western with the leather vest,
the dungarees, the cowboy boots, but on his head was a city slicker's
derby. Hanging out of his pocket was a white handkerchief. He
grabbed both her wrists.

But the nun said, "Let her go."

He did, and Joette ran all the rest of the way home.

The boy came in twenty minutes later, and she was waiting. "I
left the bag of presents outside your door," he said. He'd carried the
wagon all the way up, though, and now he rolled it into a corner, sat

down on his cot, and pulled off his shoes and socks. He could've slept in Georgie's bed—Fuzzy always did—since Georgie spent every night in Joette's room, but he preferred the cot. Army surplus.

Joette said, "Those were friends of yours?" She was seated at the table. She'd made four little squares in front of her, using cigarettes, and half a dozen triangles, using safety matches. She'd buttered a slice of oatmeal bread—to which she'd addressed her question.

"I know them." Pinfold looked at her. He smiled. Then he wasn't smiling, but still he kept staring. His eyebrows moved up. She couldn't say thank you? "You owe me," he said. "Now you owe me."

Joette began to disassemble the squares, sliding the cigarettes, one by one, back into their box. "I want to know that woman's name," she said. "For when I go to the police?" Would she? Not on your life!

"Mother Goose," Pinfold said. "Her name is Mother Goose. But did you hear what I was saying?"

With a fingertip, Joette pushed all the triangles apart, but she left the matches on the table. "Owe you what?" Finally, she looked up, looked at Pinfold. He'd taken off his shirt and trousers. Her eyes widened, and for a moment she imagined that he was going to demand—but no, he lay down on the cot and pulled a sheet over him, up to his chest. "Owe you what?"

"Got a million bucks in twenty-dollar bills?" He laughed. Then she did. "No? Well then, I'll just have to think of something else and let you know." Saying *that* without a trace of facetiousness.

Joette struck a match and lit a cigarette, smoked it. Smoked another, another, sitting at the table watching Pinfold sleep. Fuzzy watched her.

5

Georgie was dreaming, and in the dream he came—by way of a descending elevator, then through a narrow corridor and up a flight of stairs—into his studio to find Walter Geebus, surrounded by thirty-odd sketches, seated cross-legged on the floor directly under a great skylight. Scowling and chewing on a long yellow pencil, Walter quickly turned the pages of an extraordinarily large illustrated book—a mail-order catalog of some sort—that was propped open in his lap. Georgie laughed contemptuously and cast himself into a

chair. What're you searching for *now?* he asked, and Walter replied
gloomily, This picture that you told me to draw? You said you wanted
Pinfold throwing a brick, but I don't know what a brick looks like,
actually. Georgie leaped from the chair and snatched up several of
Walter's preliminary sketches. All of them were identical. They
showed Pinfold in a pitching stance, one foot squarely planted, one
foot raised, and his right arm stretched out in back of him. But nothing in his hand. If you don't know what something looks like—blast
your buttons, Walter, *go see it!* Then Georgie plucked Walter from
the floor and dragged him to the window. He threw up the sash and
leaned out. Pinfold! he called. Pinfold! Down in the yard, the boy
was just about to brain a coal delivery man with a yellow brick.
Pinfold! Run on up here, will you? And bring that with you. Georgie
turned back to Walter. If you want to know what a brick looks like,
look at a brick. You stupid dub!

Finding a picture of one's just as good, said Walter. And it's
quicker. And sticks and stones may break my bones, but names will
never hurt me. Then he looked at Georgie's wrathful face and became silent.

Pinfold ran through the door dressed in the long white nightshirt
and the original yellow derby with the bullet hole, and Fuzzy followed him, romping like a puppy; she leaped onto a couch, sprang
off, scooted under a table, then went dashing around and around the
room. The studio had grown much smaller since Georgie's arrival;
the skylight had disappeared. *This* is a brick, said Pinfold, and he
threw it. Georgie had to duck. It broke the window. That's all right,
Georgie said. This is my house. But do you have *another* one? And of
course Pinfold did, and as soon as the boy produced it—from where?
from nowhere, but then this was a dream—Georgie frowned. He'd
never seen a brick quite so big, or so yellow—golden-yellow. Let me
have that—gently! It looked heavy but wasn't—in fact, it was light
as a balloon—and stenciled across the bearing surface was this
legend:

> Official Pinfold Masonry Unit
> Portnoy & Portnoy
> New York

Damn! said Georgie. They don't have a license to make these!
Walter, come on—we're going out.

But we have work!

We're going *out*, I said!

The two of them left the house, went out the front door, and got into a horse cab. The brickyard was just around the corner. Georgie raced inside and shouted at a little clerk with hollowed eyes until at last a manager was summoned. Do you make this brick? Georgie demanded to know, and when the manager—a roly-poly Jew in baggy pants—admitted it, Georgie grabbed him by his jacket and menaced him with a fist. Do you know who I *am?* You can't just sell these without my say-so. If these cost a nickel, I want a penny. If these are a dime, I want, I want . . .

And Walter said, *Two* cents.

Two cents, said Georgie.

The manager understood and apologized. There'd been a mistake made. Now, if Georgie would only be patient, somebody would run over to the bank right away, right this minute, and bring back whatever Georgie was owed. Cash money. Sit down, sit down, Mr.—

Wreckage.

The manager smiled and disappeared through a door. Georgie went and put an ear to the panel, but heard nothing. Then he put an eye to the keyhole, but saw nothing. He finally sat down on a bench next to Walter. Walter was speaking to an old man with tufty white hair and a red rash around his mouth, and Georgie paid no attention to the conversation till he heard the old man say, But I thought *you* were Mr. Wreckage.

Not *me,* said Walter, *him,* and Georgie stood up and stared at the old man's face suspiciously.

I thought this young fella was you, Mr. Wreckage. The old man turned away and coughed. And I was just asking him how his father—how *your* father is doing. Oh, this is confusing. How *is* your father, Mr. Wreckage? We haven't seen him at all since he got fired. Or did he get sick? I forget. How's he doing?

Georgie began to pace up and down; then suddenly he said, Well, he's coming to my wedding, of course. I'll tell him you were asking for him.

And then Georgie was hurrying down a street and calling over his shoulder at Walter, Of course I meant to invite him. I meant to invite all of them. Just so busy! But I'll invite them now! And I'm sure they'd like to come. Haven't seen any of them since I left home—but I'm sure they'd like to come to the wedding! Now you'll see

where I grew up, Walter. Nothing fancy like where *you* live, but . . .
They turned a corner, and suddenly it was nighttime and the street
and pavement were filled with men and women and children shivering in their underwear and sleeping gowns—and Georgie's old tenement was on fire. Walter said, I've seen pictures of fires that looked
better than this. Georgie ran through the crowd, looking for his
mother, his father, and his brother Jack. He saw old neighbors that
he remembered, but they didn't recognize him—maybe it was his
reporter's derby? his good new suit? his burnsides? maybe it was
because he'd put on some weight? Whatever the reason, nobody
from the building seemed to know him, and Georgie didn't introduce
himself to anyone. His tongue felt thick, as though he'd been drinking raw whiskey.

He stayed there for what seemed a very long time—Walter had
vanished—and he watched the tenement house burn, making drawings till his fingers got too cold. Then, after the blaze was out, he
sneaked on a fire wagon and helped himself to a pair of boots and a
respirator that made him look like a Martian. He burnt his left hand,
though not badly, climbing up through the house—stupidly, he'd
reached for a stair rail. A tread collapsed under his foot, a tongue of
orange flame erupted behind lathing just in back of him. For a moment he thought he would be trapped, that the fire was starting up
again, and he felt more giddy than alarmed. When he finally came to
his old flat, he found the door open and blistered. He stepped inside
and discovered rolltop desks jamming the front room—each one
with its own typewriting machine, melted. No other furniture, no
beds, and the shelves where his mother used to stack dishes and
bowls and cups were filled with ledger books, with cans of lubricating
oil, and with beer mugs containing sharpened pencils. What was
this? A newspaper office? But where was his family? What happened
to them? Then he noticed several boxes of shoe polish standing
against a wall. Was Clarky here? Maybe Clarky could say where his
family had gone. Clarky would know.

He walked through the front room and into the rear of the flat,
and Walter was sitting there on a bench, speaking again to the old
man with the white hair and the facial rash. Georgie leaned against a
wall—it was warm, but not hot—and he listened to Walter say, It's
something I've always done. That's all. I've always made pictures.
Walter glanced at Georgie, but seemed not to know him, and looked
again at the old man, and said, My father—well, *you* know him!—

couldn't draw a circle. Or my mother, either. But I'll tell you who
did get me started, in a funny way. There used to be this man I'd
see. When I was a kid. Young kid. Very young. I guess he was a
crazy man, really, when I think about it now. Lived in the neighborhood someplace. Konopka? Kanaby?

And Georgie said, Konopka! His name was Konopka! And what're
you talking about, Walter—this is my story! This didn't happen to
you! Neither Walter nor the old man took any notice of Georgie's
outburst, and suddenly weak, Georgie sat down on a hill of loose
bricks.

Walter said, This crazy man always carried a big chunk of white
chalk in his apron. An apron with pockets. I think he made change at
a penny arcade, is what he did. Anyway. He'd be walking up the
street and he'd just stop and get down on his knees and take out his
chalk and draw a picture on the pavement. Some of them, *most* of
them were pretty—obscene. Dirty, you know? Filthy. He wasn't
good or anything, this crazy man, but you always knew what he'd
drawn. That was clear enough. And there was a group of us kids, not
a gang, just a group, and whenever we'd see him kneel down to
draw, we'd run over to look. He'd finish and then he'd pick one of us
out, and he'd point and he'd say, That's your mother, you little bastard. She don't do *that* for your old man, but she does it for *me*.
Once—once he picked me out and I didn't know what he was talking
about *really*, but I knew it was terrible. And I believed him. I believed the picture.

So what'd you do? said Pinfold. It was Pinfold now, and not the
old man, sitting on the bench with Walter. What'd you *do?* I
would've killed the guy.

Georgie tried to get up, but the bricks kept sliding and shifting
under his feet and hands, and he kept falling on his shoulder, his
hip—but he called out, I was five years old, maybe. Not exactly the
killing age.

And Walter said, I was five years old, maybe. Not exactly the
killing age.

So what'd you do? Hit him with a stick?

Wish I had, said Walter. No, I went home and stole my mother's
shoes. And then I threw them down the airshaft. He laughed. Jesus
Christ, I threw them down the *airshaft!* Walter was still laughing
when the brickyard manager, accompanied by an armed guard, returned with a money bag—it was the size of a laundry sack and bore

a gigantic dollar sign. He had to drag it across the floor, and he deposited it at Walter's feet. That's mine! said Georgie. Don't you give it to him! and everyone turned then and scowled at him. Walter shook the manager's hand and said, Oh, let him have it. Then he and Pinfold and the manager went into the manager's office—for a drink. The guard sat down and lit a cigarette and, with a dubious eye, watched Georgie come and open the bag. And he chuckled when Georgie reached out, not a banded stack of cash but a jar of shriveled fingers in formaldehyde, then a shirt riddled with bullet holes, then an old shabby black wallet. Georgie threw the wallet aside—it skittered underneath the bench—and, charging across the room, he began to pound on the manager's office door. He tried the knob. Locked. Pounded again. Open up! Open up! He dropped to his knees and squinted through the keyhole—and saw Walter Geebus spread-eagled on a bed with a tiny red hole in his forehead. And Joette in her wedding gown, the veil dashed with blood.

She said, "Do you feel better now?"

"I'm fine." Georgie made himself smile at her; then he rolled out of bed and turned off the lamp that Joette had jumped up to switch on as soon as his moaning broke into a howl. He stood very still now in the muggy dark and told her he was sorry that he'd scared her.

"I guess I'm used to it?" she replied. She'd been sleeping when Georgie came in; she'd waked to him kissing her breasts, his dry lips moving from nipple to nipple. Then, muttering that he loved her, loved her, he'd penetrated her without wearing a safety. But that was all right now. He'd fallen asleep on top of her and become a dead weight, and finally she'd had to get out from under him before he crushed her. And in his sleep he'd said again that he loved her— love you, Jo—and then he'd said two cents, and then he'd said that's *mine,* and then he'd started to moan. She was used to it. "What was your dream?" she asked, even though she knew he wouldn't tell her, because she felt that she ought to. Show him that she cared. He could say I love you; she could ask him about his bad dreams.

"I already forgot it," Georgie said, lying, then felt his way over to the chair where he'd flung his clothing and went through his jacket till he found a stick of chewing gum.

"How did you enjoy your party? Were you surprised?"

"Bet I was! You knew about it?"

"Certainly I knew about it."

"You keep a good secret, Jo."

In the dark, she nodded. "Did Walter show up? He didn't know whether he could make it or not. He wasn't sure if his father would still be away."

"Well, the great man must still be away, because Walter was there, all right." Georgie folded the gum into his mouth, chewed it soft, winced as sugar touched a cavity. "I'll say he was there!"

"What does that mean?"

"Oh, you know Walter. Affable as Gallegher the Office-boy. Amused the hell out of everybody, talking about his father's silly baseball machine. Even had Professor Thom rolling. And *I* had fellas all night long telling me what a cracky I'd found for an assistant. Assistant! He's going around saying he's my assistant. A month ago I'm showing the kid how to thin his ink, and suddenly he's my— right-hand man!"

Joette swallowed. "I suppose you told everybody that he isn't?"

"And embarrass him? No! I *like* Walter, I wouldn't do that to him. I just said yes, yes, I let him rule borders, do a little background drawing. I said, *Assistant?* Well, I think of him more like an *apprentice.* Don't want people getting the wrong idea." Georgie spat the gum into his palm, then pressed the sticky wad of it against the back of the chair. And then he told Joette who else had been at the party, running through a couple dozen names, most of which she didn't recognize, and then saying how surprised he'd been to see so many sketchmen from the *World*—decent of them, he said, really decent of them to put aside their jealousy, but come to think of it, he probably would've done the same thing, for a free meal. *And* a free shoeshine; three of Clarky's boys had been in attendance. "I thought *my* boy might come," he said.

"He was tired," Joette said. "He walked me home." And then she asked, "Any women?"

Georgie laughed. "At the party? Only a couple of nuns," and Joette sat up in bed, startled.

"What *kind* of nuns?"

Georgie laughed again. "I don't know what kind. *Nuns.* They're always invading the saloons. With their little tambourines. Telling everybody to get on home to the wife. *Nun-*nuns."

"*Real* nuns, then."

"What other kind *are* there?" Georgie frowned. "*Fake* nuns?"

"I thought for a moment that you meant—well, prostitutes?"

"I spent the evening at Gombossy's, Jo. Not at some perverse whorehouse. Jesus." And as he slid under the top sheet, getting back into bed, he reached out and tickled her, for being such a goose. She hated being tickled. "Just regular nuns," he said. "No women. Clarky runs a clean party. Much to the chagrin of dubs like Stolley, I can tell you." He folded his hands behind his head, exhaled noisily, closed his eyes. "I can tell you that."

Usually, after waking from one of his nightmares, he would, in a short time, start to feel blissful, as if he'd just smoked a bowl or two of sizzling opium—all because the crisis which had shaken him *had* been only a dream. But tonight, for some reason, he stayed uneasy; his heartbeat had not completely decelerated yet, and he was afraid that Joette might lay her head upon his chest and feel the kick—she didn't, though. He said, "Good night, Jo," and she mumbled the same, and then, lying awake, Georgie tried to reconstruct the dream. He remembered meeting Walter Geebus and listening to Walter pretend to be Georgie and tell someone—Sid McKeon? Clarky?—that story about Crazy Konopka. Who used to draw smutty pictures on the pavement. Crazy Konopka, Georgie said to himself now, and recalled his father telling him—years and years after the incident of the shoes and the airshaft—that Konopka was shot dead in a restaurant because he'd swiped a pork chop off a merchant sailor's plate. *Bang! bang!* said Georgie's father—*bang! bang!*—pointing his index finger at Georgie's gut. Chalk *that* bastard up!

Georgie turned to Joette and listened; she'd fallen back asleep. He touched her hair with his fingertips, then he leaned over and smelled it—perfumed shampoo. Then he stared up at the ceiling once more. She'd been wearing a bridal gown, in the dream. She won't be wearing one of those come Saturday—just a nice dress. In real life she'll be wearing a nice dress. Walter on the bed with a bullet through his brain. Why Walter? There'd been other dreams since April, other dreams of Georgie's that had sprung from that night at Mother Polk's; in most of them, Georgie peeped through a keyhole—or a window, or a crack in the wall—and saw Billy McCord again, but in a few of them—in a few of them, he saw himself sprawled out dead. But why Walter? Jesus Christ, why *not*? It was only a dream. A dream was a dream and meant nothing. He'd dreamed of Walter because—because he'd spent some time with

Walter at the bachelor party and afterwards; in fact, Walter had
been the last person Georgie talked to before coming to bed. Walter
was sleeping upstairs tonight with Pinfold and the dog.

Walter! Going around telling everybody he's my assistant! For
God's sake. And Walter—on the stroll back to Sawdust Street after
the party broke up—Walter saying that he could get over to New
York again on Saturday, that his father would be gone till next Tuesday; Walter saying that if Georgie didn't mind he'd really like to
come to the wedding. Okay? And Georgie saying, It's just going
to be a civil thing, and Walter saying, But can't I come? I'd *like* to
come. Georgie saying, There's just going to be the two of us and
Clarky and a girlfriend of Joette's from the music hall, Pearl Conselman, and Walter, sounding hurt, whining, saying, But couldn't I
come too, if I *wanted?* And Georgie saying no; saying, I told you no,
no! And Walter shrugging and then asking, Aren't your parents
going to be there, at least? And then Georgie saying, being nasty,
Walter, why don't you tell me that great story again about your father's device going *ker-plunk* at Lake Hopatcong?

Sometimes, sometimes Walter could be such a—Pinfold called
him Walter Gee-whiz-bus—such a nuisance. But he *could* draw, and
he could draw in Georgie's style—sure he could! he was *used* to
copying stuff—and for now, at least, he was good to have around; he
was useful. Walter never grew bored drawing dog, dog, dog, Pinfold,
Pinfold—while it drove Georgie almost mad some weeks. Walter
was useful—and he *did* have a few good ideas; the Bread Witch of
Awful Alley, that was his. Good one. Already, Fein & Dandley was
readying a loaf-shaped child's bank, and Perry's Drugstore in the
World Building now served a Bread Witch Sandwich—ham with a
lot of lettuce on pumpernickel. Walter Gee-whiz-bus. He'd probably
show up at the wedding anyway. Georgie smiled. He probably
would! Nervy kid. Clever kid, but nervy. Imagine him saying,
Aren't your parents going to be there, at least? At least! The nerve!
And then Georgie was thinking about his family—or rather, recall-
ing to mind some of the better sketches that he'd made of them years
ago, remembering *those.*

His father belting out his mother's front tooth plus a molar.

His mother asleep on the cot in the front room with a blanket
pulled up over her head and her corny feet sticking out.

His brother Jack standing naked in the sink and crying blue murder as he pissed.

How long had it been since he'd seen any of them? Three years—almost three years. That long? As he'd said to Walter—*said to Walter? when? in the dream,* he remembered now—as he'd said to Walter in the dream, he hadn't seen any of them since the day he moved out on his own. The morning he'd packed his things—in the footlocker he now used to store his reporter's souvenirs—his mother had said, Drop over this Saturday for supper, and he'd promised to. But something had come up. Something had always come up. And they hadn't come looking for *him.*

Georgie folded his pillow in half; he wedged it under his chest and hugged it, and he stared off into the darkness till at last he dropped off to sleep, dreamless sleep.

Recently, as part of a full-page ballyhoo for "Pinfold & Fuzzy," there'd been a biography of Georgie published in a Saturday edition; he'd written it himself, using the third person. It had made no mention of his family or, for that matter, of his life before his newspaper life. The article had begun: "In 1893, Georgie Wreckage joined the *World . . .*"

On Mrs. Bennett's walk, closer to the front porch than the fence gate, there was a galloping horse with a bareback rider, a fat man struggling to carry a block of ice, and a scrawny hobo sawing wood. And two hippos pedaling a quadricycle.

Walter stood from a crouch, rubbing his hands together briskly, then clapping yellow chalk dust from his trousers. Pinfold wandered up and down, looking at the sketches with a perturbed expression, as though he were a critic at a picture gallery. He stopped at the circus rider, and after pulling his wig off and wiping the crown of his head with a hankie, he commented, "I like that one. That one's pretty good, Walt."

Nobody besides Pinfold called Walter Walt. Even his schoolmates called him by his proper name, always had, and he'd never understood why. The nuns would call a Robert Robert, a Eugene Eugene, a Thomas Thomas, a Richard Richard, but the fellas would call

them Bob and Gene and Tommy and Dick. But Walter—he was
Walter to the sisters, Walter to his chums. (Once, he'd told all of his
friends that he wanted them to call him Geeb, but no one had, ever.)
He was Walter to his father and Walter to Nana Mary, and Walter to
Georgie and Joette; he was Walter to everybody—everybody except Pinfold. Walt. Walt Geebus. Yeah! He liked it. He never used to
sign his drawings—he'd always initialed them, in the bottom right-
or left-hand corners—but he'd started to recently, after sitting down
one day and spending a couple of hours inventing what he considered to be a crackerjack signature. Walt Geebus, boxed. When
Georgie had first seen it, he'd said, Your G looks like a number 6, and
your W, Walter—it looks like a fat lady's bottom! But Walt had decided to stick with it anyway, not that he had very much opportunity
this summer to sign many pictures; he was too busy helping to turn
out Georgie's work. He wasn't complaining, mind you—he loved
doing it, he felt amazingly lucky! For now, he was perfectly content
as an anonymous hand. From time to time, if Georgie was out or
Georgie was sleeping or Georgie was drunk or just because Georgie
didn't feel like picking up a pen, Walt had to sign some of Georgie's
pictures—advertising sketches or even the Sunday comic—and he
could do that tiny, scratchy *Georgie Wreckage* and the scrabble underneath it, perfectly. Nobody'd ever know the difference.

It was only nine o'clock in the day and already the temperature
was eighty-something degrees. Walt couldn't stand hot weather,
though he'd never in his life complained about it because all boys
were supposed to love it. He hated the way his scalp prickled when
the humidity was up. He hated being thirsty all the time. And he
hated to sweat. He left Pinfold at the front of the house—"If
Georgie calls down and wants us, come get me, okay?"—and
walked around to the backyard, where there was a hand pump he
could stick his head under and drench.

Mrs. Bennett was outside hanging laundry—nope, no underwear!
She smiled with her mouth full of clothespins, then she spat them
into her hand and dropped them back into her clothespin bag, which
bore a red stencil of a Negro mammy. She said, "How are you this
morning, Mr. Geebus?" Now, here was someone who didn't call him
Walter—but Mr. Geebus was worse. "I understand you were at that
party last night." She shook her head. "You shouldn't be going into
saloons, Mr. Geebus. Not at your age."

"I swear to you, Mrs. B, I drank lemonade all evening," he said blithely. Lemonade with beer.

As Walt was working the water pump—he didn't think he had to ask the landlady's permission to use it; he was *sure* it was all right with her, and he was correct; she brushed a strand of black hair from her eye and grinned almost tenderly—as he was working the pump, Fuzzy appeared from behind a toolshed and trotted across the yard to him. Her water dish was in the grass nearby; Walt got it, turned it over, and gave her fresh. She lapped some, then went over and lay down next to the laundry basket. "Get away, you old hound," said Mrs. Bennett, "you'll shed all over my clean wash!" She picked up a blouse and shook it, sprinkling Fuzzy and sending her back around the shed. Mrs. Bennett watched her go, then turned and looked at Walt with an expression compounded of amusement and chagrin. "Why I let that animal stay here, I'm sure I don't know."

Well, if she didn't, Walt did: The reason why was green, paper, and exchangeable for goods. Georgie was paying double rent for the dog and rent-and-a-half for Pinfold.

"Have they started moving things out yet?"

"Not yet, ma'am," said Walt, pushing his hands through his wet hair, pressing out the water, smiling with pure joy as it ran down his neck. "We're still waiting for Mr. Clark to arrive with his wagon."

Mrs. Bennett reached again into her laundry basket; pulling out a pearl-gray dowager corset with sateen strips, she asked, "You're not by any chance interested in taking over Mr. George's room, are you?"

Blushing furiously, Walt answered, "No, no, sorry, no," and hurried from the yard.

Georgie kept walking to Joette's window and peering out—where the hell was Clarky? "He promised to be here at nine."

"For goodness' sake," said Joette, "the poor man couldn't have gotten home before three. Besides, I'm glad he's late? I've still a few things to get ready." Dressed in a candy-striped shirtwaist and a dark skirt, she was sitting on the bed with a dresser drawer across her lap—she picked out a trinket box now and regarded it with a smile. As a girl of nine, she'd won it, first prize in her school's annual spelling bee—maelstrom: m-a-e-l-s-t-r-o-m; maelstrom. She tossed it into her trunk, which was jumbled with camisoles and wrappers and tights and woolen sleeping gowns, several theatre bills rolled up, a grosgrain belt with a jeweled buckle, a reefer coat, and a tied bundle of last April twenty-eighth's Sunday *World*. She put aside the drawer and went to the window; then she pressed Georgie's fingers and stood on her toes and kissed him on his forehead. And he frowned. Well, she liked that! But he wasn't frowning at her, she realized—it was something that he saw down in front. Joette looked.

Walter on his knees drawing with a stick of chalk.

Georgie said, "Do you see that? Do you?" He seemed—pained. "Do you see what he's doing?"

It looked like a dinosaur to Joette, the kind with the long neck and the little head, and she said so, after a moment's hesitation.

"No, no, no!" Georgie said impatiently. "Look at him! He's *drawing with his right hand!*"

"What's he supposed to use, his teeth?"

"He's *supposed* to be a lefty."

"Well, maybe he's both. Some people are."

Considering that possibility—that likelihood!—Georgie's eyes glittered like agates, then his face suddenly darkened. "He never let on! The conniver!"

Joette laughed: silly George. "Conniver?" she said and laughed again.

She didn't know anything about the Code of the Lefty, being right-handed herself.

Clarky arrived just before ten, and immediately Pinfold and Walt went inside and upstairs to Georgie's room and began carrying stuff down. There were a couple of drawing tables and their stools, and a brand-new Dutch easel—Georgie had announced some weeks ago that he might take up painting, paint some of his old news sketches, though so far he hadn't. There were two handsome valises, also new, but only one was going over to the house in Ninth Street; the other, already packed for the honeymoon, was staying. There were a few lamps, boxes of magazines and art supplies, the souvenir foot-locker—Joette had asked, *Must* you take that? and the answer she'd got was yes—and two paper sacks full of shoes, all pairs recently purchased.

Georgie didn't take anything down himself—he supervised, while gobbling one of the breakfast cakes that Clarky had brought. Up and down went Pinfold and Walt, up and down. A Shirvan rug, a Japenese screen. They loaded things into the back of the wagon haphazardly. A barrel-chested sorrel mare stood between the shafts. Up and down they went, up and down. Several clocks, and a palmetto plant. Up—it seemed to Walt that Georgie was looking at him, well, thoughtfully, a little sternly—and down. Bolted to the curb side of the wagon was a lacquered sign which read: CLARKY'S—THE PASTE THAT'S REMARKABLY BLACK. Walt strolled around and checked the sign on the other side: CLARKY'S PASTE—FOR THE SHOES OF NEW YORK. Up and down.

Joette had a spool table that was going, and a china closet of imitation mahogany. She'd had it two years, and it had stood empty for all that time, a reminder of what sort of life she wanted eventually. Georgie helped to carry that out; then he stayed at the wagon with Clarky, and the two of them roped everything secure. Was that all of it? No, there was Joette's trunk yet, and the gifts she'd got at the music hall. So Walt and Pinfold galumphed back into the house once more. "Jeez," said Pinfold, looking pointedly at Joette as he slung the heavy net bag over his shoulder, "I carried this up last night and now I got to carry it right back down again." Joette allowed herself a tight smile. Pinfold left, but Walt stayed, standing in the doorway with his arms dangling. The trunk lid was still open.

"Just wait a moment," said Joette, "I'm almost done?" She pondered a crepe theatrical wig, shook her head, and tossed it into the wastebasket. Then she went through the dresser drawers one last time, and finally she checked the wardrobe. Oh! good thing she did, too. There, in the back on the floor, was a tube of pictures—the Maid Bridget portfolio. She fetched it out and, glancing slyly at Walt, untied the ribbon. "Want to see something?"

She passed him the pictures. He looked them over, a few of them. "Georgie did these? Is this *you?*"

She laughed. "I'm afraid so."

"When were you a maid?"

"Oh, Walter, I was never a maid! That's a costume."

Walt looked at another picture—Maid Bridget being chased around a dining-room table by a gentleman lecher—and then suddenly he could no longer look Joette in the face; he glanced at the wig in the wastebasket.

"You don't like them?" she asked.

"I didn't say that!"

"It's all right with me if you don't. *I* don't like them. But they're the only pictures Georgie's ever drawn of me."

"Really?" Walt's fingers were damp, he realized, and he handed the full batch of drawings back to Joette, abruptly. She tied them up again and threw the tube into the trunk, then closed the lid with her foot. She handed Walt the lock. He put it on.

"Can you manage that all by yourself?"

He replied, "Sure," staring at the trunk. Then he took a deep breath and said, "Now, if *I* was to draw you, Joette, I'd draw you just the way you are." He was instantly horrified—how could he have said such a thing? Dope! Dope! Dope! He picked up the trunk—in his charged state, it seemed to weigh no more than a sandwich—and carried it, almost trotted with it toward the open doorway. You big dope!

He didn't see Joette grin, but he heard her say, "One of these days, Walter, you'll have to do just that. I'd like it."

And then he floated down the stairs—didn't he? Sure seemed like it.

7

A real dilly! Clarky repeated over and over about the house in West Ninth Street—Number 10, one hundred paces from Fifth Avenue. A dilly! A real dilly! "You've come far in three months' time, m' boyo."

Georgie nodded, and Walt, who had just staggered into the top-floor studio and deposited the big easel in a corner, said, "Well, this *is* America, ain't it, Mr. Clark? Ain't this America?"

Clarky smiled, but not Georgie. "Walter," he said, "I think P needs a hand probably with—something." P? It's what Georgie had begun to call the boy, to avoid confusion—such as this: Walter, what should Pinfold (meaning the cartoon character) do next week? Should we send him to a charity bazaar and see what trouble he can make? And Pinfold (the real one), jutting out his chin, snapped, You ain't sending *me* to no charity bazaar! Thus, for unambiguity's sake, Pinfold was paper, and paper only, while P was skin and bones. P, we're out of coffee; could you scoot down and get us some? The flyswatter, P, the flyswatter—whack that bastard! This package goes up to Twelfth and Broadway, P, and this smaller one to the World Building, eleventh floor—ask for McKeon. P! P! And just the other afternoon, Georgie had risen suddenly from his table—he and Walter had been drawing quietly for several hours—and he'd gone down to Professor Thom's room, where Pinfold—where P—was testing the Professor's kerosene-powered roller skates (too noisy! *putt-putt!* and the wheels kept locking) and he'd said, I have a question. Just thought of it. Is Pinfold your first name or your *last* name? Is it a nickname? P had shrugged, and Georgie had said, I was thinking perhaps it was John Pinfold or Pinfold Jones. John or Jonesy. P said, You want to call me John, I don't care, or Jonesy—makes no difference. And Georgie said, No, no, I just thought . . . , then, waving to the Professor, who had closed one eye dubiously and was chewing on a thumb knuckle, he went back upstairs, sat down again at his board, picked up a penholder, and sucked at the end of it for two, three minutes. . . .

Georgie said, "Let me show you around," and Clarky said, "I hear you got eight rooms."

Georgie had rented the handsome townhouse fully furnished—it belonged to a well-known painter of wildflowers and waterfalls who'd recently divorced his wife and sailed to Europe to live in sin with the infamous French comedienne Anna Madversion; he'd be in Paris for at least a year. "Or till she dumps him," said Clarky. "I've heard a few stories about *her.*"

As they wandered through the rooms, P and Walt finished unloading the wagon.

"What do you think of this?" asked Georgie. "Ain't this something?" The wine cellar. "We're under the backyard," he said, reaching up and touching the ceiling. All the shelves were empty. "P thinks it's swell. I believe he wants to move in down here."

Clarky raised an eyebrow. "Really. I heard that he wasn't coming over here with you."

Georgie gaped. "What're you talking about?"

"Well, understand, everything I hear isn't always the truth. But there's a chance—I heard—that him and the dog are going to Long Branch, 'least for the month of August."

"*Long* Branch? New *Jersey?* Whatever for?"

"To do the same thing they're doing on the Bowery. But for more money."

Georgie began to pace. He took a turn around the cellar, then sat on the bench that ran up the middle of the floor. "He never said anything to *me*. Why would he go?"

And Clarky said, "What I'd like to hear is how come you want him to stay."

"I don't *want* him to stay, I don't *want* him to go. I don't care what he does, really, it's just . . . he can do what he pleases. It's just—he never said anything." He looked at Clarky, then cleaned a fingernail with a tooth.

Clarky regarded his friend. "Let me tell you something, George. Can I?" He sat down and clapped Georgie's knee. "When I first heard that you'd took the kid home to live with you, I figured somebody got the story all mixed up. First—from everything I'd ever heard about Pinfold, he's not the sort of fella to live with *any*body. And second—there was you. I said *George?* Now, why would he bring that little arab home? What's his reason?" Clarky bent over, flicking a wafer of soot from the toe of his right boot. "And I kept figuring that sooner or later I'd hear the reason, and it would be a good one, but so far . . . ? Therefore"—he grinned at his highfalutining—"I'm asking you now: What on earth do you think you're *do*ing?"

"You sound like Joette."

"I know I do. I know it. I heard about that." He winked. "Well?"

"Well, I don't know! It just seemed like a good idea. If it hadn't been for him . . . you know?"

Clarky began to shake his head.

"And it's worked out fine. I think."

"That's not why I'm wagging the old rock."

"Why are you, then?"

"George, I can't figure you."

Georgie smiled.

"And that's *not* a compliment. People I can't figure out make me awfully nervous."

Walt ran over to Washington Square and came back a few minutes later carrying a soft pretzel in each hand. He gave one to P, who said he was obliged, and they sat down on the stoop in front of Number 10, eating in silence and watching passing gents in dark derbies and suits fan themselves with morning dailies. Walt—Georgie's pupil, still!—noticed that, but for two who were clean-shaven and one in ministerial whiskers, all the men wore mustaches; and he asked himself, So? The only women they saw were indoors, peeking out at them curiously from behind window curtains. Fuzzy began to whimper and to paw Walt's trouser cuff, and finally he broke off a bit of pretzel and fed it to her. Immediately, P gave her a much larger piece from his.

"Somebody'd probably run out and shoot you if you tried drawing pictures on the pavement over *here*," P said, getting to his feet. He looked off toward Fifth Avenue and wrinkled his nose, as though he'd caught a whiff of something gamy. He pointed at the ground. "You draw that bareback rider here, somebody run right out and shoot you, probably."

"Here," said Walt, "they'd just call a cop," and laughed, and remembered the time he'd chalked—was it elephants?—on the sidewalk in front of his own house in Morning Street. The neighbors complained—boy, did they!—and later, as he'd scrubbed off the pictures, his father stood in back of him and asked truculently, Just what's the matter with you, Walter? They've invented a thing for pictures, or didn't you know. It's called paper. You mean those white sheets, Papa? Is *that* what they're for?

"All right, they'd call a cop and the *cop* would shoot you."

Walt laughed again, reaching a hand into his pocket and taking out the stick of chalk. "This is all speculation. Should we find out for sure?"

"You wouldn't dare," P said.

"No?"

"No," P said, and after Walt put away his chalk, he smirked, then ran his gaze up the front of the red brick building, all the way to the studio at the top. There, standing at the window wall of small-pane lattices, was Georgie. If there was one thing—and at times it seemed that there was *only* one thing—that P had learned about Georgie Wreckage in two months, it was that he was a fella who liked to gaze out the window. Walt had noticed it as well, and the pair of them had spoken about it once, when Georgie wasn't around. He reminds me of old lady Italians, said P, and, smiling, Walt replied, He just enjoys watching the world go by—it's what he told me, and I told him, well, why don't you just go buy the *World*. He didn't think it was funny. And P said, I don't either. What's so funny?"

"You going to the wedding tomorrow?"

"No," said Walt dismally. "I wasn't invited."

"Me neither. But that's all right. Big deal. It's not going to be anything special. His nibs says it'll be over in two shakes of a lamb's tail anyway. Why get dressed up for *that?*"

Walt shrugged.

"Pretty cheap of him, though. *I* think. With all his loot, he could've had a nice big thing. With shrimps to eat, or like that."

And Walt said, but without much conviction, "That's none of our business, is it?"

P widened his eyes, then shut one. "I seen his chequebook. Four numbers in a row."

"He *showed* you?"

"Did not! I just know where to look."

"You shouldn't have done that, Pinfold. *That's* none of your business, for sure!" He took out his piece of chalk again—and put it away again. "What was the first of the four numbers, do you remember?"

They both laughed, and P said, "None of your business."

"One? Five? *Nine?*"

"Ain't saying."

A roundsman strolled by twirling his daystick, showing off; he nodded to Walt, gave P a hard look. When he passed, P stuck out his tongue and squeezed his crotch.

"Since we're getting personal, here," said P. "How much he pay you every week? And don't say none of my business. That's stale."

"Georgie? He doesn't pay me."

"Get off the earth! You come around, work for him—and he don't pay you? Who works for nothing?"

"*I* do," said Walt petulantly. "Me. I'm having fun." He moved his shoulders. "I'm learning a lot of things."

P frowned and sat down on the stoop again, put his elbows on his knees, pressed his fingertips under his cheekbones. Oh, Walt's learning just *lots* of things—well, la-di-da and kiss my back porch. He raised himself to look for Fuzzy—she was up the street sniffing at a tree—then he sat back down, sulkily. There'd been the day, maybe five, six weeks ago, when P had gone up to the five-and-dime on First Avenue and brought home a pad of paper and some pencils,

coming in to find Georgie—at ten in the morning!—mixing himself a
generous whiskey and water. And P said to him, If a fella wants to
learn how to draw, what should be draw first? Georgie said, What
fella is this? Me. You? Yeah, me—could you teach me? What for?
Georgie's eyes were bloodshot that morning, and his complexion was
gray. What for? Just because, said P. I could help you out. Like
Walter Gee-whiz-bus does. Georgie laughed and took a big swallow
of his drink, then a sip of tea. He laughed again and started to work,
wincing frequently over his sheet of cardboard. I can't *teach* you to
draw, he said five minutes later. You teach Walt. I don't teach Walter—where'd you get that idea? I can tell him when a line is bum or
a picture is all jumbled, but I can't tell him how to draw a *good* line,
or *un*jumble. Do you understand? P nodded, sure, but clearly he did
not. How'd *you* learn to draw? Who taught you, your father? Your
mother? Georgie gave a little start. *No*body taught me. They
couldn't draw a circle. Now, he said irritably, will you kindly amuse
yourself? I have my work here. Go memorize a new joke, why don't
you. And P said, Why don't you *write* me a new joke? I don't get
paid for writing theatre jokes, P. And besides, I don't *know* any
jokes. Then what do you call what you turn out every Sunday—
psalms? Amusing situations one step removed from tragedy, said
Georgie with a wink that was lost on the boy. Now will you
please . . . ? P shut up then and sharpened all his new pencils. Another five minutes passed, and Georgie, without looking up, said,
Drawing's like anything else—if you do it long enough . . . well! And
P smiled, nodded, then said almost inaudibly, Well, *sure!* If you do
anything long enough. . . . Then he said out loud, But what's the
best thing a fella could draw *first*, to get started? A lot of circles? A
jar? A teacup? When Georgie failed to answer, P glanced all around
the room, scanning objects. Fuzzy was snoozing below the window in
a shaft of golden sunlight, and he stared at her for a long while,
considered trying to draw her, but finally decided she was much too
difficult, and drew—a teacup. Georgie, meanwhile, made pouting
faces over his board; he pushed his fingers through his hair, he
sipped at his whiskey. P cleared his throat. Two or three times. He
held up his picture and said proudly, You want to look at this? Is this
a teacup or is this a *teacup!* It was, by his reckoning, *quite* a teacup—
good handle! You want to take a look at my teacup? And Georgie
muttered, Sure, sure, if you want to. If you'll put the water on,

yeah, I'll have another cup. P got up and left, went downstairs, and played checkers with Professor Thom.

Walt asked, "You have your own key yet?"

"What?"

"To the house, here. Have you a key yet?"

P gazed up at Walt sourly. "No. Do you?"

"Of course not, but I'm not going to *live* here."

"Well, maybe I ain't either."

"You're guying me."

"Am not! I don't think I like it much. Over here."

"You're bughouse. It's swell," said Walt, sweeping an arm in a wide arc, like a showman, to indicate the neighborhood. "Where're you going to go, if you don't come here? Back to the alley?" He asked that with an eager, almost jealous smile.

"Alley! Go to blazes! I got money. I work for a living. Me and Fuzzy work for a living—I don't need to live in no alley."

"Then what do you mean to do, get your own place?" Now Walt was truly jealous. The kid—with a flat of his own? If Walt made a list of hankerings, that would top it: his own flat. Followed closely by his own Sunday funny. His own flat, a Sunday funny, and a sexual intercourse. A sexual intercourse, his own flat, a Sunday funny. A Sunday funny, a sexual intercourse, his own flat. They were all very close—they were all up there, topping any list. "What kind of place are you going to get?"

After P thought for a time, he said, "Do I got my own key, you ask me, and I say no. And now we talk about something else—okay?"

Walt was about to protest, he wanted to pursue the matter, but two things stopped him: he looked at P, and P seemed—what's *this?*—on the brink of tears, and then Joette arrived in a hackney.

She stepped out carrying a small piece of tapestried hand luggage, and Walt dashed into the street, offering to carry it.

"That's all right, Walter, thank you. Georgie is still inside?"

"He is."

Joette addressed the potbellied driver: "Could you wait ten minutes? I'll be back." Then she walked across the pavement and up the stoop without even a glance at P. She went into the house.

Walt's sigh was loud enough to make the hackman start to cackle. "Quite a peach, I'll give you that," he observed.

Walt glanced up at him and said piously, "That's no way to talk!"
And thought: A peach? A queen! A queen! A regular queen!

9

Clarky was telling Georgie that he'd heard from a most reliable
source that shredded wheat biscuits and shredded coconut meat
looked like—and then Joette entered the studio.

She smiled. "Look like what?"

"Winners," Clarky finished. "Inside a year there's gonna be
strong markets for both things. Housewives, you know. What I've
heard. And I thought, well, your husband-to-be, here, might like to
invest a few dollars."

Georgie, standing at the window with his back turned to them
both, snorted.

"Are *you* planning to, Mr. Clark?" asked Joette, setting her valise
down on the floor.

"Am I *planning* to? I already have. And there's a cake flour company and a canned goods outfit I'm about to look into a little more.
Twenty beans here, twenty beans there—who knows?" He stared
seriously down at his shoes. "I might be a millionaire yet."

Georgie turned then and inquired, with the slightest tone of contempt, "Giving up on the shoe polish business already, are you?"

"Never! But that's my *base*, George. Which makes all other things
possible, don't it? With help, the Clarky Company pretty much runs
itself now and I don't have to bother myself with the day-to-day
routines. It's the nature of success, George, to delegate. Leaves the
sachem free to climb mountains. Or ladders, at the very least. Why,
you understand what I'm saying, George, sure."

Georgie raised an eyebrow.

"Walter, I mean," said Clarky. "You've got your help now, same
as me."

"Walter's not exactly help," said Georgie. "I let him come
around, he does odds and ends sometimes. He's not *real* help, like
you're saying."

Clarky cast a look which implied, which *announced*, that he'd
heard quite a different story.

"He doesn't draw anything, Clarky. Maybe some background, a little bit, and he might letter a balloon. But I still do everything."

Clarky pulled on his bottom lip, then nodded, and Joette went to Georgie, putting an arm around his waist and turning him completely away from the window. "I'm sure there'll be plenty of ladders—all in good time," she said. "Even if I have to run down to the hardware store myself and carry them home, there'll be ladders." She laughed.

Georgie did not. No sense of humor! He said, rather sharply, "I don't know what the two of you are talking about. Ladders! Coconut! Shredded wheat! All I intend to do is—draw pictures!" Then softening, a forced smile driving the frown off his face, he added, "And get married. Draw pictures, get married—and draw more pictures!"

Once again, as he'd done earlier downstairs in the wine cellar, and with the same mystified air, Clarky began to shake his head.

10

Walt's first efforts had been disastrous, but luckily he could, and did, erase his mistakes with his jacket sleeve. He looked up and over a shoulder at P now and asked him, "Is there an angry mob forming yet? Do you see a Black Maria? Who *says* I wouldn't dare?"

P sat on the tailgate of Clarky's wagon. Fuzzy had insinuated her head under the boy's right arm, and her muzzle was resting on his thigh; he idly rolled her dewlap between his left fingers. He stared into space and gave Walt no reply to his questions—hadn't heard them. However, the coachman had, and he called to Walt from his seat, "You gonna draw her knockers all day long?"

Walt thumbed his nose; then, picking up his yellow chalk stick from the pavement, he continued drawing. The curving lines that suggested Joette's bosoms were the most difficult; he was embarrassed to have to do them at all, but he couldn't very well just leave them off. As he'd sketched them originally, they'd seemed too voluptuous, and then on the next try, far too small. Then too pointy. His cheeks were bright red the whole while he confronted that particular drawing problem—and the damn coachman made his suffering, well, nearly unbearable. Maybe, he thought, I should scuff out the whole thing—forget it! He'd been gripping his chalk so tightly, attempting to get those—shapes—right, that his fingers began to cramp. He switched the chalk from his left to his right hand. And then, with two quick strokes, he made the breasts. Thank God. Thank you, *Jesus,* said Walt to himself and smiled. The sisters at school used to pronounce, as they compelled Walt to hold his pencil, and then later his pen, in his right hand: Jesus is a righty, Lucifer is a lefty.

Finally, Walt moved on to Joette's skirts, and was it ever a great relief to arrive there; he used the side of his chalk to indicate folds. It took only another minute to complete the sketch. Not bad! The facial features were fairly stylized, but what else could you expect? He was using chalk. All told, though, it resembled Joette, and it *was* flattering. The sketch said: Pretty Young Woman, and that's precisely what Walt wanted it to say. He signed and boxed his name at Joette's feet.

"What do you think—didn't think I'd dare, did you?" He strolled over to Clarky's wagon, leaned against the sign, then tossed the chalk into the air and caught it; tossed, caught, tossed, caught.

At last, P made a sucking noise. "Who's it supposed to be, Lady Tonsils herself?"

"Looks like lady bountiful to me," commented the hack driver, his hands swooshing feminine curves.

"It's supposed to be *Joette,*" said Walt, frowning, and P pushed out his lips. "What, you don't like it?"

P glared at the sidewalk sketch, then he laughed through his nose and said, "Sure I like it, Walt. *Gee whiz,* it's *swell!*"

"What's that tone for, you want to tell me?"

And P answered, "No. As a matter of fact, no."

Walt shrugged with phony indifference, but moments later, hearing the door of Number 10 open behind him, he stiffened like an army cadet and paled. Here she comes! And Walt tingled from head to foot, suddenly feeling very weak, weak enough to plop. Only it wasn't Joette, it was Clarky, who adjusted his cap, then trotted briskly down the steps whistling "Beautiful Dreamer." He gave up the tune, however, and just whistled a high-pitched note of approval when he spotted Walt's yellow sketch on the pavement. Scrutinizing it—he walked a complete circle around it—he pressed his lips together so hard that his chin dimpled. He went over and clapped Walt on the shoulder. "I *heard* you could draw, Hoboken," he said, climbing into the wagon. Then he glanced around at P and the dog. "You two ready?"

P nodded, and, releasing the brake, Clarky called a chirp to the horse in the shafts.

"Hey," said Walt. "Hey, Pinfold—where're *you* going?"

Lifting the front of his wig, as though tipping his hat, the boy said, "See you soon, Walt."

Soon? Hardly.

11

She'd written a list, and once Clarky left, she'd read off everything to Georgie: Remember to set the alarm for eight, remember to take the rings and the license, remember to take your *suitcase*, the train tickets, and to remind Clarky to tip the city clerk—do you think five dollars is enough? And now, folding up the paper, she looked at Georgie and said, "Promise you won't forget—" but he didn't let her finish; he touched a fingertip—there was India ink in the whorls—to her mouth; then, removing it, he bent over and kissed her, and taking her hands in his, he drew her off the stool. He began to waltz with her around the studio.

"I won't forget anything," he promised, and around and around they waltzed. Georgie was a poor dancer, Joette—naturally—a good one. She let him lead, however, and she smiled at him—Maid Bridget, ye pretty thing!—and she felt as if she might cry.

It had been Joette's idea, her *decision* to have a private wedding and no reception, and when she'd informed Georgie of that, some time ago, he'd been flabbergasted. He'd assumed always that she wanted the works: carriages and Mendelssohn, the sacrament and confetti, roast beef and a cake with figurines on top. But oh, no, she'd told him, oh, no, the quieter the better. Intimate, she said. No church, no *chapel*, no music, no hall. Let's—let's just be ourselves? No fancy dress. No morning suit. Please, George? And no wedding gown. Georgie had scratched his head, then and on several occasions afterwards, thinking about it. A civil ceremony was quite all right with him—like most newspapermen, he was a pagan—but he simply hadn't been able to fathom, and still he couldn't today, why Joette—the daughter of a minister!—wouldn't choose to get married

in a church. No dearly beloved? Georgie was baffled. But whatever
you want, Jo, he'd told her, I'll go along, sure. Whatever you want.
Or don't want.

And what she didn't want was to have to wear a bridal gown. That
was it, entirely. She knew, because she knew herself, that she
would've felt like a fool and a counterfeit putting on a white gown.
Perhaps she would've worn one—not perhaps; she definitely would
have—had Georgie been the only man she'd ever had relations, intimate relations, with. But there'd been other men, nearly a dozen
others, some of whom she'd slept with out of love and some simply
for advantage, and Joette—Joette had her pride. She would debase
neither a symbol nor herself. She had her pride, and she was done
with costumes. And so, since there'd be no dancing tomorrow, they
danced now, she and Georgie, around and around the studio, around
and around again. . . .

"I promise to remember to set the clock for eight," he said, "and I
also promise to remember—do you?—how I used to lurk in the front
hallway at Mrs. B's, sometimes for as long as an hour, praying that a
certain young lady would come down the stairs and then—Oh, Miss
Davey! Nice to bump into you! How *are* you today? And I promise to
remember the rings *and* the license *and* the time that a hornet stung
you on the thumb just as I was about to kiss you with all my might,
and for only the third time *ever*. I promise to remember that, Jo—I
love you, Jo—and I promise to remind Clarky to tip the clerk."

"And don't forget your *suitcase*—see, you've forgotten that already!"

They both laughed and kept waltzing, and some of the things that
Joette reckoned *she* would always remember, since she'd remembered them till now, passed in pictures through her mind. She and
Georgie, when he was still at the theatre drawing caricatures, sneaking off into the alley between shows just to talk—Georgie talking
about how he wanted, *thought* he wanted since the money was good,
to illustrate books one day, saying, Wouldn't it be swell, Jo, to draw
pictures for a new novel by Mark Twain or Edward W. Townsend?
And wouldn't it even be sweller to get sent out West! By a magazine!
Bet I could draw Indians good as Remington. Or China, Jo. Or Tim-
buktu! Have a look around and send back sketches! And Joette saying, You can *paint* pictures too. Why not? All artists should paint—
you'd become famous, I'm sure. And Georgie shaking his head, telling her, I don't know the first thing about mixing colors, then Joette

saying, Oh, it's all very simple, I learned it in school: Blue and yellow make green. Yellow and red make orange. Red and blue make purple. Black and white make gray. . . . Waltzing now, Joette smiled to herself, then frowned, remembering suddenly one autumn night, after Georgie had begun to work at the newspaper—remembered lifting his hand tenderly from her breast and bringing it to her lips and kissing his fingertips, then smelling the stink of the river on them because he'd spent most of the evening in a police rowboat looking for floaters. And Joette remembered the day she'd come into Georgie's room and found him hammering a cleat into the floor below the window. If there's ever a fire, God forbid, he'd said, we can loop a rope through this thing and climb right out. Don't want *us* to die young! And he'd showed her the rope that he intended to keep nearby always for such an emergency—it was a gallows rope, another of his macabre souvenirs, and she'd stared at Georgie in profound shock. And waltzing, waltzing, she remembered too the night Georgie had been sick with ague, racked by chills, and he'd leaped from bed, then stumbled to his footlocker and brought out a blanket dark with bloodstains and wrapped himself in it. They waltzed without music, around and around the studio floor mottled with hard blobs of palette color, Georgie dancing with his eyes closed, and Joette with hers open. And she remembered the day—only last April? a Sunday—the day she'd found, discarded under the drawing table in Georgie's room, those first pencil sketches of Pinfold and Fuzzy, and seen in them—believed, *wanted* to believe, she'd seen in them—a quality that she hadn't seen in anything of Georgie's for so very long. Pity? Sympathy. Then how she'd pestered Georgie later on—in the balloon!—to find out, to find out for *her,* she kept saying, whether the dog had lived or died, to find out what had happened to the small boy, pestering him till finally he'd grown sullen. Those sketches, she thought now. Two or three of them, hastily done—but because of them, here we are today, waltzing in a fine house and marrying tomorrow. And what happened to the dog? She lived.

Joette stopped dancing, abruptly.

"What?" Georgie asked her. "Have I crushed your feet?"

"No," she said, and put a wrist to her mouth.

He frowned, concerned. "What the *matter?*"

Joette shook her head. "Nothing. Really. It's just—there's a cab waiting. I'd forgotten! I should go." She was on her way to meet Pearl Conselman—more shopping to do for the honeymoon. She was spending the night at Pearl's flat. "And you've promised, don't forget, to go back to Sawdust Street later. Don't sleep here? Promise? This house is for you and me."

Georgie picked up Joette's valise and nodded. "I won't forget," he said.

And they walked together across the studio and out. . . .

12

Da-dum!

"For Christ's sake, Walter, how old are you, *ten?*"

Walt's eyebrows jumped, his cheeks turned crimson. He gulped, struggling for comic effect, then stuck his chalk into an ear—that clown!—and replied, stoutly as he could, "Seventeen. Almost."

"Seventeen," said Georgie promptly. "Well, who'd ever guess? You sure don't act it. This isn't a playground, Seventeen. And this isn't *your* house, Seventeen. And you've drawn a left hand on the right arm—typical."

But Joette, who'd been regarding the pavement sketch with much interest, glanced now to Walt, the very tip of her tongue appearing at the corner of her mouth and pushing her high lip into a subtle and crooked smile. She winked. Then ladylike, she walked to the carriage, her skirt softly swishing.

Georgie, catching that furtive wink, scratched his chin with a knuckle—and delivering the valise across the sidewalk, he scuffed, purposely blurring Walt's fancy-pants signature. *Who* wasn't acting his age, for sure?

13

"He said that?"

"He did."

They were approaching an intersection. Clarky tugged on the reins. A teacher marched her minor-school pupils across the street, and as she did, she pointed to a sewer plate and in a high chirpy voice, said—Clarky heard her say, and immediately he committed it to memory—that the plate had been manufactured in Toledo,

Toledo was in northwestern Ohio, Ohio was the seventeenth state to join the Union. "Does anyone know when? Eighteen-oh-three, of course." 1803. 1803. 1803. Of course!

"And that's *all* he said?" P climbed up front. Look at his shoes, would you! Dull, *dull,* the leather raw at the toe. Little nobody, thought Clarky. "That's *all?*"

"I told him what you asked me to, and that's what he said, yeah. It's what I heard him say. He doesn't care *what* you do. You want to go to Long Branch, you just go right ahead and go."

They were moving again, and Clarky began to roll his tongue around in his mouth, to stab it against his cheek, and against his teeth, which were clenched now. He had been planning to scoot uptown to a milliner's after lunch and buy Joette a tailored toque hat for a wedding present, but maybe that wouldn't be necessary. Maybe he could save himself the trip, *and* a few dollars that he might put to better use—Swans Down cake flour!—*and* give Joette what he'd heard she *really* wanted. To be rid of the boy. Clarky could understand her wanting that, all right. Two's company, three's a crowd. This is America, ain't it?

"So I hear it's pretty nice at Long Branch," he said. "Lots of swells there in August. Can you dip? If you can, you could probably make a lot more money just roving the boardwalk than working in a theatre every night. Can you dip?"

P frowned. Dip? Clarky shrugged. He had dips on the brain, he guessed, ever since he'd let the gangster Shag Draper talk him into hiring some pickpockets as shoeblacks to fleece the track crowds at Monmouth Park. Very profitable, so far.

"But didn't he say anything—else about me?"

"Who, George? Like what?"

"Like—oh, I don't know!"

"Well, he did say *that.*"

"That?"

"That *he don't know.* When I asked him how come he moved you in with him in the first place: I don't know, he says. I don't know. Said it seemed like a good idea. *Seemed* like."

"So, he's got some gripes, does he? Let's hear 'em!"

"Now, kid, he didn't mention anything about any gripes. Specifically. So don't you go jumping to any hasty conclusions—hear me?"

P hooked an arm over the back of the seat. "You listening to all of this, Fuzz?"

"And even if he *does* have gripes, Georgie's not the sort to complain." Chicken's gone up another two cents a pound, Clarky heard as they passed three women talking on a corner.

"Complain! Why should he? About what? His jimjams? Complain. The son of a bitch—the son of a bee has that silly doodle from Hoboken to draw for him, me to run all his goddamn errands, and *her*, her to—sink it in. And six thousand five hundred and four dollars in the bank. Aw, he's crazy anyway. I knew it soon as I met him. I did! Pegged him right away for a crazy man. Ask that Mr. Thom if I didn't."

Clarky's eyes had opened wide. *Six* thousand five hundred and *four*? *He'd* heard *four* thousand six hundred and *ten*. Georgie-porgie, pudding and pie. And pie!

"Here he's living the life of Reilly on *account* of me—and he's got the crust, the fucking crust to complain *about* me? Well, he can go to hell, *he* can!"

"Right," said Clarky. "And you can go to Long Branch."

14

Back at his studio window, Georgie stared impassively down into Ninth Street. Not much going on. A nursemaid leading a sailor-suited little boy with curled hair returned to Number 13, a butcher made a delivery next door. A few minutes ago, over at 19, a man had stepped outside, cautiously, then turned around and kissed a woman behind him in the doorway. He'd squeezed her hand before hurrying away, in the direction of Sixth Avenue. And Georgie had immediately jumped to the conclusion of adultery. She was beautiful—Georgie hadn't seen the woman's face, but he imagined now that she was beautiful—and her lover, from the spruced, clean-shaven looks of him, was a lawyer. Juicier: a lawyer for Tammany. And her husband was a—a professor of art, let's say. Chopped His Faithless Wife Almost to Pieces. Pictures by—

"That fellow Dieffer I was talking to at your party last night, Georgie? Told me that he once got Hetty Green to sit for a sketch. Fooled her by saying that what he actually wanted to draw was her dog—and she let him into her flat. That true?"

Nodding, Georgie half turned from the window wall and looked over at Walt, seated at one of the drawing tables and stretching his

arms above his head. "Yeah, that's so. It's a true story." He bared
his teeth in a small grin, nodded again, and gazed back out the window. Directly below, the pavement where Walt had drawn his Joette
was blank and almost dry. Georgie had insisted that Walt scrub off
the chalk—before the neighborhood sent a delegation, he'd said.
And Walt, on his way into the house to fill a bucket, had said, with an
edge to his voice, Aren't you going to ask me what paper is for? But
if that was supposed to be a joke or a quip, Georgie hadn't got it.
That wasn't terribly unusual, though. Their funnybones weren't in
the same place.

"Say, George, maybe—maybe if we tell her we just want to
sketch her breadbox, we could get Hetty Green to sit for *us!*"

"Why would you want to bother—when you can just go look up
Dieffer's sketch?"

"I was only making a joke," said Walt, and laughed. Back to
work. He was roughing out a series for the Sunday comic, in which
over twelve large panels Pinfold steals a fresh-baked pumpernickel
from the Witch of Awful Alley, is chased by her (over barrels, across
a mountain of ragbags, through an areaway, up the fire escape) is
tackled by her (on the roof), and is hocus-pocused by her into a
gingerbread boy. Then, just as he's about to be dunked by her into a
steaming mug of tea, Fuzzy licks him awake.

The sequence was entirely Walt's—oh! except for the part about
the steaming mug of tea; that was Georgie's contribution.

This cartoon—to run a week from Sunday, on the fourth of August—would be the fourth consecutive one to use panels instead of a
tableau, and Walt had been responsible for that change in format.
The very first day Georgie had let him help out with some studio
chores—You might as well be of some earthly use, since you're always hanging around here anyway, Hoboken; cut me a piece of
cardboard eighteen by twenty-four—Walt had brought up the idea.
You could tell a little story that way, he'd said. A little funny story
with a beginning, a middle, and an end—like it's done sometimes in
magazine cartoons. Is there some law says you can't do it in the
funny papers? What do you think? It's an idea. And Walt had kept
bringing up his idea, and for nearly a month Georgie kept dismissing
it, out of hand.

Georgie *liked* the single-panel format just fine; he was comfortable
with it. It was how he'd always drawn his news work, and besides, it
allowed for hubbub. Pinfold and his friends playing war with mop

carbines and plenty of catsup, raiding the dago's cart for lemonade,
rioting over the appearance of a truant officer or the dogcatcher,
having their eyebrows singed and their fingers blistered by a store-
bought rocket—while above them in a tenement a housewife
screamed at the noise and a man in his undershirt prepared to douse
the gang with a bucket of swill, or whitewash, or bathwater. Action
everywhere; simultaneous, sprawling, exaggerated (but not *too* exaggerated) action, with Fuzzy generally standing off by herself,
looking bemused and making some kind of wisecrack—Up goes the
rocket's flash, up goes their papas' cash, all ends in smoke. Sure! Dis
is America, ain't it? Ain't dis America? Roughhouse action and a
smart-aleck comment: that's what made a funny picture, that's what
made a picture funny. Georgie believed it, and hadn't he been
proved right? You couldn't argue with success. And you shouldn't
tamper with it, either.

But eventually he did tamper. Let Walt talk him into trying a
sequence. Because? Because several other *World* cartooners—including the well-known F. M. Howarth, who'd come over to the paper from *Puck*—suddenly began to break down *their* Sunday space
into panels, and Georgie didn't want to seem unadventurous, he
didn't want to seem *hidebound*. And because, frankly, Georgie was
running out of inspiration for his tableaux, while Walt—Listen to
this one: Pinfold buys a hen, so Fuzzy can have all the eggs she
wants, and—Walt was just brim*ful* of funny little stories. And finally
because of the great flap caused by his cartoon of June thirtieth, The
Unreliable Lifeguards of Awful Alley—ow!

Well, Georgie, Sid McKeon had said about *that* one, You've managed to offend everybody, congrats. Anarchist and Tammany wind-
bag alike—and you have the distinction of having been lambasted
by the Reverend Charles H. Parkhurst in his pulpit. And poor Mr.
Fein. You remember Mr. Fein, George, the toy man? You've put him
into the hospital. Nervous collapse. So is this the end of Pinfold, Sid?
Tomorrow I go back to chasing ambulances, do I? Oh, let's not be
hasty, George. This'll blow over. Just don't—in future, just don't
stick any more drowned children into your pictures. Could you do
that for us? And from here on, George, you're gonna have to get
your funny to us on time. No more Friday afternoon shit. If it'd
been here on time, George, maybe somebody would've had a
chance to *look* at the damn thing before it got sent to the engraver's.
Handsome Sid had nearly lost his job over that cartoon, and he'd felt

like clubbing Georgie to his knees for having drawn it, but he'd restrained himself, of course. Since he hadn't yet become engaged to a rich man's daughter, he needed to hold on to his job, and Georgie— still—was a valuable man. They said upstairs, through clenched teeth.

The *World* had apologized to its readers for Georgie's cartoon on the front page of that Monday's paper, all editions, and by the end of the week, as Sid had predicted, the hoopla died. But it had taken its toll on Georgie. He'd felt foolish, he'd felt chastened, *mortified;* nothing he'd ever done before, and of course he'd drawn some pretty raw scenes as a reporter, had ever brought such criticism down on his head. But Georgie, Joette said, looking at him wide-eyed, what did you *expect?* You're making pictures for *children* now. For *children.* You'd do well to remember that. But, but. No buts, George. But, *Jo,* have you ever seen *Max and Moritz?* That German picture book *for children?* Max and Moritz get chopped up at the end and fed to the chickens. This isn't Germany, George. This is America. So, Georgie suffered, though what troubled him the most about the whole business, and naturally he kept it a secret, was this: He had absolutely no recollection, none, of ever having drawn that particular cartoon.

He remembered being in McSorley's drinking, and he remembered thinking from time to time that he really ought to get off his duff and go home or over to the World Building, because if he didn't crank a picture out today, it would be too late. And he remembered wishing that Walt were around—but Walt was away that week, at Lake Hopatcong with his father. And he remembered talking to a reporter from the *Herald* who'd just come back from Long Island, where three small girls had drowned in Hempstead Lake. And he remembered leaving the saloon and hailing a cab on Seventh Street—but then he remembered nothing more till P woke him in his bed, saying, Another bad dream, Jim?

The Unreliable Lifeguards of Awful Alley had been followed the next Sunday—the seventh of July—by a sequence called Pinfold & Fuzzy Meet the Bread Witch of Awful Alley, and She's a Real Meany! Walt had done the script and the breakdowns, Georgie the pencils, Walt the inks and the color indications. The Bread Witch, George—I think she ought to come back from time to time. We need a few more regular characters, anyway.

We.

❑ ❑ ❑

Georgie went over and stood in back of Walt for a minute and watched him draw. Walt's hand, Georgie's style. One afternoon Walt had said with that exuberance which Georgie found so irritating, Want to see me do Outcault? Want to see me do Frost? I can do Opper too—button nose, no chin, coming right up! Georgie said, "Walter?"

"What?"

But Georgie shook his head, then walked to his own table and sat down. His supplies hadn't been unpacked yet, though, and since he didn't feel like hunting for the right carton (as Walt had done), he got up and borrowed Walt's T-square, one of Walt's pencils, Walt's pad of tissue paper. And he said, "Walter?"

"What?"

Georgie sucked on his teeth. Finally he said, "Well, when I'm away, if you'd like to come over, it'd be . . . all right. There are some things I can see we won't get to today."

Walt nodded, waiting.

"I've made a few roughs for the candy box. If you have the chance—if you *can* get over, you might redraw them. But exactly as I've done them. And you can call a messenger to take them uptown." Georgie had a telephone! He was, he'd been told by the Bell Telephone Company of New York, Subscriber Number 14,224. Hello, Central? "That is, you can call a messenger if P isn't around."

Walt nodded again. "I don't know if I'll be able to get over once my father—"

"If you can't, you can't," Georgie said and returned to his table. He sat down, flipped open the pad, and doodled Pinfold heads. Damn wallpaper. What do I know about designing *wallpaper?* The only wallpapers Georgie had ever seen had had flowers. "Walter?"

"What?"

Georgie tapped his pencil. "Did—did P say when he'd be back?"

"No, he just said he'd see me soon."

Georgie sketched Fuzzy at a gallop, stared at it, then pushing out his lips, he drew a variation: more action. "Walter?"

"What?"

"When you go back to school—in September? What're your plans?"

"Oh, I probably could get away maybe three afternoons a week. And most Saturdays. If Mrs. Cuff needs me."

Georgie lightly scratched at his scalp with his pencil point. "Walter?"

"Yes, Mrs. Cuff?"

"Walter . . ."

They exchanged a look, then Walt wet his lips. He turned all the way around on his stool, hooked his shoe heels on a rung, and leaned forward, elbows on his knees. His eyebrows moved up, moved down, moved up. "Is there something—you want to say? I'm really sorry about that business with the chalk. I don't know why I do some things. My father's right, I guess. I—"

"Walter, you never told me that you were able to use your right hand."

Walt shrugged. "I can't, really."

"I *saw* you using it to draw this morning. At the boardinghouse. If you can draw with it, you certainly can *use* it."

"Nuns, Georgie. Did you ever have nuns in school? No? Well, they won't *let* you use your left hand. They give you no peace, call you all kinds of names. A lefty's got no choice b-b-but t-to g-g-give in."

Georgie grinned, couldn't help it. "What's this business? Buh-buh? What's that?"

"It makes you stutter, George. When you're a lefty and they make you change to righty."

"*You* don't stutter."

"No, not me," Walt replied, straightening up. "Not me."

"Why not?"

"I'm just smart, I guess."

Georgie laughed then.

"I know it sounds conceited, but it just so happens to be the case here. See, a lot of lefties, *most* of them, will turn obstinate, or if not obstinate they'll get into a panic, when somebody with the clout—in my situation, the nuns—makes them switch hands. That's stupid. If you're smart, you don't let anything bother you. You go along. If you can't do anything about something, go along, I say! And something positive is bound to come from it." Walt held up his hands in front of his face. "So now I write righty fine—and draw righty okay. And if ever I was to lose a hand—well, I wouldn't starve to death, would I?" A bright gleam had shot into his blue eyes. "Would I?"

"Very fascinating," Georgie said.

"Just good sense."

"But Walter," said Georgie to his pencil point, "you never mentioned it to me. And you never have drawn with your right hand when *I've* been around."

"I don't do it often."

"Ah. Well, it doesn't matter, does it. It's just—interesting."

Walt nodded again, and his big smile faded, to be replaced by the slightest curl of his lips. "I suppose it is."

A short time later, Georgie tossed down his pencil and sighed. "I wish to heaven P was here—he could run out and get us a growler." He scanned the drawings he'd done in the pad: ten little Pinfolds in a variety of gymnastic and wise-guy poses, and half a dozen racing Fuzzies. "I'm parched," he said.

"If you'd like," said Walt, "I'll go. I really wouldn't mind stretching my legs."

Georgie was already pulling coins from his pocket. "I think there's a pail in one of the cartons you left at the foot of the stairs." He stuck out his arm for Walt to come and take the money.

But Walt, already at the studio door, shook his head, no.

"Let me get it. My wedding present to you." Then, just as he was leaving, he turned back to look at Georgie. "I *am* a true lefty," he said. "Of that there is no d-d-d-doubt." And, laughing, he ran down the stairs.

Georgie took out his cigarettes, smoked one, then suddenly he whirled from his chair, crossed the studio, sat down at Walt's table, and began to ink.

WHY P(INFOLD) WAS SURE THAT FUZZY WOULD DIE

At Long Branch one morning in the second week of August, P woke to find his dog in bed next to him and shivering. When he touched a finger to her nose, her nose was dry. She didn't eat all day—wouldn't even sniff the strawberry torte that he'd gone and bought specially for her at a bakeshop. Her stool was soft and black. The whites of her eyes looked blue. P became frightened. Around six thirty, when Alvin McCoy arrived to walk with them to the theatre, Fuzzy roused herself from a long sleep and drank a lot of water. Her legs no longer seemed wobbly then. "She's okay," said Alvin. "Don't worry about her. She's fine." But no, she wasn't. At the first show that evening, she began to bleed heavily from her nose. Then she collapsed. Several middle-aged ladies in the audience fainted. Is there a doctor in the house?

Immediately, P carried poor Fuzzy back to their attic room in Bath Avenue, and after covering the mattress with newspapers he'd found on the porch—in case she hemorrhaged again, he didn't want her to stain their landlady's sheets—he laid her down on the bed. "You're all right," he told her, climbing in next to her, fully dressed. "There's nothing the matter. Please, God." Oh, why had he ever gone down the shore? This was his fault. "What's the matter, Fuzz?" Maybe it was the salt—she was a city dog, and maybe it was the salt air bothering her. He got up and closed the window. Salt can be dissolved. "How about drinking some more water, girl?"

Later, there came a knock at the door. It was Alvin, home from
Kelly's Seabreeze Song Hall, and he was with another vaudeville
man named Taffy, who also boarded here at the widow's house. Besides being Fuzzy's stage voice, Taffy did an act in which he swallowed eighteen (telescoping) United States Army bayonets. P didn't
like having Taffy come into his room, because Taffy was a thief and
managed to steal something nearly every visit. He'd already stolen
P's lucky stone—the one that looked like a skull—P's black derby, a
few pairs of P's drawers—Taffy was a *very* small man—and P's
blond hairpiece. Now, what would *I* do with a wig? I got a fine head
of me own hair. I never took your silly wig, and I should flatten you
for even *suggestin'* I might've. It must've blowed off your head in
the storm last night. Baloney! He'd swiped the wig, all right. And
probably sold it. Alvin had said to P, Just keep your eye on him,
that's all. He's not *really* a bad sort. Different people, different brain
juices. Alvin was mild in temper and generous of spirit—Christian,
declared the Widow Orleneff; from his corns to the crown of his
head; he's a fine man, his negritude notwithstanding. Alvin was what
people back then used to refer to as Bright or Yellow, meaning a
light-complected Negro—and Alvin the Yellow would not speak a
harsh word about anyone. For that, P thought him a little crazy.
Taffy had stolen repeatedly from Alvin, yet Alvin continued to give
the bastard haircuts and shaves and to play checkers with him. Taffy
had stolen Alvin's watch, some cash, some more cash, Alvin's rain
slicker, and he'd even tried to steal Foggy, but Alvin caught him and
made him put it back. Foggy the Clown. Alvin's dummy. Alvin was
a ventriloquist.

"How's our girl?" he said now, coming into P's room. "Feeling
any better?" He walked softly to the bedside, and because of the
way that he bent over Fuzzy, gradually and with a grimace, and
because of the way he stroked her flank, using both hands, P recollected, miserably, the kitchen visit of Doctor Narcoticus, ten million
years ago when dogs could talk. Maybe she'll pull through. Maybe
she won't. And suddenly—suddenly the boy felt bee-headed, absolutely sure Fuzzy would die. When things that happened before,
happen again, they happen—with a difference. Fish-scale clouds
mean a change in the weather. A dream of smoke and fire? Your
closest friend's a liar. P jammed his wrist into his mouth so that he
wouldn't scream.

"In the morning," said Alvin, standing up straight, "we'll go find a vet. There must be plenty of them around here, on account of the horse farms."

And Taffy—who'd sidled over to the bureau and pocketed what he believed were cannon crackers but were actually sticks of Artificial Midnight—Taffy said, "What're you gonna do, kid, if she cashes her cheque? You got obligations, you got a contract—how're you gonna keep working? Have her stuffed?"

Five
WAR OF THE DERBIES

1

He did it every morning: When the toast popped, Georgie would lower his newspaper and look at the machine with grave suspicion, as if it might explode. Then, spreading the paper in his lap, he'd lean forward, elbows on the table, and stare at the Toaster of Tomorrow while chewing on his underlip. Some days he'd smile, some days he'd frown, and some days—some days he'd lean back and make a remark so completely out of the blue, so utterly unconnected to any conversation they'd had so far that morning, that Joette would laugh. He might say, If we ever needed a plumber, I've no idea who's reliable. We should ask a few of the neighbors. Or, Didn't you tell me the highboy was coming *next* week? Or, Those new shoes of yours aren't a good fit; why don't you take them back before you hurt yourself? She'd always laugh, but later—usually later the same day—she'd remember, and puzzle over, that laughter when the waste stack sprang a leak, or the chest of drawers was unexpectedly delivered, or when she twisted and mildly sprained her ankle on the stairs. What would you call it? Second sense? The things you learn about a man when you live with him every day.

It was November now. They'd been married three and a half months. Georgie had nearly ten thousand dollars in the bank, a small fortune. Joette was not pregnant, a big disappointment. Georgie had put on twelve pounds—liquor weight. Joette had changed her hairstyle (it took her nearly an hour a day to groom herself). They occasionally attended the uptown theatres, occasionally dined at Rector's or Delmonico's. Mr. Wreckage: good evening, sir. And *Mrs.* Wreckage. Joette had been learning to do crewelwork—there were classes at the Ladies' Lyceum. Georgie had started to paint— Tenderloin night scenes, mostly, and mostly in black and shades of gray.

Joette had written a letter the other week to Pearl Conselman, who'd moved to Chicago: Our future is still nice-looking. *Today,* though, I read a book cover-to-cover. And this evening? Perhaps another book as George is going out with his painter friends again. I've told you about his new friend Gulp, haven't I? Who's been arrested *three* times for disorderly conduct? I *must've* told you about him. Gulp! His real name is Jim *Sip.* But Gulp, I admit, does suit him better. George tells me that he used to be a fire artist (that's a grown man who draws burning buildings, Pearl!) for the Philadelphia *Record.* He and George and a few others—some that I know and some that I don't know—have a kind of group. Men and their groups! And this group, the whole lot of them, they paint such gloomy pictures, to my eyes. Paint, paint, paint! George's enthusiasm has taken me quite by surprise. He is not terribly good at this point, I'm afraid. And I have learned to loathe the smell of linseed oil! The Sunday cartoon still goes on, as does all the paraphernalia. Latest thing, Pearl: Pinfold galoshes, in yellow, of course. Thank goodness for Walter. He draws for George and plays Hearts with me. Write soon. That same day she'd also written to her father: I only want to let you know that I've married a successful man. Yr. daughter, Caroline. During breakfast, several mornings later, Georgie said, I guess your father still holds a grudge against you for running off, and in that day's post her letter returned marked Not Accepted.

This morning at breakfast, when Joette asked Georgie whether he wanted jelly on his toast or just butter, he replied, with a distracted smile, "I think—I *think* I have an interesting appointment today."

"With whom?"

Georgie shook his head. "Let's just see. Did I say jelly? I wanted butter."

Half an hour later, a messenger came to the door and presented Georgie with a printed card which read:

*Mr. William Randolph Hearst would be pleased
to have you call, at your convenience.*

"Your convenience," said the messenger, "is eleven thirty,
sharp."

The morning being a golden one, he decided to walk to the Row.

Since late September, when Hearst came to New York—in a balloon, rumor had it—and bought the *Morning Journal*, the *moribund
Journal*—at a discount price of $180,000, according to Clarky—
Georgie had been wondering when he'd be invited to join the paper.
There'd been no doubt in his mind that it would happen, sooner or
later. Because the Western millionaire had declared his intention to
buy all of the very *best* newspaper talent in the city: the best editors
and reporters, the best sob sisters, correspondents, *compositors*, the
best *lavatory attendants*! And the best cartoonists. He was doubling,
tripling, quadrupling salaries and throwing in bonuses. Richard
Harding Davis was paid a thousand dollars—and given a gramo-
phone, a dozen new plaid cloaks, a carbine, a Mexican saber, and a
pair of patent-leather boots—just to cover the Yale-Harvard football
game. Stephen Crane was promised Greece, Paris, anyplace on
earth he wished to go—in return for half a dozen Bowery sketches.
A.K. had demanded $500 a week, a covey of English pheasants, and
an Arabian mare, and he'd got it. He defected from the *World* in
early October. Call me Chief, Hearst told every new employee. Call
me Chief. But Santa Claus seemed more correct. And now it was
Goergie's turn to sit in Santa's lap. He'd made his list. He whistled
all the way across town. Ta-ra-ra-*boom*-de-ay.

The *Journal* had rented the second and third floors of the Tribune
Building on Park Row at Spruce Street, across from Printing House
Square, and when Georgie arrived, there was, as there'd been every
single day for more than two months, promotional rumpus in front.
A ten-piece band played Sousa marches, clowns walked around on
stilts, firecrackers popped and popped and popped. Free coffee was
available at delivery wagons lining the curb, and bandy-legged men
in *Journal* aprons stood behind giant cardboard boxes giving away
sweaters and gloves and *Journal* suspenders and *Journal* caps, and
cigarettes in specially prepared packages that said *New York Morning
Journal, W. R. Hearst, Prop.* Newsboys flew by. Uxtry! Uxtry! How

It Feels to Die—By a Man Dead 49 Days! Consuelo Vanderbilt mar-
ries dat Duke! Board of Aldermen a buncha crooks! Uxtry!

On the stairs up to the *Journal* offices, Georgie had to squeeze by
half a dozen cops eating sinkers and a clique of mustachioed Cubans
in loud conference, and then he passed, on their way down, three
jays he knew from the *World*—two reporters and a cartoonist named
Sweeney, who'd briefly drawn a Sunday comic called "L'il Massa,
the African Monkey That Came to New York." They were all grinning like fools, and one of the reporters began to wallop Sweeney on
the shoulder with a rolled-up pad of paper, and Sweeney, stifling his
giggles to cringe and to give his best Negro moan, said, "You can beat
this poor old body, but my soul belongs to William Randolph
Hearst!" They ignored Georgie.

The City Room was further chaos. Over here, two old geezers
were crouched in a corner playing marbles with gold nuggets, and
over there, a buxom woman in her nightdress and carpet slippers
and wearing a hat full of real fruit was stopping everyone to offer the
heartbreaking true story of her life exclusively to the *Journal*. "I
need the money to get to Utah," she said. A couple of athletic-
looking young men—both of them suntanned, which made them
seem, in New York at this time of year, as alien as gorillas—were
having a catch with a head of lettuce. Three other Californians were
practicing the quick-draw and shouting Bang! Bang! Gotcha! A cus-
todian painted a trestle table red. A reporter seated at a desk copied
out on paper something he'd written earlier on his shirt cuff, which,
detached now from the sleeve, was propped against a standard ref-
erence book. At the far end of the room was an elevated platform
protected by wire netting. There, a fat man in a green eyeshade
stood pecking at an invisible-action Remington. Abruptly, he
stopped typing, picked up a telescope, and trained it on the ceiling,
where heavenly constellations and all the known planets had recently been painted.

Georgie approached one of the lettuce-hurlers and asked for Mr.
Hearst. "Our Willy? That way. When you hear tap dancing, stop."

A short, muscular delivery boy was walking ahead of Georgie
down the hall, pausing at every office to call, "Anybody in here
order the Boston beans, the clam chowder and codfish?"

That's not a newspaper office, A.K. had told Georgie following his
interview, that's a lunatic asylum. Indeed. And Georgie loved it.

As he was passing a door with frosted glass, there came a sudden din of several men speaking excitedly at once. Georgie stopped and listened, and then heard *clump, clump, ka-clump.* He knocked on the door, and when no one came he opened it.

William Randolph Hearst, the most awkward-looking young man—he was thirty-two at the time—that Georgie believed he had ever laid eyes on, was doing a clumsy dance—more a jig than a tap—around a stack of *Evening World*s on the floor. As Georgie stepped into the office, Hearst kicked at the stack and the top several papers flew into sheets. He was dressed in a dark-brown suit, a hard-brimmed straw hat, a bunched ascot tie. His shoes were light brown, and his feet were enormous. His *hands* were enormous. He was long-bodied and long-faced. His eyes were deeply set and set widely apart. His skin, California or no California, was snow white. There were four other men in the room, three of them young and robust, the other elderly and sour, dressed in conservative and man-agerial black. He was mopping his brow. "Now, Mr. Porter," said Hearst to the sour, perspiring man, "would you kindly stop worrying about what my mother is going to think and start writing those cheques? My goodness, we have a newspaper to concoct." Hearst possessed a high squeaky voice—the kind of voice a boy will make when trying to mimic, with some loathing, a girl. He laughed, and as he did, he finally glanced around and spotted Georgie standing just inside the door. He flushed, he frowned and stepped quickly behind one of his associates, then, crouching, he asked over the fellow's shoulder, "Who are you?"

"George Wreckage. You asked me to call this morning, Mr. Hearst?"

"Ah, yes." With almost preternatural speed, he then propelled himself across the room, to shake Georgie's hand. But decided, at the last possible moment, not to. He folded his arms over his chest. "Good of you to come. Did you, by any chance, pass a fellow with Boston beans?"

"And chowder and codfish? Yes," said Georgie. "He was in front of me, then he was in back of me, and then—I don't know *what* happened to him."

"Life," said Hearst, "in a nutshell!"

Georgie laughed, politely.

"Well!" said Hearst then, running his hands together. He turned swiftly and gestured to the business manager, whose distress had not abated. "Write this fellow a cheque—for whatever he says, Mr. Porter. Must have *him*! He's a good lad."

Porter rolled his eyes but walked directly to a fine golden-oak desk laden with shipping crates. In one, still nestled in the straw, was a bust of Julius Caesar. A bust of Alexander the Great had already been unpacked and stood dangerously near an edge. "I've forgotten your name, sir." Chequebook out, pen at the ready, Mr. Porter glared at Georgie.

Hearst, having given the newspapers on the floor another swift kick, had gone to the window and was looking now across the park at the City Hall. On the windowsill was a gold spittoon, filled to the top with cannon crackers, and a bottle of milk.

"Mr. Hearst," said Georgie, "don't you think we should talk first about what you might want me to *do* for you?"

Hearst seemed flabbergasted, then—for just a moment—slightly hostile. "What do you *think* I want you to do for me? Review the drama?" And his three cronies all laughed. "I want you, Mr. Wreckage, to do exactly what you're doing now for—that *blind* fellow with the—" and using a finger he indicated a very long nose. "Draw your little Pinfold and his dog for the Sunday supplement."

Georgie licked his lips; he'd been afraid of that. "Frankly," he said, "I don't see how that's possible, Mr. Hearst. The World Company holds the copyright. It's not in my name. But I'm certain that I can create another comic *just* as good—"

"Maybe you can. Maybe in time you will. But right now, if you choose to come to work for the *Journal*—Mr. Porter, since your penmanship is not needed at the moment, would you please go try and find our lunch? Thank you." He watched the business manager leave, and when the door had shut, he stuck out his tongue. The cronies all laughed again. "*If* you should choose to come to work at the *Journal*, you're to do Pinfold. I want the derby and the dog. Or else we have no deal. Well?"

"What can I say?"

"Yes, of course."

"I'll be sued."

"Wrong, Mr. Wreckage. *I'll* be sued." He smiled and lightly patted Georgie's left arm. "And what a lawsuit it'll be. Front page for a month of Sundays! To the Supreme Court, if necessary!" His blue eyes glittered. "And in the end, we'll win. The copyright will pass"—he tapped a bony finger against his chest—"to the *New York Journal*. "So, are you coming to us?"

Georgie shifted from one foot to the other, thinking.

Hearst watched him, amused. "I've heard that you used to be a news artist, Mr. Wreckage. And I was wondering if you might like to do some of that again. For us. Not scene-of-the-crime things, of course. Something worthier. A prizefight—in Reno? Or perhaps you'd like to go to Havana this winter—send me back a few nice sketches of Spanish cruelty?" He leaned forward on his toes, his face just inches from Georgie's, his breath as mild, and as milky, as a baby's. "Would *that* interest you?"

Mr. Porter returned juggling tin plates. There was bean broth on his shirt.

Georgie asked for a salary of $600 a week, to start.

Mr. Porter blanched, belched, and clutched at his midriff; then, recovering enough to write out a Wells Fargo draught, he asked Georgie, "Do you spell your name with an R or a W? Ah, with a W—like the synonym for destruction! Ruination! Bankruptcy!" At his wit's end, the poor fellow.

Georgie, feeling giddy, feeling *intoxicated,* said, "When do I start, Mr. Hearst?"

"You already have. And call me Chief!"

2

Down on his hand and knees in the studio at the top of Number 10, Walt Geebus stared at his distorted reflection in the Toaster of Tomorrow—in use that afternoon as a space heater—and said, "Well, maybe it's a crystal ball," then laughed, delighted by the idea. "But without the crystal and without the ball!"

And Joette, smoking a cigarette on the couch, said, "Oh, *Walter.*"

Walt sat back on his heels. "Why not?"

"It's a *toaster.*"

"It's Professor *Thom's* toaster. Browns your bread, warms your room, tells your fortune—and if you stick it on wheels, it'll drive you around the block! All for one dollar and nineteen cents!"

Joette took the cigarette from her mouth to smile; then she blew out a cloud of blue smoke.

"There's this friend of mine in Hoboken," said Walt, getting to his feet and going to the windows. Picked that habit up from Georgie. It was late afternoon, and dark outside, and snowing. "Well, he's not really my friend—I used to know him. At school. Works in a brewery now. I mean, he doesn't boil *hops* or anything. He's in the office—his father owns the place." He looked back over at Joette, and she was staring at him wonderingly, with her eyebrows up, and he giggled at himself. "And *his* mother—you following me?—his mother used to have an adviser come to the house, a guy in a turban. Mr. Necromein! And he had this thing called the Destiny Schooner —it was exactly like a glass you drink beer from, except there was a tiny bulb in the bottom of it. Mrs. Kessler used to stare into it for half an hour every Tuesday."

"And what did she see?"

"Well, herself, of course—serving milk and cookies to worthy little boys and girls at a garden party. Or tea to clergymen and brave young soldiers. And darned if that stuff didn't happen."

"You're making this up."

"Am not!"

"You're smiling."

"I *always* smile."

Joette rubbed out her cigarette in the ashtray stand. "Yes," she said, looking across the studio at him, "you always do."

"So if Mr. Necromein could have his Destiny Schooner, why couldn't Georgie have a Destiny *Toaster*? Have you asked him?"

"Of course not, he'll think I'm mad."

"*I'll* ask him."

"You will not!"

"Well, I'm curious about it too. Do you know what he told me yesterday? Said he was going to Brooklyn this morning with that crazy friend of his, Sip, they wanted to see a guy who sells artists' canvas. And I said, I thought you had to go to *court* tomorrow, and he says, Court's going to be postponed—Pulitzer's lawyer won't be able to make it down from New Haven on account of the snow. And I said, *What* snow?"

Joette nodded.

"And *how* did he know I was coming today? I said I couldn't make it. But when I got up here before, there's a note on my table: Do this and that. I'm curious too. *Let* me ask. There's no harm. I'll be very sly. George, I'll say, take a look into your toaster, will you, and see if I get kicked out of school."

Joette reached for a pillow and strangled Walt by proxy. "Please don't embarrass me—please?—by saying *anything* to Georgie about a toaster, for heaven's sake. You're the one who brought *that* up. I simply made the comment that all these—intuitions of his seem to happen at the breakfast table." Then she frowned and asked, "Is there *really* a chance that you might? Be expelled from school?"

Walt snorted and moved away from the windows to his coat hanging on a peg. From one of the pockets he drew out his report card. It was in a dark-brown envelope. He looked at it, winced melodramatically, then read, "Religion: C. Geography: F. History: D minus. English: A. Elocution: U. That's unsatisfactory."

"And what did your father say to all that?"

"Nothing. He didn't see it. *I* signed it. I'm good at forgery."

"You'll end up in jail, Walter. With such a talent."

"It's the least of 'em!" He laughed and crouched down again by the toaster. He screwed up his eyes, pressed his lips together. "Jail? Or the White House? What's it going to be? Joette! I think I see something! It's getting clearer, clearer—darn! it's gone."

He grinned at Joette, and she shook her head. Finally she laughed. "Don't you think you should be starting back home? The snow doesn't seem to be letting up."

"Maybe there'll be another great blizzard, Jo. I'll be stranded for days. Here." He looked at Joette and she looked at him, and then they both looked away. "My father'll think I'm dead in a snowdrift on River Street."

Joette said, "I hope Georgie gets back soon." She stood up from the couch, glanced toward the studio door, then walked—*sashayed*—to Walt's table, leaned over it, and looked at what he'd been working on. Another Pinfold page in panels. Georgie's small rough was tacked above it. Walt hadn't followed it very closely. She pressed one of the thumbtacks deeper into the board and said, "I wish Georgie's mysterious intuition would tell him when all this legal business is going to be done—and what the result will be."

"You and I both, Joette." Walt came and capped an ink bottle; he looked at the wisps of yellow hair at the nape of her neck. "You and I both."

As soon as the first "Pinfold & Fuzzy" drawing (The Great Thanksgiving Turkey Hunt Down in Awful Alley) was published in the *Journal*'s American Humorist colored Sunday supplement, the *World* had gone to court, suing Hearst for copyright infringement and Georgie for his services. Since then, nothing of Georgie's (and Walt's) had appeared in either newspaper. Georgie didn't mind—in fact, he was positively in seventh heaven, since he was being paid salaries by Hearst *and* Pulitzer and would continue to be until the litigation was done.

Joette, however, was nervous. She could imagine Georgie ending up, somehow, with nothing, and the ease with which she'd slipped into such pessimism surprised her. Georgie told her, Aw get off the anxious seat, will you? but—but *already* Pulitzer had seen to it that any artwork for new Pinfold & Fuzzy merchandise was farmed out to other illustrators, Bram Hoopes for one. And last weekend, Sid McKeon had collared Georgie in some watering spot and promised him that if—no, not if, *when*—Mr. William Spendthrift Hearst failed in New York, Georgie would regret—oh! *would* he regret—his high treason. That threat had bothered Joette terribly, even though Georgie assured her it was only sour grapes; Handsome Sid hadn't been asked to join the *Journal* staff. Still, she fretted. What if the case dragged on and on and *on*—maybe people would no longer *care* about Pinfold & Fuzzy when at long last they returned, in one paper or the other. She worried and worried. She cashed cheques, she made deposits in savings accounts, she lost sleep at night, and she worried.

Walt was just impatient. He'd gotten used to seeing his work reproduced, and he missed it. He wanted the whole mess to be over. The *World*, the *Journal*—he didn't care *who* won the case, he didn't *care* who legally owned the characters—he simply wanted to see them back in the funny sheets, where they belonged.

Against the court's order (but who was to tell, eh? and didn't the lady wear a blindfold?), Hearst had insisted that Georgie turn in a new cartoon every Saturday. The following morning (not *too* early) it would be delivered by a *Journal* newsboy to Hearst's bachelor suite at the Holland House Hotel, and it gave the millionaire enormous pleasure to be the only person, man, woman, or child, in all of New York to have Pinfold & Fuzzy with his Sunday breakfast. And Walt was grateful to him for being that sort of oddball. Because if Georgie suddenly had told Walt that he wasn't needed, if suddenly he hadn't been able to come over to New York after school whenever he wished and draw his—his? well, *ours,* he'd concede—boy and dog at a nice table in a proper studio, and if suddenly he wasn't seeing Joette three, four times a week, wasn't getting squiffy on her cologne and heavy with the Urge at the sound of her voice, her slightest gesture—well, young Walt would've felt plain bum about it.

Now, he capped his bottle of ink and watched Joette read the speech balloons he'd lettered a short while ago. She grinned. He'd known that she would. He thought about touching her—lightly, and on the waist. But what then? What would she do? Oh *Walter?* would she say? You're such a silly? Or would she slap him? Or would she, like the women in the spicy novels he'd been dipping into of late, *suspire with ardor?* He didn't dare find out. You don't *do* such a thing. Mash a married lady. The wife of your friend and model. But then, neither do you spark up the housekeeper—and Walt had done *that.* Nana Mary *started* it, though. Barged into his bedroom, interrupting him at self-abuse. Standing over the chamber pot he'd been, and not *five* strokes from completion. *Wal*ter, she'd said, closing the door, Walter, if you *must* relieve your tensions, must you relieve them like a monkey? And she'd opened her blouse and untied the strings on her petticoat and white bodice. Men have certain desires, I understand that. And *young* men, such as yourself, also have a certain curiosity about things in nature. Now, these are my *teats,* she'd said, and promptly fainted to the floor. Walt had revived her, and she'd flung an arm around his neck and pulled him down on top of her. And *that's* my vagina—it's a Latin word, I believe. And *now,* Walter, you may cross the Rubicon. Have you spasmed yet? Oh, good! Don't worry about hurting me, I'm fine. So was Walt. Later, though, he had a bad moment. Shouldn't I have put *on* something, Nana? To prevent—you know. It's all right, Walter. I've been through the change. And Walt said, Change? What were you before, a duck? Walt, ever Walt. He couldn't help it. Oh *Wal*ter, Nana laughed, then she tried to kiss him on the mouth, but he turned his head. That had happened on his seventeenth birthday, in October. Think of it as my present to you, Nana had said before leaving his room. All right, I will. Thanks. His father had given him a suit of clothes and a pocket watch. Georgie had given him a book called *Anatomy for the Artist,* inscribed: *To Geebus, who wouldn't know a real muscle if it hit him.* Joette had given Walt tickets to a musical extravaganza at the Herald Square Theatre. He'd asked her to come with him, but she'd declined, so he'd taken Professor Thom—on an evening when Mrs. Cuff was in desperately low spirits, Papa, and needed a friendly face.

Joette said, "Really and truly, Walter, you should be on your way. What if the ferries stop because of the weather?"

"All right, all right, I know you just want to get rid of me."

"Don't be silly." Then she touched him, a playful poke to his upper arm, and when she saw him flinch, saw the color rise in his face, she drew back her hand, quickly. "The ferries *might* stop." She frowned and went and sat on Georgie's stool, at Georgie's table, where there were several charcoal studies haphazardly strewn. An ancient crone sweeping the pavement, a tipsy hack driver, a derelict gazing through a pastry-shop window at a wedding cake. Standing under the table in a kind of bin were three of Georgie's paintings in oil, pictures that she didn't like and that Walt thought—But don't tell him I said so, I'm *only* joking—should be exhibited at the "Morgue Museum": a picture called "Hoboken Sunday" (an unconscious, so probably drunk, baseball player being gawked at by a scrofulous blond girl-child), a picture called "Noon at Cooper Square" (half a dozen policemen laboring to get a fat woman—anarchist?—into the paddy wagon), and the picture that Georgie had varnished only yesterday called "Nathan Hale" (a tramp asleep on newspapers under the statue in City Hall Park). Do you seriously expect to find collectors for these? Joette had asked. These? Not for these, Georgie replied. These are very poor. I'm just *learning* to paint. But there'll be other pictures. Better pictures. Less depressing? said Jo. *Better*, said Georgie.

Walt put on his coat and his muffler and his cap and his gloves. "Out into the storm," he said, and then trudged across the studio as if through a snowdrift. He stopped when he came next to the toaster. "Let me just check about the ferries," he said, and squatted down.

"Walter, I think I've heard quite enough jokes about toasters. Come on. I'm turning off the light."

"Say, will you look at *this*," he said, pointing and grinning at the blurred reflection of his finger. "There's *me*—I'm going to grow a mustache. Handsome. And there I am learning to drive an automobile. Bet it's French-made. Well, well, well! And there I am again—on a steamship to Europe. Bon voyage!"

"Walter . . ."

"Seems I'm going to do all *right* for myself. Successful man!" He started to get up, then stopped. "Wait! There's more still. Look at those children! Are they mine? They're mine! And blond. What do you know—they're both blond. A boy and a girl."

"Walter."

Walt looked—harder. "Blond—just like their mother." He waved at the toaster. "Hello, dearest!"

Joette came and pulled the electrical wire. "Sometimes, Walter," she said, "you do go *on.*"

The ferries were still running, and Walt got into Hoboken shortly before seven. He walked home through the snow, *crunch-crunch.* As he turned into Morning Street, he was struck in the back of the head with an iceball; his cap flew off, and for a moment he saw stars. Then he whipped around, hearing his assailant laugh at him from across Hudson Street, and for an instant he thought it was—little P. But no, it was only an Irish kid in a Pinfold winterized derby. And Pinfold earmuffs. And Pinfold boots. Walt scooped up snow, packed it and shaped it, and fired it off—missed.

Mrs. Meerebott, all excited, met him in the foyer. "*Walter—this* came for you." A telegram. For Walt? It was the first one that he'd ever received, and not bothering to take off his gloves, he tore open the envelope with his teeth.

3

Some weeks later, only a few days after the start of the New Year, Georgie received a morning telephone call: Hearst himself on the wire with news of the court's decision, and Georgie said, "Really? Really? Wonderful!" But since breakfast he'd known that today would be The Day. When Joette had refilled his coffee cup, he'd said, The characters are mine! How can you be so sure, George? And he'd shrugged.

He took a cab to Park Row and spent an hour with Hearst and his lawyers; he'd listened to a reading of the actual decision, he'd heard it explained in layman's terms, and then he'd asked questions. But I don't understand. If the judge says the *characters* are mine, since I created them—how can the *World* continue to hold the copyright to the characters' *names?* It doesn't make sense. I can *do* Pinfold and

Fuzzy for Mr. Hearst, but I can't *call* them Pinfold and Fuzzy? That's correct, sir. And you may no longer use the terms Awful Alley, or *Down* in Awful Alley, or *Up* in Awful Alley. *Awfully* sorry, Mr. Wreckage. You may *draw* Awful Alley, but you may not call it by that name. Since it's a legal copyright of the New York *World*. Then we've really *lost* the case, said Georgie. Lost? cried Hearst. We have not! Your services have come to me, and you may now go ahead and draw your little boy and his dog again. Simply under new names. And everybody in this city will know that it's *still* Pinfold and Fuzzy, that the *Journal*'s got the original and clear McCoy. We'll see *to* it that everybody knows that—trust me. And if Choseff Bulitzer should choose to run a cartoon called Pinfold & Fuzzy Down in Awful Alley—why then, we'll call *it* every name for bogus in the book. Porter! A few synonyms for bogus, quick! False, fraud, counterfeit, fake. Enough, Mr. Porter, said Hearst, doing another jig around his office. Fake, counterfeit, *bas*tards! But in the meantime, Chief, said Georgie, what am I supposed to call *my* characters? And Hearst, who'd obviously thought about it already, replied: The Little Nobody and His Dog Pal. *Pal?* said Georgie. Short for Palaver, said Hearst. Palaver the Talking Dog! And so, Mr. Wreckage, it's settled at last. Go have a drink, and have one for me, since I am not a drinking man.

Georgie went downstairs and just around the corner to Andy Horn's saloon. There, and till three in the afternoon, he stood rounds for all the clientele, and the clientele was wholly newspapermen. At ten of three, Clarky appeared, dressed in a felt hat and a black chesterfield coat, very stylish, with the fly front concealing the buttons, striped trousers, and shoes with spats. He carried a walking stick and came through the swinging doors followed by three bodyguards in white suits—gorillas in vanilla. When the reporters at tables and standing along the bar saw him, they glanced at one another and winked, and a few of them joked, in very low whispers, It's Clarky—his crimes are remarkably black. Hearsay had it that he'd poisoned Shag Draper with atropine and buried him in the swamps of Jersey.

"George! I came soon as I heard the news!" He put out his hand; he was wearing kid gloves. "Congratulations! Now—who do I see about getting permission to open a billiard parlor called 'Little Nobody's'? And I want you to personally paint the sign." Georgie didn't know whether he was serious or not. It was entirely possible that he was, since already Clarky held at least part ownership in a couple of downtown pool halls, one in Bleecker Street and one in Canal. But as it turned out, he wasn't serious, he was kidding, and after peeling a twenty from a roll of bills to blow everybody in the place to one last free drink, he nudged Georgie—who by now was several sheets to the wind—and said, "I got a coach out front. Come on, and I'll give you a ride uptown."

"Uptown?"

"Aren't you going to Thirty-fifth Street? Fifty-three West? It's Wednesday, George. Don't you go to the Café Moon every Wednesday? It's what *I* heard."

"Will we all fit into one carriage?" Georgie asked with a nod to the bodyguards.

Clarky smiled. "I'll leave one behind. I'd leave 'em all behind, but if I were to be attacked, could I count on you to defend me? No, you'd probably only reach for your paper and pencil."

"And who, exactly, is after you, Clarky?"

"Oh, I've heard a few names mentioned. It comes with success, George. Enemies. But I'm not crying on my shoes." He steered Georgie through the crowd and out the doors to the pavement. The air felt especially cold now, after the almost suffocating heat of the saloon. Clarky's carriage was illegally occupying a cab stand. It was a herdic built of mahogany. The door handle was a perfect imitation of a paste tin, only in gold. Climbing inside, Georgie commented, "The ladies of America must be buying a lot of shredded wheat biscuits," and Clarky laughed, saying, "Yes, and a lot of cake flour too." They sat together opposite the two strong-arms. One of them loudly chewed bubble gum till at last Clarky made him spit it out the window.

"So, George, you're with Mr. Hearst now. Do you happen to remember that day last spring when I mentioned him to you? Told you he was coming to New York? You didn't seem very interested then."

"No," said Georgie. "I suppose I wasn't."

"What really interested you that day, as I recall, was the banquet. Lucky thing, too. Because if you hadn't gone there, where would you be today?" He patted Georgie on the knee.

Georgie looked thoughtful, then he said, "Over in the meadows sketching the cops as they looked for Shag Draper?"

A deep frown settled on Clarky's brow. He drew his lips into his mouth, held them there for a moment, then blew them out. He shrugged. "Good way to get your trousers wet."

"I never minded."

"No," said Clarky. Then following a heavy silence, he asked, "You've never heard again from your little Pinfold, have you? The one of flesh and blood?"

Georgie didn't reply; he looked through the window. Then he took out his cigarettes, and as soon as he did, Clarky came up with a match and struck it on his thumbnail. And Georgie said, "The ungrateful little bastard—no, I never heard from him again. The last time I saw him was the day he helped us to move out of Sawdust Street. And if you hadn't told me where he was going, I wouldn't have known *what* happened to him."

"You sound almost like you miss him, George. Is that what I'm hearing?"

"I thought we were friends, that's all."

"I figured you'd be glad he was gone, now you're married."

Georgie grunted.

"You heard the dog died, didn't you?"

Georgie flinched, and turning his face to Clarky, he seemed— stricken. "No! How would I've heard? When?"

"In the summer. She got sick and she died."

"Are you certain?"

The bodyguards smirked.

Clarky looked pitying, or perhaps he was just feeling slightly guilty; he *had* manipulated the kid, a bit, and was in some way responsible for his having left town last July with the dog. But say! Clarky'd thought he was doing Georgie and Joette—Joette especially—a kindness, a big favor. The dog was dead, too bad. But her going to Jersey had had nothing to do with it. What he'd heard, the animal died of old age. Collapsed. Clarky said to Georgie, in a sympathetic chapel whisper, "I had a few fellas that worked at Monmouth Park July and August, you might've heard. And two of them took a hike over to Long Branch one evening, just to do something. They happen to pass by this theatre and see on a rat sheet that Pinfold and Fuzzy out of the funny papers are appearing on stage. So naturally, being faithful readers of your cartoon, George, they buy tickets. Only when Pinfold and Fuzzy don't show, they get mad and go looking for the manager. Who tells 'em the dog got sick of a sudden the night before and died that very day."

"And what about P?"

Almost sheepishly, Clarky replied, "I don't *know,* George. Haven't heard a thing about him, not a word. But I can't be expected to know everything. New Jersey—but don't tell this to any cop with a shovel, he might get mad—New Jersey ain't really my territory."

"But maybe P's not *in* Jersey anymore. Maybe he's back."

Clarky shook his head. "I would've heard."

Georgie looked out the window again, a thumb knuckle between his teeth. Then he glanced again at Clarky and said, "If you do hear anything about him, let me know."

"Really?" Clarky sat back and stared at the roof for a moment. "Sure." Georgie, Georgie, he was thinking, I can't figure you out. If you were a . . . competitor, I'd consider you dangerous. "How's Joette?"

"All right."

"And the painting—how that's coming along? Have you mastered the chemistry yet? Have you heard that your friend Gulp has syphilis?"

"He insists it's ague. And my paintings are still god-awful, but thanks for asking."

"Well, if you ever happen to do a picture of Mother Polk's cadets and a certain phony nigger lugging a truck through the streets of New York, I want to come see it."

Georgie laughed. "With what, an ax in hand?"

"Not necessary, George. I'm not such a shrinking violet anymore. Success changes a man."

Georgie laughed again.

"And besides, who'd exhibit it? Last time I was in a picture gallery, the walls were still covered with nancy-lookings guys dressed in Greek robes and holding laurel branches."

"That'll change."

"By then, I'll be too old to care, George."

At Thirty-fifth Street, as Georgie was pushing open the carriage door, Clarky suddenly leaned forward and pulled it closed. "Two more quick things." He put out his hand, and one of the bodyguards, after emptying his topcoat pocket of a revolver, several pieces of bubble gum, and half a brick, took out a can of boot paste. He passed it across to Clarky, who gave it to Georgie. "For Gulp. When you see him." Georgie frowned: he knew what was buried in the

paste—a tiny dropping bottle filled with a dark-brown narcotic.
"And the last thing, Georgie. Your friend Walter."

Georgie blinked. "Walter?"

"When was the last time you spoke to him?"

"Why are you asking me this? I guess I haven't spoken with him
in a few days. The weekend just past, I think."

"What'd you talk about?"

"Nothing, really."

"Well, I believe, George, that the two of you might have a lot to
talk about this coming-*up* weekend. The *World*'s hired him to do
'Awful Alley.' He starts Sunday."

Georgie's mouth formed a perfect O.

4

Wednesday afternoons at the Café Moon, the front door was hung
with a CLOSED sign, and if you were not a member of the Black
Gang, go away! Now, the Black Gang may've *sounded* criminal—the
Black Gang, didn't they use to hang around Vest Pocket Wedge?
thugs and petty thieves, weren't they? no, you're thinking of the
Devil Boys—but in fact it was only a group of young artists, num-
bering roughly twenty, that had formed because its members shared
a similar point of view regarding what was good painting and what
was bad. They all painted scenes of the city they lived in, boldly,
quickly, often clumsily, never bothering with fancy, mannered high-
lights; they were concerned only with expressing the idea, with energy. That was *good* painting. And all those noble Greeks currently
hanging in the galleries and exhibited annually by the National Arts
Club—that was *bad* painting, and necrophilia to boot. Why would
they want to paint another Leda and the Swan, for goodness' sake,
when they could paint Fifty-seventh Street full of slush and banked
with gray snow, a carriage tipping in the March wind? What did they
care about Cephalus and Aurora? Charlie the Egg and his girlfriend
Pickles were a lot more interesting. And so they painted Charlie and
Pickles, and hogs at the slaughterhouse, and gutter children splash-
ing in the shallows alongside trawlers down at the Fulton Market,
and women having their hair curled at a cheap hairdresser's; they
painted men at their carousing, men at their trowels and spades,

they painted whitewings sweeping the street at dawn. They considered themselves revolutionists and talked always of going to Paris,
since the painters *there* weren't still painting the Nativity, the Cruci-
fixion, and the Resurrection; *those* fellas weren't still painting the
Death of Socrates. Only a handful of Black Gang members had any
academic background, which meant at that time having spent a few
years copying the Venus de Milo and the Dying Gladiator. No, for
the most part, they were newspaper artists and magazine illustrators. Billy China and Teed Preston were on staff at *Puck*, Ernest
Fistick, Jack Wynn, Peter McCormick, and Aaron Method all free-
lanced for the *Evening Telegram*, the *Commercial Advertiser*, and the
Trib, William Klotz contributed to the *Herald* and Andy Gillick to the
World, Sandy Young drew for *St. Nicholas* and illustrated novels for
boys. And Jim Sip—Gulp—used to sketch for the *Record* in Philadelphia. Now he painted full-time and sponged off his friends. It had
been Gulp who'd organized the Wednesday get-togethers, sweet-
talking Richard Bunner, who owned the café and whose brother
Leonard was a member of the Gang, into closing down one afternoon
every week.

The Gang would drink a lot of coffee and eat a lot of sandwiches;
they'd bring along their newest paintings and lean them against the
walls. And they'd talk. You've *ruined* it, Jack, with that red, there,
y'know. I like it, Peter, but do learn to control your temper; the
holes still show where you stabbed it. That—that—*that* is—trash!
Take it back, Teed. I will *not!* It is trash. Trash is trash. You've done
the roller-skating rink: *damn* you! *I* was going to paint it *next* week. I
told you, too. You did like hell! I did, I *told* you! In between the
squabbling, though, some genuine, some *thoughtful* criticism would
be tendered, and praise given, and of course there'd always be time
for general theorizing.

So far—and he'd been coming to meetings since October—Georgie had brought only two canvases to show: "The Blade" and
"Mother's Parlor." But everyone realized that he'd only just started
to paint and so treated both Georgie and his works kindly. Try to
paint like you were sketching a riot for the daily press—simply *go* at
it. Use the flaked white, George, don't bother with sublimed—no
stability when you're mixing with other pigments. Georgie listened
carefully to every word said at the café, and out of a reporter's habit
he often took down notes. Don't overpaint high-oil color (lampblack)

with low-oil pigment. Can cause cracks. Alizarin red for blood?
Teed's suggestion.

He was always happy and frequently elated those afternoons
spent with the Black Gang, and he felt that among these painters he
had, in the term of the day, found himself. He could remember
laughing at Joette whenever she'd called him an artist, and he could
remember dismissing her suggestion that he try to paint. All artists
should paint, shouldn't they? she'd said, and he'd made a face. How
stupid he'd been! But not really. He'd always believed, along with
people like Clarky, that artists painted sissies in robes with more
folds in them than there were grains of sand on a beach—or else
they painted the Blessed Mother. But then he'd met Gulp, and then
he'd joined the Gang. Paint what you see—that's your obligation,
Wreckage. Obligation? At first, Georgie hadn't liked the sound of
that. It sounded politically radical. If he painted a knife fight or a
whorehouse parlor with a fat girl sitting on the lap of some thug, it
was because he wanted to, it was because the images were strong,
not because he hoped that some do-good one day would stare at the
pictures on a gallery wall and be inspired to launch a crusade to close
all the dives and brothels in New York. But that's not what Gulp and
the others meant by obligation. They weren't political at all. (Well,
there *was* one Anarchist in the group, Bruce Banks, but he painted
the mildest pictures of anyone: snowball fights, a fruit vendor ogling
a pretty woman.) They didn't mean *social* obligation. They meant
personal obligation. Oh. Take it in and give it back. What's beautiful, paint beautiful, and what's ugly, paint ugly. It's your eyes,
your hand, your life—your obligation.

Georgie was sold.

Once in a while, Billy China would bring a model to the meeting—
he would always introduce the girl to the Gang as So-and-so, my
daughter; he used to be a pimp. Everybody would sketch her for an
hour, and then Gulp would try to convince her to leave with him.
None of Billy's daughters ever would, even though Gulp was still
handsome, corruptly handsome but handsome, with a tapered bony
face, red lips, and hazel eyes that were set unnaturally deep in his
skull. The models all had been warned about Gulp's affliction.

If Billy wasn't bringing a girl to model nude, then Gulp would
generally arrive at the café with some drunkard or tramp that he'd
just plucked off the street and promised a meal if he'd sit half an

hour and let the Gang draw him. Once, Gulp had showed up with a patrolman, and another time with an obese Cockney girl who'd *insisted* on disrobing, though the artists assured her that it wasn't necessary. And still another time, Gulp had dragged in a young poet by the name of Edwin Arlington Robinson, and the poor man, too shy to demand to leave, had suffered his time on the model stand.

Today, when Georgie stepped into the Moon and saw Gulp introducing his latest "found" poser to all the others, his eyes popped. "Well, I'll be hanged!" he said. "*P!*" But it wasn't—it was simply a small, dirty boy with blond hair, who looked at Georgie, frowned at him, then said, "And pee to *you*, too."

Gulp was saying, "Ah, Jesus Christ, Georgie, why should you care? Somebody was bound to get the job—why *not* your friend from Hoboken?"

Georgie spread his hands over the café table, about to explain why not, but then he clapped them together and just stared at his cup and saucer. And shook his head. How could Walter do it? he thought. Just turn around like this and stab me in the back. It's—unbelievable. He said, "Unbelievable," and Gulp rubbed his cheek slowly with the back of his hand. If McDougall had grabbed the assignment, or Dieffer, Stolley, Bram *Hoopes* even—anybody else at the *World*, or anybody else, period—Georgie wouldn't have cared. He was sure he wouldn't have. But Walter Geebus. Didn't he have a smidgen of loyalty, didn't he feel any obligation to Georgie, after what Georgie had done for *him?* All those surprise visits he'd put up with, all those drawings, hundreds of drawings, that he'd looked at, commented on. He'd taken Walter sketching, he'd—he'd showed Walter how to dry an ink picture quickly, over a candle. *Lots* of things.

Including how to draw "Pinfold & Fuzzy."

Georgie felt betrayed and sick at his stomach with rage; the more he thought about it, the sicker he felt. Gulp watched him make and unmake fists.

"So this kid's got a job—good for this kid, it seems to me. Artists ought to stick together," said Gulp. "Don't you think artists ought to stick together?"

"Walter," Georgie said to the table, "is a cartoonist. At best."

Gulp laced his fingers together, then cracked his knuckles. "So now I guess you'll have to find a new assistant."

"Walter has never been my assistant. He's just a kid I let come around and watch."

"Sounds like a great position. May I apply for it?"

Georgie looked at him.

"I'm serious, George. And it would be fun, wouldn't it? The two of us? I did a package of comic pictures once. For a magazine in Philly called *Your Back Garden*. It didn't last. Never got paid, either."

Georgie leaned forward and blew gently on his cold coffee.

"Think about it, would you? My application. And forget Walter Stevens."

"Geebus."

"Just forget him. Wish him well. We'll have a better time. The Little Nobody! We'll have a *grand* time of it." Gulp stood up and took his tiny bottle from the table—earlier, as soon as Georgie had given him the tin, Gulp had thumbed off the lid, then eagerly dug his fingers through the paste. "And now I'll leave you to your misery, if you don't mind."

Georgie nodded.

"And I would like the job."

"I don't *need* an assistant."

"Well then, just think of it . . . as a way of saying thanks to the man who told you that red and blue make purple."

Georgie made a face. "My wife told me that."

"Yes? Then I'll try this: I'm the man that brought you into the Gang, remember. And I *can* draw. I'm not asking for charity. For once. George. I do need the money."

Georgie looked up at him again. Money?

Gulp came around the table, stooped, said, "Shhh," and leaned toward Georgie. "Do you hear that?"

"Hear what?"

"That hissing. It's my heart. Honest to God, it is, and heart medicine costs money." He held up, in the palm of his right hand, the bottle from Clarky. Heart medicine! Then he stood up, shrugged, and wandered over to the far side of the café to join the rest of the Black Gang, everybody laughing because Gillick had just stuck a rose petal on his nose and was harrumphing and muttering and making his eyes look beady—pretending to be J. P. Morgan, the banker. "My nose is red and my heart is black," said Gillick, "and my ass is made of gold."

The street kid that Gulp had dragged in looked stupefied as he ate a corned-beef sandwich.

Georgie suddenly banged the table with an open hand.

5

"*Walter?*" said Joette. "Walter *Gee*bus? But he's a schoolboy— he's barely seventeen."

Georgie said, "Well, he's convinced the *World*, somehow, that he's all grown up!"

And Joette said, "*Walter? Walter?*"

6

Professor Thom got a late start that Wednesday. He slept till nearly one in the afternoon, since he'd worked all through last night; he'd been trying to convert an old typewriting machine—that he'd scavenged from a trash barrel in Wall Street—into a sort of player piano. Imagine! *Typing* "Oh, Promise Me"—easy as A-B-C, X-Y-Z. Though success had eluded him overnight, he'd try again one day. Maybe. Professor Thom, alas, hardly ever saw a project through to completion—and when he did, *pfff!* But don't forget the toasters, he'd tell himself whenever he began to feel like a—a *tinkerer*. He'd built twelve from the bathtub, sold them all, and not one complaint. Does that sound like a *tinkerer?* Sounds like an inventor/business-man to *me*, he'd say. To himself. His friend, his *former* friend, Doctor Geebus, had called him a tinkerer, hurting him deeply, and demor-alizing him—in a letter the Professor had received just yesterday. A tinkerer who has never amounted to anything and never will. And what brought *that* on? This: I hold you responsible—not entirely, but still, responsible—for the grotesque *adventure* in which my son has become involved. Walter has informed me that he intends to quit school, and I inform *you*, sir, that should he go ahead with this very dangerous plan, the incubus of his ignorance will sit squarely on your weakling shoulders, now, tomorrow, and forevermore. The *what* of ignorance? thought Thom. I am aggrieved and I am angered that you misrepresented to me—though *not* to Walter—your "friend,"

Mr. Wreckage, and that you abetted Walter during his clandestine visits to New York City. Consider yourself rebuked, tinkerer. My God! thought the Professor, how can a man of science be such a . . . such a . . . such a . . .

Professor Thom ate a package of dried apricots; then he lit his pipe and went quickly downstairs, passing Joette's former room on his way. An old-maid public-school teacher lived there now. And up in Georgie's room there was—well, no one in the house knew for sure *what* he was. Young fella, quiet, shabby dresser. The Professor suspected he was a cardplayer. No substitute for Georgie Wreckage—even though sometimes the Professor had thought Georgie crazy as a bug. But who am *I* to call somebody bugs. He missed Georgie. He missed Joette. And he felt quite injured that they'd not once come to see him since the wedding, or had him over to their house. They had sent a thank-you note. Last time he'd heard from them. Thank you, Professor, for the electric fan. We will use it and cherish it since we know that you made it yourself. And you're right, its special vibration does keep away the mosquitoes.

He got his wheelbarrow from the front porch and headed for the gate. It was already going on two o'clock, but he'd try to hurry, finish as quickly as he could at the dump, so that he might have time to go by the financial district again. This was a new resource, Wall Street. He'd found, in only three visits, a broken ticker-tape machine and plenty of tape (he'd think of a use for the stuff, eventually), that typewriter, and several discarded umbrellas. And oh, a bowler hat.

As it turned out, though he did get to Wall Street, the afternoon was not very profitable, as far as raw material was concerned. He enjoyed his wanderings, nevertheless. Exercise. Good for the blood. When he got back to the house in Sawdust Street, it was dark, and with the coming of nightfall the temperature had dropped, rapidly. A wind blew. It was wonderful to come inside; Mrs. Bennett always kept her house cozy in winter. Professor Thom trudged up the stairs, pulling off his gloves. He'd left a light burning in his room? And then he jumped, a foot.

Because there was Fuzzy the dog, sitting on his bed.

"So what've you been doing, Mr. Thom?" she asked. "Building the better mousetrap?"

7

"But why should he be angry at me? Are *you* angry? Boy, *every-body's* got it in for me. You should hear my father!" Walt punched himself in the forehead with a gloved fist; then he pressed his lips together, filled his mouth with breath, and rolled his eyes.

"Oh, stop it, Walter," Joette said. She was standing in the door-way of Number 10. He couldn't come into the house? He wasn't welcome?

"Is Georgie home?"

"Upstairs."

"In the studio? May I see him?"

Finally, she stepped aside, and as he passed her by, going into the hallway, she could feel the cold coming off his overcoat. His cheeks and forehead were bright from the wind. He unwound his muffler and started up the stairs. Then he stopped and turned around, a hand on the balustrade. His expression, for once, looked entirely serious. Grown up, thought Joette. He pulled off his cap. "They offered it to me about a month ago," he said. "But they said it was all—what's that word? That it all depended on Georgie going to the *Journal* finally. They said that if he stayed at the *World*, decided to or *had* to, then there was no job for me. You see? Now, what if I'd told Georgie all about this . . . then? And what if he'd gotten mad at me *then* like he's mad at me *now*—and ended up staying on at the *World?* I wouldn't have had *anything.*"

Joette looked at him with surprise. "I don't know what to say. But I think you should've told him about it when they made the offer. Why would he have gotten angry? You didn't go looking for the job, did you? *Did* you?"

"No! I swear."

"Well, then," she said, only to say something.

"Jo, it's not as if I'm stealing his cartoon. He doesn't *own* it. I didn't decide *that.* And—and when he went to Hearst, he didn't tell *me.*"

Again, she was surprised. *Walter?* She said, "Why don't you go talk to George about all this."

And then Walt poked his tongue into the corner of his mouth, and suddenly he was the old Walt again, and he said, "Anyhow, why's

George so shocked by what happened? Did the toaster break down
or something?"

She set her mouth and walked up the hallway and into the back
parlor.

Walt bit his tongue.

Gulp had arrived at the house earlier that afternoon—Friday—
bearing a heavy auctioneer's carton, and when he'd lugged it up the
stairs and into the studio and unpacked it, it proved to be filled with
rolls of artist's linen, stretchers, pliers, brushes, spatulas, and a paint
box, as well as about a dozen bottles of gin and rye whiskey. He'd
lined those up on the long windowsill. And Georgie had said, I
thought you were supposed to help me draw cartoons. But of course
he hadn't really thought any such thing. He'd been on to Gulp since
the proposition. Gulp needed a place to work; that's what this was
really all about. He'd been thrown out of his studio on the grounds of
moral degeneracy; the landlord had been notified—"by a friend"—
of Gulp's syphilitic condition.

Gulp had stretched a canvas, he'd primed it; he'd drawn a charcoal sketch of Georgie bent over his table, he'd dated and signed it;
he'd broken open a bottle of gin and poured himself a glass, and a
glass for Georgie; he'd fiddled with the toaster/heater, he'd fogged
up eight or nine windowpanes with his breath, he'd lain down on the
sofa, and finally he'd said, If there's anything that you want me to do
special . . . ?

And Georgie had replied, testily, Yeah. Think up a new name for
the Bread Witch.

Who's the Bread Witch?

Georgie closed his eyes. She's in *our* cartoon, Gulp. She's mean.

Mrs. Meanie, said Gulp.

Georgie shook his head. She's got a lot of money and she keeps it
all under her bed. She lives in a tenement.

She does? said Gulp. Why?

She just does, said Georgie. He'd almost said, Ask *Walter* why.
And Pin—Little Nobody's always trying to get a few bucks from
her.

I like him already. All right, let's see. Call her . . . The Rich
Lady.

Gulp, come on. She likes to bake. Cakes and bread and cookies. It's the only thing she likes to do.

This is a strange woman, George. She needs a man to fuck her. *Then* she'd discover there are other things to like.

Georgie reached for his glass and took a swallow of gin.

Gulp, his forearm slung over his eyes, started to chuckle. She's got a billion dollars and she likes to bake cakes? Call her Mrs. Cake. Jesus Christ, George, call her anything. It's a *job*.

Ma Billions, said Georgie, and with his index finger made an ex- clamation mark in the air.

There, said Gulp. Call her Ma Billions. Amen. And he'd turned on his side, to nap.

He was still napping when Walt came in.

They exchanged a look for a long, long minute. Then Walt smiled and Georgie said, "Don't. Don't give me any of the Hoboken-kid-in- woolens crap. Just don't."

"All right, I won't." And like that, the smile was gone. He took a further step into the room, and Georgie slid off his stool. Walt had unbuttoned his coat on the way up; now, he found himself rebutton- ing it, and stopped. "If you think—if you think I did something underhanded, I'm sorry."

"Underhanded."

"Underhanded. Wrong. Terrible. Awful." Again, he bit his tongue. "Whatever you want to call it, if you think I'm guilty—I'm sorry. But George, it's an opportunity. When you were my age, you went to work for the paper. Why can't I?"

Gulp had finally woken up. "You, I take it, are Walter Remus." He swung his legs to the floor. "Jim Sip."

"Ah, sure. They call you Choke? Georgie's mentioned you."

Gulp frowned, he glanced at Georgie, then he said, "*Gulp*."

"Walt Geebus," said Walt. When he turned back to Georgie, he lifted his eyebrows. Georgie's expression remained stony. "I really didn't think this would happen—that you'd be this upset."

"That's a lie," said Georgie, matter-of-fact. "Why didn't you tell me about this last weekend? Last week? The week before last? Be- cause you're a sneak."

"That's not fair."

"You're a sneak. You come around here, you just start coming around here anytime you please—what's this, what's that, how do

you do this? And the next thing I know, you've taken everything
I've taught you and turned it against me."

Walt knuckled little white balls of spittle from the corners of his
mouth; his throat was dry. He said, "*What* have I turned against
you? How? This is stupid, George. This is a stupid conversation."

Georgie's face darkened; he stood a little straighter.

Gulp said, from the couch, "I'd like to interject just one—idea. A
thought. A consideration. Before tempers . . . whatever. Georgie,
you've taught this young man some things—that's wonderful. Isn't
it? One artist helping another. And the younger artist grows,
and . . ." Gulp gestured with his hand like a thespian tossing daisy
petals, ever so fluidly, ever so meaningfully.

"Oh, shut up," said Georgie.

Walt started across the floor. "If you don't mind, there are some
things I've left." He squatted at the table he'd used and pulled out a
pebbled black portfolio. The Toaster of Tomorrow was standing
close by—close enough that Walt could lean toward it and see his
reflection. He pushed down a lick of hair. "So what's the future hold
for us, George? We're not going to be friends anymore? Ever?"

"I don't like ingratitude. And I don't like theft."

Walt bristled then. "*Don't* call me a thief, George. Because you
don't *own* Pinfold, never did. And as for being ungrateful! You make
it sound like I did nothing at all for the past half a year except ask,
Daddy, why are there clouds? Ungrateful? I never heard you thank
me when I saved *your* ass time and again. When you woke up with
such a bun on that you couldn't even *look* at a sheet of paper, much
less *do* anything with it. *Thank* you, George, for everything you
showed me. Thank you, George. Thank you very much. And
George? You're welcome."

"Get out of here, Walter."

Walt said, "Nice to've met you, Choke. He doesn't like too sharp
a point on his pencils, and you have to keep an eye out that he
doesn't forget he's got a cigarette burning on the edge of his table.
We've had a few small fires. *Good*-bye, George. And mea culpa. Mea
maxima culpa." He opened the studio door, startling Joette. She
moved back toward the head of the stairs. When she started down
ahead of Walt, Georgie told her, "He knows the way."

Walt muttered something.

"What?"

"I *said*, George, aren't you afraid that I'll steal something else on the way out?"

Joette said, "Enough. Enough's been said, I think?"

Walt was nearly to the foot of the stairs, when suddenly Georgie leaned over the top rail and shouted down, "I give *your* Pinfold a month."

"That's what you *hope*, George. But you *know* better." He looked back up as he tugged on his cap. "You *know* better." He opened the inside front door. "Because *I'm* better." And left.

He wanted to walk and walk and walk, and it didn't matter where; he crossed Ninth Street on a western diagonal, so west he headed, toward Sixth Avenue. As he was going by one of the brownstones, the front door opened and a man stepped outside; when he saw Walt, he dropped his eyes and then averted his face. Walt smiled, but only for a moment. Number 19—Georgie's house of adultery. Tuesdays, Thursdays, and Fridays, Walter. She's a hot one.

Somebody was calling him.

Georgie, coatless and hatless and signaling him to stop, to wait. He came running across the street, his frosted breath ripping away over a shoulder. Walt tensed. But as Georgie got closer, he was smiling, and so Walt smiled. And pulled off his left glove and stretched out his arm. "I say stupid things sometimes."

Georgie took a hard sock at the side of Walt's head, knocking him down. Never in his life had Walt been struck with any force, and he was thoroughly disoriented. He saw a shimmering curtain of red, and he felt a sharp pain in his skull and a rising nausea. He was on his knees, and though he tried, he couldn't stand. For God's sake, he said to himself over and over. For God's *sake!*

The situation quickly improved, however. He heard Joette shouting at Georgie to leave him alone, leave him *alone,* and then he heard Gulp arrive tsking, and then Georgie wasn't there anymore: Gulp pulled him away, forced him back across the street, Georgie saying, "*Ho*boken, Ho*bo*ken, Hoboken nancy!"

Joette stooped. "Are you going to be all right?"

Walt didn't reply at once; he tried to think of a particularly winning remark, which was not easy to do, what with his head throbbing and spinning. No, it would not do just to say that he was all right; he had to say something that Joette would remember—forever. Something witty, even courageous. While he was trying to think, though, he briefly lost consciousness. And when he came to again, he found himself confused—about what had happened, about where he was, even about who was there with him, and as he tapped at the aching ridge just above his right ear, he said, "Shit."

And Joette said, "Oh, *Walt*er, I'm so very sorry."

8

Sunday, Professor Thom rose before daylight and quietly, as quietly as possible, slipped out of bed. On tiptoes, he went and checked the boy: sound asleep—in the cot that Georgie had left behind when he moved. Fuzzy was under it, also sleeping. He got down on his knees and stroked her gently. She opened her eyes. Green. "Come on," he whispered. Then he grabbed his coat and went to the door. "Come on." She hesitated, but went finally. Noiselessly, they left the house. It was a Big Secret—Fuzzy and P's return. The boy had been emphatic. I can trust *you*, Mr. Thom. But somebody else sees us, don't matter who, and that Clarky bastard'll hear. And then that Wreckage bastard will. And P had his reasons for not wanting *him* to know *anything*.

Just as the Professor had his reasons—besides wanting to let the poor animal stretch her legs and do her business—for taking Fuzzy out now. He wanted to be alone with her, wanted to see her away from P, for a few minutes.

She followed him down the front steps, then started to go around to the backyard. No, not there. She'd be seen if someone should look out a window. Professor Thom unlatched the gate. They walked up Sawdust Street to the corner, where there was a vacant half-lot. Fuzzy trotted across the frozen grass and peed on a small mound of old black snow. And the Professor said, "I'll bet it feels good to be outside again. Dogs don't like to be cooped up. Isn't that right, Fuzzy?"

She trotted through the lot, sniffing at the ground.

"Isn't that right?"

She looked around at him, then continued her sniffing.

The Professor smiled, nodded. "You know, Fuzzy, I'm in a plight —truly—because of your young master. Because of those designs of his. What do *you* think about them? Do you think he should go ahead? Fuzzy, what do *you* say?"

Fuzzy returned and sniffed at the Professor's shoes. He bent over, thumping her on the side. "Finished?" he asked her. "Go back now? Yes?"

Well! The scientific method prevails again: She doesn't talk, he thought. And laughed to himself, following her down the street, back toward the boardinghouse. She doesn't talk. Which *meant?*

That P was, somehow he'd become—a ventriloquist.

Why not? the Professor could almost hear Georgie say. Why not? The kid's smart.

On Wednesday, after he'd come into his room and Fuzzy startled him, and P, laughing, had jumped up from behind the bed, Professor Thom said, Now, I want to hear everything, where you've *been* all this time. But first, let me fix you both something to eat. And P said, Anything is fine with me. But Fuzzy's got special food. Then, from a small wigbox, he took a piece of raw liver wrapped in paper, unwrapped it, and drenched it with molasses. The Professor gave P cold franks. And then they'd talked, all three of them, for several hours.

So what was his name, this friend of yours?

Alvin McCoy, said P.

Sounds like a nice man.

He is, said Fuzzy. He's a colored man.

Is that so.

He doesn't *look* very colored, said P. He almost looks white. You could mistake him.

And this Mr. McCoy helped you when Fuzzy got so sick?

Did he! He sure did—didn't he?

And Fuzzy said, Yes.

And here is the story they told, P telling a little bit, Fuzzy taking over for a time, P suddenly interrupting and continuing:

The day after Fuzzy's collapse, Alvin McCoy went with P to find a doctor of veterinary medicine. One of the Widow Orleneff's almost-grown daughters was kind enough to borrow a neighbor boy's slat-sided wagon for Fuzzy, then the landlady herself gave them the names of two vets she knew of and pointed them the way. They were to walk inland, toward Oceanport and the Monmouth Park Race Track. It was half past nine when they set out. The sky was overcast. P was afraid that it would storm on them, but Alvin was

confident it wouldn't. You mustn't worry about the animal, he said.
It'll be all right.

P shook his bald, uncovered head: he'd lost faith.

Stop worrying. She's okay, really.

They located the house of one of the vets, a doctor named Henry
Irons, and Doctor Irons, after taking his fee, examined Fuzzy—
pretty damn hastily, P thought—and then shrugged. I'd put her
down, he said. She's sick and she's old.

She ain't old! said P.

I'd guess she's twelve, and that's old. Seven times twelve . . .
seven times twelve, seven carry the one . . . is eighty-four. If she
was a woman, she'd be eighty-four. Who's healthy at eighty-four?
You're dead at eighty-four. *Been* dead forty years. I could put her
down easy, for another dollar.

They left then, to find the second doctor the widow had told them
about, Doctor Gaily. He lived in a fine gingerbread house right on
the main road. He would not, however, agree to look at Fuzzy, as
she was not a thoroughbred horse. But his housekeeper suggested to
Alvin and P that they trudge ahead another half mile, and when the
road forked, take the left fork, along the Shrewsbury River. On
their right they'd see an old green house. Try there. Mister Shuttle.
Not *Doctor* Shuttle? No, *Mister*.

They found the green house without difficulty. The property was
overgrown with weeds, and the building itself looked about to tum-
ble down—the chimney already had. The front porch slouched. The
steps were rotted. The elderly and carelessly dressed Mr. Shuttle
answered their knock promptly; then, looking past them to the
wagon in the yard, he moaned and hurried directly outside. Six tiny
fur-ball kittens clung to his trousers. He knelt and rested one ear
against Fuzzy's flank; he sighed. Let's carry the old girl inside, he
said.

P said, She's *not* old.

Alvin touched P gently on the shoulder, and Mr. Shuttle grinned
at the boy around teeth that were as crazed as an antique vase.

As soon as Fuzzy was laid on the table, Mr. Shuttle listened to her
heart with an ear trumpet. Then he looked into her ears. And then
he turned and walked to a glass-fronted corner cabinet, the kittens on his trousers bobbling as he moved. He took out a jar of fine
yellow—sand? and carried it back to the table. Pouring some carefully into his palm, he pursed his lips. Then he bent over and blew

the stuff into Fuzzy's face. The dog immediately closed her eyes and
went to sleep.

Sit down, my friends, sit down, said Mr. Shuttle to Alvin and P.
I'll be a few minutes. He pointed to a sofa. Alvin sat down, but
jumped right up again. Out from under a cushion emerged a sleek,
white-footed gray tom. A live owl perched on a valance. The walls
were covered with unframed—tacked-up—animal lithographs,
hand-colored. Here a Baltimore oriole, there a trotting stallion, here
a dragon, there a dromedary. Something with thick reddish fur and
a short leathery tail, something with a pointy face, something about
the size of a man's shoe ran suddenly from under a chair, across the
floor, and disappeared into a pile of newspapers. Seeing that—something, P decided to remain standing where he was, beside the table.

Mr. Shuttle pried open Fuzzy's jaws and looked into her mouth.
He fetched an electric torch for a better look. He pressed a finger
against her gums and frowned at her tongue, now swollen and
flabby. He worked a bit of cotton into her nostrils, collecting a few
flakes of dried blood. Then he filled a pan with pale-blue fluid from
an old wine bottle. He dropped in the cotton and swirled it around
with a tongue depressor. Hmm! Finally, he unknotted Fuzzy's red
neckerchief and examined the scar. Shot, was she?

I didn't do it, said P.

Of course you didn't. How long ago? Meanwhile, he was prodding
and poking at her throat with both his thumbs. *How* long ago?

Last spring.

Did she bleed a lot? Did she lose a lot of blood?

Well, I didn't *measure* it, but it made a big mess.

Mr. Shuttle smiled. Then he wasn't smiling. Who'd shoot a dog!
The people of this world! The people of this world!

The boy was thinking, said Alvin, that it might be the salt air. Is it
the salt air, do you suppose? She's a city dog, you understand.

Mr. Shuttle shook his head. You want to feel something? Come
here. He took Alvin's hand and drew it down to Fuzzy's side. Feel
that? Feel big? It *is* big. Spleen. Anemia. I'd say anemia *of course*,
but I'm not licensed to. So I'll just say—I think.

But she's a dog, said Alvin. *People* get anemia.

She's an animal. Animals get anemia.

What's anemia? said P. Sounded to him like some foreign country,
the hot kind where people wore fezzes.

Troubled blood, said Mr. Shuttle.

It goes away, does it?

Sometimes. But with her spleen all blown up like that—it's serious, my boy. She's got to rest. And she's got to eat good. Liver—feed her liver. And turnip tops, beet greens. Will you remember all this?

I'll remember, said P.

Liver, turnip tops, *molasses,* beet greens. And eggs. See if she'll eat some scrambled eggs. But before she can rest and before you can see to it that she eats right, I got to take that bullet out.

What bullet? *I* got it out. I got it out first thing.

Then there were two. Because there's still one in her neck.

And you let this man operate? Professor Thom had asked, incredulous.

I trusted him, said P.

We *both* trusted him, said Fuzzy.

He knew what he was doing, said P. I watched him real close.

The Professor smiled. So he performed this surgery right then and there?

On the living-room table, said P. Didn't take but half an hour. Less than that. And I got to use the sponge. Wasn't much blood at all. He knew what he was doing, Mr. Shuttle did.

And later? asked Professor Thom.

She was pretty sick.

I guess I was, said Fuzzy. I don't remember.

Mr. Shuttle said she had to stay, we couldn't take her back to Long Branch in the wagon—the sewing might've come undone. He said she couldn't be moved for three or four days, at least. Said he'd take good care of her for me, but I wouldn't leave her.

He wouldn't, said Fuzzy. Not for a minute.

But Alvin had to get back. To go to work. So I said to him, Anybody asks, you tell 'im Fuzzy died.

Why did you want him to do that?

Just so nobody'd try to make Fuzzy go back to work again. There was still a month left before the theatre closed.

Good lord, Pinfold, they couldn't *make* her do anything. A dog?

I think he was really afraid I might *want* to go back, said Fuzzy.

P shrugged. The thought crossed my mind. Mr. Shuttle said you had to rest. You can't rest staying up till three o'clock every night.

And Fuzzy said, He treats me like a child, Mr. Thom.

And the Professor, relighting his pipe, looked from P to the dog, then back to P, then finally asked the question. The Question: What's going on? Since when does Fuzzy talk?

You mean, when did she start talking again? About a week after Mr. Shuttle took out the second bullet.

Pin*fold*.

Sure! That was it all the time. It's just like that story my mother told me—about the German girl that got poisoned. You must've heard that story. Somebody didn't like her looks, her sister or somebody, and gave her poisoned leberwurst to eat? The girl takes one bite and falls down dead. This must've happened on the Bowery or close to it, because who should come along but Steve Brody. And he picks the girl off the pavement, and soon as he does, the chunk of meat pops right out of her throat. She says, Steve, I'm alive! and kisses him all over his big ugly face. You *must've* heard that story, it's famous.

I daresay, said the Professor.

Same thing happened to Fuzzy. Soon as the bullet comes out, she's her old self again. Well, not *right* away. Took about a week, like I already told you. One day I'm trying to get her to eat a plate of scrambled eggs, and she looks me square in the eye and says—

Don't you have a piece of chocolate? said Fuzzy, quoting herself.

Professor Thom sucked on his front teeth for a moment, then he shrugged and stood up and went to get his tobacco pouch. He was remembering Father David and his Adventure in the Valley of the Pagan Dogs. He was smiling. He wanted to believe the boy's story, the boy and the *dog's* story, the *whole* story, the happy ending in particular. But what would Thomas Edison say? Don't believe anything till you've seen the proof! So the Professor gave P a slice of raisin bread, and when the boy's mouth was full, he asked Fuzzy a direct question. She failed to reply. Instead, she lay down on the rag carpet and closed her eyes.

He'd asked her, So what are your plans now?

P was awake, dressed, and jamming his feet into his shoes when the Professor returned from taking Fuzzy for a walk. An ashy light backlit the window shade. A pot of water hissed on the kerosene cookstove. "'Morning," said P. "I hope nobody saw Fuzzy."

The Professor shook his head. "I'm pretty certain no one did."

And Fuzzy said, "It sure felt good to be outside again. After being cooped up."

The Professor glanced at the dog; he raised his eyebrows, then he ran his tongue across his top lip.

A few minutes later, he and the boy sat down to breakfast: yesterday's rolls and cups of mint tea. "I've been thinking, Pinfold," he said. "What if *I* went to see George?"

"No. That's a bad idea." He scraped back his chair, stood up. "A real bad idea." He went and cut more liver into small pieces and put them on a plate, and the plate on the floor. Fuzzy ate everything. *Good* dog! "And for lunch, scrambled eggs—your favorite!"

"Very funny," said the dog.

The Professor clenched his teeth: he'd seen her mouth move. *Certainly* her mouth moved, he thought, she's *chewing*. He reached for another roll, broke it in half, then reached for the butter knife. And just when he'd thought he had the proof, doubt returned. No, no—there's *no* doubt. It was the boy doing it, the boy. He'd said that his friend Alvin had come to visit him every day that he was living at Shuttle's house, waiting for Fuzzy to recover. And the two of them often went fishing together in the river, or swimming. It was very easy for the Professor to imagine this Alvin giving the boy lessons in the art of ventriloquism; he could imagine the boy *asking* for them; the boy was like that. Now, take a deep breath, swallow. And try to say—don't open your lips, but try to say . . . Say what? thought Professor Thom. A cylinder can stand on one of its flat faces and it can roll on its round face. Mary is going to feed the chickens. She feeds the chickens every day. The Professor could just *see* the boy, mumbling, mumbling, as he sat on the riverbank with his feet in the water or hunkered next to Fuzzy, watching her eat, making sure that she ate *every*thing. The boy would practice, he was the sort to. Practice and practice. But then the Professor said to himself, Why? He could learn, he would practice, but why would he *want* to? For what possible reason? Just to learn? No, he didn't think the boy was *that* sort. Alvin, the kindly Alvin saying: Papa gave me this pony this morning. Now, *you* try it. And P swallowing, closing not only his lips but his eyes, and beginning: Bahba gay be . . . The Professor smiled. Sure! It must've been like that. (But *why?*) Six months he'd been away. There would've been plenty of time for lessons, for practice. (But *why?*)

P suddenly interrupted the Professor's musings. "I came to you because I thought I could trust you. Say you won't go see Georgie. Promise me."

Professor Thom sighed. "Pinfold, what you intend to do will get you into a lot of trouble. And it's so thoroughly pointless. And it's *spiteful,* and for the life of me, I can't imagine what wrong you think Georgie has done you. He was always kind to you. He was *always* kind to you."

P turned and looked out the window.

"Pinfold. Listen to me. If you simply were to go to Georgie and tell him what you wanted, and why, he'd *help* you. I'm certain that he would. He'd probably give you what you need."

P shook his head. "I don't want him to *give* me nothing. I'll just take what I figure is rightfully mine. He owes me."

Again, the Professor sighed, but louder this time. "Well. I can't allow you to stay on here—once you've started all this nonsense. It wouldn't be right. And I wish to be no part of it."

P replied, "I know that. And don't worry. Don't worry about it."

But he did, the Professor did worry: as he finished drinking his morning tea, as he smoked his first pipe of the day, as he made his bed and tidied up his room a bit. He worried as he watched the boy sit at the workbench playing mumblety-peg with a small yellow pen-knife, and he worried whenever the boy suddenly laughed out loud for no reason that the Professor could discern. Finally, he was so overwrought from all his worrying that he decided to go out and walk. He put on his heavy coat, the one he'd lined himself with goosedown. By then it was late morning, and you could hear the pealing bells of several churches in the area. "I'll be back in a few hours," he said. "Can I get you anything while I'm out—either of you?"

P folded his knife closed.

And Fuzzy said, "I'd like a little piece of cake, but only if you pass a bakery. Don't go out of your way."

The Professor smiled. "Pinfold?"

The boy rubbed a palm over his scalp. "You're not going to see him, are you?"

"I'm off to the dump."

"You wouldn't do that, would you? See him?"

"Can I bring you anything *back?*"

"I want you to promise me that you won't talk to Georgie."

The Professor heaved his shoulders and let them fall. "I promise," he said.

As he was coming down the stairs into the main hallway, Mrs.
Bennett emerged from the front parlor and said, "Professor! Have
you seen Pinfold?"

He stopped dead in his tracks, then proceeded the rest of the way
down, struggling to appear—innocent.

"Come in here for a moment, please," she told him, and, turning
around, waddled back into the parlor.

The Professor tapped his tongue against the roof of his mouth, his
teeth. Had someone told her? Maybe the schoolteacher, in the room
just below his, had heard Fuzzy's pacing—she was a terrible pacer.
With a shrug, he walked after Mrs. Bennett and found her bending
over a piecrust table with her back to him. "Look at this," she said.
"It's that nice Geebus boy—*he's* drawing the cartoon now." And she
pulled the colored wraparound from the Sunday *World*.

The Professor opened his mouth, shut it. Opened it. "*Walter?*"
Walter, indeed. Look at that signature: Walt Geebus. With a puzzled
smile, he took the funny sheet from Mrs. Bennett. Then "Good
heavens!" he said, and snorted. "That's my toaster!"

And it was; see for yourself: The Bread Witch, in Panel One, leans
over the appliance on her kitchen table and says, "Toaster, toaster,
burning bread, where's that boy I hate and dread?" And in Panel
Two, there are Pinfold and Fuzzy clearly manifested in the toaster's
shiny surface: He's scaling the tenement wall, while the dog peers up
at him from the alley below. In Panel Three, Fuzzy says, "If dat ol'
witch catches you comin' in tru dat window, you're gonna *get* it!"
And the boy replies, "Five *bucks* is what I'm gonna get!" Panel
Four: "Well den," says Fuzzy, "bring *me* back some shortbread!"
And in Panel Five, the Witch is cackling. In panels six through
eleven, Pinfold is caught in the act of larceny, is brained with a
rolling pin, is trussed up in his own rope, and pitched out through the
window, head first. In Panel Twelve, the final panel, Pinfold is dangling helplessly, while Fuzzy down below is rolling around in hilarity
and saying, "If you don't watch out, da rope you shinny up today,
you'll swing by tomorra—'cause dis is America, ain't it? Ain't dis
America?"

The Professor folded the Comic Weekly in half and gave it back to the landlady. "But why is Walter doing this now? What's happened?"

"Professor Thom, don't you know anything besides engines? Georgie is drawing for the *Journal* now. It's on billboards all over town—up in the Elevated, even."

"And what's he drawing?"

"Same thing as this. Miss Franny showed me a copy."

"There're two Pinfolds now? In two different papers?"

Mrs. Bennett said, "There are. But the *Journal* is saying that Georgie's is the genuine one—even though it's called something else. Little So-and-so."

"So-and-so?"

"I think that's it. But just between the two of us, Professor, young Geebus gave me the bigger chuckle. And he's such a nice young man. He must be thrilled."

The Professor said, "Yes," raising his eyebrows. So *this* was the "adventure" referred to in Doctor Geebus's nasty letter, the one certain to ruin Walt's life, the one the Professor was being held culpable for. Well, well! And he'd assumed only that the doctor had somehow discovered Walt was assisting Georgie. But he was drawing the cartoon *himself* now. Walt *must* be thrilled. Adventure, thought Professor Thom. I'll say! And he wondered whether Georgie had recommended him for the job. Must've. And then he wondered, again, whether he should go and have a little chat with Georgie. About? Well, they could start with Walt, and then proceed to . . . other matters. "Good morning, Mrs. Bennett," he said, tipping his homburg.

He didn't stay long at South Dump that day; weekends had never been his favorite time for browsing there—too many hoboes, and much too much competition from out-of-town inventors. He thought it unseemly that two or more men of science should struggle over, even come to blows over, a clothes wringer, say, or a rusty crank. He did pick up a small clock, though, and a fireplace grate before leaving. He wandered through several neighborhoods after that, snooping into the alleys and rummaging in any trash barrels which happened to be out. By then it was going on two o'clock, still early, and since it was a mild afternoon, he decided to make another visit to Wall Street. He'd never been over there on a Sunday and reckoned he'd find it deserted as the moon. In his prevailing state of mind, his perturbed state of mind, the idea of solitude appealed.

It was a long walk, and, with his wheelbarrow so laden—the grate must've weighed twenty pounds, easily—a slow one. But he used the traveling time well, to think. To ponder the question of responsibility. He'd promised the boy that he wouldn't run to Georgie Wreckage and spill the beans, he *had* promised, but. But was it a *legitimate* promise? Should he feel bound by his word? Didn't he have a responsibility to Georgie? To tell him what he knew? To warn him. After all, Georgie was a friend—neglectful, but still a friend. Must you feel obligated by promises made to children? But Pinfold is *not* a child, he thought. He's really not. He is! He's not. He *is*. All right, forget whether he is or isn't. Think about this: If Pinfold gets caught, he's going to be in a lot of trouble. So didn't the Professor have a moral responsibility to prevent that from happening? He had the opportunity to stop it—did he have the obligation? He did. Didn't he?

Yes, he did.

And so he decided finally to break his promise to Pinfold and to go see Georgie. As soon as he was done peck-and-sniffing in the Wall Street district, he'd go. He could almost hear Georgie's initial reaction: laughter. He intends to do *what*?

It was as empty in lower Manhattan as the Professor had imagined it would be, and he created echoes rolling his wheelbarrow up and down the narrow and winding little streets. He stopped occasionally to explore an areaway or peek into a carton of rubbish set out at curbside. He was delighted to come upon almost two dozen typewriter-ribbon spools, ecstatic to find a box filled with broken panes of window glass. But as he moved from one street to the next, Cedar to Nassau to Pine, he kept noticing the same large yellow broadside plastered on building walls and telegraph poles, on postal boxes, on plate windows, and he thought it was disgraceful. Who would blemish property like that? Thoroughly uncivic-minded, to say the least! What was it, anyway? A rat sheet for some third-rate melodrama, an advertisement for a celery nostrum, a catsup, a beer? He was so annoyed at it, and at the profligacy of whoever had done the pasting of it, everywhere, that he refused to stop and read it.

Coming along Wall Street at last, he discovered that several of the broadsides were pasted to the statue of George Washington. An outrage! He looked around for someone to complain to, but there was no one. Except for pigeons, he was the only living thing in the street. And finally, he could resist no longer: he had to see what someone thought was so goddamn important—and if it were a product, he'd shun it for life. Oh, lord, he thought when he'd read it, *I should have known. Anarchists.* The sheet consisted of several slogans and a crude drawing, a cartoon: A mob of angry men, built like smithies and collectively labeled THE WORKING CLASS, thrashing, clubbing, trampling, and kicking skeletons in black cutaways and striped trousers and top hats—this skeleton labeled Rockefeller, and this one Carnegie, this one Huntington, that one Harrington. . . . Death to the Captains of Industry, Corruptors of America! You Can Not Run from Nemesis. We Will Strike You Down in Your Counting Houses! Next Time It Will Not Be on a Sunday!

The Professor shook his head. *Why do they let those people into the country?* And then, just as he was turning away to walk on, he noticed a small satchel leaning against the base of the statue. He picked it up and opened the flap. Inside was a cut-glass candy dish wound with sticky black tape. He turned the dish upside down. Heavy. Something was in the dish, he couldn't see what. He began to unravel the tape, but it was so sticky he decided not to finish. He could do it later, with gloves on. He returned the dish to the satchel, and put the satchel—*No! Professor, don't do that!*—into his wheelbarrow.

And then he proceeded on his way, turning up Nassau Street, fully intending to go have that little chat with Georgie Wreckage. But he made it only as far as Golden Hill.

It flabbergasted nearly everyone who knew her when, upon the death by misadventure of Professor Thom, Mrs. Bennett, long recognized throughout the precincts of Sawdust Street as a flintheart, became so—*afflicted* with grief. At the news, she'd fairly swooned. Nobody knew quite what to make of her terrible pallor, her hand-wringing, her sobbing and blubbering, all her lamentations, because as far as anybody knew, she and the Professor had not been, at any time, confidential or even particularly friendly. Nevertheless, she mourned—for the boarder who'd twice (three times?) set fire to his room while conducting some experiment, who'd stained, bleached, and warped the floor with a thousand varieties of chemicals over the years, who'd disturbed the woman's sleep on countless nights *(click-click-click, whirrrr, sputter, putt . . .)*, and who'd once, in exchange for six months' rent-free living, painted the boardinghouse with a surface coating of his own manufacture, a cadet-blue guaranteed not to blister or peel and to last till the Second Coming (or the demolition of the property, whichever happened first) but which turned black as ink within a month. She mourned that man; she wept for him. Had she been in love with him, secretly? It was possible, of course; everybody admitted that it was possible—this being America, and all—but still they felt it highly unlikely. And then the Metal-Eater recollected that, about two years earlier, the Professor had devised a do-hinky that he called the Thomson Bunion-Burner—a thimble connected to a zinc battery—which Mrs. Bennett had used several times and found to be extremely satisfactory. Ah! Maybe that was a clue to the woman's grief, or maybe it was the reason entirely. Simple gratitude. As the Metal-Eater said to Byrnsie the Tenor, The Lion bawls for Androcles.

The initial barrage of reporters had showed up at the house late Sunday afternoon, long before the police and about half an hour before a white-bearded inventor by the name of Elmer Dreezle, who offered Mrs. Bennett a ten-dollar bill if she'd allow him twenty undisturbed minutes alone in the Professor's room. She'd thrown him out and slammed the door. He'd gone away, unlike the newpapermen. Not fazed by the landlady's refusal to let them inside, they had turned the porch and front yard into a kind of bivouac—some had found (where? God knows) tables and chairs for cardplaying, others had fetched cookstoves and were grilling sausages, still others were resting on portable cots, playing catch, pitching horseshoes, and one extraordinarily muscular fella had lugged a stuffed grizzly bear, pedestal included, across the street from a taxidermy shop and was dancing it around the lawn.

When the police—a pair of young patrolmen in ill-fitting tunics—finally did arrive, Mrs. Bennett demanded that they clear her property of riffraff, and they were only too happy to oblige her. The reporters were ordered back behind the picket fence; dawdlers and wiseacres got a swift kick to the seat of their trousers. The patrolmen had been sent to give the Professor's room a thorough going-over, a task they were clearly reluctant to perform: After you, O'Keefe, said the one to the other. No, no, I wouldn't *think* of it—after *you,* O'Hare. Finally, Mrs. Bennett opened the Professor's door and led the way in. Their behavior baffled her until she realized that what they were expecting to discover was evidence of a bomb-making factory: they opened every drawer in the dresser gingerly, they walked on tiptoes, they handled even a shaving mug, even a dish of liver they found on the floor as though it were detonable. The strain quickly became unbearable. What's in that wardrobe, missus? Just clothes? Ah, fine. And so they didn't find P. And that trunk? *More* clothes would you say, missus? And so they didn't find Fuzzy, either. They kept wetting their lips, sleeving their foreheads. Finally, O'Keefe—or possibly O'Hare; the landlady was too distraught to get them straight—asked, Might you tell us, missus, the precise nature of the gentleman's grudge against the United States of America? Mrs. Bennett narrowed her eyes bitterly, drew up her shoulders, and spat. I'm sure the poor soul never even realized that he *lived* in the United States of America! she said.

As they were leaving, the patrolmen hung a card on the outside doorknob: Under Police Scrutiny, No Admittance.

P took it and pocketed it on his way out with Fuzzy, shortly after midnight. He carried down Georgie's Army surplus cot, as well. Several reporters were still loitering on the pavement when they quit the house, but guess what—nobody noticed them.

According to Monday's papers, Professor Thom—and the suggestion was made in several news articles that the victim's name might've been changed from Thomski—was a mad bomber, an *incompetent* mad bomber who'd inadvertently blown himself to kingdom come before he could leave his infernal device at the door of the Stock Exchange. Unidentified "acquaintances" were quoted as recollecting that the Professor had thought highly of Marx and Bakunin, and a sketch which appeared in the *Journal* showed the poor man black-bearded and dressed in a greatcoat with a spherical bomb, fuse sputtering, jammed into each pocket. Sketches in the *World* depicted the mangled wheelbarrow, the hole in the pavement, and the Professor's flaming left shoe; it was noted in the caption that the shoe had been flung a quarter mile by the concussion—that it had smashed through a window, landed on top of a desk in the offices of Lissenden and Lissenden, Shippers, where it started a small paper fire. In the press, much was made of the discovery that the Professor's pipe was constructed from a bullet mold; an alienist interviewed in the *Sun* declared that it was precisely the sort of talisman adopted by the most vicious of assassins.

Monday afternoon Mrs. Bennett took a carriage to the city morgue to claim the remains; there, she came upon four or five sketchmen making drawings of the few parts of Professor Thom still in existence, while fortifying themselves with drafts of liquor. She had to wait till they were all finished. The man in charge of the morgue then released the Professor to her in a gimcrack suitcase that he happened to have lying around. And Professor Thom was buried in it the following morning, in Mrs. Bennett's own cemetery plot and alongside Mr. Bennett, who'd died of influenza a decade ago.

There was quite a large crowd at the interment, large enough to bring out the pretzel vendors and the coffee wagons, and at least a dozen of Clarky's shoeblacks. Several Anarchists bearing pictures of Professor Thom were arrested, as was a drummer from the Fein & Dandley Company who attempted to sell toy bombs. All the boarders at Mrs. Bennett's house attended the ceremony, and so did a contingent of the Professor's fellow inventors—one of whom placed on the mound a wreath of artificial lilies, which, after being sprinkled with a patented yellow solution, sobbed and keened like a proper widow for a full fifteen minutes. Georgie and Joette were there. Joette kept knuckling tears from the corners of her eyes, but you couldn't see Georgie's eyes; he was wearing those spectacles with the dark glass, the ones he'd got from Professor Thom to hide the shiners P had given him.

Walt was there, too—but not wanting to come face-to-face with Georgie, he stood away from the gravesite: he'd watched the lowering of the battered blue suitcase from in back of a large granite statue of Michael the archangel.

Thus, the father of the modern toaster was laid to his final rest.

10

Later that week, when Joette stuck her head into the studio to say that she was going out for a few hours (up to Fourteenth Street, to Macy's, if asked), Georgie, with his back turned to her and dressed in a smock, was dabbing at a new painting. It was to be called "The Discovery"—he'd told her at breakfast yesterday—and portrayed a scene so revolting to Joette that she could not bear to look at it.

Late last evening she'd come up to the studio in her dressing gown to ask Georgie to come to bed with her, and he'd been sketching out the picture on canvas, in charcoal. Two small children, a boy and a girl, obviously twins, excitedly scooping cinders from an ashcan, while a slightly older child, another boy, danced around them holding up the leg of a human being partly wrapped in a strip of tablecloth with a cabbage-rose pattern. Do you remember me telling you about the Bits and Pieces Murder Case, Jo? That's how it broke— three kids. And Joette had said, You're not going to paint that, you're not. And something moved inside of her, some feeling she didn't recognize, couldn't define. How *can* you? How can you—*especially* after what happened to poor Mr. Thom. Georgie! And he'd grown angry with her. Angry! Telling her that he had a perfect right to paint whatever he pleased; it was his experience. She'd gone straight downstairs to bed, alone. He'd finally crawled in under the covers about four in the morning. She'd waked, wondering whether he would touch her, hoping that he wouldn't. And he hadn't. Then, a short time later, when he'd bolted up in the bed—another nightmare—she'd waked again. Of course. But said nothing to him.

"Georgie? I'll be going out for a little while. Will you be here when I get back, or are you going over to the *Journal?*"

He still hadn't turned to her, and he made no reply, but Gulp was staring at her with a toplofty grin, the corners of his eyes crinkled tightly. He also was dressed in a smock—the pair of them reminded Joette of mechanics—and standing at an easel. *His* painting, at least, she could look at, though she didn't much care for it. A heavy-set man with a crimson mouth, bald except for just a fringe of black hair above the ear that showed, clutching another, smaller man by the coat lapels and shaking him; the victim's hat had fallen off and was in the air, between the head and the floor, but closer to the floor. There was a rolltop desk. "Have a nice time," said Gulp to Joette, and he winked. God, how she despised that man!

And feared him. Not that she felt in any personal jeopardy because of his reputation as a lecher—he wouldn't dare to try anything, and besides, she'd strongly expressed to Georgie her demand that Gulp not be allowed into the house, except when Georgie himself was present. No, she wasn't afraid that he might suddenly—

assault her, her trepidation was far less specific than that. The man, she believed, was insane, or was *going* insane, rapidly. The other morning when she'd brought up a tray of coffee, Gulp was talking to Georgie about the properties of some particular pigment—didn't they ever talk about work? didn't they ever draw cartoons?—when suddenly, and without his being aware of it at all, he began to speak in Latin. On and on in Latin he'd rambled—presumably about titanium green, but who could tell?—and Joette had begun trembling, she'd had difficulty swallowing, she'd stared in amazement and loathing at the madman, seeing the droplets of perspiration appear on his forehead and below his nostrils. Then, abruptly, he'd wiped his face on a sleeve and stopped speaking. He'd frowned, he'd chewed on his underlip, he'd gone and lain down on the sofa, where he'd become flatulent.

Joette had turned to Georgie, and Georgie had shrugged diffidently. He'd looked away, then said, Imagine remembering your Latin after so many years. Gulp used to be in the seminary, he tells me. *Georgie!* And Georgie had said to *that,* I just thought I'd inject some humor into the situation. Don't worry. He's harmless. The poor bastard.

And now, after winking to Joette, the poor bastard went and nudged Georgie, saying, "Your beautiful wife is here, maestro."

Georgie turned finally, deliberately blocking his painting. "Anything the matter?"

She shook her head. "I'll be back around four. Maybe earlier. Will you be here?"

"Probably," he replied, with a glance at his drawing table. "I'm due to drop off a picture at the *Journal* later, but I don't think it'll be done. Probably I'll be here. Have a nice time."

She was glad not to have to lie but, just the same, ruffled that he didn't ask her where she was going. She moved to leave, but stopped. "George? Have you found your purse yet?"

"No. Do you need money?"

"Did you leave it someplace?"

"I haven't been anywhere to leave it. It's got to be in the house. It'll turn up."

When Joette stepped outside, two husky men in yellow newsdealer's aprons were tumbling cartons into the street from a delivery

wagon standing in front of the house. The large sign on it read:
JOURNAL READERS ARE BIG CASH WINNERS! PLAY SUPER-JINGO,
DAILY & SUNDAY! Joette scowled, watching the cartons fall. Six,
seven, eight. One of the men jumped down from the back of the
wagon and began to stack them on the pavement. He noticed Joette
then, and grinned; his teeth were bad. "Missus? Do you want to sign
for these?" He plucked a blue flimsy from his apron pocket, and a
stubby pencil. "And tell us where you want us to put it all?"

"Put *what* all?" she said. "What *is* all this?"

The man still in the back of the wagon threw down the ninth—or
was it the tenth?—carton. Then he straightened up and laughed.
"You won't believe it, ma'am. *No*body does. And we've been delivering these things all morning."

"Delivering *what?* I will not let you bring anything into my home
until I know what it is?"

She thought, with a pang, about Professor Thom once again.

The man with the flimsy—it was now in his teeth—bent over one
of the cartons and tore open the flaps. "What is it?" he said. "It's a
million dollars, ma'am." Snickering. He came across the pavement
and handed Joette a sample stack of currency, banded.

And *she* handed it to Walt in the dining room of the Fifth Avenue
Hotel (quite swank).

"*How* many boxes?" he asked.

"I believe there are twelve in all. A dozen."

He laughed, breaking the band with a finger, spilling the twenty-
dollar bills across the table in front of him. "I think I'll pay for our
lunch with one of these, if you don't mind. And I'll be generous with
the gratuity."

"I'd advise you not try it, Walter." She smiled at him. "One day
you're a forger, and the next, a green-goods passer. You're a very
dubious character, Walter Geebus."

His eyes glittered. His hands scooped up all the money and made
a neat pile of it. His heartbeat accelerated. Dubious character! But
she'd forgotten to mention backstabber and thief. "So what does Mr.
Hearst expect everybody to *do* with all this stuff? Paper the walls?"
He picked up the top bill, which bore a flattering portrait of William
Randolph Hearst himself. On the reverse side was a picture of the
Pulitzer Building in debris, the dome upside down and cracked.

"He expects, I *imagine,* everybody to have a good chuckle. And eventually to burn it—as *he* seems to be doing with the real stuff."

Walt sat back in his chair as a waiter appeared. Natty little fella with slicked-down hair and a trim mustache; his eyes widened slightly at the stack of twenties—they seemed real, till you looked closely—and then he scowled at the ostentation. He said, coolly, "Would you care to order, sir?"

"Yes," said Walt. "We'd like the beefsteak, And a bottle of cha-blis." He'd looked up Wine in the *Illustrated Book of the Known World,* picked out one that sounded—sophisticated. And he'd repeated the name to himself a couple of hundred times on his way to meet Joette. And a bottle of cha-bliss.

The waiter said, "I'd recommend a red with your steaks," and *Walt* said, "Recommend what you like, just bring us what I said."

Joette concealed her grin by taking a swallow of water. When the waiter left, she reached over and took the money off the table and put it all into her handbag.

"So Mr. Hearst has promised to make everybody a millionaire, has he?" said Walt.

"I guess that's the idea. I've never met him—I don't suppose I ever will, either—but he certainly sounds like the queerest duck. George told me a funny one? Seems that Mr. Hearst overheard Richard Outcault say that his wife wanted a mink on her birthday. So he sent her one. A live one."

Walt liked that. "Well, just don't let it get around that you want a bearskin rug."

The waiter returned with the wine and poured a taste for Walt, who said, "Yes, this is fine." Then, after his glass was filled, and Joette's too, he proposed a toast: "To my favorite lady . . ."

Joette blushed.

" . . . the Bread Witch!"

And she laughed, waving a hand at Walt.

"Did you see the cartoon last Sunday? What'd you think? How many copies did you buy?"

"Of course I saw it."

"How many copies?"

"One."

Walt made a face. "Did you like it?"

She looked at him. "You really shouldn't have done that, you know. Use the toaster." But she was grinning.

"What did Georgie think?"

She shook her head.

"No. Tell me—please?"

"He said, there you go again—stealing somebody else's work. The toaster. Because it looked exactly like Professor Thom's."

"Ah." Walt picked up his glass and took a sip. "Professor Thom. I feel badly." He smiled, remembering the day he'd helped carry the bathtub upstairs; the sticks of Artificial Midnight. Poor Professor Thom.

Joette said, "I hadn't seen him in months. He should've come by sometime."

Walt nodded. "Last time I saw him was on my birthday—or I guess it was a few days after. He gave me a hammock with a small motor that rocks you to sleep. And if I don't buy a bedstead by tomorrow, I might end up actually sleeping in the thing. I'm using the floor at the moment."

Joette stared at Walt across the table, then she blinked. "Buy a bedstead?"

"I got myself a flat. A floor-through. Waverly Place. Number Ten." He squared his shoulders and beamed.

"*Waverly* Place? How on earth can you afford to live there?"

"I got a nice salary now, in case you've forgotten. And I convinced my father to sign the withdrawal papers for a savings account my mother started for me when I was born. Baptized. That's over two thousand dollars right there."

"And how'd you talk your father into doing that?"

"Oh, he's suddenly very glad to be rid of me."

"Threw you out?"

"I suppose." He smiled slowly. Then lunch came, and they began to eat, Joette with not much of an appetite, Walt with a hearty one. And while he chewed a piece of meat, methodically—twenty-three times, exactly—he glanced around the dining room. He'd been told that the place would be swarming with politicians, Republican politicians. And there they were, a fair number of them resembling his father. A certain brutal complacency, and a similar thickness in the neck.

Walt had surprised himself, a little, when he'd said to Joette yesterday on the telephone, Will you meet me at the Fifth Avenue Hotel? He could've said the Waldorf. That was fancy too. Fancier. He *should've* said the Waldorf. But he'd said the Fifth Avenue.

Around twelve thirty? You know where that is, don't you? She'd said,
Of course. But Walt had had to ask Handsome Sid. What is it,
Twenty-fifth Street? Between Twenty-third and Twenty-*fourth*,
Walt. Everybody at the *World* called him Walt. Sure—it's how he
signed his cartoon.

Joette cut a piece of steak. She stared at her dish, then smiled.
When she lifted her eyes to Walt's, she was smiling still. "Your father
actually threw you out of your own home because you started pub-
lishing cartoons?"

"That too."

"What?"

Walt put down his knife and fork. "It's just been bloody murder at
home since all this started. It's been just—bloody murder. But—
what's that word that means not literally?"

Joette frowned. She shrugged.

"I mean, it's been bloody murder in a figure of speech. But then
Sunday night . . . we had *another* argument. This one really loud.
And Papa"—Walt blushed—"my *father* said by hook or by crook
he'd stop me from continuing. He said I was still under his authority.
That I was still a minor—and that he was going to see a lawyer. He
was going to make trouble for the *World*. Which they wouldn't like,
so they'd naturally fire me."

"Could he really do that? Stop you, legally? You *are* seventeen."

"I'm twenty-one over at Waverly Place." He laughed.

"Nobody in his right mind would believe that *you* are twenty-one,
Walter."

He shrugged.

"But tell me what happened? You didn't *strike* him, Walter! Please
don't tell me anything like that?"

"Of course not. I didn't do a thing. But the housekeeper tried to
suffocate him in the middle of the night with a pillow."

Joette choked on a piece of meat. She began to clap on her chest
with her right hand; then she reached for her wine and took a swallow. Her eyes had begun to water.

"Are you all right?" Walt asked, and when she replied that she
was, he laughed. "She tried to suffocate him, yes."

"She just slipped into his room with a pillow?"

"Well," said Walt, "she's been known to make visits there in the
past."

"Only without the lethal pillow."

"Yes," Walt replied, chewing. "This was absolutely the first time she tried to smother him to death."

"And she was doing this all for you? Or is she in his will?"

"All for me," said Walt.

Joette lifted an eyebrow. "But she didn't succeed."

"You've seen her. She weighs about fifteen pounds! No, she didn't succeed. But what a tumult! And of course, my father thought, still thinks, I put her up to it."

"He doesn't!"

"I'm afraid he does." Walt seemed—boastful?

"So *that's* why he threw you out."

"*And* for being a cartoonist." He pushed his dish away. He discovered that he had some wine still left in his glass and quickly drained it. Now *his* eyes began to water.

"You're lucky your father didn't call the police on you."

"He wouldn't dare. It'd be in the papers."

"And what happened to the housekeeper? Also thrown into the street?"

"I should say not. He'll probably end up *marrying* her."

"Walter!"

"I wouldn't be a bit surprised. Dessert?"

"I think not." She watched him take out a cigar and light it.

"You'll have to come over and see my flat. When I get my bedstead."

"*Walter!*"

"I didn't mean *only* my bedstead. It was just a way of saying my furniture. When I get my *furniture*, will you come?"

"No," she said, "I will not."

"You have to see it."

"Draw me a picture?"

"I'll draw you a map."

"A picture," she said, "will be fine."

"How about next Tuesday? Say ten? In the morning? I'm getting Pinfold wallpaper."

"You're not."

"Sure. I can get it all free," he said, just as the waiter put down the check. He picked it up and looked at the sum, and just to be the clown, he opened his eyes as wide as they'd go and stuck out his tongue in horror.

Joette chose to ignore that. "I've enjoyed this, Walter. Thank you? Very much?"

"You're welcome." He paid the waiter.

"I didn't know—I didn't know whether I'd see you again after what happened last week. Did your headache stay very long?"

"Stay long? I still have it!"

She smiled. "I couldn't believe Georgie would do that to you."

"I shouldn't have said what I did."

"No. You shouldn't have."

"But he's really got no sense of humor. Sometimes."

"You weren't making a joke, Walter. Don't pretend you were."

She pushed her chair back, and instantly Walt was on his feet, coming around the table, a perfect gentleman. And then the waiter returned, saying, "Might I have a word with you, sir?"

"What about?"

"*This*." He held up a William Randolph Hearst twenty-dollar bill.

"Yes? What's the problem," said Walt, feigning bafflement, and Joette—Joette began to laugh, so loudly—for a lady—that she attracted the attention of other diners. Some of them smiled at her, but most of them glared.

11

Georgie sat at the kitchen table in the middle of the night, eating toast. Eating toast and nursing a highball.

He'd brought down a sketchbook from the studio and a Pabst beer bottle that he'd cut the top off to use as a pencil holder, and every so often he would rough out several panels on a clean page, stare at what he'd done, and end up doodling around their perimeters—small boxes, stars, isosceles triangles. The toast popped, his fifth and sixth slices since coming downstairs. He leaned over the table and looked at the machine, saw his reflection: his eyes were red-rimmed, his beard was heavy, his cheeks seemed puffy. He rubbed his forehead with the heel of his hand. He felt . . . totally blank. No ideas. He'd thought that perhaps getting out of the studio might help, he'd hoped that sitting at the kitchen table, where of late he seemed to get a lot of ideas and intuitions about a lot of different things, might start the juices flowing. But no. He was blocked. And at this bleak hour of the morning, he had the terrible feeling that he'd never, *never* draw another Pin—Little Nobody cartoon; never be *able* to. And wouldn't he love not to *have* to. He took a swallow of his drink.

Jesus, when this all had started, he'd figured that, at most, he'd have to do maybe half a dozen Sunday pictures. And how many had he done so far? How long had this been going on now? He took a bite of toast. "Come on," he said out loud, "come *on*," his voice sounding loud, strange, a little spooky. The house was so quiet. Joette was asleep. He hardly ever went to bed when she did anymore. Always up late, most of the time painting. She'd ask, Can't you get your work done in the daytime, like normal people?

He sketched another box. Another. Box, box, box. Nothing. And he had to get *three* finished drawings to the *Journal* by tomorrow afternoon. He'd already done the funny for this coming-up Sunday; these others—the ones he'd hoped to do tonight—were to cover himself while he was away. Hearst kept his promises, and he'd informed Georgie—only on Monday, which didn't leave him much time to get ready, much less get a jump on his cartoon work—that he was sending him to Cuba for a month. Havana. And I expect some good shockers—don't draw the *harbor*, unless there are bodies floating.

Georgie was looking forward to being away—he'd never been *anywhere*—and doing news work again. He was going with a writer named Canfield, Arch Canfield. He'd asked if Joette might come along—after all, this was Georgie's *bonus*, as well as being an assignment—but Hearst said no. War might break out in that pitiful island at any moment. Wishful thinking. And Joette had said, It's just as well. Standing around for two and a half weeks, or three, watching you draw sweaty Cubans doesn't particularly interest me. Oh? and what *does* interest you? he'd asked. I don't know—want to make a baby? And Georgie had done all he could. But she'd got her monthly a day later.

Georgie took another swallow of his drink. Looked at the clock on the wall. "Come *on*," he said, desperate now. He rapped on his skull with his knuckles. If Gulp were a *real* assistant, he thought, there'd be no problem. He could simply tell him, *You* do the next three pictures, and leave it at that. But he couldn't depend on Gulp; either Gulp wouldn't do the cartoons or he'd do them so poorly the *Journal* would bounce them. And Hearst would be very angry when Georgie returned. I hired *you*, not some second fiddle. The Chief had a temper, and a mean streak. Already, he'd become disenchanted with several of the high-priced reporters and editors that he'd pirated from other newspapers—but what could he do? He'd given them all iron-clad contracts. What could he do? This: There were currently at least half a dozen very tall newsboys hawking the *Journal* around lower Manhattan, not one of them earning a salary less than $400 weekly. Georgie wasn't about to be humiliated.

Gulp was hopeless. As a cartoonist. Now, if Walter—

Damn Walter.

Georgie made a small sketch of Little Nobody.

A sketch of Palaver.

Do something, you two!

It was nine minutes past three. He dropped two more slices of bread into the toaster.

At eleven minutes past the hour, the toast popped, and as it did, Georgie leaned over the table: he looked into the metal—and saw Fuzzy. Then Fuzzy *and* P. P was carrying something in his arms, something large. And Fuzzy had—something in her mouth.

Georgie stared, amazed. It was after three in the morning, he was tired, but there *had* been a few times before when he'd imagined he'd seen—*Images* in the side of the toaster. . . . He shook his head and then suddenly felt a tingling in his spine, across his shoulders. He turned in his chair.

P was standing in the kitchen doorway. P as he *used* to look, without the yellow wig, and wearing a pair of overalls. In his arms he held a palmetto plant in a cachepot. And Fuzzy had a small pillow in her mouth.

Georgie stared, and the boy and the dog stared right back.

But then they were gone, and where they'd stood a moment before the darkness seemed deeper than it should've, and the darkness seemed to . . . move, a little. Georgie continued to stare, until his eyes began to sting, and he coughed. He took a sip of his drink. He frowned and picked up a pencil. Looked around at the doorway again. Then quickly he drew P—Little Nobody just as he'd imagined him a minute ago: carrying a potted plant. And what was he doing with a potted plant? Where was he going with it? Georgie drew Fuzzy—Pal—with the pillow held in her jaws. He stared at the drawings, made a box around them. Made a second box. And in it, drew Nobody standing at a door. *Whose* door? A third box: Nobody enters a house, immediately trips on a runner. And from there,

Georgie had no problem constructing a scenario: nine panels in which Nobody struggles to regain his balance and not fall and break the vase. Pantomime. The vase finally lands on Palaver's pillow, safely.

Then Georgie asked himself, again, *Whose* house?

Why, Little Nobody's, of course! There was no more Awful Alley, his character had to live *some*where.

And that's how Number 10 Slum Gardens came to be the Little Nobody's permanent address.

Georgie, in twenty minutes' time, sketched two further series around the theme of Moving In. And in the third one, he even gave Little Nobody a neighbor and little sweetheart, a blond girl in a dirty pinafore and straggly ribbons in her hair. Katie Crackernut. With Palaver commenting at the end of the sequence, "I guess there's somebody for everybody, if there's somebody for Nobody!"

Georgie got up and stretched, then he turned off the light. He'd transfer everything to cardboard in the morning, ink it, and run it over to the *Journal*. And tomorrow he could leave for Florida, as scheduled. As he was going out of the kitchen, he stood for a few seconds in the doorway, touched the doorframe, shook his head.

He tried to wake Joette when he got into bed; he pressed himself against her from behind, spooning her, cupping her breasts, but she only muttered, asked him what time it was, and refused to wake up. He shrugged and, throbbing with exhaustion, turned over and went to sleep.

It wasn't until late the next day, after she'd returned from seeing Georgie off at Grand Central Station, that Joette realized that the potted plant was no longer in the back parlor. She'd gone to water it. Why would Georgie move it? And where had he moved it to? She went through the entire house.

She didn't find it.

12

First thing Walt said when he opened his door and Joette was standing outside clutching last Sunday's funny, rolled up, in a fist, was, "You know what I found out just yesterday? Richard Harding Davis used to live *right here!*"

And she replied, "He's always had a reputation for being an absolute gentleman."

And Walt said, "Well, I haven't made *my* reputation yet." Then he grinned at her and asked, "So you got my invitation?"

"I and half a million other people in New York." She waggled the comic under his nose. "Pinfold & Fuzzy," Panel Seven: See the toaster on the table in the Witch's flat? See what's lettered on its side? TUESDAY. 10 A.M.

"Won't you come in?" said Walt.

She hesitated for just a moment, then said, "Well, since I'm here . . ."

During her walk over—and it was a relatively short distance, from her Number 10 to Walt's—Joette's mind had entertained a bewildering assortment of discrete and complementary thoughts, speculations, alarms and fancies, likely conversations, and potential consequences of her visit, and one of the most intriguing of her meditations, while at the same time one of the least ominous, pertained to Walt's taste, or lack of it, in the matter of decoration and home furnishings. What would his first bachelor apartment look like? Like a boy's room? She hoped not. Would he actually hang Pinfold wallpaper, and if he did—if he had—what would she think? Would there be pinups? Would there be a pipe rack? (Please, no!) Would there be exercise paraphernalia? Joette at one time had had a brief affair of the heart with a boy who'd graduated (he said) from Dartmouth, and in his hermitage (his word) on lower Fifth Avenue (not far from where she and Georgie lived now) he'd had weighted grip pulls bolted to a wall, and three punching bags; he'd also had snowshoes crossed over the mantel. She hoped that Walt had not gone out and bought punching bags, though she asked herself why it should mean anything to her if he had.

Walt had no punching bags, no physical-training equipment of any sort. He had a morris chair with an adjustable back; he had a tufted lounge—dark maroon; he had a low wicker table and a square library table, a mission rocker, and an enormous, an absolutely enormous alabaster vase; he had a brass reading lamp with a sunny-yellow shade, and a majolica cuspidor. Everything crammed into the parlor. It was a hodgepodge. The stuff was simply—there. Picture molding ran around the walls just about a foot above eye level, but so far he'd hung nothing up. The wallpaper was dark green, plain. The draperies, also green, were open and the winter daylight through the window was powerful. The place, for some reason, made Joette feel giddy. It was awful! It was wonderful. It was very much Walter. She asked, "Did you buy everything yourself?"

"I did," he admitted, going over and touching the rocker, making it rock. Then he reached a hand up and scratched his head. "I had no idea what I wanted. I thought I'd just—fill the rooms."

She laughed.

"I'd be the first to admit I don't know what I'm doing. I bought that silly old vase and I didn't buy andirons. It's no easy job."

"No," said Joette, unbuttoning her coat. He ran around behind her and helped her off with it.

"And I forgot to buy a coat rack." He folded it carefully and laid it over an arm of the lounge. "I've spent a fortune, I'm afraid."

She looked at the furniture again. "You didn't," she said. "You did?"

He nodded sorrowfully. "I don't know how anybody can afford to stock an apartment from scratch."

"Furnish."

"And a whole house must be just murder," he said. "Sit. Please. Take your pick."

She smiled but remained standing. "I've had to buy very little so far. Hardly anything in Ninth Street belongs to us. Just the things you brought over that day." She went to the library table and touched her fingertips to the edge. She saw a small gray flowerpot on the window seat and frowned for just a moment. Then she said, "All in all, I think you've done *fine*."

"Thank you," he replied, his cheeks coloring.

Now what? They stood looking at one another till finally Joette said, "Well!" and turned to admire the brick fireplace. She said it was "very masculine." And again Walt thanked her, taking it as a personal compliment.

"Would you like a cup of coffee?"

Joette looked at herself in the chimney mirror. "I must apologize," she said. And then she looked around at Walt, across the room. "I'd bought you a little present last week—for your new apartment? I'd intended to—send it over."

He nodded, grinning.

"But somehow, I must've misplaced it. I have no idea what's become of it."

"A likely story," said Walt.

"I *did* buy you a present!"

"Only joking. What was it? I hope it was a stuffed osprey—I need one of those."

"It was a pillow."

Walt hated himself for blushing.

"A decorative pillow—it had a picture of a pheasant on it."

"A pheasant!" Walt exclaimed. "Well!"

"I can't imagine *what* happened to it."

"It'll turn up. And then you'll have a good excuse to come again." Walt crossed the room, carefully avoiding any contact with the tall vase, where for the time being he was keeping his dirty laundry. He said, "Would you like a cup of coffee now? I bought sticky buns. Would you like to see the rest of the place? There's nothing to see. Would you like me to tell you the names of the pet turtles I had when I was a boy of seven?"

Joette laughed; she took his hand and squeezed his fingers. "And I thought you wanted me to come here so you could kiss me. I thought that's what this was all about." Up until a moment before she spoke, Joette had not known that she would say such a thing or, saying it, use the very words of the heroine in a story she'd read last evening in the *Ladies' Home Journal,* Romance Number. Hopelessly unoriginal, but quite possibly wise: now, if Walt showed any scruples, she could claim to be parodying cheap literature—making a joke. She could send him the magazine with the dialogue underlined.

Three, four, five seconds passed.

And Walt, shaking off his astoundment, functioned: he tried to pull Joette into his arms, but the decision to do that had come so suddenly that he didn't coordinate himself well. He nearly tripped her, his shoe scooping around her ankle, his full weight bearing down upon her. Joette caught her balance just in time.

He kissed her, then broke the kiss prematurely so he could tell her that that had just been the first kiss of his life.

Joette said, "Richard Harding Davis would *never* say that to a woman."

"Well, it wouldn't be true for Richard Harding Davis."

"I'll bet you he never said it even when it was true," said Joette, and she poked him with two fingers, between his ribs.

Walt grabbed her wrist. "My name is Walt Geebus. I'm a forger, a thief, a backstabber, a green-goods passer, and a cartoonist. I love you!"

Joette said, "I knew that was coming. Let's get comfortable, *Walt.* We have to talk about this declaration of love."

Walt whined, "Don't make me feel ridiculous, Jo. I'm *serious.*"

She laughed—and for her, wasn't *that* what this was all about?

13

They'd come over on a steam launch from Key West—that had been three days ago, and since then Georgie had had nothing to do but drink beer on the porch of the Hotel Inglaterra. Hearst had expected him and Canfield, somehow, to get to Santa Clara province, where the rebel forces were supposed to be strongest and best organized, but they'd been denied passes. The Spanish weren't stupid. They knew where the sympathies of the American newspapermen lay. And so Georgie sat, drinking and perspiring and slapping at mosquitoes. He wanted to return home, immediately. He'd already wired the *Journal,* asking for permission to do just that, but had received no answer. *Slap! Slap!*

Canfield didn't mind having nothing to do, nowhere to go. Lazy bastard, Georgie thought. Overweight and lazy, and he liked it fine plopped down in his cane chair with his eyes shut. He had a reputation for being a good reporter, but he was nothing of the sort. What he was good at was taking a tidbit, a rumor, and turning it into something two thousand words long, full of thrills and sentimentality and large and small intestines spilled on the pavement—or, in the case of this assignment, on the verdant countryside and in the hard-packed yellow dirt of little towns a hundred miles from Havana. Canfield had made his name during the Great Blizzard of '88, when supposedly he'd slogged around New York in snowshoes seeking out and filing stories of poignancy and humor, courage and self-sacrifice; in fact, he'd been in a hotel room around the corner from Park Row, nipping from a bottle to fuel his imagination. Every several hours he'd cranked out a few more stories, then run over to the various papers and sold them at space rates.

If Hearst wanted open warfare to break out here in Cuba—and oh, he did, for circulation's sake—then Arch Canfield would try his damndest to do whatever he could to incite it. And that meant cabling long juicy horror stories, the longer the better, the more the merrier.

Georgie found the man contemptible, and he was starting to feel that way about himself.

At half past three each afternoon, a group of Cubans, never the same ones twice, would appear at the hotel, and for a small fee—and it *was* nominal, since they *were* patriots—they would describe for the reporters, and in the richest detail, the massacres since yesterday of peasants by soldiers; they also bore tales of canefields torched, track sabotaged, prisoners at Morro Castle fed alive to the sharks, and yellow fever in the reconcentration camps. They checked the spelling of names and made corrections, absolutely free of charge. Canfield filled notebook after notebook. Georgie listened, chewing on his pencil. How do we know what to believe, Arch? What do we care? The stuff is great, George. Now, give me a big heap of corpses, would you, for this one? Women and children on top. Georgie kept spitting splinters.

Today, Georgie was sitting with his feet up on the porch railing and a pad in his lap, doodling Little Nobody, when the Cubans came. He didn't budge, not until Canfield finally called him from the opposite end of the porch. Then he sighed and stood up.

There were several clusterings of Cubans and Americans, and Canfield's Cubans were dressed in white shirts and trousers; their handsome faces were brown as cordovan, their mustaches long and lush and needle-sharp at the tips. One of them had a large yellow dog on a short rope. When Georgie came and sat down in an empty chair, Canfield was petting the animal and finger-combing wads of hair from her thick coat; he blew those away like dandelion fluff. "You ever have a dog, George, when you were a boy?"

"No."

"Were you ever a boy?" Canfield laughed, then leaned back in his chair. His notebook was open on his lap, and a half page was covered with his indecipherable handwriting. "These two señors have been telling me a wonderful story. I'll write it up and you can do some drawings, all right?"

Georgie shrugged.

Canfield glanced at his notes. "All right. Seems there was this jail-keeper right here in the city, wonderful man, sympathetic to our side, and while the Spanish bastards were trying to starve all the

poor rebels in the jail, this fella was sneaking them chickens to eat."
He looked at Georgie. "*Pollos*. Sneaking them *pollos*." He winked.
"Okay. The Spaniards couldn't figure out how come the rebels
weren't just wasting away, how come they were staying so goddamn
healthy—some of them even put on weight. Well, they set a trap.
And they caught the old hero one night—last night?—and took him
and hanged him." Canfield clapped his hands enthusiastically.

Georgie glanced to the Cubans, standing there gravely nodding.
He asked them, "This really happened?"

The smaller of the pair, the one who had a straw hat, replied,
"Oh, yes. I swear to the Mother of God."

"You said this happened last night. There'll be a funeral." He said
to Canfield, "We could see that."

"No funeral," said the Cuban wearing the hat. "They took his
body and burned it. No funeral."

"What about a wife? Did he have any children? I could go sketch
them."

Both Cubans shook their heads. And the taller one, the one with
the dog, said, "No wife, no children, no family."

"Georgie," said Canfield, fed up, "we got a hanging here. What
do you want to draw a funeral for, when we got a hanging?"

"The old man," said the Cuban with the dog, "should be known in
all parts of the world where men breathe free. His heroism must not
be forgotten."

Georgie said, "Sure."

After the Cubans left, Georgie made sketches of the hanged man
on the same page where he'd doodled Little Nobody.

A short time later, Georgie's back began to bother him—too much
sitting, and he already had a headache and he was tired of killing
mosquitoes, so he decided to go on up to his room. Take a short nap,
then do a couple of finished drawings for Canfield in the coolness
after nightfall.

Passing through the hotel lobby, he saw the U.S. Consul General
telling more of his cowboy stories to the barman. A pretty whore
smiled at him on the stairs. He pretended not to notice her. Jesus,
this had been a complete waste of time. And Jesus, he felt lousy all
of a sudden. To draw what he'd been drawing for the past three
days, he could've stayed in New York. In future, he'd tell Hearst
thank you, but no thank you, to special assignments. And he'd been
bellyaching for months—months!—about how much he missed be-

ing a news artist. Well, here he was, a news artist once more, and it was—shit. Now, wait. This isn't quite the same thing. This isn't the same thing at all. No, it's really not. When I was at the *World*, I drew what I'd seen for myself. Oh? And what about the marvelous machine that cured, what was it, asthma and catarrh? All right, once in a while that sort of thing did come up. But it was *only* once in a while. He hadn't done that sort of thing often. Really! And then he thought of that first sketch of P. The *sketch* had been honest; maybe the *story* hadn't been, but the sketch was. And the second sketch? The third? The fourth?

And then he was thinking just about P, wondering where he might've disappeared to. Anywhere. He might've gone anywhere.

He might even be dead.

And suddenly, imagining the boy dead, Georgie clutched up inside, and he had to put out an arm to brace himself against the stair wall. He's *not* dead, Georgie thought. Why should he be *dead*, the little bastard? He felt woozy now. Too much beer.

He'd taken out his room key and was fitting it into the lock when he realized that the jamb was splintered; there were chips of dark-stained wood on the carpeting. He pulled open the door—startling a small Cuban boy in a long and soiled white blouse who'd been just about to climb out through the window with Georgie's valise; the Instant Camera Georgie had been given by Hearst was slung on the boy's shoulder.

Georgie froze, and the boy jumped.

Going after the little thief, Georgie became lost, quickly. The back streets were narrow, and the whitewashed houses old, jammed together, and whenever Georgie glanced up, he saw a dozen lined faces in a dozen tiny windows peering down at him. He passed a crowd of men huddled around two teenaged boys fighting with knotted ropes: he'd remember it. And he passed a small church where a mule draped in purple vestments stood on the steps, untended. He walked and he walked, and his head throbbed and his back spasmed; his mouth felt dry as dust. He stopped and leaned against a wall. His clothes stuck to him. He touched his forehead and it was hot. Flies buzzed aroud his face, mosquitoes; he waved them off, listlessly.

He began to walk again.

This is foolish, go back.

He kept walking, and night fell, the moon so low and large that he thought if he kept walking straight he would walk right into it. It appeared to be just another street away; its silvery light nearly blinded him. He put a hand to his eyes, just as a deluge of soapy water came crashing down in back of him. He spun around, and then he thought he saw the boy who'd been in his room disappear down an alleyway. Georgie began to run.

The alley was full of old beggars who sat on the ground with their backs to hovel walls; votive candles, statues of the Virgin, and tin cups stood between their bare feet. The candles flickered weirdly, and the beggars clutched at Georgie's trousers as he passed them. At the end of the alley was a high board fence, and lined along the fence were several barrels of stinking trash. No sign of the boy. Georgie walked up to the fence and peered over it. Another alley, more beggars. No sign of the boy. He felt so weak now that he was afraid he might be stricken—and what would happen to him then? He forced himself to walk, taking one step at a time, holding himself erect. He glanced down at one very old man whose face was raddled with scars. In his cup was a tin of Clarky's polish.

14

It was Clarky who first heard the news about Georgie; don't ask how. Immediately he went to Ninth Street to tell Joette, but when he arrived at Number 10 two policemen were standing at the door. He felt it wiser to take a stroll around the block and come back later.

"So you know," he said to Joette after he'd returned. "They told you?"

"Told me what? The police, do you mean? They came about a burglary I've had. Know *what,* Clarky?"

Clarky's sober, almost grieving expression alarmed her. Her stomach turned.

"May I step inside, Jo?"

"You're alone?" she asked, knowing it was a silly thing to ask—who cared? "Georgie told me you never travel alone anymore."

He allowed a smile; in fact, he wasn't alone: that pretzel vendor at the corner of Fifth Avenue had a loaded double-action .32 Colt concealed in his pushcart. "So I may come in?" He stepped past her into the hall. "A burglary?"

"Mr. Clark: Do I know *what?*"

"Georgie got sick in Cuba."

"Oh, my dear God! How sick?" She sat down heavily on the long cushioned bench outside the front parlor.

"A fever, I heard. One of those fevers they got down there. He'll be all right, I'm sure."

"He's still *there?*"

"In a hospital."

She raised a knuckle to her lips.

Clarky touched her on the shoulder.

The telephone rang then.

"That'll be the *Journal* probably. To tell you."

She stood up and slowly walked down the hall, into the back parlor. She lifted the metal cradle from the side of the box mounted on the wall and said, "Yes, I'm here," into the protruding mouthpiece. Then she frowned. "Walt, I can't speak to you. Really." Clarky had followed her in. "Yes," she said, "something's the matter." She replaced the cradle.

Clarky asked, "That was our friend, Walter *Geebus?*"

Did she answer? Did she nod? She didn't know—she didn't know what she was doing. She turned to sit down, and when there was no rocker where it ought to have been, she began to cry. One rocking chair, three blankets, and an oval mirror: missing when she'd gotten up this morning. First that, now this. Joette sat down on the sofa. Now this.

"I wouldn't worry too much, Jo."

"I don't want him to die."

"Don't be silly. It's just an old fever."

15

It was yellow fever, and Georgie nearly did die of it—at least that's what Arch Canfield told Joette when he called at the house, the week following Clarky's visit. By then, Georgie had been taken by boat to Florida. He was still in a hospital there.

"It just came on"—Canfield snapped his fingers—"like that. It was terrible to see. He had the chills. He had that high fever. And his skin went all yellow. Hits the liver, they tell me. He was vomiting like a sailor."

"Mr. Canfield," said Walt, who'd been at the house when the *Journal* man arrived. "I think you might spare Mrs. Wreckage all the details."

Canfield looked momentarily cross; then he smiled. "Sorry! I talk like I write, I guess. Sorry. But he's coming along swell, missus. They say. And Mr. Hearst sent down two doctors of his own to have a look at Georgie. Isn't he a crackerjack fella?"

Joette managed a tiny, the tiniest smile.

Canfield snatched his hat from the table. "I won't take up any more of your time. I only wanted to give you a kind of a personal report—and this, too." Georgie's sketchbook. He passed it to Joette. She put it down, and Walt immediately picked it up, began flipping through it, idly.

"And the rest of my husband's things. Are they at the hospital in Key West, Mr. Canfield? Would you happen to know?"

Canfield set his mouth. "I'm afraid they were stolen, missus. Awful thieves they are, those Cubans. Great patriots! But a bunch of thieves." He nodded to both Joette and Walt, then Walt went with him to the door.

"Are you the lady's brother?" Canfield asked, as he was stepping outside. "I see a resemblance."

Walt said yes, her brother.

16

Joette would've taken a train down to Florida immediately, but she'd been advised by everyone—Walt, Clarky, even Hearst himself, who twice telephoned the house—to wait at least until Georgie's recovery had begun in earnest. I'm his wife, though, I *should* be there! Well, if you feel that you must go, then *go*, certainly. Do what you feel is right, Mrs. Wreckage. I'll pick up a train schedule for you, Jo, and you can leave first thing in the morning. Well . . . if you *truly* believe that I can't do any *real* good down there at *this* point . . . , and she'd let herself be talked into staying at home. The reports she got on Georgie's condition—via the *Journal*'s man in Key West—were cautiously worded for about the first two weeks, but then, quite suddenly, they turned sanguine. He looks much better. His color's improved. He's eating some food and keeping it down. Joette thanked God.

One afternoon she received a call from a man named Monk Brown, of the *Journal*'s art department. He wanted to know whether, by some chance, Georgie had left behind any sketches, or jotted down some ideas, for upcoming Little Nobody cartoons. The Sunday pages Georgie had done before leaving for Cuba would be exhausted after next weekend, Brown told Joette, and he told her as well that Mr. Hearst was quite anxious that the feature appear in *every* colored supplement. If there are some sketches, we can send a messenger over to get them, Mrs. Wreckage. And we'll have a staffer here do the finished drawings. Joette felt a throb of panic. What if that *staffer* should turn in highly satisfactory cartoons? And what if Georgie's convalescence were protracted? Might not Georgie eventually lose his cartoon, might not this *staffer* inherit it? She told Walt of her fears later, and he said, Oh, don't worry, Georgie's got a contract. Contract, said Joette, wrinkling her nose. Show me a contract that can't be broken, somehow. All right then, said Walt, *I'll* do the drawings. Oh, you can't! I certainly *can*. And who'll know? Call the *Journal* back and tell 'em you found a couple of finished pictures. Say you'll send them over tomorrow. And I'll have them ready for you. But Joette said no, she couldn't let Walt do that. Georgie would, Georgie would . . . Georgie wouldn't *like* it, she was certain. So finally Walt suggested that she contact Jim Sip. Tell *him* to do them. Joette thought about it, and at last she agreed it was a good idea. At least worth a try.

Gulp arrived at the house on a rainy Thursday morning, and after Joette had explained to him what she wanted, three—three ought to do it—Little Nobody cartoons, to tide things over till Georgie returned, he bowed and snapped his fingers—he *tried* to snap his fingers, but his coordination was groggy. He promised Joette the pictures by the end of the day. Could he use the studio? Of course. She gave him the key, and he went trudging up the stairs, keeping a hand on the banister all the way.

Walt was down in the kitchen having a slice of jelly toast and a cup of tea. Well? He's gone straight up to work, Joette said. Thank you, Walt. For being here. I know it's silly, but I didn't want to be alone in the house with that man. *I* certainly didn't mind coming over, he said, taking one of her hands and patting it. He stayed there at the kitchen table for the rest of the morning. He did some of his own drawing, while Joette cleaned the house.

Shortly after one, Joette climbed to the studio to check on Gulp and found him sprawled out on the sofa, asleep and snoring—the sound a high-pitched whistling. There was a sheet of cardboard, still blank, on Georgie's table, and a wet painting of Gulp's standing on the Dutch easel. A palette and an empty gin bottle lay on one of the twelve cartons of counterfeit money ranged along a side wall. Joette shook Gulp awake, roughly, thanked him very much, threw him his coat, and showed him the door. He swore that he'd intended to get to the cartoons—How long can they take, really?—after lunch. Joette said, Good day, Mr. Sip.

That afternoon, Walt took his pad and pencils and the toaster/ heater up to the studio and completed a Pinfold page of his own and two Little Nobody pages. By Georgie Wreckage. Joette asked him to stay for dinner. He did, and stayed for the night, too.

Next morning, when Joette went to prepare oatmeal for break-fast, she discovered that nearly all her pans and pots and prepa-ration utensils and ordinary cutlery were gone from the kitchen cabinets and drawers. Joette, said Walt, are you sure that the man who owns this house left it for love? Are you sure he wasn't chased out by a ghost? Joette said, *Walt*, please. And Walt said, But I *read* about ghosts like this. *Walt*er: What would a ghost want with an egg-beater? Walt said, What would a *thief* want with one?

So Walt climbed to the studio and brought down the toaster, and they toasted rye bread and had that for breakfast.

Several night later, Walt came over to the house around nine o'clock in the evening. They played cards in the parlor, both of them playing sloppily, unable to concentrate. In the morning, Joette would be leaving for Key West; Georgie was deemed fit enough to travel again, and she would bring him home. And *then* what? Joette kept looking over her pasteboards at Walt, and he kept pressing his lips together and widening his eyes. Every so often, he rubbed a fist across his forehead and sighed heavily; then Joette would bite on her thumb. When it was nearly midnight, Walt threw his cards down. "I should be going home," he said.

"Yes?" Joette smiled weakly.

"But I'm not."

"Yes," she said. "All right."

Sometime later, as Walt lay quietly with his head on her breasts, Joette—winding and unwinding a lock of his hair around her finger—asked him in a whisper, "What would you like to see happen, Walt?"

His head moved.

"I mean—would you want me to come visit you on certain days of the week? Like that man visits the wife in the house across the street? *Tell* me."

His head moved again, and a shoulder. "I guess not," he said.

"What then?"

He rolled over on his back, then reached down and pulled the bed sheet over them both. He stared at the ceiling. He wet his lips. "Are you still in love with George?"

And she replied without any hesitation, "Yes. Of course."

He breathed down through his nose.

"Did you honestly expect me to say no?"

Walt shut his eyes.

"Well, *did* you? Yes, I love George. *Yes.*"

"And me? Do you love me?"

That time she did hesitate; and finally, instead of making a reply, she spoke Walt's name again, as a question.

"Then you *don't*," he said.

"Oh, Walter, you want everything to be so simple, don't you? I don't love him anymore, I love you. Just like that. But things aren't always simple. And people aren't cartoons, Walter. I'm sorry to have to tell you that."

"You're calling me Walter," he said.

She smiled. "People aren't cartoons, Walt."

There was a long silence. Then Walt asked, "Do you love me a little bit, at least?"

"Would you be here if I didn't?"

"But *just* a little bit?"

"Walter," she said then, testily, "please turn off the self-pity. I like you much better when you're being funny."

He put a finger in his ear and stuck out his tongue.

But it did nothing for Joette, and then, sadly, she watched him as he turned over in the bed, on his side, and sulked. She moved to touch him—oh for goodness' sake, she was about to say, sure I love you, a *lot*—when there was a loud crash, downstairs. Walt pushed himself up on his hands, and he and Joette looked at each other in

surprise, each seeing imperfect pores and blotchy spots. Walt's eyes
seemed about to fly from their sockets. "What's *that?*" he said.
Joette noticed a tiny scratch above Walt's eye. "Should I lock the
bedroom door?" he said.

Joette stared. "If you think that's what you should do." She
touched her own cheek, then drew back her hand; it hovered in the
air, then the fingers curled into a fist.

"You don't think I should go *down*stairs, do you?" said Walt, his
whisper a hiss. "All right, I will."

"Walter, I didn't say you should do *anything.*" A pulse was beating in her throat.

Walt got out of bed then, pulled on his trousers, reached for his
shirt. "Do you happen to have a gun?"

"No."

"*No?*"

"I wouldn't let George keep one in the house."

"You *wouldn't?*" Walt seemed in physical pain; he kept pressing a
fist against his solar plexus.

"Walter, you don't have to go downstairs. I don't *want* you to. Just
stay here."

"And lock the door?"

"Yes."

Walt stood next to the bed, indecisive. "You really want me to go
downstairs."

"I don't!"

"Would Georgie? He would, wouldn't he?"

Joette threw off the sheet; she crossed the bedroom to the door,
cocked her head, and pressed an ear to the panel. Then she turned
the key in the lock. Walt came and turned it the opposite way.

"Listen: if I get killed down there, don't do anything till you've
got in touch with Clarky. He'll know how to get rid of my body so
there'll be no scandal."

"Wal*ter!*"

He smiled—it was a strained one, but a smile nonetheless. "I'm
only kidding, Jo. I'm only being funny." Then he wiggled his eyebrows. She could see how hard his throat was working to swallow.

Before he slipped out into the upstairs hall, he took a hairbrush
from the dresser, as a weapon. He crept to the head of the stairs; he

crept down them. As he came into the foyer, the darkness there seemed as absolute as in a cavern. How could that be? There were fanlights above the front door. His heart was beating crazily, and now his throat and lungs began to feel scorched with every breath that he took. He stepped barefoot across the foyer, then stopped and listened. Heard nothing. He continued on into the front parlor and immediately slammed a knee against a bookcase door that was open; the door banged shut. His heart leaped into his throat. He raised the hairbrush.

As soon as the throbbing in his head quieted, he listened again, and this time he thought he heard a noise down in the kitchen level. He dropped the brush to the carpet, felt his way over to the fireplace, and grabbed a poker. That emboldened him. Ready or not, here I come. . . .

He made his way slowly down to the bottom hallway, where there was an electric light. He reached across himself with his right hand and switched it on. Nobody. He checked in the dining room and in the kitchen. Nobody. But then, just as he was about to go back upstairs—Oh, Penelope! Brave Ulysses has returned!—he noticed that the door to the wine cellar was ajar.

He tingled from head to foot; a bitter juice squirted up his throat into his mouth.

Promising Cartoonist Murdered.

He stood at the wine cellar for half a minute; then, setting his teeth, he pulled the door open.

Nobody.

The hall light yellowed the dirt floor. There! Over *there*, what's that? Walt bent and picked it up: a piece of red paper, charred around the edges. It looked like the wrapper from a cannon cracker. Walt sucked in his cheeks. He almost smiled. Then he glanced around him, at the shelves lining three walls; finally, he looked up. And *did* smile. Dropping the poker, he stepped onto the bench which ran up the center of the vault, raised both arms—and shoved.

In the ceiling, a trapdoor gave. Walt almost expected that it would be kicked right back down into his face, but it wasn't. He clambered up through the opening. A tool shed, and as soon as Walt stood, he banged his head on the roof. Then he stepped on a garden rake. The handle shot forward, hitting him in the collarbone. He tried the shed door, but it was padlocked from the outside. There was a small diamond-shaped pane of glass in the door, and through it you could see the back of Number 10 and the short yard. Nobody out there, nobody that Walt could see.

On his way back through the wine cellar, he stopped and selected a bottle of—something, something French from one of the shelves. And then he began to laugh.

WHO (P)INFOLD BEFRIENDED AT THE PICKLEWORKS

When Georgie Wreckage had given him a tour of the house in Ninth Street last summer, P had been much taken with the wine cellar—because of its secret exit. A way out in case of fire. He'd said then to Georgie, Sure, here's the place to sleep—one, two, three, and you're safe! Georgie was amused.

The first time the boy had sneaked into Number 10 in his capacity as—burglar? he didn't really think of what he was doing as stealing, but burglar would do; housebreaker—the first time he'd gone there, he'd found, as he'd expected to, the shed door secured by a padlock. He'd broken it—Taffy from Jersey had shown him how to do just that, and with only one strike of a hammer, a hammer wrapped in cloth. And on his way out—he'd taken Georgie's wallet that first trip—he'd locked the shed with a padlock of his own. Who'd notice the switch? Who did any gardening in the middle of winter?

This night, P had taken an armload of books. Taffy had told him, Lots of people stick money between the pages, though hardly ever in Bibles. You can skip those. And make sure you always slice out the bookplates. I once found a hundred-dollar bill pasted back of one. Books, he'd said, are rich. And pillows—you never know what might be sewn up inside of 'em. And flowerpots. I found a diamond ring in geranium dirt. And check in back of drawers—dresser drawers, kitchen drawers. Just stick your fingers behind; you might feel tape, if you're lucky. P had had to pay Taffy for all the lessons.

Twenty dollars. Alvin McCoy had been horrified—not only because P had taken such instruction, but also because he'd actually sprung for the charge. This is America, he'd said. Education should be free! Now, close your mouth, Pinfold. Swallow! And repeat: Education should be free. . . .

At the corner of Canal and Brine, two drunks were arguing loudly in separate languages, and they began to cough and wheeze as P walked past them with his stack of books, but neither man noticed him. P continued on Brine for half a block, then cut into an alley which led to the old pickleworks, Maloney & Grue's. He dumped his books on the loading platform and climbed up there himself. His arms ached. He wet two fingers and used them to pinch out—*ssss!*—the sticks of Artificial Midnight jammed into wads of chewing gum on the toes of his shoes. He took off his derby—he'd found a new one, gray—and snuffed yet another stick, on the crown and similarly anchored. Then he removed the handkerchief that had been covering the bottom half of his face—so he wouldn't choke to death—and wiped his sooty forehead with it. He took a deep breath and filled his lungs.

The padlock on the shipping door looked closed, but wasn't quite.

Inside, it was cold and gloomy, an enormous, empty space; P heard several rats, felt one. His footsteps clanged and echoed as he climbed to the office level, and before he reached the top, Fuzzy had come out on the balcony and was waiting for him. The first two times that P had gone into Georgie's house, the dog had gone with him—but he'd started leaving her behind after the night she'd wandered away from him and he hadn't been able to find her for twenty minutes. Now, *there* was a night! It had almost made him quit. First, he'd lost Fuzzy—and then Georgie had seen him. He'd expected Georgie to make a grab for him, but the son of a bitch had just sat there like a stone; later, when he and Fuzzy were walking back to Brine Street, safely enveloped in their black cloud, it had occurred to the boy: The bastard figured he was just imagining things. Bet he was drunk. P had felt incredibly lucky, but nevertheless very cross with Fuzzy. You stay home from now on. She hadn't given him any argument.

"What'd you bring tonight, Pinfold?"

P lowered the stack of books, so he could look over the top: in silhouette behind Fuzzy stood Gertrude Gal.

"Books!" he said. "When I'm done with 'em, you can read 'em to your ma, if you like." Then he said, "How're you doing, Fuzzy?"

"Fine," replied the dog, and Gertrude laughed and clapped. She always did that, whenever Fuzzy talked, and then she always turned to P and beamed at him like he was—like he was *Steve Brody,* or somebody. P liked it. He liked it very much.

Gertrude was fourteen or fifteen. She had a small, narrow face and a nose that was slightly crooked, with a bump— But it wasn't never busted! That's just how it grew—and kinky yellow hair to the backs of her knees. She and her sickly mother had been living at the pickleworks since Mr. Gal went to prison, nearly two years. He had another thirty-three to go. I am greatly disappointed in him, Gertrude had told P. He promised Ma he wouldn't get caught. He promised me the same thing. And then he never even made it out of that old bank. Never even got through the doors. I am greatly disappointed, still! And P had replied, 'magine you *must* be.

As P lugged the books down the corridor, he passed the small secretary's office which the Gals called home. He glanced through the doorway and saw Gertrude's mother asleep on the floor, her head resting on a small pillow with a pheasant on it. Alongside her stood a leafy palmetto plant in a pot. Several little candles were burning in saucers. P had promised Gertrude that he'd try to bring back a lamp some night, but so far none of the lamps that he'd seen at Number 10 were at all familiar to him—and he was taking only things of Georgie's that he remembered from the rooms in Sawdust Street, or things that obviously were new—such as the pillow, which he'd found with a price tag on it. And cash money, of course, any cash money, though there'd been precious little of that left lying around—a two-dollar bill in the kitchen, probably intended for the milkman, mixed change in a jeroboam, and the five singles from Georgie's wallet. The boy knew that the house had been rented furnished and didn't want to remove anything belonging to the owner. That would've been stealing. He was certain that once he'd had a chance to get up into the studio, he'd find one of Georgie's own lamps. Gertrude said, There's no hurry. She admired him for being so scrupulous in his pilfering. She didn't pretend to understand it, but she admired him for it, nevertheless.

The last time P was a squatter at Maloney & Grue's, the fortune-teller Canary Ella had been living in the office that he bunked in

now, the one whose door said VAT FOREMAN. (He'd thought it said
NO ADMITTANCE, till Gertrude told him otherwise: Whenever you
see the letter V, it's the *vuh* sound; vuh-*at*. Vat. Vat foreman.) After
dropping the books on his cot, which he'd taken with him from the
Professor's room in Sawdust Street, P lit half a dozen candles, then
crawled into the kneehole of a desk for his wigbox. He kept Fuzzy's
vegetables in it. He brought out the wigbox and cut a turnip.

"I got her to drink some cold soup before, with an egg stirred in,"
said Gertrude.

"You did? You shouldn't give her any of your food. Honest. She
ain't your responsibility. She really drank it?"

Gertrude nodded.

"Well, thank you," said P, and turning to his dog, he said, "Did
you thank Gertrude for being so generous?"

"Thank you," said Fuzzy.

And Gertrude laughed again and clapped her hands together.

Fuzzy lay down on her pallet of newspapers.

Gertrude sat on an up-ended dry-goods box; she crossed her
skinny arms on her knees. Her dress in the gloom looked black; it
was actually gray. "Did everything go all right tonight?"

"I'm here, ain't I?" said P. He tried eating a piece of turnip himself but spit it right out. He cleaned his knife on a sleeve, then knelt
down and flipped through a book; when no money fell, he sliced out
the bookplate. Nothing concealed. He handed the book to Gertrude;
she turned the spine toward a candle and read, "*A Connecticut Yankee in King Arthur's Court.*"

"I *did* get a little clumsy, though. Knocked over an ashtray
stand—I think that's what it was. Crash! And Georgie came down,
almost caught me."

Gertrude asked, "How long do you think you can keep this up?"

"Well . . I still got about forty sticks of Artificial Midnight. Till
they run out, at least."

"You think you'll find any money?"

P finished going through another book and shrugged. "Taffy said
that even people with bankbooks keep money around."

"But what if these people don't?"

"There's still rocking chairs." He laughed.

Gertrude wagged her head. "But what do you want with their
rocking chairs?"

"You have to sit on something."

"No," she said.

He looked at her, candlelight and shadow in motion across her face. "No? What do you mean, no?"

"I mean, I don't think you care about chairs . . . or pots, or knives and forks . . . or books. You're just taking these things—to *take* them." She leaned forward, and P placed another book into her hand. *"Allan Quartermain,"* she read.

"I'm entitled to anything of his that I want."

"Who says?"

"I do."

"But why do you want this stuff? You don't need it."

"Could sell it. Later."

"What you'd get from what you got—so far—wouldn't buy you a train ticket to Philadelphia, much less California."

That's where Alvin McCoy was now, California. San Francisco, California. He'd said, Why not come? And P had said, Maybe I will. Alvin said, With me? *Now?* And P said, Later. Maybe. He'd told Gertrude, I want to get out to California—that's why I'm doing all this. I need the money. It sounded good, it sounded reasonable; he'd told Professor Thom the same thing. I want to go to California. In fact, he had about as much desire to go to California as he had to go to the moon. So, if he didn't need traveling money, why *had* he begun to rifle Georgie's house? Because. It made perfect sense to him, if to no one else. Because. Just because. Sometimes, tiptoeing through the hallways at Number 10, or staggering back to the pickleworks with a sack full of pennies or clickety cutlery, or even sometimes in his cot, his arms folded behind his head, P would ask himself, Because *why?* Because he owes me, because he used me, because he didn't—didn't *what?* And he'd give it up right there and turn his thoughts to other matters, plain matters: Is the cloud still around me? I'm hungry. That's a rat I hear.

Gertrude was saying, "If you think this man, I don't know, cheated you or something, maybe you should bring a lawsuit."

"Bring it where, the cleaner's?"

She laughed. "Really. If you think he owes you something, you ought to sue him. It's the way of the world."

"Is that a fact," said P, "or is that a rule?"

"It's just—the way of the world."

P shook his head, sliced another bookplate. "I like my way better. And maybe tomorrow I'll find a million bucks in twenty-dollar bills." He lifted his eyebrows. "Tucked away under the sink."

"Tucked away!" Gertrude glanced at the latest book she'd been handed: *Huckleberry Finn*. "You don't believe that."

He shrugged

"Well, at least I hope you're *enjoying* yourself."

And he laughed.

Later, after he'd gone through all the books (nothing in any of them, except a letter to Joette from her girlfriend Pearl Conselman in Chicago), P shared a cigarette with Gertrude, and then Gertrude lay down with him on the cot. They kept their clothes on and all they did was hug and cuddle (That's *not* cuddling, Pinfold, please remove your hand). Eventually, they both fell asleep—but Fuzzy came and nipped at Gertrude's ankle till finally she woke and stood up to leave. P was snoring. "Good night, Fuzzy," said Gertrude.

The dog said nothing, and when Gertrude was gone, she lay down on the floor under the boy's cot.

Six

ARTIFICIAL MIDNIGHT

1

"'The lamp flame jumped. One of the candles on the mantel was blown out, and the little machine suddenly swung round, became indistinct, was seen as a ghost for a second perhaps, as an eddy of faintly glittering brass and ivory; and it was gone—vanished! Save for the lamp, the table was bare. . . .'" Joette paused; then, seeing that Georgie had fallen asleep, she laid the purple ribbon across the page and closed the book. *The Time Machine*, by H. G. Wells. She had bought it at Brentano's, just a day after returning from Florida. Actually, Walt had made the selection. He'd scanned a few passages here and there, then read one out loud to Joette: "You can scarce imagine how nauseatingly inhuman they looked—those pale, chinless faces and great, lidless, pinkish-gray eyes!" Buy this one, Jo. George'll love it.

But Georgie seemed neither to love it nor hate it; he just . . . listened. He lay in the bed—and how small he looked there! almost like a child, he'd lost so much weight—and gazed up at the ceiling, hardly any expression, but fatigue, on his face. Joette would ask, Do you want me to continue? And he'd nod, but almost imperceptibly. She only got to read a page or two at a time, he kept dozing.

Joette herself didn't much care for the story. It made her think of poor, sweet, luckless Professor Thom, and thinking about the Pro-

fessor naturally led her to think about Pinfold the thief. See this, Jo?
Walt had said the night he'd gone downstairs to investigate the
crash. See this piece of paper? Remember the day you mistook me
for a Negro? Artificial Midnight. Found it in your wine cellar. Whoever's been sneaking in every other night is burning these things.
And who do you suppose that might be? Who do you think might've
helped himself to the Professor's supply? Who do we know bugs
enough to burgle a rocking chair, a stock pot, and the ordinary
cutlery?

Joette placed the book on her dresser and crossed the bedroom to
the window. She brushed the curtain aside and peered down into the
yard, then at the shed. Before leaving for Key West, she'd had a
locksmith come to the house; he'd removed P's padlock and replaced
it with another—a sledgehammer couldn't break this one, missus,
and it can't be picked either, I guarantee that. Joette had considered
going to the local precinct—they'd station a man in the yard, surely,
if I asked them. If I *paid* them. But she'd hesitated. It was strange,
but she'd been unable to summon the indignation, the anger, the
sense of violation which she'd supposed she ought to feel. What P
had been doing simply—baffled her. Why on earth—? If he'd
showed up at the front door, Georgie would've invited him in. You
need a mirror, you want a plant—here, take them. That's what
Georgie would've said. Didn't the boy *know* that? Joette did. She
did, indeed. She'd wondered again that day, as she'd wondered the
evening when Georgie had first brought P to Sawdust Street—
wondered whether the boy was insane. If he could walk in through
the front door, *why* would he sneak in through the cellar? And steal
books! Blankets! A pillow! Was it some kind of game? What did he
really want? Joette had not gone to the police. The new padlock
would suffice. It would keep P out, keep him away. He'd told her
once, Now you owe me. Well, she no longer did. . . .

She leaned over Georgie now and unfolded the pillow behind his
neck, she pulled the blanket up to his throat, she felt his forehead.
He had a temperature again. The doctor she'd spoken with at the
hospital in Florida told her, It'll come and go, come and go. For
several more weeks, possibly. And then suddenly it'll be over. And
he'll be immune to the disease forever. Joette had said, trying to
make it sound as if she were joking, Please, don't let *him* know
that—he'll be back in Cuba by Easter.

"George? Do you want a cup of tea? Anything?"

He opened his eyes, the whites tinged yellow. When he ran the tip of his tongue across his top lip, Joette could hear a faint crackling sound. He shook his head, no, he didn't want anything.

"In a little while I have to go out. Mrs. Trager from next door is coming in. All right?"

He smiled, and she pressed her lips together, glanced away. He reached for her hand then, and stroked it, his fingers unpleasantly warm and dry. "Love you, Jo."

"And I love you," she said, then left. A few minutes later, after Mrs. Trager arrived, she put on her coat and walked across town to see Walt, who met her at the door with a small bow in his hand, a quiver of toy arrows slung across his back, and cardboard wings glued to his shoulders.

"You're looking much better this afternoon, Mr. Wreckage, I'm pleased to see."

Georgie, in carpet slippers and a robe over his pajamas, was sitting in the big uncomfortable spool chair by the window—he'd asked Joette to bring up the rocker but she'd told him she gave it away in a charity drive. *My* rocker? He sipped at a cup of tea Mrs. Trager had fixed him. He felt so tired—all he *did* was sleep (and dream: Gulp dragging a corpse with a broken neck up the steps of the Hotel Inglaterra, for the Black Gang to sketch . . .), and still he felt so tired. And so—foggy. What time of day was it? What day of the week? Was it still January? "Mrs. Trager, do you happen to know today's date?"

"It's the fourteenth, Mr. Wreckage."

"Of *February?*"

She nodded. "Valentine's Day."

"Is it *really?*"

"Till midnight."

Georgie glanced out the window: nothing to see in the yard, nothing to look at. "Valentine's Day," he said. If Joette had let him have today's paper he would've realized: red hearts on page one, for sure. He hadn't looked at a newspaper, though, since getting back to New York. No news is good medicine, Joette kept saying. "Mrs. Trager, I wonder if you'd do me a great favor. Would you go upstairs to my studio—the key is on top of the dresser, there, it's the one with the dab of white paint—would you go upstairs and bring me back a pad of paper? And a bottle of ink. And some pens. And there should be a lap board. I believe it's in the closet."

"I don't think your wife would like it. You're not supposed to work."

"And a scissors! There should be several around."

Mrs. Trager smiled regretfully and shook her head. She was a plump woman, in her early forties, plain-featured; she wore a tiny gold cross on a chain around her throat, and her dark hair in a French twist. "There'll be plenty of time to draw pictures again, when you're better."

"Mrs. Trager, you've just told me that it's Valentine's Day. I'd like to make a card for my wife."

She got up then, from the chaise longue, and, smiling, said, "In that case, I suppose it'll be all right. Like your Little Nobody made for his sweetheart last Sunday, eh? Hope yours isn't as great a mess! I laughed—everything sticking to the glue on his fingers. Mr. Trager enjoyed it too, and he's not one for the funny papers, ordinarily." Mr. Trager worked for Tammany—Superintendent of this or that. Sanitation? "We both thought it was very cute. I cut it out of the paper, as a matter of fact. And I was wondering if you might autograph it for us sometime."

Georgie stared at the woman.

"I didn't realize that you people prepared your drawings so far ahead of time. But it's lucky for you that's the case." She frowned at him then, and with a parental edge to her voice added, "Running off to Cuba!"

"And there's a glue pot I'll need. Thank you for reminding me." He looked out the window again. "Don't try to carry everything at once. If it's too heavy." Valentine card? Little Nobody?

When Joette returned, just before seven, Mrs. Trager told her that Georgie had been up for perhaps an hour, that he'd had a cup of tea, but then had gone back to bed, complaining of a headache; he was still sleeping. Joette climbed the stairs and went into the bedroom, quietly. She noticed at once, on the table, the scissors and pens, ink bottle and paste pot, as well as a sheet of paper with a heart cut out of its center. And then she saw the heart, what must've been the heart, crumpled in the wastebasket. She pressed her wrist to her mouth, then walked around the bed and sat down on the edge.

Georgie was mumbling in his sleep; he still felt warm. "I'm back," she said.

His eyes opened quite suddenly, and wide; he stared at Joette for several seconds before blinking. And then he said, his voice hoarse, sticky, "I have a question for you. And I want you to tell me the truth."

Joette felt cold. "Tell you the truth?" She forced a laugh. "About what?"

"About Walter Geebus," he said.

2

In a letter to Pearl Conselman, dated March 19, Joette wrote: . . . so my life is not quite the fairy tale that you seem to believe it is, dear friend. I must tell you that, but for occasional afternoons away from the house, I am almost always in low spirits. Georgie is still angry with me, and nothing that I say to him, *try* to say, makes a difference. He calls me disloyal. Disloyal! When I only wished to make certain that his cartoon would not be taken away from him. He says there was never any chance of that happening. I am supposed to believe, as he apparently does, that Mr. Hearst is the fairest of fair men. But I am beginning to believe that—no, I won't finish the thought. Perhaps it was foolish of me to let Walter Geebus draw Georgie's cartoons for those several weeks; certainly it was foolish to think he'd never find out about it. (Did I tell you how that happened? I don't believe so: a neighbor of ours brought one of Walter's pictures to Georgie, so that he might autograph it for her! And after all the trouble I'd gone through to keep him from seeing anything!) I tell Georgie, at least three times every day, that I *tried* to get his friend Gulp to do the pictures. It makes no difference. Walter Geebus is a villain. *I'm* a villain.

You ask about George's health, but I don't quite know how to answer you. He is up and around again. He goes out. He has an appetite, and some of the weight that he lost he's regained. He does continue to run a slight fever almost every night, but it is certainly nothing dangerous. So, is he well again? He is getting his strength back, and his stamina. But in other ways, Pearl, I am convinced he is not healthy, and sorrowful about it.

He has resumed his painting. I'd hoped he would abandon it, now that Jim Sip (Gulp) is no longer around to influence and encourage him. I told you about that, didn't I? About Gulp? (Pearl, you must forgive me if I keep repeating things from letter to letter—last week I paid the gas bill twice, on Monday and again on Wednesday!) Mr. Sip, the "realist" painter, is now confined to a sanitorium; he *was* in jail—for biting a woman, a perfect stranger, on the arm, in the Elevated! (Georgie won't admit it, Pearl, but I'm almost certain that he is paying for that man's—treatment?)

At the beginning of the month, Georgie exhibited a painting, for the first time, at a small picture gallery on East Fifty-third Street. His so-called Gang convinced an art dealer named Hamlet to show their work. Not surprisingly, those newspapers that chose to send critics published highly unflattering reviews. The kindest word I read in any of them was *vulgar*. In the *World,* Georgie was singled out for particularly harsh remarks, and naturally they made mention of the fact that he is the artist of a cartoon appearing in the Sunday *Journal* which is read by thousands of children. They did not, however, mention that Georgie used to draw for them. It was very cruel, but not surprising. The *World,* after all, is managed by men, and men hold grudges. Georgie was so incensed that I truly feared he would march down to the Pulitzer Building and assault the art critic; he actually spoke of doing it. Is *that* healthy? This coming Sunday, his cartoon is entitled The Great Art Show in Slum Gardens. A sissy critic is bitten by the dog and brained by the Little Nobody. I honestly think that cartoon is the first in months which Georgie enjoyed drawing. And it *is* very funny. When I saw it, I laughed out loud— and, Pearl, it's probably the first time I did that, in this house, in God knows how long. I wish I was happy. I wish Georgie was. I wish this was a time when wishes still came true.

3

In Clarky's dream, he was strolling down the middle of lower Broadway, listening to the cobblestones cry out: Boston Telegraph's in jeopardy, sell all your holdings! Have you heard about the Mayor of Filch Hall? It's c.a., not pleurisy! Nick the Nose is skimming the receipts at Canal Billiards; you should do something! Wilma's sister—

"—is coming to New York to live with me next week, Clarky. Do you think you might find her a job?"

The warm breath in his left ear tickled him awake, and turning his head on the pillow, he swallowed, grunted, opened his eyes.

Wilma—a cashier at a penny arcade on Avenue A that Clarky had recently bought into—leaned over him and kissed him on the nose; then she crawled on top of him and collapsed. Such a buxom thing was she—two hundred and fifty pounds if she weighed an ounce—that Clarky felt as though he'd been struck by a falling safe. He was struggling to get his wind, and to untrap his arms so that he might box her ears, when there came a loud knock at the door. Wilma, her expression pouty, flopped off him and onto her back, and her breasts—Nature has been too kind, she'd say—slapped loudly against each other. Clarky breathed in, breathed out, then got up and put on his robe. He was halfway down the hall when he stopped, abruptly, and turned to go back to the bedroom. He'd forgotten—

Wilma had remembered, though: She'd followed him out, and now, holding it by the barrel, she extended his revolver to him. He took it, gave her a wink, and went to answer the door.

"Who's there?"

"Cheese Feet, Mr. Clark. You want to hear something?"

Clarky unbolted the door but left the chains on; he opened it slightly and put an ear to the crack. *Pss—sst—sst, sawasawa.* He leaned away then, and Cheese Feet's hand appeared. Clarky found two bits in his robe. He closed the door and locked it again.

There was a boot-shaped clock on a gateleg table next to the door. It said twenty past eleven. Today was a Sunday, the last in March. Before returning to the bedroom, Clarky opened the drapes in the parlor. The sky was overcast, it looked like snow, but he'd heard rain. Down on the pavement in front of the house, two of his employees loitered, one of them dressed in a white bootblack's uniform, the other in a suit of good clothes. When Clarky raised the sash, they both looked up. "Hey, Mr. Clark," said the fella in the uniform, "didja hear the Commissioner of Bridges swallowed a bone last night and choked to de't?"

No, Clarky hadn't. That was interesting. He nodded, then called down, "One of you run around the corner and get me the papers. And listen: I'm expecting a visitor later. Either of you know George Wreckage on sight?"

They shook their heads.

"Well, you'll know him because he's been sick and looks it. Let him come right up." He started to close the window, but stopped. "Why the hell did you let Cheese Feet in?"

"Gee, we thought it was okay, Mr. Clark," replied the fella in street clothes with a foot up on the shoeshine box. "He said he'd heard something important you should know."

"That human beings once had tails? I think I could've waited till after breakfast for that particular bit of news." He slammed the window.

Earlier that morning, sitting at the kitchen table reading the newspaper (a story headlined Experimenting with an Electric Needle on an Ape's Brain), Georgie had suddenly intuited that today was jinxed. It came all at once, the feeling, like the kick of a drug, and his stomach clenched. The toast had popped then, and Joette put down her section of the paper—she was reading the new Timely Topics for Women supplement in the *Journal*, all about spring hats. She reached for the toast, and as she did, she happened to glance up at Georgie, and the almost wild look in his eye frightened her; he reminded her, at that moment, of her father, on mornings when he preached, or evenings when he summoned first her older brother, then Joette, out to the woodshed for chastisement. Can't you ever smile anymore? she asked Georgie. And then he did, for exactly one second. She'd been relieved when he left the house about noon, carrying a new painting in a wrapper of brown paper. He said he didn't know when he'd be back, maybe in the later afternoon, maybe not. He was off to see Clarky first; then, depending on how he felt, he thought he might go up to Billy China's studio. Joette had said, Fine. In that morning's *World* comics—she'd had to buy the paper herself, then sneak it into the house—Walt had put another message on the Witch's toaster: Sunday? 6? If Georgie was still out at five thirty, perhaps. . . .

This was the first time that Georgie had been up to Clarky's new townhouse on Twenty-second Street, near the corner of Eighth Avenue. It was narrow, four-storied, and the color of American mustard. A bootblack was crouched on the pavement in front, vigorously buffing a gentleman's brogues. Both of them watched Georgie climb the

stoop. "Wreckage?" He'd expected to find it was the bootblack
who'd called him, but it was the gentleman. "Your name is Wreckage?" Georgie nodded, and the gentleman came up the steps to un-
lock the front door. "Mr. Clark is at the top of the house."

The foyer was not lit. Neither was the parlor off it to the right,
which had a parquet floor, an astonishingly busy crystal chandelier,
and a white marble mantel, but no furniture. The room was filled
with cartons labeled CLARKY'S PASTE stacked halfway to the ceiling.
When Georgie stepped in there—he'd noticed what appeared to be
scenes of the hunt carved into the mantel, and wanted a closer
look—a boy in his middle teens suddenly appeared from behind one
of the stacks, with a shotgun. It was the Armenian Georgie had
talked with at the Blade, the night he'd first seen Fuzzy. The boy
didn't seem to remember Georgie; he scowled, he tightened his grip
on the slide handle; his finger was on the trigger. Georgie took a step
backwards, ludicrously shielding himself with his painting, then he
turned his back on the boy and hurried up the stairs.

The top floor of the house had been converted into a flat. Georgie
had to knock at a door, then wait while Clarky released the deadbolt
and undid several chains. "Bear with me, George," said Clarky on
the other side. "Safety in all things." Finally it was open. Clarky still
had on his pajamas—red flannel, with what Georgie took at first
glance to be a pattern of smiling dentures; upon closer inspection,
however, the dentures turned out to be caterpillars. "So I own a
house now, George. I think next I'll join a club." He laughed, drawing Georgie into the hall.

"There's a boy downstairs with a shotgun."

Clarky nodded.

"He's guarding shoe polish?"

Clarky's underlip overslid the upper, as he closed one eye. Then
he shook his head, but Georgie couldn't tell if that meant no, it
wasn't shoe polish, or if it was supposed to be an expression of mild
surprise at Georgie's naiveté, or both. Finally Clarky led the way
into the parlor. It was a very small room—originally it must've been
a child's bedroom—and Wilma, who was lying on her stomach on
the carpet, looked particularly stupendous in there. She was surrounded by newspaper supplements, and there was a slice of toast
with drippings on a blue plate by her elbow. Her red hair flowed
down her back, and her throat was blotchy yet from Clarky's ardent
kisses of an hour ago. She was dressed in a pale-yellow combing

sacque with a fancy yoke. Her feet were bare and her ankles were crossed. "Georgie, Wilma. Wilma, Georgie Wreckage," said Clarky. "This is the famous man I was telling you about."

"Who does the cartoons," said Wilma, impressed. "Pleased to meet you." She smiled at Georgie till Clarky caught her eye and gestured, gestured as though he were brushing away crumbs, and then she reached for a section of the newspaper.

Georgie took off his overcoat and hung it up while Clarky poured out two cups of coffee from a pot on a warmer. "So how're you doing, George? I heard you were feeling much better. You don't look sick." He patted his own cheeks. "A little sunken, but not too bad." Then, after Georgie had replied that he was doing all right, feeling fine, Clarky said, "Well—let's see it!" and eagerly rubbed his hands together.

He had telephoned Georgie immediately after reading the review in the *World* of the Black Gang's exhibition at the Hamlet Gallery. How about painting something crude and indecent for *me?* What he'd suggested was a picture he thought might properly be titled Wisdom: a depiction of Young Clarky standing by a carriage as an old codger leaned through the window and pointed a scolding finger at his scuffed shoes. But Georgie had had another idea: a portrait of Clarky on the brink of success—seated behind his poker-table desk at the old storefront in Avenue B. Clarky had said, Yeah, that might be more interesting. And then they'd talked about Georgie's fee. You have to be joking! You may be a hot-dog cartoonist, but according to the papers you're the worst painter since—since Ugg the Caveman! ("Ugg the Caveman" was a new cartoon appearing in the *Journal* and drawn by a young German named Ira Karp.) Two hundred and fifty dollars? I'll give you a hundred, George. They'd settled on one seventy-five. "So, let's see this masterpiece," said Clarky.

Georgie tore off the wrapper and leaned the painting against the wall. Then he sat on the sofa; he reached for his coffee but decided at the last moment to leave it on the table and bite on his thumb, instead. Clarky stooped, as if to polish someone's shoes. His tongue started tapping on the roof of his mouth.

In the painting, Clarky was staring straight ahead, looking right at you. He was wearing a red shirt with a brown stain on its front, and a green necktie. On the table in front of him, and stacked like poker chips, the world's largest poker chips, were tins of paste. The scene was lit as though by a searchlight, and Clarky's shadow on the wall was grotesque.

"Well?" said Georgie.

Clarky stroked his jaw, slowly. "It's me," he said at last. "But it's not." He shrugged. "It's a funny feeling. I guess I'm just not used to seeing my picture. What do you think of it, Wilma?"

She'd been staring at the picture since Georgie put it on display. "It's all right," she said. "But you should be smiling in it. You're always smiling in real life. You're a smilin' fella." ("The Smilin' Fella" was also a new cartoon, this one appearing in the *World* and drawn by a former sign painter named Jack Crosse. The Smilin' Fella was a hobo, well-meaning but hapless, guilty of nothing, blamed for everything: in the last panel every Sunday, he ended up in jail.)

"I *am* a smilin' fella," said Clarky, smiling. "Why didn't you paint a smile on me, George?"

And Georgie replied, "If you don't like it, you don't have to take it."

"Hold your horses! Hold those horses! Whoa! I'm not saying I don't like it. It's just a simple question."

"I felt you shouldn't be smiling. That's your simple answer."

"*You* don't think I'm a smilin' fella, deep down, is that it?" He turned to Wilma. "Artists always go for the soul, like guard dogs go for the jugular. That's what I've heard." She lifted an eyebrow, then reached for a comic supplement. "All right, George. I like it. I'll hang it! You've made your first sale."

And then Wilma began to laugh. When she noticed Georgie and Clarky both staring at her, she covered her mouth with a hand. She'd been looking at "Lydia & Lafcadio," yet *another* new cartoon series, in the *Journal* and drawn by Clarence Devine, for ten years a regular contributor to *Judge*. Lafcadio was an oily, unpleasant little man—a furniture remover by trade—who tried each week to convince Lydia—a scornful beauty of the middle class—to marry him. It's high time you and me lived happily ever after, he'd say.

Their business settled, Georgie and Clarky sat down together and chatted, Clarky wanting to know what Cuba had been like, saying he'd heard it was mosquitoes that carried yellow fever, and Georgie saying mosquitoes? the doctors hadn't said anything about mosquitoes. Clarky mentioned several investments he'd recently made but evaded almost all of Georgie's questions about his business, his business*es:* Things are swell, in general—say! I hear that your Mr. Hearst is sweet on a showgirl! Clarky never mentioned Joette, but Georgie didn't notice. They each had a couple of drinks. Wilma continued to read the funnies, giggling often, laughing out loud occasionally. Finally, Georgie said he had to be going, and as he was buttoning up his coat, he asked Clarky, "Still haven't heard anything about the boy?"

"No. If he's back," Clarky said, "he's invisible."

They were shaking hands at the door—"On your way out, George, don't stick your head into the parlor again"—when Wilma called, "Mr. Wreckage?" She came into the hall shaking a comic supplement at him. "Since you're here, I should ask you. Are people supposed to understand what all those days of the week and numbers mean? Are they part of the joke, or what?"

Georgie frowned. "I don't quite understand what you're asking me."

"Here, in your cartoon. The days of the week. Sometimes it says Monday or Tuesday. Today it says Sunday. And then a number. Six. Is that a private joke? On the *toaster,*" she said, when he continued to look at her blankly.

Georgie glanced at the funny sheet, then curtly said, "That's not mine, so I can't answer your question."

"Not yours? I thought Clarky told me you drew Pinfold. I'm sorry." She blushed. "I misunderstood. What *do* you draw?"

Georgie said, "A paycheck," and then he left.

On his way down the stairs, he heard Wilma cry "Ow!" then ask, "What did I say that was so wrong?"

Georgie hailed a cab on Eighth Avenue. The carriage had rubber tires, and it was a smooth ride uptown to Billy China's studio on Thirty-seventh Street—a minimum of jars and sudden jolts, just the steady *clip-clop, clip-clop* of the horse's hooves. *Clip-clop, clip-clop,* six o'clock, thought Georgie. Six o'clock? It can't be later than one, one fifteen. His stomach knotted, quite suddenly, as the feeling returned that today, somehow, was jinxed. He looked out the window and saw a mechanical man carrying a chessboard and a box of chessmen; its smile was made of rivets, and there was a red light bulb, not burning, on the top of its boxy head. Its inventor strolled several paces ahead, arrogantly tapping the pavement with an ebony stick.

Several members of the Black Gang were at Billy China's when Georgie arrived, and they were all excited because an artist named Henri Droit was expected. Georgie had never heard of the man, but according to the others, he was supposed to be—well, quite a remarkable painter. His name notwithstanding, he was American, from Philadelphia, but he had lived in Paris for seven years, in Brussels the past two. The gangsters kept chattering about how wonderful was Droit's technique, how startling his color sense, how real his subject matter. Georgie began to anticipate the visit along with the rest. He wished he'd brought a picture—Teed Preston had, and Leonard Bunner and Sandy Young and Pete McCormick, too. Waiting for Droit, everyone drank a gin punch that one of Billy's "daughters" prepared in a washtub.

Droit appeared shortly after four, a small, thin man in his late thirties with long arms and almost tiny hands; he walked with a sprightly step, like a boxer. He puffed on stinking cigarettes no longer than suppositories. He gave an air of great energy, he spoke often in abstractions which Georgie found difficult to understand, and he used terms Georgie was unfamiliar with—negative space, for one—and he grabbed and squeezed Billy's daughter on the buttocks every time she walked by. She walked by very, very frequently.

Henri Droit talked Art, and the afternoon stretched on.

It was around five thirty, and Billy's daughter was sitting on his lap, when Droit said, "I happened to see the exhibition at Hamlet's Gallery." He smiled coldly, then shook his head. "Morbid. Morbid. Morbid."

Mouths opened and stayed open.

Then, directing his gaze at Georgie, Droit added, "*And* gruesome—without being in the least ontological." His eyes narrowed, and Georgie felt his cheeks flush. "Or even very well painted." He continued to stare at Georgie, while everyone fidgeted. "Now, some of the work I quite liked. Mr. Bunner's pigs, for example. They were good pigs. And Mr. Young's bricklayers. And Mr. McCormick's union orator—very fine! Some of the other work, however . . ." He moved a hand to the young woman's breast; she removed it and giggled. "But then, I have always been interested, as an artist and as a man, in life. So . . ." His hand returned to the breast; she let it

remain. "There is a museum in Brussels, the Wertz Museum. Great
big paintings of coffins falling to pieces and rats running about." He
glanced toward Georgie again. "I visited it once and never went
again. You might find it interesting, Mr. Wreckage."

The studio then was absolutely quiet—until finally, and thank
God! Billy China's daughter squealed and said, "If you don't stop
that, sir, I shall tell my daddy!"

Georgie left, shaken, only a few minutes later.

The saloons of New York, because it was Sunday and by order of
the law, were closed. Their front doors were, at any rate. Georgie
found one in Thirty-fifth Street with a side entrance. A young
woman in abbreviated tights sat on the bar, banging a tambourine
against a thigh and singing church hymns. There was spongy sawdust on the floor, smoke thick in the air, and a crowd of mostly
Irishmen, whose expressions vacillated from anger to robust cor-
diality and back to anger again. Free corned beef was available.
Georgie paid for two schooners and carried them to an empty table.
Almost all the tables were empty, though the place was crowded.

He smoked and drank with his right hand, and kept his left
clenched in his lap. Droit! Who the hell was he? Georgie ought to've
thumped him. Just—thumped him! Georgie had never claimed to be
a terrific painter, but he took his pictures seriously, and that—that
frogified bastard had simply dismissed him. Humiliated him. And
none, not one of the gangsters had gone to his defense. Oh, no! They
were too much in awe of the Great Man. Some revolutionists they
were. You watch, they'll all be painting their Madonnas before the
century turns. To hell with them! And to hell with the Great Man—
he could just bend over and kiss Georgie's back porch! A woman
with her face painted like a Jumeau doll appeared at the table then
and, smiling, touched Georgie on the arm with commercial intent.
He flinched. She winked at him, reached for his hand. "You have
nice long fingers, darling," she said. "And I bet you know how to use
them." She tried to press the hand against her thigh, but Georgie
snatched it back. The whore made a spitting sound and strolled off.
He watched her go, memorizing the lumpy curve of her hip, noticing
the tobacco spittle on the hem of her dress. Bet I *do* know how to use
'em! He opened his fist, spread his fingers as wide apart as they'd go,
and looked at the lines in his palm. The lines were white, and the
palm was slightly yellow, still. He got up and left the saloon to find a

cab. It was dark by then and drizzling.

When he got back to Ninth Street, he was no longer in a bad temper, he was simply—tired. He paid the hackman; then, as the carriage pulled away, he noticed a crowd of perhaps twenty, twenty-five people milling on the opposite pavement and slightly down the street. There was a police wagon and an ambulance. He felt compelled to find out what was going on, or what *had* gone on, and as he was crossing Ninth, the door of Number 19 opened and a detective that he recognized from his days at the *World* stepped out. Immediately, a dozen reporters swarmed around him, but he shook his head—he shoved one man and sent him reeling—and then he jostled his way down the steps, strode to the wagon, and climbed in.

Georgie spotted Stolley—a *Journal* man now—jotting a word or two in his pad above a rough pencil sketch of—Georgie couldn't make out what. Stolley clapped the pad shut, jammed his pencil into an overcoat pocket, then, turning, nearly bumped into Georgie. He grinned. "Ah! Bloody Wreckage," he said. "Still have the nose for it, do you?" He flipped back through his pad, then stopped, and Georgie peered over his shoulder. A woman sprawled awkwardly, brokenly, and face down across a four-poster bed.

"Only the woman?" Georgie asked. "What happened to her boyfriend?"

"How the hell did you know about the boyfriend?"

Georgie moved his shoulders. "He in there too?"

"No, but he's dead. After I finish here, I have to run up to Twentieth Street. Mr."—Stolley glanced at his notes—"Mr. Howard shot him in his own house."

"Howard? That's the husband's name? Where is he?"

"Nobody knows. But I figure he'll turn up sometime tomorrow. In the river, maybe. Or in some flophouse, shot through the temple or blue-faced from some poison he took. Surely, you remember human nature, George. You haven't been drawing funny papers that long. The poor bastard's a judge—he's going to let himself be hanged or strapped into the electric chair? He'll turn up tomorrow. Guys like him always do—remember?"

The front door opened again, and two morgue workers—dressed in uniforms quite similar to those worn by Clarky's boys—came out carrying a stretcher. Stolley looked, then grabbed for his pencil. Georgie only looked.

❑ ❑ ❑

When he finally let himself into Number 10, he called out that he was back, but Joette wasn't home. She *wasn't?* Georgie frowned. Where could she be at this time on a Sunday evening? What time was it, anyway? He stepped into the parlor to check the clock on the mantel but for some reason it was no longer there. Now, where the hell had she moved *that* to? Or had she donated it to charity, for Christ's sake, like she'd gone and donated so many other things of his. He still couldn't believe that she'd given away his rocking chair—and his *razor strop?* He looked in both parlors, then upstairs in the bedroom and downstairs in the kitchen (the clock there said twenty minutes past seven) to see if Joette had left him a note. Was she next door at Mrs. Trager's? No, Sundays the Tragers visited relatives in the Annexed District.

While he was in the kitchen, he cut white meat from a chicken and made a sandwich; he washed it down with milk. He considered going up to the studio—there were a couple of paintings he might've worked on—but he couldn't muster the energy. (If Gulp had been there at Billy China's studio, he wouldn't have just sat by and let that artificial frog spout like that!) And then Georgie thought perhaps he should try to work up some new cartoons. Ideas were getting harder and harder to come by (I can't keep this up for the rest of my life, I can't), and he was delivering his pictures later and later every week—and the Art Chief at the *Journal*, Monk Brown, wasn't as lenient about that as Handsome Sid used to be. With a salary like yours, we expect promptness, at the very least. Brown was a Californian—he was built like a lumberman, and that's what he'd been. One evening several years ago—so the story went—he'd saved William Randolph Hearst from drowning, after Hearst was pitched off a wharf on the Barbary Coast by a merchant marine who mistook him, on account of the falsetto, for a fairy queen. Said the sopping Hearst to the dripping Brown, You want a job? Maybe—what have you got? At the *Examiner* in San Francisco he'd been Circulation Manager, but when he came to New York, he wanted something different—no more numbers. Art Chief all right? It'll do. Brown was tolerant, though just barely, of sketchmen, but he was intolerant, utterly, of cartoonists. He thought the color presses should be used to publish lovely pictures of America's mountain ranges. Cartoons! Is this supposed to be funny? he'd ask each and every cartoonist, each and every week. It is? Why? Brown was a stickler for promptness and would send memos to the Chief whenever anyone was late with his work. To Brown, nobody except Hearst, and naturally himself, was a valuable man. So far, Georgie had been reported three times, and once Brown had tried to have a Little Nobody cartoon rejected—the one where Little Nobody blackens his girlfriend's eye for having a soda with a towheaded German boy from Slum Gardens. Mr. Hearst, he'd written, I find this disrespectful to the Female Species. Hearst had let the cartoon run but later informed Georgie, in writing, that in future the Little Nobody should restrain himself from using his fists so often. He suggested that Georgie occasionally try a more—whimsical approach to humor. Let's not forget the suburbs, where different values obtain. A *harmless* prank once in a while might be in order. Georgie had gritted his teeth.

Now he picked at them with a toothpick, sitting at the kitchen table. Whimsical approach to humor? Definition, please. A pie in the face instead of a club? He decided to go on upstairs and confront the problem of whimsy—when *bam! bam! bam!* What's that? He stood up and walked into the hall. *Bam!* From the wine cellar? He opened the door—nothing. Then *bam!* And he raised his eyes. It was overhead. Outside. *Bam!* He went back into the kitchen, switched the light off, and squinted through the window. Nobody out there that he could see. *Bam!* Georgie unlocked the kitchen door, stepped into the yard. The noise suddenly stopped. Frowning, he started across the yard, and just as he did, he began to cough. He walked around to the far side of the tool shed, but nobody was there either. He checked the door. It was locked. And then he felt the lock itself, and it was warm and badly mangled. He spun around then, quickly—but nobody was there. He examined the padlock again. Hammered at. He peered over the back fence into the next yard. Nobody.

On his way back to the house, he tripped over something—it really felt as if some*body* tripped *him,* with a foot, but that was nonsense, since nobody else was in the yard. He fell and landed hard on his arm, the right one, and then his head struck the ground, and he saw stars. He may even have been knocked out for several seconds. When he stood up again, his forearm ached terribly and his fingertips tingled, and one cheek felt raw. And he thought, Well, here's the jinx—ow!

He'd not been expecting to find anyone in the kitchen, so he jumped when he came upon Joette there. Still in her coat and gloves, she was scraping the crusts of Georgie's sandwich into the garbage sack—and *he* startled *her*."What's the matter with your face? What were you doing out in the yard?"

He looked at her and was suddenly angry with her. He didn't know why. Then he thought he did. "Where the hell have you been?"

She looked at the floor, the lamp, the toaster, the sinks. "When you didn't come home, I thought—there was a concert at St. Michael's Church."

He pushed out his lips. A concert at St. Michael's Church?

"When did you get back?" she said. To the calendar? Either that or to the wooden draining board. Hard to tell.

"Around seven thirty. When did you leave?"

"A little before six o'clock,"

And Georgie thought, *Clip-clop*, and frowned, and pressed his left thumbnail to his lips.

5

A week and a half later, a Wednesday morning, Georgie came awake suddenly, mouth dry, both hands clenched at his sternum. He'd been dreaming but couldn't remember about what. He lay there, waiting for the peace to come, as it always did finally. But it did not come. Because today was— He looked over at Joette, still asleep; he touched her, ran his fingers down her upper arm, then withdrew his hand. He got up and dressed and then went out for the paper. It was early April now, and the weather over the last several days had been exceedingly fine, springlike. The sun had lost its winter pallor, and you could no longer stare into it without seeing spots that burst.

When Joette came into the kitchen for her breakfast, Georgie had already finished his and was reading a story in the *Journal:* Dead Rather Than Be a Burden/Calls His Wife and Daughter to Watch Him Drink Carbolic Acid. Joette poured out a bowlful of Granose, a flaked cereal, and sat down at the table. She started to read a story on the *Journal*'s back page—Seven Curious Ways in Which Men Ask Women to Marry Them—but she didn't finish it. She ate a spoonful of cereal, then suddenly felt nauseated and pushed the bowl away. After perhaps five minutes, she said, "Good morning?"

Georgie looked over the top of his newspaper. "Good morning."

"Georgie, what's the matter? You don't even look at me when I walk in the room anymore. Are you angry with me about something? Why don't you talk anymore?"

"I talk. And nothing's the matter," he said, then picked up his coffee cup and tipped it to his mouth, but the cup was empty. "Of course I talk to you. Listen: How're you feeling, Joette? Are you feeling . . . all right?"

She widened her eyes. "Don't I look all right?"

He shrugged. "You look fine."

"Then why did you ask me?"

"*Just to talk!*"

They stared at one another for a long moment, then both glanced away at the same time, and toward the toaster.

Then Joette said, "If you want to know the truth, however, I'm not fine."

He sat back in his chair and lifted his palms.

"Georgie," she said, and stopped. "Georgie, I'm not fine— because you're not." Then she looked exasperated. "Fine! Not fine. All right. *Not* all right. We sound like children."

He narrowed his eyes.

"Georgie, I'm your wife."

"Yes," he said, "you are."

"And I don't want—"

"What? You don't want *what?*" Jammed down between his knees, the newspaper rustled.

"Let me finish. Let me speak? I don't want you to be so miserable! Do you know what it's like, living with you? You're successful! Doesn't it make you happy—at all?"

"Successful," he said.

"Oh, Jesus Christ! Can't you be happy with what you have, who you are? You draw a cartoon that everybody loves—everybody but you. You're only happy drawing murders. And painting those— paintings! Georgie." She dropped her voice, her tongue swept across her lip. "Can you tell me what would make you happy? Do you know?"

"Making pictures makes me happy." He looked down at his lap, flicked away toast crumbs. "And you."

"I don't think so, George."

He looked at her, miserably. He was speaking the truth—and she said she didn't think so! It *was* the truth. It was.

"Nor do I think your pictures—any of them!—make you very happy anymore, either."

He said, "They saved my life."

"I don't believe that either. You may, but I don't. I think they wrecked it."

He smiled—at the pun? But when Joette started to get up from the table, his expression changed swiftly; his eyes seemed bright with a new fever, in a split second, and the color in his face darkened. "You're going out this afternoon?" he asked her.

Something trembled inside of her, and her wrists throbbed; she couldn't look at him, she looked at the bag of cereal lying on its side. "I'm going out before that. At eleven? I have my class at the Lyceum."

"Do you? I thought that was Friday."

"I'm going twice a week now—why not?"

Georgie's tongue pressed against his cheek, along the jaw. "And you'll be back when—by *two*, do you think?"

"No, after that. Why? Do you want me home?"

He took the newspaper out from between his knees, smoothed it, refolded it.

"It's Wednesday, anyway," said Joette. "Aren't you going to the café?"

"I don't think so."

"Why not?"

"I just—don't think so, that's all."

Joette sat down again in her chair. "George. If you want me back. If you need me for something—or you want us to do something to-gether . . ." She shrugged. She smiled. "I could be back by two. I could be back sooner."

But he shook his head. "No," he said, "that's all right. Enjoy your pyrography."

"Crewelwork," she said.

Just before eleven, Joette left the house and took a cab to Murray Hill, to see a highly regarded physician named Martins, who in Penalty Street, and Penalty Street only, went by the name of Narcoticus.

❑ ❑ ❑

□ □ □

Whimsy. Georgie had looked it up. Anything fanciful or quaint. Odd. Charming. Whimsy, now Hearst wanted—whimsy. He hadn't said it in so many words, but what he *really* wanted was the Little Nobody to be closer to what Walter Geebus had been making of Pinfold. Whimsy. Anything fanciful, charming, or geebus. The Stuttering Leprechaun of Awful Alley. The Genie in the Magic Schooner. The Bread Witch's Cousin Zwieback, the Incompetent Necromancer. Whimsy, all right. Remember the middle class. Well, thought Georgie, Geebus would have no trouble remembering. Whimsical Walter Geebus. Georgie stubbed out his cigarette, the seventh or eighth he'd smoked in a row.

In his billfold—somehow, he'd lost the billfold he'd always had and for quite a while now had been using the one he'd got from Spit in the Church of Eleven Martyrs and One Virgin, Billy McCord's billfold—he had one of Walt's cartoons. The previous Sunday's. He took it out now, unfolded it on the kitchen table. Pinfold & Fuzzy Meet the Zwieback Ghost. Now *there's* whimsy, thought Georgie. Oh, that's just whimsical as hell. Count Zwieback, visiting the Bread Witch, decides to assist in ridding her of Pinfold. He conjures an evil spirit to chase the boy from the alley, only the spirit (who talks like a vaudeville German: Is dot der kid you vant me to eat?) is frightened of—what else?—dogs. Boo, says Fuzzy. And in the final panel, Count Zwieback and the Bread Witch themselves are being pursued through Awful Alley by the spirit. How could he *do* this to my characters? thought Georgie. How could he do this to *me?* And then his eye went—for perhaps the hundredth time since Sunday—to Panel Two: a scene in the Witch's kitchen, the spirit rising from the toaster, and on the side of the toaster, printed small: WED 230?

Georgie stared at the panel, still not believing that his suspicions could be true, and at the same time believing them utterly. He refolded the cartoon and put it away. The phone was ringing upstairs. It had been ringing every ten minutes for the past hour. Monk Brown. Where the hell's the picture? But there was no sense answering the telephone, because there was no cartoon this week. Georgie hadn't done one. Sorry, no whimsy.

Walt called them thingamajigs, and each time he'd had to go out and buy some, he'd been mortified. At school, he'd seen them occasionally—say, if a classmate had gone into his father's top dresser drawer, where they were usually to be found concealed under stockings and knee garters. Walt's father did not keep any—possibly he had when Walt's mother was still alive, but then Walt wasn't curious in those years. Where thingamajigs came from, where you might purchase them when you, ah, matured and found yourself in a situation that called for them, Walt had never had any idea. Drugstores seemed the logical place, but no, they were not available there—unless specifically prescribed by a physician, a friend had once told Walt. And Walt might've risked stealing one of his father's pads and forging a prescription *if* he'd ever had any real reason for doing so. But before Joette, he'd never had, of course. And it was too late to steal prescription pads now.

He'd asked Joette about—thingamajigs, and she'd laughed. I can't help you out, Walt. You're on your own.

At the *World*, he'd been too embarrassed to ask any of the fellas in the art department, or any of the editors and reporters he saw almost every day—but there was a lavatory attendant on the tenth floor who seemed, to Walt, likely to know about such things. Walt couldn't explain to himself why, exactly, he thought this old codger would be a good man to ask about thingamajigs—perhaps it had something to do with the occupation he was engaged in, or perhaps it was the man's furtive, slightly unsavory appearance. At any rate, Walt decided to chance a snide remark and speak to Roy Euringer in his lavatory about . . . thingamajigs. Where do you buy them, supposing you want some? Supposing you *need* some, do you mean? said Roy with a leer. Then he scratched his scrawny throat. There used to be a little boy in City Hall Park, you could buy 'em from him.

Is he there anymore? said Walt.

Don't think so. Now lemme see. You want to prevent disease? Or children?

Disease? said Walt, astounded. I'm not worried about disease! What, are there different *kinds* of thingamajigs?

Roy Euringer nodded. If all you're worried about is disease, you don't care if it leaks a little. Get my drift? So you can go for the cheaper kind.

I don't want the cheaper kind, said Walt quickly.

Roy placed a finger on the side of his nose. Used to be a nigger, *big* nigger, lived not far from here. *He* made a good product, I understand. I don't know if he's still in business, though.

A features editor stepped into the lavatory just then, and Walt gestured to Euringer, *ssh!* While they waited to be alone again, Walt scrubbed his hands at the sink. Taped to the mirror was one of his Pinfold cartoons; The Plunderer of Awful Alley and His First Mate That Talks—Pinfold and Fuzzy playing pirates in a rocking chair fitted with a union suit as a sail. Finally, the editor left. Well, said Walt. Do you or don't you know where I might find . . . thingama-jigs. And Roy Euringer, thinking some more, said, I believe there's a fish market on Varick Street.

A fish market!

Tell them you're interested in the *guts,* and give a wink. See what happens.

In the guts?

And give a wink, don't forget that.

Well, Walt had gotten his first supply of thingamajigs at this fish market—somehow he'd managed those words and that crucial wink. But the products were highly unsatisfactory. They smelled—of fish! They *were* fish—the intestines. Joette had roared with laughter when he'd dumped them out of the sacks. I even see the scales, she'd said. You do *not!* There are no scales—come on, Joette! She'd wrinkled her nose and laughed some more. No, Walt, she'd said. No? *No.* They'd played Hearts, instead.

Then it so happened that Walt heard about a bachelor party to be thrown for one of the staff writers, and in the course of the conversation, it was mentioned that somebody had been put in charge of purchasing . . . thingamajigs, since half a dozen horizontales had been hired to entertain throughout the evening. And Walt asked casually, making a joke of it, Where's he going to get them, at a fish market? Ha, ha! Funny Walt. No, not at a fish market—at a penny arcade in Avenue A. A penny arcade? said Walt? Yes, Uncle Lenny's Penny Arcade.

Thus, without knowing how he would make his purchase, or even whom to approach, Walt walked over to Uncle Lenny's. He wandered through the place, watching tough kids play the gambling machines, bowl, crank the kinetoscopes. He perspired heavily. Finally, he was approached by a wavy-haired Irishman wearing a change apron. You looking for somebody? Or something? And Walt, blushing furiously, shook his head and turned away. He went to the cashier—just about the largest woman he'd ever seen in his life, flame-red hair and breasts like bolster pillows—and got a quarter's worth of pennies. And then he wandered around some more, the coins clutched tightly in his fist. The suffering you must go through for love! The Irishman kept looking over at him. He stepped up to Walt once more. If you don't want to play any games, I got a shoeshine stand in the back. Maybe you want your shoes clarked. Walt said no, no thanks. The Irishman grinned then, and taking Walt gently by an elbow, ushered him through the arcade and into a back room, where indeed there was a shoeshine throne, a Clarky's boy standing beside it. See if you can help this fella, said the Irishman, and left. The Clarky's boy smiled. Have a seat. I don't want a shine. That's all right. Walt sat, and then the boy proceeded to open paste can after paste can, to show Walt various narcotic substances in pouches and vials, assorted jewelry, poison spiders in glass bubbles, and, at last, thingamajigs. They were sold three to a can. The boy said, Only one can? Where's your stamina? So Walt bought two.

He'd gone back twice since then, and each trip had been an ordeal of embarrassment. He wished he didn't have to buy them, he wished he didn't have to wear them. But he did have to, for the time being. He had to act responsibly.

It was twenty past two, and Walt was waiting for Joette to arrive; as always, his stomach was in knots, but at the same time he was euphoric. He'd dusted and swept the flat. He'd aired it out. He was sitting on the lounge, one leg crossed over the other. He'd tried to read a little bit in *The Time Machine*—which Jo had loaned him—but hadn't been able to concentrate. The excitement of love! When he heard Joette's knock, he leaped up and flung himself across the room.

But as soon as he saw her face, his heart seemed to clench. She raised her eyebrows. "Walt," she said, "we have to talk."

Walt had been chewing on the side of a pencil for the last ten minutes—chewing, then wiping the bits of wood from his lips with the back of a hand. He hadn't spoken yet. Finally, he said, "But Joette—I've always used one of those thingamajigs. Always! Except for that first time, and that first time, remember, I—"

"Walt, it's all right. It's okay. I *know* you did." Then she looked at the ceiling. "I'm *glad* you did." And she heard his pencil snap in half.

"This is for certain now, Jo. The doctor told you?" He jammed both halves of the pencil down behind the lounge cushion.

"No," she said.

"No?"

"He won't know for sure until—he said I could call him on Monday."

"Then you're *not* sure."

"I've never been late, Walt."

"Say—everybody's late sometimes. I'm even late today." He flung an arm toward his drawing table, which he'd set up in front of the window. There was a sheet of cardboard tacked on it, and daylight bounced off the masses of black ink." And *I've* never been late, either." He smiled, leaned forward to touch Joette's knee, but she rocked away in the rocker. Then he wasn't smiling. "Are you going to take off your coat? Or are you going to leave it on?"

"I haven't decided yet."

"Okay," said Walt. "Fine." He lifted a hand, then let it drop. Then he stood and went to the fireplace, picked up the screen, and set it aside. He squatted and rearranged the logs. "Well, let's suppose it's true," he said.

"All right."

"I have to tell you, Jo, and you might get angry at me: but I'm glad."

She looked at him levelly; an eyebrow flicked. "Why would I be angry? I'm glad too."

"Do you think—is there any chance at all that it's Georgie's?"

And Joette laughed—unkindly, Walt thought. "*Any* chance? It *is* Georgie's."

And Walt said, "Oh." He sat down again on the lounge and pulled at the tufts.

"There's no question of that," said Joette.

Walt kept pulling at those tufts. Finally, he looked at her. "No," he said. "No question in my mind, either." He began to gnaw on his cheek. Half a minute went by. "I've been reading that book," he said.

"Have you?"

"I jump around in it—it's pretty good, though. I like reading about the future."

"Pretty bleak, isn't it?" said Joette.

"It's only a story." Walt got up then and walked over to the drawing table; he picked up a knife and scratched out some ink, bent over, and blew it away. Then he put his hands flat down on the board, and looked from one to the other, right to left, left to right. "You asked me once: what would I like to see happen. Now I'm asking you." He turned and looked at her.

She said, "*Walter* . . ."

And he laughed. "Well, there's my answer."

She crossed the room and kissed him on the cheek.

Game of Hearts? Or two or three or four . . . ?

7

Georgie could picture it; he could picture everything, and as he paced the little street, up and down, across the cobbles and back, his chest tightened and the hands in his pockets clenched, unclenched. He'd seen her go inside, almost two thirty exactly! So, he hadn't been mistaken—it *hadn't* been a little private joke of Walter's. But then—oh, yes, it *had!* A joke on Georgie. Jo and Walter's joke on Georgie. He felt flushed and sick and empty, and he kept pacing, his body so rigid he might've been that mechanical man with the chessboard. His nostrils kept flaring involuntarily, and when they did that, his eyes, the *corners* of his eyes began to tingle. But he stopped himself from crying.

By picturing everything.

He could see them, Walter and Joette—see them as if he were looking at them through a keyhole.

He walked up onto Walter's porch suddenly and was about to pound on the door, his fist was raised—but then he forced his hand to fly open, he turned around and went back down the steps. He ran to the corner, where he slowed, his breathing becoming more regular. He continued on to Abingdon Square. A Clarky's boy approached him, asking if he wanted a shine. Then he found himself in Bank Street, in Bethune. And then back in Waverly Place. It was late afternoon now, going on five; the air was turning cool already.

Joette had been inside Walter's flat two—nearly two and a half hours. Unless. Unless she'd come out and gone home while he was wandering around. No, she was still in there.

Because he could picture it.

Georgie began to have difficulty swallowing.

A few minutes before five, a carriage came around the corner, stopped, and then someone called from inside it, "George?"

It was Clarky, all dressed up. He leaned through the window. Reluctantly, Georgie crossed the street, and when he came up to the carriage—as he walked now, it felt as though he were floating, just an inch or two above the ground—Clarky grabbed him by the wrist, squeezing bone. "George. Get in."

"You knew?"

"I'd heard, yes."

"So others know?"

Clarky shrugged, and Georgie pulled his hand free. "Everything that's done in this world, everything, including a shit in the woods— at *least* three people know about it. Clarky's Law. Get in the carriage, George."

Georgie shook his head.

"So what do you intend to do?"

"That's none of your business, Clarky."

"But it is, George. It truly is. I'm your friend."

"You didn't tell me."

"I wouldn't have been your friend if I did."

Georgie started back across the street.

"George!"

He stopped but didn't turn around.

"Don't do anything—please?"

Georgie laughed bitterly and then he did turn around. "What *can* I do?"

Clarky raised his brows. "I know what you're *capable* of doing. I heard about—I heard about Connie Dwyer, what happened after I left you that day. You thought I hadn't?"

"Go away, Clarky—let me think."

"*Don't* think. Just get in the carriage. Think *later*. Look, we'll spend the evening together, discuss the problem. Friend to friend. Come to the Filch Hall Banquet with me." He smiled, a little. "And this time you don't have to wear any blackface. You can come as my guest."

Georgie said, "Good-bye, Clarky."

Clarky glanced sorrowfully at Georgie's shoes, then he shook his head. Finally he thumped his stick three times on the carriage floor, and the carriage went away.

Georgie could picture this: Killing Walter Geebus, killing Joette. And he knew exactly what they'd look like once he'd done it. Knew what their eyes would look like, their hands, he knew the forensics. And as he was picturing it all, sitting on a stoop directly opposite Walter's door, Georgie suddenly hugged himself, bent forward, and wept.

Because picturing them dead, the two of them, made him clutch up inside, clutch up so much he couldn't breathe.

Yet he knew now that he *could* do it, that he could murder them both.

With? The small revolver that was buried in the bottom of his souvenir locker—the revolver that had been used to kill Billy Mc-Cord. He knew exactly where it was: he knew he could find it, he knew he could use it.

He knew he could do it, that he could murder them both. He was capable of it. He could picture it. He dragged himself to his feet—it was full dark now—and with a hand pressed to his stomach, he walked west, toward home.

Coming along Ninth Street, he had to stop and brace himself against a tree. He glanced across the street and saw that Number 19 was dark.

At 10, he went slowly up the stoop, unlocked the front door, and walked inside; he didn't shut the door after him. . . .

His vision began to blur as he climbed the inside stairs to the studio. He dragged his footlocker out from under his drawing table, then sat down on two cartons of Hearst money. He opened the locker. Picked out and threw aside the shirt with bullet holes, the scarf, the hammer, a couple of spigots, Clarky's suit. He set the jar of fingers on the floor. He took out the revolver, laid that also on the floor. Then he reached back into the locker and took out a long metal hook—used once in a gang killing at Five Points; the long metal hook, finally a gallows rope.

Into the middle of the studio Georgie carried a chair; he stacked several Hearst cartons on the seat of it, then he stood on the cartons and hammered the hook into one of the exposed beams in the ceiling. He tied the rope around the hook. He fitted the noose around his neck.

And then he hanged himself.

UXTRY! UXTRY! READ ALL ABOUT IT! P(INFOLD) FINDS A MILLION BUCKS!

Mrs. Gal died in her sleep, rest her soul. P was up and frying liver for Fuzzy when Gertrude burst in, weeping. He ran back down the corridor with her, and there was the woman, lying on her back with her mouth open. P thought it was better to die with your mouth open than your eyes; best not to die at all. He bent over, covering Mrs. Gal's face with a blanket, one of Georgie's. Early daylight filtered weakly through the newspaper sheets tacked over the window: the New York *Times,* a tombstone format, no banner headlines. P said, taking Gertrude's hand in his, I'm sorry.

And Fuzzy said the same thing.

That time, Gertrude neither laughed nor clapped. Thank you, Pinfold, she said. Thank you, Fuzzy.

Though grieving, Gertrude maintained a clear head that difficult morning. We got to move her. She has got to be buried. But where do we take her?

P thought, The morgue, but he didn't like to speak that word, so didn't.

I think, said Gertrude, we should take her to a church.

P thought, And leave her?

But that wasn't Gertrude's idea at all: she meant bring her mother to a church and ask there for assistance doing—whatever had to be done.

P remembered then, as best he could, his own mother's death: men came, men wrapped her, men carried her off. Strangers.

Gertrude said, We need something to get her there—to a church.

P promised to take care of it and went out, bidding Fuzzy to stay with Gertrude and keep her company. Very rarely did the boy go out in the daytime anymore; even after the newfangled padlock had appeared on the shed door, ending his housebreaking career, he'd kept mostly to a nighttime schedule. He scavenged, from ten till perhaps three, three thirty. He still had some money left from his work at the theatres, not a lot, but some—he wasn't desperate. He'd discovered that he preferred to stay up all night, or almost all night, and sleep half the day. Music-hall schedule. Gertrude usually went out once in the afternoon to buy food.

Less than an hour after he'd gone out, he returned, telling Gertrude that he had a vendor's cart down in the alley. She didn't ask how or where he'd found it. They bundled Mrs. Gal as snugly as they could in three blankets and then negotiated their way slowly down the stairs. Into the cart—gently, gently. They pushed the cart into Brine Street. Gertrude said she knew of a church not too far; she'd passed it a few times. The Church of Eleven Martyrs and One Virgin.

The priest there, a powerful-looking man named Reverend Poole, answered the door himself at the rectory, and though P, by nature, did not trust men of the cloth, he had to admit that this big fella was extremely sympathetic to Gertrude, very kind. He said he'd take care of everything, and he did. There was a brief service the next morning, followed by interment in the small graveyard behind the church. P looked there for a statue of the Archangel Michael, but didn't find it.

Afterwards, Reverend Poole invited Gertrude back into the rectory for a chat—he was, he said, concerned about what would become of her now. P started to follow them in, but the reverend turned him away at the door. This is a private matter, he said. Could you possibly come back in—an hour?

Instead of going away and coming back, P stayed with Fuzzy by the cart, alongside the church. And about twenty minutes later, no more, Gertrude and the Reverend Poole emerged together from the rectory. The reverend seemed annoyed to find P, who immediately asked, Where're you going, Gertrude? She shrugged. Reverend says he might know a nice place for me to live. She nodded her head at Poole, opening the carriage-house doors. Where's this place? said P. Nearby, I expect. Let me come with you, said P, alarmed all of a sudden. I'll be all right, she said. Always have been before. We're just going over to some lady's house to talk to her—I'll see you later in Brine Street. Tell you how it all worked out. Gertrude then climbed into the carriage with the reverend, and she blew a kiss to P, another to the dog. I'll see you jays later, she said as the Reverend Poole said gid-yap! P called after her, All right! And then as the carriage turned the corner and was lost to sight, Fuzzy said, Good-bye, Gertrude.

She did not return to the pickleworks, and when P returned to the rectory, the Reverend Poole frostily informed him that Miss Gal was living now in a respectable house and that it was in her best interests to disassociate herself as completely as possible from her former life on the street. He started to close the door, and P said, Respectable house. Is that a two-dollar house, or a five-dollar house?

Slam!

So P and Fuzzy were alone again. The pair roamed together at night and stayed at the pickleworks, mostly, in the daytime. The boy often rocked in Georgie's rocker, looked at himself in Georgie's mirror, and flipped through Georgie's books, staring at the unintelligible black marks, looking for V-words. Fuzzy seemed—well, certainly spry for her age. P couldn't say when it happened, but he'd come to accept what everyone had been telling him for the past year: she was an old hound, twelve if she was a day, but maybe fourteen, even fifteen. He wouldn't have her all that much longer. A year? Two years? And then she'd be gone like everybody else he'd ever met, known, been with. P was not in the highest of spirits as April began, as Easter approached. So much had happened to him, changed during the past year—and whenever he tried to think about it all, in sequence, he ended up feeling sad and angry, awfully confused, hurt. Georgie Wreckage!

The boy had no idea what he should do next, where he should go—*if* he should go somewhere. Tell me, Fuzzy, what the hell should we do?

But the dog would only look at him and seem to wink.

One late afternoon, just after it grew dark, P and Fuzzy went out. They still had the vendor's cart, and the boy wheeled it up Brine Street and through Salt Alley, looking here, there, everywhere, for anything. Anything at all. Half a grapefruit, a million bucks. He picked up trash-can lids and put them back down. They went slowly, taking it easy. P had been feeling poorly all day—he'd had an ache in his chest, as though his ribs were stretching, and his shoes no longer fit him properly. Nor did his shirt and pants. Hardly any of his clothes fit well any longer. About the only comfortable thing was his derby.

As he was digging through a barrel in Hogan's Alley, he found a fish skeleton wrapped in Sunday comics. He started to toss it back, when he noticed one of the pictures, one of the panels: It was stained darkly with fish oil but still recognizable as his and Fuzzy's cartoon selves. He hadn't looked at a Pinfold sequence since—since he'd left for Jersey. Shaking out the bones, P unfolded the supplement, and then he frowned. Something about it was—funny. Not *funny*-funny. Odd. And he didn't know what. He glanced quickly over the first two, three pictures. There was the Bread Witch—he remembered her, remembered the day Walt Geebus had convinced Georgie to stick her into the cartoon. There was the Bread Witch—and there was Professor Thom's toaster! He laughed, then scanned the remainder of the sequence: Pinfold climbing the side of a tenement, crawling through a window, making a grab for a breadbox full of cash, crowned by a rolling pin, tied up by the ankles and thrown out the window, to hang upside down.

P didn't think it was so funny—it didn't make him laugh, but then, he knew he wasn't a fair judge: He couldn't read the words. He was just about ready to toss the paper, but then he took another look, and in the last panel, in the right-hand corner, he saw Walt Geebus's signature. *That's* why it seemed so—funny! *Walt's* signature? P had been in the room the day Walt had spent something like four hours trying to perfect it. Like this *W?* like this *a?* Nice— isn't it?

P scowled, looked at Fuzzy, scowled even deeper.

And then, quite abruptly, he turned his cart around and headed it toward the Village. Why? Because. Because *why?* Just because.

He left the cart under a tree in Washington Square; then, jamming sticks of Artificial Midnight onto his shoes and derby hat and lighting them, he crossed the park, cautioning Fuzzy to stay close by. Everyone they passed coughed.

P didn't know why he was coming here now, or what he expected
to do once he arrived—as recently as last week he'd tried to bust
open that new padlock, and he just couldn't. So there was no sense in
climbing over the back fence again—especially since he didn't even
have a hammer with him now. All he had was a sack of butterscotch
candies and his penknife. He turned into Ninth Street just as
Georgie Wreckage was crossing Fifth Avenue. He was—staggering. And P, squinting through his black cloud, made a face. Drunk
again. He watched Georgie pass him by, then go up the steps
and into the house. He waited for the door to close, and when it
didn't he looked down toward Fuzzy and whispered, "Come on,"
almost giddy.

So the night entered into Georgie's house.

The hall, the entire main floor was dark. Georgie hadn't switched
on any lights. P listened and heard the sound of footsteps going up.
If Georgie was going up, he was going down. "Come on, Fuzz—and
don't stray." He was hoping he wouldn't bump into Joette, but no
one was downstairs, and it was dark there, too. He took off his derby
then and blew out the wick. Then he rubbed one shoe across the
other. He untied his bandanna and Fuzzy's. Fuzzy trotted directly
into the kitchen. There, P turned on a small wall lamp, then found a
sack of clothespins, which he emptied into the sink. Carefully, he
began to fill the sack with cups and saucers. There was one that he
took—it had a yellow rose on it—that he remembered Georgie
drinking from afternoons in Sawdust Street. It was, as a matter of
fact, the teacup which P had drawn. Teacups, saucers—what else?
He looked around. And saw the toaster on the table.

No, he wouldn't take that; anyway, it was Joette's.

And he wasn't an Indian giver.

He continued to stare at the toaster, not quite sure why—until
suddenly he frowned and came a few steps closer to the table. He
bent from the waist—and looked. Then he straightened, his eyes
wide, a hand going involuntarily to his throat. He backstepped,
banged against a chair, lifted his eyes to the ceiling.

"Go up!"

P flinched and glanced down at the dog. "Go *up*, you said?"

The dog only looked at him and seemed to wink.

Georgie was twisting at the end of the rope, his feet were kicking—the noose had jammed just under his chin. His face was red, his

eyes bulged, his nose was bleeding—his tongue was slotting back and forth, wildly.

The boy stood below, gaping up, his breath all violent.

"Climb up!"

He glanced to Fuzzy in the doorway—then jumped on the chair, and reached, and could do no good. Then he saw several cartons tumbled on the floor. He stacked two of them on the seat of the chair, climbed them—and still he couldn't reach high enough to cut Georgie down.

He stacked two *more* cartons, and as he climbed those, they tottered, and the chair tottered. And *still* he couldn't reach.

He jumped down, grabbed two more cartons, now a stack of six, and climbing them, going slowly, P felt all start to rock—and then one of the cartons slid out, the chair tipped—and the boy hit the floor, winded.

Georgie continued to twist; his fingers were splayed, stiff.

"Try again!"

He uprighted the chair, stacked three cartons, stood on the rim of the seat and stacked three more cartons—and then very . . . very . . . carefully, he climbed.

At last, he was face to face with Georgie, but Georgie didn't see him: his eyes had rolled.

P thought, *Now* what?

And panicked, realizing his knife was still in his pocket, and that he didn't dare reach for it. And he was afraid to try to move the noose: what if it slipped from Georgie's chin—his neck would snap in a second.

He stood there on the top carton, unable to move, to act.

And Fuzzy the dog said, "Pull the rope out of the ceiling!"

And the boy screamed, "You don't talk, *I* talk!" and leaped into the air, kicking the boxes away—and grabbed hold of the rope. The hook came free. And the boy and the man crashed to the studio floor.

When Joette came home, she found them both where they'd fallen, banded stacks of phony twenties scattered every which way. Fuzzy was on the couch, muzzle resting on her paws.

The dog looked up, then her mouth opened in a big yawn.

THE DEEF BIRD

1

The Scoundrel's Cup—a silver chalice enameled black—was awarded biennially to the badman who, in the opinion of the voting members of Filch Hall, best embodied the ideals of jugglery, ruthlessness, and greed, and just as Clarky had heard, days ago, that the banquet meal would be sauerbraten, the dessert vanilla ice cream with butterscotch sauce, the dessert wine a grappa from California, and the cigars corona chicas, he'd heard that the cup would pass to him. Quite an honor! Previous winners had included such fireballs of the underworld as Receiver Newman, Old Father Hubbard, Charlie Lewis, the Diamond Swallower, and, ironically, Shag Draper, may he rest in peace. It was a career milestone, and Clarky had been looking forward eagerly to this night in Penalty Street, but now, now practically all his joy was spoiled: Because of Georgie Wreckage, he sat in a funk in Mother Polk's dining room, staring miserably at the red cabbage on his dish, and when at last his name was called, he failed to hear it; one of his bodyguards had to give his chair a good shake. He was then invited by the new Mayor of Filch Hall to say a few words—he'd heard that he would be, so he'd prepared some brief remarks yesterday, thank goodness, jotting them on the flap of an envelope—and as he stood, nodding this way and that, he hoped he looked jubilant but suspected he didn't. He cleared his throat. The room fell quiet.

Now, Clarky had heard that it was customary to begin a speech with an anecdote, something pithy yet fashioned to get a big guffaw, so following his very sober expressions of appreciation, he said, "About two years ago, I went to a hanging." He paused while, instinctually, all the badmen caressed their necks. "It wasn't anybody professionals such as yourselves likely ever heard of. Just some poor nobody, a *bigamist* of all things! Married about two dozen women, I gathered—and killed one of 'em. The amazing thing to me is that it was *only* one." That earned a laugh; Clarky had figured it would: he'd heard that any joke about marriage as an unhappy institution was certain to get a chuckle, at the very least, from an audience of men. He continued, "Two dozen women, gentlemen. Dozen! And him just about the homeliest of jays. Bad skin just full of pits, a mousy little mustache, squinty eyes, and big ears—even bigger than mine!" Again, a laugh: he was doing well. "So there I was, gentlemen, watching this unfortunate brother climb the gallows, and I'm wondering, I'm wondering how in the name of Hannah did *he* ever get so many peacherines to fall for him? What was his secret? It wasn't his looks—maybe his palaver? But then he opens his mouth to say his last words, and I can't even understand him. It's half English, *less* than half English, and the rest is—God knows. And his voice! Even allowing that he's scared shitless, it's a croak, if you'll excuse the pun. So, if it's not his looks and it's not his voice, what's the secret? Charm? Mesmerism? And I think, well, whatever it is, it's going to the grave with Joseph. That was his name: Joseph. Joseph Penfield. They stand him on the trap, they put the hood over his head, and then—*then*, gentlemen, before they can tie his ankles together, do you know what Joseph does? He lifts one foot and rubs it against the back of his trouser leg, and then he does the same thing with the other foot. The last thing he did on this earth was to put a shine on his prison slippers! There! *There* was his secret—eh? And I said to myself, Joseph, have a good trip. You're a man after my own heart!" The banqueters roared laughing, as they were supposed to, and for just a moment Clarky felt that his triumph tonight might be delish, after all—but then, ah, Jesus, then he was thinking about Georgie once more, about what Georgie might do, about what Georgie might already have *done*, and the dismals recaptured his mood. Was it so apparent to the Filchers? Clarky hoped not. "Gentlemen.

Gentlemen, while I'm on the subject of footwear, let me just say this: Keep them shining! In fair weather and foul, in good times and bad. Keep them shining, no matter what you wear—brogues or brogans or even, God forbid, prison slippers!" Georgie Wreckage had been at that hanging too, the hanging of Joseph Penfield—as a matter of fact, *he'd* taken *Clarky* there. He'd sketched the prisoner cleaning his slippers, he'd sketched the prisoner dangling; he'd paid the hangman five dollars for the rope, a souvenir. Clarky said, "Gentlemen! Mind your shoes! And keep your ears open! That's all there is to it. That's all there is to it. I thank you again." The Scoundrel's Cup, filled with red wine, was delivered to him, and he raised it high. "Thank you all so *very* much! You've made me a most happy fella! Now. Please join me in drinking a toast to—to Joseph Penfield!"

To Joseph Penfield!

The presentation of the Golden Bludgeons took the better part of the next hour, and while he applauded every time a giddy winner extended gratitude to his fence or to his mother, Clarky found it increasingly difficult not to fidget and nearly impossible to pay any real attention to the ceremony, to give it more than the most casual ear. Georgie Wreckage! Twice, a latecomer showed up—the first an arsonist reeking of kerosene, the other a yegg with his fingertips still oily—and each time Clarky wet his lips and clenched his fingers, half expecting the new arrival to stop at his table, bend down, and whisper. Have you heard about your friend . . . ? *Damn* Georgie, anyhow! As soon as all the awards had been given out, dessert was served and coffee poured; then about a dozen of Mother's girls, every girl with her own miniature gravy boat, entered the dining room and immediately crawled underneath the tables; those revelers desiring a complimentary fellatio were invited by Mrs. Polk to unbutton their flies. Clarky passed. Then the guest speaker, a sportswriter for the *Sun,* was introduced and began reminiscing about his salad days as a robber of the Union Pacific. It was probably very interesting, the talk, but Clarky didn't listen. Tried to, for a short time, but it was no good. Utah, he heard. Pinkertons, he heard. Charlie Siringo, Bob Ford, all noise, no reception. "Mr. Clark? I wonder if you know—" And Clarky cringed, glanced over a shoulder, then impulsively he chopped his bodyguard at the sternum with the edge of his hand. "Mr. Clark? I only wanted to know if you knew—" And Clarky scowled the gorilla—who'd only wanted to know the whereabouts of a toilet—into baffled silence. "Excuse me, Mr. Clark," he murmured, flushing brightly.

After the former Ukiah Kid concluded his speech and left the rostrum, there were a few skits (The Death by French Disease of Police Commissioner Roosevelt; a High-handed Outrage at the First National Bank; Rub & Dub Loot the Weaverville Stage), then a sing-along ("The Bowery, the Bowery/They say such things and they do strange things/On the Bowery, the Bowery . . ."), and a raffle (the prize being sample signatures of the fourteenth through the nineteenth richest men in New York), then every banqueter was given three house tokens, and finally the mayor declared it was time to troop upstairs and mingle with the parlor girls. But Clarky didn't feel in the mood for catting and so remained in his chair, while all around him badmen rose and stretched, buttoned flies, used spittoons, hastily finished their ice cream, drifted out. Kitchen girls appeared to clear away the plates. Then Clarky saw a panel worker named Silvers gliding toward him, and he paled, agitatedly stubbing his cigar. They're dragging the river for your pal. They got him in custody. They're watching the bridges and ferries. They're—"Mr. Clark, congratulations again. I voted for you." And Clarky, whose earlobes had started to prickle and whose feet had gone numb, exhaled loudly, dizzy with relief. He gave Silvers a tin of paste, then a crisp two-fingered salute.

Upstairs, the piano man began to play "A Hot Time in the Old Town."

Clarky sat with his chin in a hand and licked his lips nervously. Three, four minutes. Then, relighting his cigar, he turned in his seat and crooked a finger at the bodyguard he'd struck earlier and who was now standing against the wall with his legs pressed tightly together. "Mr. Clark?" And Clarky, with an apologetic smile, pressed his tokens into the fella's hand.

"You and Vogt run upstairs and enjoy yourselves—all right?"

"But we can't leave you alone, Mr. Clark."

"Did you hear what I said?"

"Yes, Mr. Clark."

"And Elmo."

"Yes, sir?"

"Stay away from the girl named Carlene."

"Carlene."

"She'll leave you with a drip, is what I heard," said Clarky with a kind and gentle smile.

When at last he was alone in the dining room, he stood up, tipsily, and then walked from table to table, emptying whatever remained in the wine bottles into the Scoundrel's Cup. He sat down again, but this time at the head table, where he found a package of machine-mades. He slid one out and lighted it. He heard loud chatter in the kitchen, so started humming "Beautiful Dreamer." Then, as he crossed one leg over the other, his right shoe collided with something—something that complained with a groan, then scrabbled out from under the table on all fours. A young blond girl with a thin face, a thin everything, and kneeling up suddenly, she reached behind her and grabbed hold of her gravy server by the base, then aimed the spout at Clarky as though it were the barrel of a pistol.

He was astonished, so much so that, reflexively, his hands flew up—don't shoot! Then he laughed at himself, and at the girl, rising slowly to her feet, bitterly squinting, her eyes gray as pewter. Her nostrils quivered, the tip of her tongue, anemic, paper-thin, showed briefly, was pressed back by her lips. At both corners of her mouth were clusters of tiny yellow-headed pimples, sore-looking things. But scarcely as sore-looking as the welts on her wrists. There was a glazing of dry ejaculate across one of her cheeks, and her petticoat was stained with the stuff. She sidled away, moving around the table, banged her hip against a chair. Vaguely, Clarky heard a squealing—someone being tickled, somewhere. And the girl was hurrying across the room now. "Hold your potatoes!" he called, and she stopped, her elbows digging into her ribs, as though she'd been lassoed. She turned and looked back at him, her face no longer challenging but doleful. He raised a bowl of melted ice cream. "Have you had dessert?" She stared, swallowed. "Don't feel like talking? Good! Good, I don't feel like listening. Sit." When she didn't, he half rose, pressed his knuckles against the table, thrust his jaw. "Sit *down,* my girl." She obeyed then, slowly coming back around the table and sliding onto a chair, two up from Clarky's. She picked at dead skin at the base of a thumbnail.

"I take it," said Clarky, "that you're the new girl."

She moistened the pad of her thumb, and ducking her head, laved a cheek, the sticky one, with it, almost like a cat or dog.

"New girls never talk, that's what I've heard. Too much murder in their hearts—eh?"

She looked at him, looked away.

"Well, the worst of it's over—I should think. At least you're out of the cellar now—every girl's welcome. Up from the cellar, untied. Full belly?" He frowned, studied his cigarette for a moment, then extended it toward her—would she care to take a draw? No. "My name is Clark," he said then. "There are plenty of us Clarks around, but I'm the one whose paste is remarkably black. You've probably seen a tin. Every room in the house has one. You're in twelve, aren't you, Gertrude?"

Her eyebrows rose, and he saw his cue, shrugged. "You're Mother's new girl, and I just happened to hear that Mother's new girl was named Gertrude. Trudy, she wants you to call yourself." Smiling, the corners of his eyes crinkled; he got up and moved one chair closer to her. "See, that's the thing about me, Gertrude. I hear all sorts of things. I hear everything, it seems. It's my career, when you get right down to it. Joe Jackson's got lockjaw. Al Cummings is blackmailing Sy Worth; once in a blue moon it snows in the desert; evaporated cream will sell for five cents a tin, starting Monday." He reached for his cup, had a swallow, then offered it to Gertrude. She shook her head. "I'm sort of like a daily newspaper, you might say—the only difference being you can't swat the dog with me or line the parakeet's cage." He grinned, she nearly did. Then he set his mouth tightly, and his brows lowered, pensively. You can't swat the dog, line the parakeet's cage, and Sundays I don't come wrapped in a colored supplement. "Somebody mutters something, I hear it. Somebody whispers—somebody gossips in the next ward, I hear it. Somebody confesses, somebody snitches, somebody sits down with his mother, his uncle that owns the fruit and vegetable stand, his second cousin, I hear it. Maybe I can use the information, maybe I can't. But there it is." He gestured toward his ears with his index fingers, then tapped them against his temples. "There it is. I fill my shoes with my feet, and my head, my head I fill with facts, wholesale. Everybody's got to fill his head with something, Gertrude. Otherwise, he starts thinking too much. I'm a scavenger." She'd been watching him closely, and now her lips separated, and Clarky, afraid she was about to say something, told her, "Don't," sharply, causing her to jump in her seat. Immediately, he apologized, and picking up a dish of ice cream and a spoon—he checked to be sure the spoon was clean—he passed them to her; she accepted.

"But you know, Gertrude, it's funny. Maybe you're trying to figure out—or maybe you're *not*, I don't know—but maybe you're trying to figure out what in hell I'm doing sitting down here all by
myself. The party's upstairs! Well, I'll tell you. Tonight I just don't
want to hear anything. I don't care to hear what Stogy Meyer or
Slim Philip thinks he's going to do next Thursday. I don't want to
listen to a couple of housebreakers discuss architecture of the Second
Empire style. That's a joke, Gertrude." She smiled, faintly. "And I
especially don't want to hear about this certain acquaintance of
mine. This certain friend. I don't want to know what he's gone and
done. Now, I pretty much can figure out for myself what he's done,
he's ruined everything, wrecked the engine, but I just—Gertrude, I
just don't want to hear about it. And if I *don't* hear it, maybe—"
Clarky broke off there, bit down on his tongue, shook his head self-
deprecatingly. "But that's stupid, ain't it, Gertrude? As if me
somehow not hearing about the thing might cancel it out, undo it.
Make it so it never happened. Go ahead, Gertrude, stare at me like
I'm drunk—I am! Like I'm bugs—I deserve it!" She blushed then,
and began to stir her melted ice cream with the spoon. "But just
imagine! The very idea!" Clarky's laughter squeaked. "Say you got
a brother Claude, just say you do, and one day Claude's out walking
where they're fixing a street and he happens to fall into a trench of
molten solder. But nobody thinks to tell you about it, or nobody can
find you to tell you—and so in saunters Claude at suppertime, fit as
a fiddle! Think of it!" He pursed his mouth, lifted his brows,
blinked, blinked, and shrugged. "Or—or the silk weavers go out on
strike, only you don't *hear* about it, so when you go shopping for an
Easter blouse, there they are, there they all are! Silk blouses galore!
Brooklyn loses to Washington, nine runs to nothing. *Who* says? Nobody told *you! You* didn't see today's paper! Brooklyn, still unde-
feated!" Clarky had begun to gesticulate wildly, like a Chautauqua
lecturer, and his eyes were squeezed tightly closed, his forehead
glistened. Suddenly, he clapped his hands over his ears and pressed.
He drew a breath, held it. Finally, he let it hiss out.

The girl, spoon in her mouth, watched him with a mystified
expression.

Clarky finally opened his eyes again and looked at her, levelly.
He tried a smile. "People shouldn't drink so much," he said. "It

makes them stupid. Or do I mean think? Think or drink? Drink *and* think?" He shrugged again.

Gertrude stood up and walked across the dining room. At the double doors, she turned and looked back. "Mr. Clark," she said, "thank you. For dessert." Then with a nod, she went out and on upstairs, quickly.

"Don't mention it," said Clarky, and he finished her ice cream.

2

Roughly an hour later, inside Room 12, Gertrude Gal rose from her bed, carefully, so to not disturb the naked man—naked but for a cherry-red prophylactic—asleep and snoring there. She tiptoed to the valet chair then and began to dress—in Elmo's white shirt, white trousers, white jacket. They were voluminous, but she stuffed the sleeves and the shoulders and the legs with nightgowns and corsets and camisoles and petticoats, rolled up. She put his shoes on after wadding newspapers into the toes. Then she took a scissors and cut her hair. It fell in clumps about her feet. With a towel, she rubbed her face clean of cosmetics. A glove! She'd seen a pair around, someplace, churchgoing gloves. In a dresser drawer, with bars of soap! She found them, drew on the left one only, then prying the lid from a small tin that was on the dresser, she scooped out boot paste and rubbed it through her hair. She slicked it back dandy-fashion. She drew a mustache on herself. Nellie Bly! But glancing into the mirror, she quickly abandoned such pretensions, and nearly all hope. It wouldn't work. She'd probably never make it up the hall; for sure, she'd never make it down the stairs. And she would never, never be able to get past the cadets in the foyer. It wouldn't work, and she'd end up in the cellar again, or in a tighter spot, a worse predicament—quite possibly a final one. She trembled. She pulled off the glove and dropped it into the wastebasket, and then her thoughts went back to that peculiar man she'd listened to in the dining room, that Mr. Clark whose paste, it was true, was remarkably black. And she tried to tell herself—she *did* tell herself, finally—that her father, miles away in Sing Sing Prison, surely had not heard of her travail: as far as *he* knew, she was still where she'd been when she'd written to him last, at Maloney & Grue's, living with her mother. Thus for-

tified, she went to the door and opened it. She checked up and down
the hallway. It was empty. So she walked. And nobody saw, or even
heard of, Gertrude Gal ever again.

3

Alone, unable to walk without lurching, and with a pelagic boom-
ing in his ears, Clarky left Mother Polk's at half past eleven. His cup
he carried underneath an arm. He was surprised to find that it was
drizzling out—last he'd heard, the weather was supposed to stay fair
through the weekend. He climbed into his carriage, standing in front
of the house, to wait for his bodyguards. He dozed and dreamed a
very peculiar little dream: He was a boy again—Little Clarky—and
he was with his older brother, they were kneeling on a metal grating,
fishing for something, a penny, with a string and a wad of sticky
clay. Suddenly, they were struck by a pair of shoes which came
plummeting down an airshaft. Claude grabbed them, shoving
Clarky to do it. But as soon as he discovered they were a woman's
shoes, he tossed them away. And Clarky, Clarky picked them up
and, since he was barefoot, put them on. Claude jeered at him, then
Claude vanished, then Clarky went and fished out the penny, only it
wasn't a penny, it was a twenty-five-cent piece, only it wasn't that,
either, it was a silver dollar. Only it wasn't a silver dollar, it was—it
was a goddamn penny, after all. Clarky woke, his mouth sour and
his bladder full, thinking again of Georgie Wreckage, sorrowfully.
He had no idea how much time had passed. He craved a drink of
water. He climbed down from the carriage and relieved himself
against one of the wheels. Just then, half a dozen newsies appeared
at the corner of Penalty Street with armloads of first editions, and as
though responding to a signal, they all began to holler at once. Kid
falls off Reservoir Wall! Roosevelt nabs a pickpocket! Washington
beats Brooklyn, nine to nothing! Clarky buttoned up and ran, away,
away, with quick-taken breaths, before he could hear any more.

He flagged a cab on Broadway at Mumm Street, and after clam-
bering in, he removed his necktie, then his collar, with which he
began to fan his face. "Twenty-second and Eighth," he'd said before
the cabman could ask him. *Clip-clop, clip-clop.* Briefly, Clarky's
thoughts went back to the banquet, and he cheered up some—the

Scoundrel's Cup, the Scoundrel's Cup! He was the youngest man ever to receive it, and what was even more remarkable, he'd got it his first year as a bravo. Only in America. And then, as the hansom jounced through a chuckhole, he thought of Shag Draper, who'd brought him into the life, who'd been his mentor, then very nearly his assassin. Fortunately, Clarky had heard in time of the plot against him, of Shag's scheme to do him in and take over the shoe-shine business, replace all of Clarky's boys with his own crew of dips. Clarky had been far more depressed about it—at first—than outraged. He'd trusted Shag, he'd liked him, he'd felt almost broth-erly toward him. Nevertheless, he'd acted—dashing atropine on Shag's lemon sherbet. With a dispassion which later troubled his mind, he'd stood and watched Shag's horrible agony—the paralysis of the eyeballs, the swelling lips, the incontinence, the loss of motor control—a weird dance. Hail Mary, full of grace, the Lord is with thee, blessed art thou among women and blessed is the fruit of thy womb, Jesus. Holy Mary, mother of God, pray for us sinners now, and at the hour of our death, amen, said Clarky, once Shag's heart had stopped. All right, get him out of here. So, he'd killed a man. And since then he'd killed two others—rather, he'd had them killed, but to Clarky, no moral idiot, there wasn't a speck of difference between doing murder yourself and having it done for you. Murder was business, and business was business, and nothing black that he'd done since last summer, since re-creating himself, had been done out of spite or pique, but still, in his secret heart—the heart no dues-paying member of Filch Hall, obviously, had any inkling of—Clarky was uneasy. In his secret heart—whose auricles and ventricles Georgie Wreckage had painted in oil, poorly but truth-fully—Clarky was no smilin' fella. George! In the cab now, Clarky touched his neat new mustache, then his lips, then his chin, then his throat, then he pinched the flesh there, and tugged, slightly. Ah, George, you bastard. You know. *Knew?* And drawing his legs up, bending his knees, Clarky hooked his heels on the seat opposite, then discovered—and in his depressed state of mind, the discovery struck him as particularly ominous—that the toes of both his boots were scuffed raw: He'd been stepped on, goddammit! He let his feet drop heavily to the floor rather than keep looking at them. And sud-denly thought, The cup! He'd left it in Penalty Street, in his car-riage. And he hoped, fervently, that no Filcher heard about it. He wouldn't want it said about him that he was careless, that he was absentminded, that he wasn't always, *always* on top of things. That he wasn't, in all respects, everything they'd ever heard he was.

As he was climbing his front stoop, somebody whispered his name urgently from an areaway two houses down, toward Seventh. And Clarky's heart stopped. Your brother's dead. *Claude?* Claude's *dead?* He clenched his fists and continued up the steps, and the caller ran from the shadows. It was the Armenian boy. "Mr. Clark," he said, hissing, "Mr. Clark, I have to tell you something."

"Tomorrow," grumbled Clarky, digging out his key. He flung his other arm, as though throwing a ball at a batter.

"No, Mr. Clark, it's important."

Clarky widened his eyes. They're dragging the river, they're watching the ferries. "Tomorrow. Go away!"

"Mr. Clark, it can't wait! It's important. Please listen."

And Clarky, sticking his house key into his mouth, jammed a finger into each ear, then he glared at the Armenian, until finally, with an expression that was a mixture of puzzlement and dismay, sadness and disappointment, *big* disappointment, the boy shook his head, took a kick at the bottom step, then turned and ran off—Eighth Avenue, Ninth Avenue, Tenth Avenue, whatever came next.

Clarky had watched him run, and his stomach knotted, and the thought struck him, struck him like a surface car, that he'd erred, that he'd made a mistake. You can't close your ears, ever. It was a mistake to think that you could—and he, of all jays, should've known that. But it was too late to call after the boy, he was gone. And besides, it was the whole evening, his behavior all evening, that had been a mistake—hadn't it? A mistake. And one was all you were allowed. That was the rule. Or was it a fact? One man, one mistake. This is America, ain't it? Ain't this America? Georgie, he thought, damn you, and unlocked his door.

Immediately, he came face to face with four uniformed coppers with semi-hammerless shotguns hefted.

Did you hear about Clarky? they said. Did you? Pinched soon as he came home from the whorehouse supper Wednesday night. Made

all the evening papers, Thursday. And did you hear what they found
in his house, what the cops found in his parlor? You saw them, then—
the drawings in the *World*. Well, there were even more pictures in
the *Journal*, they said. All those crates! they said. And not a tin of
paste in any of 'em. Jewels and seal sacques and black squirrel-tail
boas—all stolen, of course. Solid sterling tea sets, Colt revolvers,
spring-back knives—blank college degrees! Golf clubs and golf
balls, golf bags, and a thousand tintypes of French Jane performing
the French Trick on a Shetland pony. Heard the cops helped themselves! Poor Clarky, they said. Such a thing to happen, and on such
a night, too—he won the cup this year, had you heard? Clarky,
Clarky, Clarky, they said. Did you hear about Clarky? Did you?

5

Under arrest, he'd been walked to the closest station house, then
delivered by a patrol wagon down to Mulberry Street, police headquarters, where several detectives—along with their chief, Paradise
O'Day—took turns maliciously trampling on his boots, mashing
them. Clarky never winced; he stared, unblinking, at a meandering
crack in the wall. For the record, is your name Clark? they said.
First name Jilly? He made no reply. So they pulled the boots from
his feet and clubbed him with them, they nearly garroted him with
the laces, then asked again: Your name Clark? First name Jilly? And
Clarky continued to stare, like a dummy. What's the matter with
him—can't he hear? Ach, that's a laugh. He can hear, all right. Then
one of the bulls quietly opened the door and suddenly slammed it—
but Clarky didn't jump, or turn his head, or even bat an eye: he kept
staring, while the cops scratched their heads.

Clarky was detained overnight in a cell with a half dozen other
men; he gave them all a slight nod upon his arrival, then found a
spot on the floor, squatted, hugging his knees, and stared, for hours
and hours, at the slippers that he'd been issued. His cellmates argued among themselves, they boasted of, bitterly cursed, loudly
pined for their wives or bundles, they complained about the swill
passed under the door come morning, the sour milk, the watery
eggs, and of course, they asked Clarky his business, his felony. Say,
dub, we're talking to you—hey! They snapped their fingers, raised

their voices, they looked directly into Clarky's face when they spoke—one of them even dropped into German, another into Irish. By midmorning, they'd begun to refer to him as the "deef bird."

It was quite a circus when the so-called Deef Bird was arraigned in Criminal Court—remember now, Clarky's boys, Clarky's Paste had become, in a small but very real way, New York institutions; people talked of having their shoes clarked. Reporters and sketchmen from all the dailies were there, expecting the prisoner to swagger and sneer, to crack jokes and wink, to roll his eyes and blow lewd kisses to the ladies, but they were mightily disappointed. Criminal mastermind? He shuffled in with all the flamboyance of a—of a litterer! Where was the dash, the insolence? This was a villain? Say, Clarky, they called from the press gallery, you're innocent, right? This is incredible, right? Travesty of justice, right? But he never even glanced at them; he sat down and gnawed at his hangnails, then stood and approached the bench when his attorney nudged him to. The judge addressed him, but he didn't respond. His attorney did all the talking, all the listening. And Clarky never heard a single charge brought against him: he simply closed his ears to them. How many counts of this or that, were any of the offenses capital? Clarky didn't know because Clarky didn't hear. He was led back to a cell following the proceedings, so that meant he'd been denied bond, but why, what the reasons were, Clarky had no idea.

He was brought to the Tombs that evening, and from then until his trial, he slept a good fourteen hours a day, undisturbed by the commotions and altercations around him. Sometimes he played a hand of cards with his fellow prisoners, but he was so desultory about it, so uncommunicative, and it was so obvious that he cared not a whit whether he lost or won, that eventually they quit dealing to him. He's spooky, they said, though Clarky never heard them say it. He was a spook, and further, a terrible disappointment to them. Some gangster *he* is! Scoundrel's Cup! What a disgrace! First time he's pinched, he caves in.

But that wasn't fair, or correct. Clarky wasn't depressed by his sudden reversal of fortunes, he wasn't even particularly dismayed. In fact, when he thought about it—and he was doing a lot of thinking, now—he felt almost content; having shut his ears to the noise of human speech, to the noise of the daily news, he felt almost content. If it hadn't been for the occasional throb of guilt, clouding his mood like a drop of ink in a saucer of water, he would've been truly content.

The press had lost interest in Clarky by the time his case was tried and gave it a minimum of coverage; file sketches were used to illustrate the brief reports, even though by then Clarky's appearance had changed considerably: his mustache was gone, as was his smile, he'd lost weight, and his ears, once elephantine, had become, over the course of several weeks, as bantam as a chimp's. The trial lasted only part of an afternoon. Clarky toyed with a chewing-gum wrapper for the duration; he never responded to any of his chagrined attorney's whispered remarks, nor did he pay the slightest heed to the prosecutor's arguments or to the testimony of witnesses, none of whom he recognized. And he didn't hear the verdict, announced by the foreman of the jury, but obviously he was found guilty, because his chains were not removed. Then, as he was being taken away, Clarky happened to notice—how could he miss her?—Wilma Milhauser at the back of the courtroom, and he smiled at her, he raised his shackled hands as best he could in a wave. She called something to him, and he raised his shackled hands again, again he smiled.

A convict, he wore black-and-white striped daytime pajamas, a white pillbox hat, and a twenty-pound ball-and-chain whenever he left his cell for the prison yard to pulverize boulders with a sledge. *Crack! crack! crack!* he heard from early morning till late in the evening. *Crack! crack!* During rest periods he heard the *snick* of safety matches on strikers, an occasional bird singing; in the dining hall, he heard the scratch of cutlery on tin pans. He wasn't unhappy. He was on the moon, and while he was there, the earth cycled closer to the sun—or was it the other way around? Years passed. There was war with Spain in Cuba, bubonic plague in California, the brassiere came into existence, also the Wassermann test for syphilis. But Clarky didn't hear about any of that. Barnum's Animal Crackers, Jell-O, the inauguration of the World Series in baseball, the assassination of President McKinley in Buffalo, the bioscope, instant coffee. America was changing, it changed, and Clarky didn't hear about it.

Automobiles, automobiles—license plates for automobiles! Girls menstruated younger, the modern submarine was invented, a gasoline-powered aircraft was invented, air *conditioning*, a cellulose fiber, your grandmother fell in love. *Crack! crack! crack!* Joseph Pulitzer, that altruist, endowed a school for journalism at Columbia University, and journalism became a profession, like medicine, dentistry, advertising. William Randolph Hearst served four years in the United States House of Representatives. Headlines shrunk, the skeletons of prehistoric giants were debunked—it's plaster of Paris!—in the daily press, and the passage of the Pure Food and Drug Act was front-page news, not the girl in the whipped-cream cake. There were more suburbs, more and more suburbs, where little girls dressed like mothers and little boys like businessmen. Buster Brown was the most popular Sunday funny now: Dick Outcault's prankster with clean hands and a guilty conscience, two roosters, one lamb, and a bulldog, and a violin that he could actually play. Resolved, said Buster in his sailor cap and big bow tie, his belted jacket, knickers, and button shoes; Resolved, said the firstborn son of the Browns of Yonkers, of New Brighton, the Oranges, Leonia; Resolved—that we never realize just how comfortable or happy we are until the toothache or some other thing comes along. Why don't we stop once in a while and tell ourselves how thankful we ought to be for our sight and our hearing and our good digestion? He lived, did Buster, in a household with a maid and a cook, and his mother was a Gibson Girl before she married. Buster Brown! Prince of the Funnies! But what about Bram Hoopes's Little Nobody, the orphan of Slum Gardens? Gone, gone. He'd missed the train to Hunter's Point, the ferry across the Hudson, and besides there was no welcome for heartless ragamuffins in White Plains or New Rochelle, Montclair, Englewood, Tenafly, where Foxy Grandpa and the Newlyweds read Booth Tarkington in their hammocks and gliders, and grilled chopped beefsteak—or hamburger, as people were calling it—outdoors on barbecues. No welcome there for Little Nobody. And Pinfold? Pinfold was different. Pinfold survived because Pinfold changed.

In 1901—Clarky didn't hear about it, of course, but in 1901, Walt Geebus, upon the death of his father, moved back to Hoboken, back into the brick house on Morning Street. He was twenty-three, and financially quite well off; he'd invested in apartment buildings, trolley systems, the Eastman Kodak Company. And with syndication, the income from his Sunday pages—now appearing in Boston and St. Louis, Chicago, Indianapolis, and Toledo, as well as in New York—had multiplied several-fold. Quite well off? Frankly, Walt was stinking rich. Geebus richer than Kernochan? Not *that* rich. But rich.

Doctor Geebus had died in his bath, suddenly, and without having reconciled with his son, never knowing that Walt, casting his first ballot the year previous, had voted for McKinley, the Republican. Walt wept bitterly at the funeral, then went and saw Ethel Barrymore in *Captain Jinks of the Horse Marines*. I feed my horse on pork and beans, and often live beyond my means. Afterward, he took out a pretty, the *prettiest* chorist—took her to supper, then straight back to Waverly Place. So, this is where you draw your funny sheet? Yes, and this is the hand I draw it with. Now would you like to see my pencil? Here, let me fetch it. Oh! Mr. *Gee*bus!

Walt's father had left his entire estate—which included the valuable patent on the Geebus Hurler, and by then what amusement park didn't have at least one? The new Steel Pier at Atlantic City had half a dozen—to his second wife, the former Mary Meerebott. And it was on account of Mary, it was because Mary asked him to, that Walt returned to Hoboken. I don't want to be alone, Walter. I won't cook for myself, I won't clean. I'll starve to death in a house full of dust. The neighbors were saying that she'd gone strange, but Walt couldn't see anything much different about her. She looked older, of course, and she perhaps smoked more. Beyond that, she seemed—just the same. In fact, once Walt had moved in, she once again offered herself to him. He turned her down—kindly, he thought. Why, Nana, is it the first day of spring already? No, I don't believe it is—so let's wait. And speaking of vaginas, do you think we could have fish tonight? I was reading in the *Saturday Evening Post* that red meat is very bad for us. Heart congestion.

Walt made the doctor's consultation room his new studio; he didn't bother to remove either of the eyeballs or the giant nose, or even the optometry chart. He worked four hours in the morning, two or three in the afternoon, every day. He still loved what he was doing and hadn't wearied in the least of his characters. As a matter of fact, since making all the changes in the strip, he liked it better than ever. Derby, it was called now. Derby & His Dog That Talks. Pinfold sounded—well, it sounded too much like slang. The name change was decided upon—and Walt concurred with the editorial decision—

a few years earlier, just after the war, when suddenly there'd been twenty different clergy-led crusades against the funny papers and a variety of anti-cartoon bills pending in the New York State Legislature. Derby & His Dog That Talks. Derby's ears were a lot smaller than Pinfold's had ever been, and miraculously, he'd gotten a full set of teeth. And somehow learned grammatical English. Fuzzy, too. This is America, isn't it? Isn't this America? Yes! America! where a slum boy and a cranky old hag could become—in only seven days, one Sunday to the next—a suburban rascal and his young legal mother. Derby, I'm Mrs. Bredwich, and this is your home now. Derby and Buster Brown might've been neighbors—certainly the barns the two jumped from, using umbrellas as parachutes, and the ponds they fished, the bulls they dodged, the girls they teased, the tutors they pranked were close to identical. Derby gave up his coveralls for a blue tricot vestee suit, the kind Walt himself had been dressed in, and grumbled about, each and every Sunday of his boyhood.

Crack! crack! Clarky cracked rocks.

Walt, naturally, was a celebrity in Hoboken; people pointed to him, as they used to point at Hetty Green, whenever he was out for a stroll or for a drive in his French automobile. He enjoyed the attention and always carried a pencil and a stick of colored chalk— happy to give autographs, to make quick, impromptu sketches for children on their copybook covers or right on the pavement. Nana Mary told him often, You should have children of your own, and he replied—well, sometimes he replied, I *should,* and sometimes he replied, All in good time, and sometimes, with the slightest curl to his lip, he replied, I do already.

One day, after Walt had finished a morning's work, he went and stood at the bay window and looked out into the side yard. It was spring and the dogwoods were in bloom. His gaze happened to drift to the next yard over, to the yard belonging to a house which fronted on Afternoon Place, and then to the clothes hung on a dryer there. Glory be to God, brassieres! He'd never seen brassieres hung outside before, and as he gaped with adolescent bug-eyes, he was seized by a profound erotic impulse. Without considering any of the potential consequences, he left the studio, trampled down the stairs, and raced out the front door, and half a minute later, he was trespassing in the adjoining yard, circling the dryer, and coveting his neighbor's wife? daughter? The house, he'd heard from Nana Mary, belonged to people called the Hamiltons, but he didn't know the family, since they'd bought the property—it used to belong to a brewer named Kohl—after Walt had moved to New York. He reached, with his left hand, and touched one of the brassieres—there happened to be four out—and as he did, he lifted his eyes and was looking directly back at his studio window: for just a moment, he seemed to see his father standing there, scowling. Walt laughed. Just then, a young woman— the girl next door—pushed up the root-cellar doors, and discovering Walt in her yard, she frowned indignantly. And Walt—he couldn't help it, he couldn't—looked to her bosom before he looked to her face. And the bosom matched the brassieres, of that there was no doubt in his mind. Cinderella. What are *you* laughing at, said the girl, who was pretty, although her chin did come to a slight point. And who *are* you, anyway? What are you doing here? Walt introduced himself, nodding toward his house. Oh, yes, she said, smiling then. *Derby!* And you're Miss—Hamilton? Ann, she said. *Crack! crack! crack!*

Not in a million years, a trillion, would he have ever dreamed that Joette Wreckage would show up at his wedding. But there she was. There she was. Throughout the exchange of vows—whoops! wrong finger!—Walt kept glancing over at her; she was in a pew on the left-hand side of the nave, Walt's left, standing with her two children, the twins, a boy and a girl with shining blond hair. They would be almost seven. During the nuptial mass, Walt felt on the brink of passing out—perhaps there was some incense burning? Incense had always made him ill. He kept sneaking looks at Joette. Her hair had darkened. Joette. On the kneeler beside his, Ann turned and smiled at him through her veil. Smoothing his new mustache, he smiled back. Then again, he looked at Joette, and it seemed incredible now that he'd—been with her, all those many times, all that time ago. He'd felt such passion, but could no longer remember what that passion had felt like, nor could he remember her breasts, if they'd been soft or if they'd been firm. All that he could remember clearly was a large pore in her right cheek.

After the recessional, Walt stood beside Ann in the vestibule, receiving congratulations, shaking hands, kissing faces, and thinking, Who the hell *are* these people? Most of them were Ann's relations— she came from a large family. Obviously. Her father owned a tool

company which recently had become a vacuum-cleaner company.
The Hamilton Sweeper—If You Care About Your Carpets. Best of
luck! Lucky man! She's your little girl now—take good care of her.
Yes, I will. Thank you, thank you, thank you. And suddenly, there
was Joette. I hope you don't mind that we've come. . . . She kissed
Walt lightly, and, as she started to pass by, steering the twins toward
the doors, Walt felt that he'd—what?—just greeted, been greeted
by another stranger, another one of Ann's relations? Almost. Not
quite, but almost. He'd looked for that pore, hadn't found it:
makeup. One of the children, one of Georgie's children, the boy,
half turned before going out, and filling his cheeks with breath and
rolling his eyes, he made a funny face, just for Walt. And Walt made
the same funny face right back at him.

And Georgie? What of Georgie? Clarky, way up there on the
moon, never heard, and that's too bad: At the very least, he de-
served to hear that Georgie survived; that, saved that night, already
years ago, by the strange small boy with the stick-out ears, he'd
examined his life, from the outside in and the inside out, then
changed it. He never drew for newspapers again. And after buying
back his contract from the *Journal,* which took a great deal of
money, he left Ninth Street, he left New York and moved with Joette
to a small green house on the Shrewsbury River in central New
Jersey. Pinfold—that's what Georgie began to call him again—Pinfold, of course, went along, and about the next two, three, even four
years, there is almost nothing to say, really. Marie and Thomas
Wreckage were born, Pinfold learned to read—Joette taught him—
Georgie did sign-painting, and Fuzzy died quietly one September,
adored by everyone, especially the two children. Eventually, Georgie began to paint in oils once again, but this time he found his sub-
jects at the racetrack, the seaside, in the pine barrens, and at home.
He painted his children, he painted Pinfold (a terrible fidgeter), he
painted Joette, and he painted self-portraits. The family liked everything that he did, and in time Georgie began to agree with their
opinions.
    Not long before Walt Geebus's wedding, he went up to New York
with about a dozen canvases, which he traipsed around to picture
galleries; Pinfold accompanied him, naturally. He went everywhere
with Georgie. It turned out to be a thoroughly unsuccessful trip.

Georgie's work was politely rejected everywhere, even at the Hamlet Gallery, and on the evening of their second day in the city, as Georgie and the boy—who, while he was still quite short, was certainly not a boy any longer: seventeen? nineteen? twenty?—as they were leaving their hotel, they were approached by a portly beaming Negro, a giant of a man. Suddenly, he threw his arms around Pinfold and hugged him. Albert! cried Pinfold. Albert! It was, indeed, Albert Shallow, and dressed in a very smart-looking suit, too; expensive cigars were lined up in his shirt pocket. What're you doing here, Albert? Business, replied Albert. As usual. Then he drew from his coat a small white square box with fancy printing: Shallow & Sons—Health Products for the Deepest of Loves. You need a job?

No, said Pinfold. But thanks! I *got* a job. But thanks! Working with this fella right here. Georgie nodded at Albert, and Albert at Georgie. Everyone shuffled for a moment, then Pinfold asked Albert how were his boys, how was Dick, and Albert said fine, fine. Albert said, I got a building in Brooklyn now—you know Brooklyn? I got a building there where I do my work. You should see—it's just like the pictures in the drugstores. There I am with my beakers, stuff is always bubbling. You should come by sometime, Pinfold, we'll talk. The boys are with me.

Maybe we'll *both* come by, said Georgie, if that's all right with you, and Albert pursed his mouth—and Pinfold, Pinfold laughed happily, then swept his tongue across his top lip. Albert then shook Pinfold's hand and, warily, Georgie's. He said good night, heading around to the back door of the hotel. But he stopped suddenly and turned around. You made it, huh?

Pinfold looked at him.

That day I last seen you. The train. You made it okay?

Then Pinfold grinned and nodded. Yeah, he said, I made it. There was a door open, Albert, and like you said I should, I didn't think, I just went ahead and I jumped.

ACKNOWLEDGMENTS

As a boy, I covered my bedroom walls with Sunday funnies and saved comic books in cellophane wrap so the paper wouldn't flake; you can check that with my mother—she'll remember. Then sometime around fourth grade, after seeing my idol Chester Gould interviewed on *Person to Person*, I decided, Hey neat, I'll be a cartoonist. A comic strip in a jillion papers, a trademark signature and all my characters on a grape-jelly glass! That's what I wanted. I wanted to create a strip and draw it every day for seventy-five years. So what happened? I wish I knew. I was drawing funnies right up until the time I went to college. I took one art course there, as a freshman—Introduction to Drawing—and have never drawn since. Like Georgie Wreckage, I had no idea what the hell they were talking about when they talked about negative space. But even though I haven't bought a pad of Strathmore paper in about fifteen years, or a bottle of India ink, I still love the comics, obviously. And with this book, I feel that finally—finally!—I've created that comic strip I'd dreamed of doing ever since I was ten. Thank God.

And thanks are due to some other folks, as well.

First, and foremost, to Santa, who's always been *my* favorite artist, my favorite everything, who's shared my life for eighteen years and shared hers with me. None of my novels could've been written without her support and love (without her raised eyebrow, her rolling eyes). And thanks also to my daughters, Jessie and Kate. *Nobbles? Daddy makes nobbles? That's* what he does up there every night? Thanks for going to bed at eight, kids. Thanks for your gooniness and your sweetness. And thanks to Chuck Verrill, my editor—for all the nice notes, the enthusiasm that never flagged, the patience. (We can laugh about the missed deadlines now, can't we, Chuck? Chuck? Can't we?)

Before *Funny Papers*, I'd never written anything that required very much research, and while this book is a delirious, not actual, account of the birth of the funnies in turn-of-the-century New York, I couldn't have put it together if it hadn't been for the wonderful articles, interviews, and books by a great many historians of the comic strip, especially Stephen Becker, Bill Blackbeard, Jerry Robinson, Martin Sheridan, Coulton Waugh, Maurice Horn, and Ron Goulart. I owe a very special debt of gratitude to Rick Marschall, that walking encyclopedia of cartooning, editor of *NEMO: The Classic Comics Library,* and just a wonderful fella, for all his assistance, and for the loan of some bound copies of *Puck* and *Judge* (whence, incidentally, come a lot of the cartoon gags used in the novel). I'm also indebted to Alvin F. Harlow, Allen Churchill, and William Morris for their social histories of Park Row and old New York, and to Ira Glackens for his prose portraits of the so-called Ashcan Painters. I hope none of these good people holds it against me that I've taken more than a few liberties with the facts they've labored so hard and well to get straight.

Thanks to Harriet Wasserman for a most encouraging telephone call a couple of years ago, and to the other Clarky I happen to like a whole lot, Michael Clark the actor, for reminding me one night just how much fun it is telling stories. And to Chris Rowley, Anitra Brown, Sam Koperwas, Evelyn Brodsky, Jim McTague, Walter Gallup, and Julia Markus: You'd ask me, So how's *Funny Papers* coming? and I'd groan and you'd say, Well, I'm sure it's going to be fine. I needed that, and I appreciated that, more than you know. Thank you, my friends.

And finally, thanks to two people no longer with us, but who, in widely different ways, mean so much to me:

To Richard F. Outcault, creator of The Yellow Kid and Buster Brown, the *real* father of the Sunday funnies.

And to my grandmother Mary O'Hare, who used to sit me on her lap and read me all the comics in the *Daily News*, the *Newark News*, the *Journal-American*, the *Jersey Journal*, and the *Bayonne Times*.

> Tom De Haven
> Jersey City
> June 1984